# PRAISE FOR CATHY

## ISRAELIS AND PALESTINIAN VOICES: A DIALOGUE WITH BOTH SIDES

Standing in the shoes of those who face each other daily across this dangerous divide forces us to see beyond media stereotypes often reduced to terrorist and victim. This fast-paced narrative and compelling interviews brings to life a conflict whose complexities Americans must try to understand.

Sarah Harder, President, National Peace Foundation

## THE SYRIAN

In *The Syrian*, Cathy Sultan has achieved a master trifecta of political thriller, historical fiction and romance. This wickedly smart novel reminds us that politics is all about relationships and dares us to conceive that women are just as capable of sexual power plays as the men who have made careers by them for millennia. Sultan's expertise about the contemporary Middle East brings a breathless authenticity to the surprises that come at every turn.

Antonia Felix
*New York Times* Bestselling Author

## A BEIRUT HEART

There is nothing like an intelligent woman, spouse and mother of small children, to carry one into the midst of war, with its horrors as well as its capacity for soul-building. Sultan's narrative enfleshes our disjointed 'news' of the Middle East.

David Burrell, C.S.C, Hesburgh Professor in Philosophy and Theology, University of Notre Dame; Director, Tantur Ecumenical Institute, Jerusalem

...a view drawn from a camera obscura that moves behind the screen of invading armies, détentes, and broken treaties...a compelling story of survival that settles for no less than the promise that this family will remain together and safe at all costs...

Colleen McElroy, Professor of English, University of Seattle; author of 14 books including *Over the Lip of the World: Among Storytellers of Madagascar* and *Queen of the Ebony Isles*, which received the American Book Award

## TRAGEDY IN SOUTH LEBANON: THE ISRAELI-HEZBOLLAH WAR OF 2006

*Tragedy in South Lebanon* provides vital information about a topic often misreported by the mainstream media. I particularly liked the interviews with both Hezbollah and Israeli soldiers describing the same battle. This is an important book that should be read by anyone interested in Israel and Lebanon.

Reese Erlich, foreign correspondent and author of *The Iran Agenda: The Real Story of US Policy and the Middle East Crisis*

As someone who works with other organizations to ban the use, sale, and transfer of cluster bombs, I applaud Cathy Sultan's discussion on the effects of these lethal weapons on Lebanese civilians, many of them children, who continue to be killed and maimed by these odious, unexploded Israeli cluster munitions.

George Cody, Ph.D., Executive Director, American Task Force for Lebanon

Finally, finally, finally, there is a book that looks at the complex issues in Lebanon for what they are—complex. And even more importantly, Sultan has taken her experience and transported all of us into the region to better understand the complexities from the people themselves. We have had enough of the bumper sticker slogans and five second sound bites. Great.

Jack Rice, journalist and former CIA officer

Sultan gives a fair and accurate account of what went on in South Lebanon. As a UN official who has spent 24 years in South Lebanon, I say she also lends refreshing voice to those who would otherwise never be heard.

Timor Goksel, Senior Advisor and Official Spokesman for the United National Interim Force in Lebanon

# An Ambassador to Syria

## Cathy Sultan

**CALUMET**

Minneapolis, Minnesota

# Other books by Cathy Sultan

## Non-fiction:

*A Beirut Heart: One Woman's War*
*Israeli and Palestinian Voices: A Dialogue with Both Sides*
*Tragedy in South Lebanon: The Israeli/Hezbollah War*

## Fiction:

*The Syrian*
*Damascus Street*

# An Ambassador to Syria

## Cathy Sultan

**CALUMET EDITIONS**

Minneapolis, Minnesota

FIRST EDITION OCTOBER 2021

Printed in the United States of America.
10 9 8 7 6 5 4 3 2 1

ISBN 978-1-950743-62-9

Book design by Sue Stein

Map of Syria © Nations Online Project

*To my late Syrian-born husband Michel Naim Sultan*

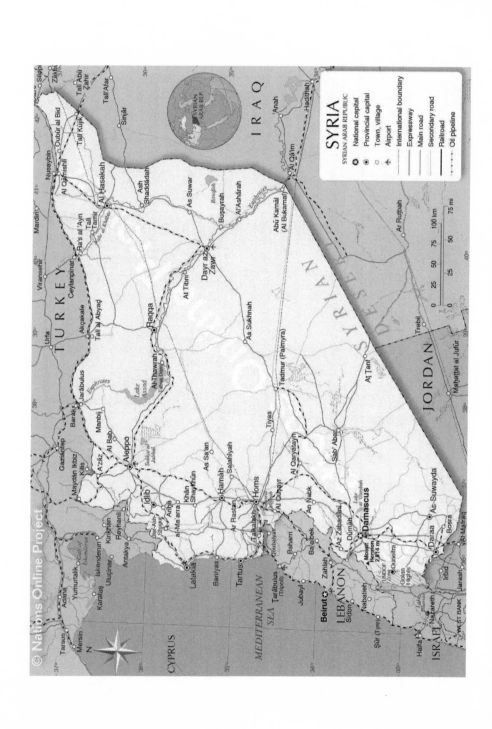

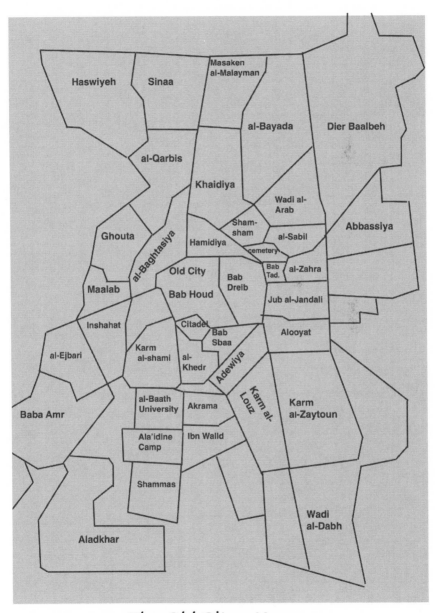

The Old City – Homs

*Never think that war, no matter how necessary, nor how justified, is not a crime.* – Ernest Hemingway

*We'll know that our disinformation program is complete when everything the American public believes is false.*
– William Casey, CIA Director, 1981-1987

*War is manufactured by political leaders, who then must make a tremendous effort—by enticement, by propaganda, by coercion—to mobilize a normally reluctant population to go to war.*
– Howard Zinn

# ACKNOWLEDGEMENTS

To my editor, Ian Graham Leask, who continues to support my effort to not only challenge mainstream media for its biased coverage of the Syrian conflict but the US government for its reckless attempt at regime change that has needlessly cost the lives of tens of thousands of Syrians. To my daughter Nayla, who recommended important changes to the manuscript, and to my readers Sheila Perelman, Joe Golibart, Marie-France Strohschanks and Kim Ayres for their invaluable input.

# CHAPTER ONE

AT 8 A.M., UNITED STATES AMBASSADOR ROBERT JENKINS, accompanied by his security officer, entered the gates of Bashar Assad's presidential palace. While he found it curious that their early morning meeting had been so hastily called when previous visits had been planned weeks in advance, Jenkins reassured himself that there was nothing to be concerned about. He expected no immediate backlash. He had successfully contained the coordinated insurrection to the Daraa region, and at least for now, Damascus remained calm. Morning traffic flowed normally, and his driver had been able to follow his usual route unhindered from the embassy in the Abou Roummaneh neighborhood, past the National Museum, Damascus University and the Opera House to the white marble palace atop Mount Mezzeh.

Jenkins was not supposed to like the young, affable Bashar Assad, but he did, and this unsettled him, for he was no ordinary ambassador, nor was his mission one which could be called routine. He was charged with initiating civil unrest to generate regime change, and the trouble in Daraa was just the beginning. By and of itself, the issue was not Syria, which, in his mind, made his job even nastier. It was about dealing a crippling blow to Iran and Hezbollah; Syria, as their linchpin, needed to be taken out, even if such actions were to trigger a wider conflict.

He first met Bashar in January 2011, when he presented his credentials as the new US ambassador. Alone in the back of his black Mercedes sedan, bearing the flags of the United States and Syria, he had sat erect as a monarch about to begin his reign. Confident, and yes, feeling quite smug, as he recalled, he had done his job well. The insurgents had been recruited and trained, the weapons transported, stored and ready. He was an American patriot, as had been his father during his long career in government, and he was confident in his mission. It was an integral part of preserving American hegemony across the Middle East.

Bashar had shaken his hand vigorously that morning, and after the usual pleasantries, had confided:

"I'm pleased that President Obama has decided that diplomacy and not war is the means of conducting international policy. We don't pretend that we're a democratic country, nor do we say we're perfect, far from it, but we are trying to move in the right direction. And," leaning close to Jenkins, he had whispered, "even if this isn't a job I ever wanted, I love my people, and I'm trying to do my best."

Jenkins had found himself so charmed by Bashar's British manners and speech, and particularly by his earnestness, that he could scarcely recite his prepared falsities. "Thank you, Mr. President. I come in friendship and hope, determined to make the road to Damascus a road to peace. My president's belief in you as a reformer will help make that possible."

\*\*\*

At the palace gates, the military guard directed Jenkins' chauffeur to a nearby helipad. "The President is waiting for you there," he said.

A helicopter? That's a spoiler, thought Jenkins. He would have preferred, as was their habit, to meet in the president's elegant, wood-paneled sitting room and have their cardamom-spiced coffee there. Disappointed, he directed the chauffeur to follow instructions.

As they drew closer, Jenkins saw President Assad, dressed in his customary dark suit and trademark Windsor-knotted tie, standing alongside a Russian-made, twin-bladed helicopter, talking to the pilot.

Jenkins got out of the car and walked toward the president, followed by his security officer.

"*Marhaba,* Mr. Ambassador, I appreciate you coming on such short notice."

Jenkins was momentarily taken aback by both the frostiness in Bashar's voice and his use of Jenkins' official title. On past visits, Bashar had addressed him as Robert. Undeterred by the snub, Jenkins offered the president a hearty handshake and replied in Arabic:

"*Marhabtain,* Mr. President, I'm happy to meet with you anytime," and pointing to the helicopter, "but this is a surprise. Are we going somewhere?"

"On a little tour of southern Syria," and pointing to Jenkins' security officer said, "you're welcome to come along, too. There's plenty of room."

Jenkins looked around. "It's going to be just the three of us and the pilot?"

"That's right."

"Very well," Jenkins responded uneasily, still confused by Bashar's cold reception.

Once they climbed aboard, the pilot started the rotor blades.

"Ahmad is our pilot today," said Bashar, shouting over the noise. "He's a career air force man, so no worries. Mr. Ambassador, you and I will sit in the two middle seats," and turning to the security officer, he asked, "What's your name?"

"John Jones, sir."

"Why don't you sit behind your ambassador. You'll have a better view."

"How high will we be flying?" asked Jenkins.

When Ahmad heard the question, he turned and said, "About two thousand, seven hundred feet. We want you to enjoy the scenery and," handing him a headset with speakers, "be able to converse with either me or President Assad, depending on which button you push."

"Ahmad," said Bashar, as he motioned to Jenkins to buckle himself in, "let's fly toward the Lebanese coast before we head south. I'd enjoy a look at the sea. It's beautiful this time of day."

In less than fifteen minutes, Jenkins saw the turquoise Mediterranean before him, glittering in the morning sun like specks of diamonds, its waves gently hugging the shoreline. As they flew over Beirut, he was reminded of his Lebanese mistress, Nadia Khoury, who was waiting for him at his official residence. Ahmad continued south, flying over the Phoenician cities of Sidon and Tyre.

"Sidon's crusader castle," Jenkins said, marveling at the archeological wonder. "What is it? Thirteenth-century?"

Bashar nodded. "You know your history."

"I'd be remiss if I didn't know at least some of this region's history."

"Ahmad, circle around again, please, only this time get a little closer."

"Are we allowed to fly into Lebanon's airspace without permission?" asked Jenkins.

"I notified them of my flight path before taking off," said Ahmad. "In the air, at least, we're good neighbors."

Poor Lebanon, thought Jenkins, it did not have much say in anything its neighbors did. Both Syria and Israel had not only interfered in its internal politics; they had each occupied the country. Syria for thirty-five years, Israel for twenty-two.

"Thanks, Ahmad. Now, on to Daraa."

"Daraa?" asked Jenkins.

"Yes, Mr. Ambassador. A disgusting massacre took place there during the night. I thought it important we see it together."

Bashar's cold, hard stare produced an uncomfortable sinking feeling in Jenkins' stomach.

"Mr. President, I need to be back in Damascus for a meeting at noon."

"Don't worry about that. This is more important. We'll also have a little chat later about Hassan Jaafar who was blown up under suspicious circumstances along with your attempted assassinations and coups, an impressive record, indeed."

"Very well," Jenkins responded uneasily, unsure if Bashar actually had the evidence to prove Jenkins' guilt regarding the assassination of that swine Jaafar or if he was simply on a fishing expedition.

As Ahmad left the coast and flew back inland for the thirty-minute flight to Daraa, Jenkins watched the face of the young Bashar, peering down at his territory, his sunglasses reflecting the sun. What was he thinking, Jenkins wondered? Did he grasp the full extent of the plot against him?

To stage and sell a regime change to a skeptical public, Jenkins needed a villain the world would come to fear and loathe. And unless he had a complicit media willing to promote his government's narrative, he would have a hard time convincing the world that Bashar Assad was evil and capable of killing his own people. In fact, the majority of his citizens supported him, as did his army. Even his fiercest critics called him a decent man trapped in a bad regime. Jenkins would have had an easier time of it had he chosen Bashar's brother, Maher, as the villain in his plot. While his hot temper and reputation for brutality had disqualified him from assuming the presidency, it had qualified him to command the Republican Guard and the elite Armored Fourth Division, charged with defending the country from inside and outside threats, both of which he ruled with an iron fist.

In the absence of anyone else, Jenkins was left to somehow create an antihero out of a spindly, six-foot-two, blue-eyed, thirty-four-year-old, London-trained ophthalmologist who had been summoned to Damascus to succeed his autocratic father and groomed for a position of power he had no desire to inherit. Even his age should have disqualified him, but the country's constitution had been amended to allow the young Bashar to take up his new role.

Upon assuming the presidency, Bashar had had to take on multiple reins of power. His father's cronies had suggested he had neither the political moxie nor the necessary financial acumen to lead such a complex country into the twenty-first century. Bashar set out to prove them wrong and was on the cusp of implementing a far-reaching set of reforms when the uprising began.

In foreign affairs, Bashar made every attempt to comply with Washington's world order, never fully grasping the extent to which he had, all along, been sowing the seeds of his own demise. John Bolton, serving at the time under George W. Bush, had already designated Syria as one of a handful of rogue states that, like Iraq, could expect to eventually become a US target. By the time Bashar became fully aware of the US-NATO plan to trigger social chaos to discredit his government and destabilize Syria as a nation-state, he was powerless to do anything about it. And here was Robert Jenkins, an instrument of that plan, working behind the back of a man he had reluctantly come to respect.

During his tenure as Deputy Ambassador in Iraq, his job was to arm and train al-Qaeda-like insurgents and then clandestinely move them into positions in the Daraa province and elsewhere across Syria. On day one of the uprising, the key narrative was that Assad indiscriminately killed innocent civilians in a popular, peaceful revolution and he needed to step down. When Bashar blamed the presence of foreign fighters, his accusations were rejected as propaganda. And the reforms he had initiated? Dismissed as "too late" and "window-dressing." Eighty-eight soldiers had been killed in the first month of protests. Who cared? Weren't they the same Syrian soldiers who had been killing innocent civilians? Many journalists, whether from *The New York Times, The Washington Post,* the major US news channels, were complicit, too, as Jenkins knew they would be, all pretty much relying on the same sources—the White House, the Pentagon and the State Department— reporting, as if on cue, their government's script—Assad was a dictator killing his own people. Jenkins had tried to tamp down his discomfort with all this but could not seem to hold off the feeling of personal dishonor and disgust with much of the journalism he once admired. Most American correspondents believed in the liberal order, in US exceptionalism, and, if necessary, interventionism to secure America's national security interests. In all fairness, Jenkins also knew that when journalists were given information, they wrote it down and reported it as told to them because they wanted to maintain their access to power. Most did not take the time to verify information or sources, leading, in most cases, to a black-out of anything pro-Bashar Assad.

Over the previous five months, Jenkins had made several unauthorized trips, including one to the Daraa province, the epicenter of anti-regime protests. The other to the flashpoint city of Hama, still a hotbed of opposition that dated back to the 1982 crackdown by Hafez Assad, Bashar's father, against the radical Sunni-based Muslim Brotherhood after it had tried to assassinate him.

***

Jenkins sought to warm things up between them. He hated this frostiness with a man he liked and hoped they could somehow conduct the rest of their field trip on a more conciliatory note.

"Mr. Ambassador, what's your favorite Shakespeare play?"

What an odd question, thought Jenkins, coming over his headset after a long stretch of silence, each of them still a bit ill-humored. What did he mean? Was this Bashar's way of placating him, or was it a ruse for more discord? Jenkins erred on the side of caution.

"Offhand, Mr. President, I'm not sure. What's yours?"

"Othello. How could it be otherwise with so many people trying to undermine me."

Robert felt an ominous bank of dark storm clouds closing in on him, and his breath quickened. Bashar thinks of me as Iago, the man who betrayed Othello. While Jenkins was saddened by his insinuation, Assad was right. That was exactly what Jenkins was doing, and he hated himself. Assad knew all along that Jenkins had been assigned this job, and he played him at every step, aware of everything. The insurgents, the planned uprising in Daraa, the massacre, the orchestrated international outrage to come. The full script, written and directed by Jenkins.

"You realize, I'm sure, that had my father still been in power, he would have already shut down your embassy and sent you packing, or worse, charged you with subversion and thrown you into prison. I prefer to handle things differently."

What a brilliant contriver, thought Jenkins. No temper tantrum, no expulsion, at least not yet, just level-headed calmness from a supposedly naïve, inept leader. Jenkins wondered if Bashar's unwillingness to be severe with him was an indication of how much he had come to like him. With great admiration, Henry Kissinger had called Bashar's father a wily fox. The reluctant leader of his people had inherited his father's trait.

\*\*\*

The weather was already boiling hot. It was only the middle of May, and the presiding drought made everything brown and dead. As the helicopter approached the Daraa region, Jenkins saw the vast swaths of baked, barren earth, its cracks etched wide and deep, like some macabre work of art. As they descended, a cloud of dust, stirred up by the helicopter's approach, obscured the view but not enough for Jenkins to miss a thick, sickening plume of smoke. A fire, or was it from the massacre? He was about to point it out to Bashar when Ahmad shifted the direction of the helicopter to prepare for landing, and he turned his attention to the group of people assembled near the helipad.

"No need to worry, Mr. Ambassador, they won't throw stones or tomatoes at you. I believe that already happened, didn't it, when you and the French Ambassador visited Hama."

Jenkins knew not to respond. It would only aggravate an already volatile situation.

When the pilot switched off the engine and slid open the door, the sudden quiet felt ominous. Jenkins waited for Bashar to exit before whispering to his security officer. "None of this conversation is to be repeated, John. Do you understand?"

"What conversation, sir? I couldn't hear a thing over the engine's noise," and that was when Jenkins realized that his security had not been given a headset.

He stepped off the helicopter and fell in line behind Bashar as he shook hands with the mayor of Daraa and his staff. By the time Jenkins had blundered his way through the reception line, Bashar had already trotted off in the company of an army officer.

When Jenkins finally caught up, Bashar made the introductions.

"This is Colonel Suliman. Colonel, this is Ambassador Jenkins."

The colonel gave a cursory nod in Jenkins' direction as he, too, tried to keep pace with his president.

"The colonel is going to show us the crime scene, Mr. Ambassador, so do keep up. Time is of the essence."

Bashar abruptly stopped, turned and looked at John. "And do ask your security guy to lag behind. He's like a puppy trained to follow his master. Our conversation isn't his business."

Jenkins turned, and putting his open hand up in front of him, motioned to John to fall back.

Bashar watched to make sure the man had stopped. "That's better," he said. "Now that I've got my head out of the sand and have figured out what's really going on, I can only assume it's the usual suspects at regime change again.

"Why an intelligence agency would repeat the same mistakes over and over again is beyond understanding. Your CIA's been at it here for the last seventy years, attempting coups and assassinations, and they have yet to succeed. Why do they think this time will be different?"

"I wouldn't know, sir."

"Your own president commissioned a report on the CIA's track record on covert activity and concluded such efforts seldom worked, and yet, he went ahead and approved their operation here. What does that say about the whole miserable lot of you?"

Jenkins' startled look was not lost on Bashar.

"You look surprised, Mr. Ambassador. You didn't know about Obama's report? Let me spell it out for you. The CIA can try all it wants, but it will never succeed. Syrians are a proud people. They love their country, and they abhor outside interference. Now then, come along. Colonel Suliman is waiting for us."

The closer they got to the plume of smoke, the heavier the air, the darker the cloud. As they walked past the government office, Jenkins noticed that the top two floors had been badly burned, the façade blackened and pockmarked with bullet holes.

Bashar saw him looking up. "According to Western press reports, my security forces were responsible for damaging their own building. You and I know that wasn't the case, don't we, Jenkins."

He ignored Bashar's comment. He was more troubled by the pervading foul odor as he walked past the shops, their doors and windows shattered, shelves broken and trampled, then vandalized. In some other context, he might have thought the smell reminiscent of tanning leather over an open fire, but not here. It was coming from decaying human flesh left in the boiling heat for eight, possibly nine hours. He took quick, shallow breaths, hoping the stench would not pass to his lungs.

"Such a pity." Bashar shook his head. "There was no need for any of this destruction unless the organizers' aim was to create chaos, instill fear and encourage more violence. I suspect the latter, don't you, Jenkins?"

It took Jenkins a second or two to clear his throat before he could respond. "It would appear so, Mr. President."

Beyond the commercial section and off to the left, Jenkins saw through the fog of smoke a row of run-down, two-story apartment buildings around an open field, used no doubt in calmer times for neighborhood soccer games. And the vast plains he had seen from the helicopter looked even more irreparably fissured.

Jenkins knew by the intensity of the heat that they were getting closer to the site of the massacre, and finally, when Colonel Suliman turned one last corner, he saw the two transport trucks, a team of security officials examining the site, forensics taking photos and preparing to bag up body parts. One truck was riddled by bullets, its canvas covering torn to shreds, some of the bodies carelessly slouched forward in a heap while others dangled freely over the side as if attached by hinges. The other truck had been set on fire, some of its bodies still smoldering like slabs of burned meat.

"Mr. President," said Colonel Suliman, "if I had been given the choice, I would have spared you this grotesque scene, but I was under strict orders not to remove any of the bodies until you got here. Everything is exactly as we found it, and for obvious reasons, we have kept the public away.

"Indulge me for a moment, if you will, sir, while I explain a bit about this area. If you were to drive up that hill," he said, pointing to the left, "past those apartment buildings, you'd discover the once beautiful Harrir Valley. Before the drought, you'd have seen lush orchards full of pomegranate and citrus trees. And over that hill," pointing off to his right, "that's part of Syria's breadbasket—a curtain of tall, green wheat stalks, enough, in normal times, to help feed our nation.

"Last night, under cover of darkness, these newly graduated military officers in the company of some of their superiors were on their way home to visit their parents."

"Which means this had to have been an inside job," Bashar said, looking at Jenkins, "which makes it even nastier."

Bashar thought it was the CIA, and Jenkins was relieved this had nothing to do with him. It was his job to get uprisings started. He did not order massacres.

Colonel Suliman continued, "We estimate that it was probably shortly after midnight when the two old Russian-made military transport trucks rolled down the hill from Harrir Valley. Unbeknownst to the young army officers and their superiors in those trucks, the road had been slickened with oil. When they discovered the potential for a major accident, I assume the drivers pumped their brakes as hard as they could but were unable to stop their vehicles. The ambush began just as the two buses collided here at the bottom of the hill. All twenty-four were killed. Local authorities were home and asleep at the time, and the crime was only discovered around six o'clock this morning. That's when we notified you, Mr. President."

Jenkins followed the colonel as he approached the bus, and when he turned to see if Bashar had followed, Jenkins noticed he had lagged behind, his face white as death. In the heat, the blood had curdled into thick blobs, its smell still pungent in the hot, stale air. In Iraq, he had only ever seen videos of massacres, never up close, and nothing like this. Bile rose in his throat and gagged repeatedly. In the sun's merciless rays, the bodies had begun to decompose, distend, the flesh around the lids and pouches under the eyes already swollen. And the flies, great hordes of them, nibbling on open flesh, coming from everywhere, trying to lay eggs, and literally covering the men's faces black until waved away by forensics so they could see who was under those dark clouds. The pieces of clothing melted into skin, the crooked positions of the bodies, the putrefaction powerful and foul-smelling, the odor not just of burning flesh but open bowels, all of it unbearable, smells his olfactory nerves would never forget. Jenkins turned his head, bent over and vomited.

"Mr. Ambassador," Bashar shouted from behind. "I would have thought you'd have seen plenty of massacres in Iraq."

"I've never seen something like this, have you, Mr. President?"

"No."

And in that moment, in all that horror, Jenkins felt that they had momentarily come together.

Colonel Suliman was polite enough to continue. "In so far as I can determine, once the trucks collided, insurgents moving in from all sides, machine-gunned the occupants, then dismembered their corpses."

"Why the fire?" asked Jenkins. "Did the bullets hit the motor or…"

"The one truck was hit with an incendiary grenade. The bodies fried in the fire and look," pointing to the side of the vehicle, "even the metal melted. It's impossible to identify most of the victims."

"What will you tell their parents?" Bashar asked.

"Sir, what can I possibly tell them? Would you want a parent to see his child in this condition?"

"Certainly not."

"We have the names of everyone on the bus and have notified each family. We're not allowing anyone here until we've taken up all the body parts, prepared them for burial and hauled away the trucks. We've informed the families that given the nature of the attack, we'll conduct a mass burial."

Jenkins nodded. "That's the only merciful thing to do." Good God, Jenkins thought after saying this, aren't you the one talking about empathy and compassion.

"We'll leave you to your work, Colonel, and thank you for your delicate handling of this tragedy," said Bashar. "Jenkins, are you coming?"

Jenkins had moved on to the other truck. He stood there, helplessly staring at a young man, a boy really, the awe of imminent death in his dazed stare, seated in the cabin, embraced by the older officer next to him, attempting, no doubt, to protect him when they were both shot.

"Jenkins?"

When he heard his name, he said, "Yes, I'm coming." He turned, and with the image of the boy in his head, caught up with Bashar.

When John lagged behind to take photos, Bashar called out to him. "No photos, please."

"Has the press been informed of the massacre?" Jenkins asked.

"For the moment, I've ordered a news blackout. I thought it best to calm things down. Emotions are already high here since the uprising. As for the opposition, no one's taken credit for the attack. Maybe they thought it best to hide how well-armed and trained they were. If you'd been in charge of those insurgents, Jenkins, would you have kept this attack secret?"

"Since I wasn't in charge, sir, I couldn't say."

"And if I do finally call a press conference and announce the death of twenty-four of my soldiers at the hands of rebels?"

"If the US is attempting regime change, as you've suggested, then they'll call you a liar."

"Are you insinuating that whatever I do, I'll be called a liar? Using lies as a point of war is unconscionable."

"Wars are premised on lies, Mr. President, and truth is its first casualty. It's naïve to think otherwise."

"All the more reason for such lies to stop. Where's the logic in that kind of thinking?"

"I'm not the one who calls the shots. It's debatable, as you suggest, if such decisions make sense, but I've not studied the nature of arguments or what constitutes good or bad reasoning. I was a political science major."

"If you'd had some good solid courses in ethics and philosophy, you'd more thoroughly understand the nature of good decision making and have better counter-arguments for your government's unwise decisions."

"Clearly."

"You know the irony in all of this? This is mostly a social media war, and I'm responsible for my own bad press. I opened up my country to the internet, and its users have turned on me like a pack of mad dogs."

"No doubt, the propensity for lying has expanded because of the internet."

"I fear for the human race," said Bashar. "We won't continue to evolve if we can't control our penchant for lying. The internet is Pandora's box. It might seem invaluable but, it's actually a curse."

Bashar finally spread his arms wide and asked, "In the end, what is it your government wants, Mr. Ambassador? The Muslim Brotherhood or Al-Qaeda sitting in the presidential palace?"

What could he say, wondered Jenkins? Did any of this make sense?

"You've already seen what's happened in Iraq," said Bashar. "Isn't that enough of a debacle to know that regime change doesn't work?"

"I can't speak for my government." I just carry out its dirty work, Jenkins thought.

"But you can deliver an important message. Tell your president I'm a proud Syrian. I love my people, and yes, I'm their reluctant leader, but I'm the best they're going to get right now. You'll get sucked into a quagmire here just like Iraq, only here my people aren't divided. My army is eighty percent Sunni, many of them highly paid officers. They're proud, and they love their country, and they'll fight to the bitter end to save it." Bashar looked at his watch. "Enough talk about things that get us nowhere. I have a condolence visit to pay. I've already kept the mourners waiting too long."

Jenkins felt strangely relieved by their frank conversation even if it had unmasked him. Sadly, Bashar would never know how badly he felt

about betraying his friendship. Did this mean he was any less committed to carrying out his assignment? No, although he did wonder at the
reasoning of perpetual wars, especially if none of them were ever won.

Jenkins followed Bashar into the mayor's reception room. John
joined him, and together they stood along the back wall and observed
the gathering. From his years in Iraq, Jenkins knew that in such a mi-
lieu, it was customary for the men to present their condolences to their
counterparts in the village while the women received their visits elsewhere. He found it difficult to watch grown men openly weep, but
when he saw an elderly man in tears collapse on the floor, he had a hard
time containing his emotions. Could the young man in the cabin of
that truck have been his grandson? Perhaps, in the absence of parents,
he had raised that boy to manhood only to learn he had died a senseless death, unarmed, unable to defend himself. Fuck all wars, thought
Jenkins, this is bullshit. What am I doing here?

When Bashar had finished his condolence visit, Jenkins and John
discreetly followed him out of the reception hall.

"The mayor's wife has prepared us coffee and knafeh," Bashar said.
"Come, we'll have them in the office."

As Jenkins started to follow Bashar, John stepped smartly to his
side.

"Shall I join you, sir?"

"That won't be necessary, John," said Bashar. "Find somewhere quiet to have your coffee and dessert while your ambassador and I finish
our discussion."

Jenkins juggled his cup and his knafeh and followed the president
into the mayor's office. Bashar closed the door behind them. "Take a
seat, Jenkins," he said as he pulled out the chair behind the mayor's
desk and sat. From the open window behind Bashar, Jenkins saw a
small patio, its contour a wall of flowers, a lovely touch of beauty, he
thought, in an otherwise drab place where the carpet was frayed and
the chairs plastic.

By this time, it was already late-morning, and Jenkins desperately needed a boost of sugar. So he took a bite of knafeh and, closing

his eyes, savored both its syrupy sweetness and the crunchiness of the shredded wheat. And it was not until he had finished his knafeh and taken a sip of coffee that Bashar spoke again.

"There's the matter of Hassan Jaafar's murder I'd like to discuss with you."

Jenkins knew this was coming. Bashar had alluded to Jaafar earlier, but he still choked on Bashar's words when he heard them, and once he stopped coughing, Bashar's blue eyes looked across the desk and asked, "How did you manage to get past our security and blow up our friend Jaafar?"

"I have no knowledge of how it happened, Mr. President."

Jenkins had no pang of conscience. Jaafar not only killed a CIA agent in Beirut but had also held Nadia captive four years, and with Jaafar dead, she was now his mistress.

"Hassan confided in me weeks before his assassination that you'd leveled threats his way. That wasn't a very smart move. We're family here, Jenkins. Not only was Hassan our Intelligence Czar, he was also related and worked closely with my brother Mahar, and no one, especially Mahar, forgives you for having killed Hassan."

"Mahar, the hothead who arrested those poor children in Daraa when they wrote graffiti on the walls?"

"Yes, the very same, and as soon as I found out, I not only reprimanded him, I fired the governor who arrested the children and had them set free. Don't ever underestimate Mahar. Even if I can't control him at times, and Allah knows I've tried ever since the uprising began, he'll do whatever he thinks is necessary to protect the government. And say what you want about Mahar, at least he doesn't behead people like your Sunni allies in Saudi Arabia."

"I'll keep that in mind." Jenkins regretted saying that. It sounded flippant and, given the circumstances, totally out of place.

"There's also the little matter of a confidential file that Hassan kept in his safe. It contained some rather incriminating evidence, wouldn't you agree? Information about your assassination plots, the murder of a drunkard in an alleyway in Georgetown, the attempted killing of a sheikh in downtown Beirut. Need I say more about your criminal activities?"

"No," Jenkins replied, shaking his head. "None of it's pretty."

"It was my understanding there were two copies. Hassan gave me one which, when the time comes, I won't hesitate to use. The other he kept in his safe."

"I wouldn't know..."

"And yet, you visited Hassan's villa shortly after he was assassinated."

Robert looked surprised.

"I'm no longer your fool, Jenkins. Mahar's men reported that Hassan's safe had been opened, presumably your work, but no files were found. It would be a pity if they fell into the wrong hands, wouldn't it."

"Yes."

"There was a woman-friend of Hassan's. Maher didn't find her either when he got to the villa."

"Yes, that would have been Nadia Khoury. She'd already left. I stopped her car on the highway. I searched her bag and found nothing."

Except a lot of Jaafar's stuff, he thought—money, gold—items Nadia had insisted she needed to buy her way across the Syria-Lebanon border since she had neither ID nor passport.

"Was she the one driving?"

"No, it was a man, presumably someone who had worked for Jaafar, and beside him a woman."

"Did your men search the car?"

"Yes, but they found nothing."

"The man and woman. Were they searched?"

He lied and said, "Yes," and from Bashar's icy stare, Jenkins could tell he, too, knew he was lying.

As Jenkins glanced out the window past Bashar, he replayed the scene where Nadia had begged him to let them go, insisting the man and woman had simply been trying to help her escape. He suddenly realized that in that exact moment, he had already fallen under the spell of her green eyes and had foolishly given in to her request, never examining the woman in the front who had probably stuffed the file under her blouse.

***

Jenkins accompanied Bashar back to the helicopter. As he stood aside to allow the president to climb on board, Bashar turned and, giving Jenkins another cold, blue-eyed look, said, "My pilot will fly you back to Damascus. After everything I've discovered, I'm half expecting someone to come forward and put a bullet in my head. Maybe it'll be you, Mr. Ambassador. In any case, I won't be riding back with you in the helicopter."

"That's nonsense, Mr. President. How else will you return?"

"I'll drive myself home," he said and walked away.

Wounded, Jenkins allowed John Jones to help him into the helicopter. While John opted for a seat next to the pilot, Jenkins was left alone and weirdly bewildered as they took off without Bashar. He was already sufficiently traumatized by the massacre, by the image of the boy soldier who wouldn't leave his head, the stench, and by the president's anger. Might Bashar's fury lead to his possible arrest, he wondered, for any number of crimes, not least meddling in Syria's affairs like the CIA had been doing since 1949? Had Bashar gone home alone so he would not have to be present when Jenkins got arrested on arrival in Damascus? And how awful that would be for Nadia sitting in his house waiting for him to return and she with him in jail. She had already suffered such an ordeal when her husband was arrested and thrown into a Syrian prison for thirteen years. Should he send her a message, warn her that he may not be coming back? He pulled out his phone but thought it best to wait until he saw what happened when he landed.

The thirty-minute flight seemed a lifetime, and as the helicopter prepared for landing, he dared not look down, afraid he would find the security police waiting to haul him away. When Ahmad landed on the helipad and slid open the door, Jenkins stepped out, relieved to find no one there except his chauffeur.

# CHAPTER TWO

SONIA TUCKED HER SUNGLASSES inside her hijab to better hide her eye patch before leaving the hotel to explore Daraa, which, at its height, had been an important Canaanite city in what was today southern Syria. It was Friday, but the muezzin in his minaret had not yet called the faithful to prayer, so she had time to re-discover a town she had visited years before. A lot had changed. A coffee house which, by mid-morning, should have been full of boisterous men sipping thick Turkish coffee, was empty. The local greengrocer offered only the most basic food staples, the butcher, a paltry selection of meat, and a clothing shop, dresses five years out of fashion. New to Daraa, however, were large numbers of al-Qaeda militants, their weapons slung over their shoulders, appearing to feel right at home, and Sonia felt grateful for her modest attire.

Her phone rang several times before she could retrieve it from her shoulder purse.

"Good morning, Sonia. Are you settled in?" asked Father Frans in his peculiar Dutch accent.

"Yes, I arrived last night with my friend, Joe Lavrov. And I'm still wondering what the hell I'm doing here. You didn't exactly give me an accurate description of what was going on, Frans. An uprising doesn't necessarily mean pitched gun battles lasting an entire night. You knew I had sworn off combat zones after that car bombing last year nearly killed me."

"I know, and I apologize, but I felt it was urgent you come, Sonia."

"Why? I could have stayed in Beirut and followed events from there. It's obvious from all accounts that Bashar is as brutal as his father."

"But it's all lies," Frans insisted, "and I have the proof. This is a huge story, Sonia, and you need to tell it." He rattled off a few elements of his story, astounding her, then said, "I'd intended to meet you this morning, but something important has come up. I'll meet you at the café adjacent to the al-Amari mosque at noon. Ask the hotel for directions."

"Does the café have a name?"

"Yes, but I don't remember. It's not important. I'll watch for you and stand when I see you arriving." He hung up.

***

Sonia was about to return to the hotel when she spotted Joe walking toward her—black baseball cap, bushy hair, dark beard and sunglasses.

"I hardly recognized you," she said.

"You fit right in yourself."

"I wouldn't be caught dead wearing this outfit in Beirut, but I didn't get whistled at or called out while walking around, and I liked the security it provided, especially when I met up with al-Qaeda."

He nodded. "I saw them, too."

Whether it was because they had both resided in Washington or because Joe had worked for the CIA, their chosen language was English, even when it would have been just as easy to converse in Arabic or French.

"By the way, Father Frans just called. We're to meet him at a café at noon."

"Good," said Joe, looking at his watch, "which means we have almost an hour to waste."

"You're an easy-going, no-fuss travel companion. I'm glad Fouad insisted you tag along. I've lost my appetite for dangerous situations, and after last night, I'm not sure I'm up for this."

"Fouad knew that. It's the reason he entrusted me with the love of his life. And as his fellow intelligence officer, I take my assignment very seriously."

"As you should," she laughed as they began their walk down Jumhouriyeh Street.

"Tell me about your friend, Father Frans."

"He's a Dutch Jesuit who's been serving the Christian communities around Syria for the last fifty-five years. He's convinced outside forces are trying to destroy the country. He wants them exposed and has asked for my help."

"Is he playing warrior-priest, or is he for real?"

"He claims that the media is lying about what's really happening here—that the protest wasn't peaceful, that armed men marched alongside the protesters. He saw them open fire on both sides. If that's true, it means this uprising has all the hallmarks of a deliberately planned covert operation. And since he was an eyewitness, I owe it to him to hear what he has to say."

"Fair enough. In the meantime, let's stroll a bit."

"Have you been here before?"

"I've had occasion to visit the area a few times."

"Of course, you have. It's close to both the Jordanian and Israeli borders. Hell, you probably know more about what's going on here than Father Frans."

Joe looked at her and winked.

"So, tell me about Daraa. Why did the uprising start here?"

"If the intent is to create havoc, the instigator looks for the perfect storm or produces one, like Beirut in 2005 with the assassination of Rafic Hariri. The Lebanese were told it was the Syrians who had killed their former prime minister. It was an easy lie to believe. Most Lebanese had grown tired of thirty-five years of Syrian presence in their country. They demonstrated *en masse* and demanded the expulsion of Syrian troops, something Israel and the US had sought for years. Here in Daraa, nature did most of the work. Syria's experiencing its worst drought in nine hundred years."

"I hadn't realized it was that serious."

"With minimal effort, those preparing this uprising had all the necessary components. A million and a half angry, unemployed men, most of them displaced Syrian farmers who came to Daraa in search of work. They found none, and now, with a little encouragement, they're ready to blame Assad for their woes."

"What was Daraa like before all this happened? I haven't been here in years."

"Daraa and the surrounding area produced most of the wheat and barley for the country. Now, because of the drought, Syria has to import much of its food supply. As a result, it costs more, and people can barely afford even their most basic staples."

Suddenly aware of how late they were, Sonia and Joe found themselves jostling for a space on the crowded narrow sidewalk as hordes of men poured out of the Amari mosque after Friday prayers. Joe grabbed hold of Sonia's hand, and walking ahead of her, pushed his way into the oncoming crowd. Sonia did her best to keep up, weaving as Joe did through the swarm.

"Frans said the café was somewhere near here," she said when they finally stopped alongside the mosque. She turned around in place, and standing on her tiptoes, looked over the heads of the men. Off to her right, she saw Father Frans standing tall and lean beside a table in the café, waving his hands in the air.

"There he is," she said, taking hold of Joe's arm. "Follow me."

Just as she had remembered, Frans was dressed in his trademark black leather jacket, polo shirt, jeans and a black stocking cap.

"Sonia," he cried, embracing her and speaking Arabic, "What a pleasure to see you again." Then, holding her at arm's length, exclaimed, "Still the beauty I remembered. How's your eye? I see you're still wearing a patch."

"*Ahsan*, I'll be getting my robotic eye soon."

"*Nishkurallah*."

Continuing in Arabic, she said, "Frans, I'd like you to meet my friend, Joe Lavrov."

"Any friend of Sonia's is a friend of mine, welcome."

Joe extended his hand. "*Shukraan*," and Frans shook it warmly.

Gentleman that he was, Joe chose the chair under the green umbrella for Sonia that offered her the most relief from the noonday sun.

"I've had quite a busy morning," said Frans, taking off his stocking cap and stuffing it into his jacket pocket, "and I've worked up quite an appetite. Shall we order before the restaurant gets too crowded? Friday after prayers is a busy time here."

"I've had nothing but coffee since breakfast," said Sonia. "I could eat just about anything. I'm famished."

Joe nodded. "Me, too."

"Then let me recommend the shish taouk with fries. The chicken's marinated with yogurt, lemon and garlic. For a more intense flavor, they add cumin, cilantro and Aleppo pepper. It's awfully good."

"My favorite kind of lunch," Joe said. And Frans gave the order to the waiter standing nearby.

Sonia had not seen Frans in ten years. Since then, the band of hair around the base of his head had turned white, making him look much older.

"Is this your first visit to Daraa?" asked Sonia.

"No," said Frans, "It's been a few years, but I'm shocked by how rapidly the town has declined. This whole region was Syria's breadbasket. Work was plentiful. Besides a thriving agro-business, there were mills and poultry farms and a major power station. Now, work has come to a standstill, and food insecurity is a real issue. If that wasn't bad enough, thousands of foreigners have begun to descend on this poor town, stirring up trouble. You have only to look around here and listen. And worse, they're recruiting Daraa's jobless youth. When you're hungry and penniless, who can refuse a two-hundred-dollar a month salary."

"That's a lot of money," whistled Sonia, glancing around the crowded cafe. The cacophony of dialects—local, Saudi, Iraqi, others unfamiliar—was obvious, their conversations ranging from loquacious nonsense to tirades against the Assad regime. Her ear was drawn to a conversation at the table bordering hers. Four brawny bearded men, dressed in fatigues, three wearing drab-colored turbans, one a tight-fitting black cap, sat with their heads together, shoulders touching, cigarette smoke as thick as dense fog hovering over them, their hushed voices emanating a conspiratorial hissing. Alongside each of their chairs leaned an AK-47 some thirty-four inches in height. From her days covering foreign wars, Sonia knew that at the full cyclic rate, each clipped-on magazine, while not particularly accurate, could fire a minimum of 600 rounds per minute. The rifle closest to her, beautifully cleaned and smelling of freshly applied oil, brandished, in addition to an improvised magazine capable of firing more rounds, a grenade launcher. She glanced at Joe, who was watching as she took in this frightful display of firearms. He nodded and rolled his eyes.

When the waiter finally brought lunch, he exchanged civilities with Frans, a frequent customer there. She knew that Syria had accepted over a million Iraqi refugees following America's invasion of that country. Here was one of them, willing to take any job to feed his family, waiting tables when it was apparent from his speech that he was well educated.

Ravenous, Sonia pulled off the bite-size pieces of chicken from the skewer and dove into her lunch, wishing she could just enjoy her food, drenched in garlic, olive oil and Aleppo pepper, without having to worry about missing something the four men next to her were plotting. She hoped Joe was doing a better job of listening. Words like "shipment" and "munitions" caught her ear. Libya was mentioned, too. Was that the accent she could not identify? One of the men, younger than the others, spoke a faulty Arabic. She glanced up from her plate to see Frans staring at her. With a knowing glance, he indicated that he knew the man.

At the end of the meal, it was Sonia who settled the bill. Frans protested, but she put up her hand. "I insist. When I visit you in Homs, it'll be your treat."

"Then the least I can do is offer you tea at the apartment I'm using. Joe, would you mind if I steal Sonia away for an hour or so?"

"Not at all, Frans. Take your time. We only need a couple of hours to get back to Beirut. In the meantime, Sonia, I'll check us out of the hotel."

"Thanks, and don't forget my overnight bag. It's still in my room. Here's my key," she said, tossing it to him.

***

Sonia and Frans left the café and walked at a steady pace past the shops with their iron shutters still sealed shut, a custom after Friday prayers, before reaching a quiet, residential area where two and three-story drab cement buildings lined either side of a narrow, pock-holed street. At one point, Frans stopped, pulled a set of keys from his pants pocket, and, choosing one, opened a door. They entered a bare lobby, walked across a dirt-strewn tile floor and up a short, dimly lit staircase, the walls a faded metal grey, to the first floor, where Frans used a second key to open another door.

"This apartment belongs to a friend," he explained as he led Sonia inside.

"Whenever I'm in town, I have use of it. As you can see, it's nothing fancy."

When he removed his jacket, Sonia stared at Frans's rail-thin arms and slim waist, his belt fastened into the last hole, making him, with his almost-bald head, look frailer than his seventy-five years.

Compared to Frans' kitchen with its small fridge, countertop burner, coffee-stained sink, single overhead cupboard and rickety table with four plastic-padded chairs, Sonia's fully equipped kitchen in Beirut was embarrassingly luxurious. Along the opposite wall stood a table and small lamp beside an unmade bed. Beyond, a closed door, presumably the toilet.

Frans inclined his head toward the bed. "I'm not the tidy type."

"Who cares. You're here alone."

"Please, have a seat while I make us some tea."

"Let me help," said Sonia. She opened the cupboard, which contained two mugs, a few glasses, mismatching silverware, two dinner plates and a pot with its lid.

"I don't see a teapot."

"Look in the sink. I washed it out this morning and left it there to drain."

"And your tea?"

From a drawer under the burner, Frans pulled out a small plastic bag.

"Camomille leaves from my garden in Homs. Add them to the pot once the water's boiled."

Sonia emptied a handful of leaves into her hands, crushed them and threw them into the hot water. The room was suddenly awash with the aroma of sweet, ripe apples.

"My mother made jams and tisanes from her chamomile flowers," said Sonia, "and she swore the flowers calmed frayed nerves."

"She was right. After a stressful day, I often drink a cup before going to sleep."

While the tea steeped, Frans and Sonia sat at the table.

"As you know," Frans said, "there've been allegations of snipers targeting crowds and security forces in Tunisia, Egypt, and Libya over the last few months, and now here."

"That's what Bashar's claiming but..."

"Sonia, let me ask you this. What could be more effective at turning populations against authority than the unprovoked killing of unarmed civilians?"

"Nothing."

Frans stood, poured the tea and brought two mugs to the table. Then said, "By the same token, what could better ensure a reaction from the security forces of any nation than the gunning down of one or more of their own?"

Sonia wrapped her hands around her mug, brought it to her nose and breathed in the camomille. "Go on."

"In Beirut, you probably get your news from Al-Jazeera, like everyone else. They're saying the protests were purely peaceful. It's not true. I know what I've seen, Sonia. Armed men, marching alongside the protesters or on the rooftops. They didn't seem to care who saw them as they open-fired at both police and demonstrators.

"By the look on your face, I see you're skeptical," he said. "It's the mark of a good journalist, but ask yourself this, why would the Syrian government go about killing vulnerable civilians in places like Deraa while at the same time initiating reforms to quell tensions?"

"Simple, to cover up its crimes. Bashar just had a few kids arrested for writing graffiti on a wall. His security forces beat the shit out of the poor buggers."

"It wasn't Bashar. It was Maher, and the provincial governor just followed orders. When Bashar discovered what had happened, he had the man sacked and the boys released. He also agreed to new elections and to the formation of a new government. And he's willing to lift emergency law, something that's been in place for forty-eight years. Look, I haven't always liked what the Assad's have done, but I can't turn a blind eye to what I see happening here."

Frans stood and paced around the small room.

"I regret having excluded Joe, but I had to. I've invited someone to meet you. I was afraid he wouldn't open up if he saw someone else here. He should arrive any minute."

"Sounds like a trope out of a spy thriller."

"Even better," he said, "but listen to what he has to say. I think he'll challenge everything you thought you knew about what's going on. Mainstream media has done a miserable job, presenting the conflict as good-guy protesters versus bad-guy government. It's much more complicated. Hell, you know that. This is the Middle East where nothing is as it appears, and a one-sided version of events makes the chances of restoring law and order extremely remote. We have a chance to tell the real story, Sonia, and to save lives."

Excited, Sonia said, "It's one of the four men who sat at the table next to us at lunch, isn't it? The one in the stocking cap, speaking faulty Arabic."

"Yes."

"Where's he from? I assumed he was from Turkey or Afghanistan," she said excitedly, without waiting for an answer. "I knew you knew him. I saw it in your eyes when you stared at me."

He was about to say more when a bell rang. Frans walked to a panel alongside the front door and buzzed in his visitor. A minute later, they heard a soft knock. Frans opened the door and ushered in the bearded young man.

As a gesture of courtesy, Frans spoke in Arabic. "I've agreed that we wouldn't use his name, Sonia. Are you okay with that?"

"Of course."

"And just so you'll know, it was by happenstance that I made this man's acquaintance," Frans continued, "and after a bit of persuasion, something I've become fairly good at over the years, he agreed to tell me his story. And now, Sonia, I want you to hear what he has to say."

"Am I allowed to ask questions?"

The young man's flippant stare sent a chill through Sonia as he stood before her—arms folded across his broad chest, shoulders erect, full beard—seemingly ready to take her on as adversary.

He nodded.

"And do you know I'm a journalist?"

His response this time was more deferential. "Frans told me. He also said that when you write something, people pay attention."

"Where are you from?"

"Iraq."

"I heard you speak at the café. Your accent didn't sound Iraqi."

He lost his composure and glanced forlornly at Frans.

"Look," said Sonia, "it makes no difference to me where you're from or whether or not you speak Arabic. If it's easier for you to talk in English, say so. Both Frans and I are fluent."

"Okay, my Arabic's rusty. I've tried to keep it up, but it's been a challenge because lots of my friends only speak English. Besides, these days, with so much prejudice in the States, no one wants to be heard speaking Arabic."

"Wait, now you're telling me you're American?"

"I was born in Iraq but moved to the States when I was a child."

"Okay. That makes more sense."

"My father was Iraqi. All hell broke loose after the American invasion, and Shiites began raiding our Sunni neighborhoods, feeling empowered after Saddam's fall. They ransacked our houses, intimidated the women. On one of their forays, they dragged all the men on our block into the street and one by one shot each of them in the head. I was forced to watch my father die. I was six years old."

"I'm so sorry. And your mother?"

"She's second-generation Iraqi Christian, born in Dearborn, Michigan. She met my father while on a family visit to Baghdad. After his death, we moved back to Dearborn, where she had family."

"Why aren't you still there where you belong?"

"I answered al-Qaida's call to come kill the infidels."

"Why Syria? Why not go back to Iraq and kill Shiites there?"

"Our Sheikh in Dearborn declared war on the Alawite Muslims who dominate the Syrian government. 'By Allah we shall mince the Alawites in meat grinders and feed their flesh to the dogs.'"

Sonia and Frans exchanged anxious looks.

"Does your mother know you're here?"

"For her sake, I didn't tell her. Our community's closely watched by the FBI. A lot of our older residents have turned informants. It makes them feel more secure, I guess. Anytime an Arab does something in the US, the FBI comes down pretty hard on our neighborhoods, so no, she knows nothing."

"Would she approve if she knew?"

"She made the decision long ago to put the past behind her. Is she bitter? Of course, why wouldn't she be? If the US hadn't invaded our country, we'd still be living there. My father was an engineer with a well-paying job. My mother, a psychologist. Neither was particularly religious, my mother Chaldean, my father, a non-practicing Sunni. Until the Americans came, Saddam had kept a lid on sectarian violence. If you respected the laws, you enjoyed a good life. Now it's a jungle. Anything goes."

"What do you do here? Do you just hang out at the mosque all day?"

"No, one of my jobs is to desecrate Sunni mosques. I scrawl, 'There is no God but Bashar' on the walls."

"Whatever for?"

"Sunni soldiers will see it. They'll blame Bashar and defect."

"But Bashar has the support of his army, and for that matter, the majority of his people."

"Not for long, he won't."

"Have many answered the call to jihad?"

Distracted by a fly buzzing around the dangling bare light bulb above his head, he did not immediately respond.

"Many," he finally said, looking back at Sonia. "They've come from all over the Middle East, from Afghanistan and as far away as Chechnya and China. Libyans, too. They brought weapons from Benghazi. We just finished storing them in the al-Omari mosque."

"From Libya? How's that possible with the NATO bombing campaign going on there?"

"The bombing's the perfect cover. Their operators in Benghazi, where most of the government's weapons had been relocated, arranged the shipments to southern Turkey. From there, they were transported across the border and distributed."

"You mentioned operators in Benghazi. Who are they?"

"You're the famous journalist," he scoffed. "Surely, you know the answer. Who orchestrated the Arab uprising across the Middle East?"

"The CIA?"

"Who else!"

"How do you know all of this? For a young man from the US, who speaks poor Iraqi Arabic, you're incredibly well-informed about what's going on."

"I spent many months in Saudi Arabia studying how the destruction of Syria would be carried out."

"The Saudis are only supplying weapons and paying salaries. Surely you know that the masterminds of this entire operation are the same people who destroyed your country. You're working with the devil."

"Yes, and I know they consider us fodder, but little do they know the force we're about to unleash. We're unstoppable. We'll soon have our caliphate, and even more jihadists will join us."

"Why are you telling me all this?"

"I'm anonymous and one of many. I walk out of here, and you'll never see me again. I want our message spread far and wide. You'll tell this story. It'll scare people, but they'll believe you because you're famous. I'm using you as our recruiter."

"And us?" she asked, pointing to Frans and herself. "We're infidels in your eyes. What will happen to us?"

"Your time will come," he said as he walked toward the door. "Thank you for helping our cause."

Sonia stared at the door long after the young jihadist had closed it. "He's dangerous, Frans. You need to be careful."

He shrugged his shoulders and fished in his pants pocket for something, finally holding it up in front of Sonia.

"A flash drive...where on earth..."

"Remember the Iraqi waiter at the café?"

"Of course, I was sad to see him serving tables."

"Don't be. He's an IT specialist working with the Syrian army. We've become friends, and now he shares information with me, too."

"How does he do this?"

"He carries his cell phone in his pocket and leaves the recording device on. He's the perfect inconspicuous spy. Who pays attention to a waiter? After a day's work, he goes back to his apartment and downloads pertinent conversations."

Frans handed her the flash drive. "Take it back to Beirut and listen to it."

"I'll do that."

"I hope that means I'll see you in Homs soon."

"Yes, you will, Frans. I have a story to write."

He smiled. "I ask only that you give up your prejudices and admit that none of us owns the whole truth."

\*\*\*

Frans accompanied Sonia back to her hotel. Joe was waiting in the lobby with her overnight bag. They said goodbye to Frans and set out for Beirut.

"How was your visit with Frans?" Joe asked as he started the engine.

"Powerful! I have a lot to share with you and Fouad."

And as they turned the corner to pick up the main highway, they saw the graffiti scrawled in large letters across a long wall. Joe slowed the car while they read it.

"Christians to Beirut, Alawites to the grave."

# CHAPTER THREE

From his balcony overlooking the eastern Mediterranean, Andrew Sullivan reveled in the early morning quiet. It was here that he began each day, leisurely sipping his first of many coffees while nibbling on a warm zaatar toast. His lovely Leila usually joined him, but she had opted to sleep in after working late on a camp project. The air was refreshingly cool at this time of day with a breeze that generated a soothing, almost hypnotic sound of waves caressing the shoreline. Even the beach, the only public space along the Corniche, and usually full of joggers, fishermen and retirees in no particular hurry to get anywhere, was unusually quiet.

With a thermos of coffee tucked inside his backpack, Andrew hopped on his bike. Leaving the western shoreline, he pedaled east up a gentle hill, steep enough to get his heart rate going yet hardly comparable to the rigorous combat training Joe had put him through during his rehab a year earlier. By contrast, at day's end, he enjoyed the thrill of soaring effortlessly down the hill back to his apartment. His early morning route took him past the new eighteen thousand capacity all-purpose sports stadium to the Kuwaiti Embassy intersection. The policeman, a regular on his route and dressed in his dark grey uniform and mid-calf black leather boots, smiled and tipped his cap when Andrew arrived. And, as a courtesy to him, by now the neighborhood hero for his work in the camp, the officer brought the traffic to a halt to allow Andrew to pedal safely to the other side. Those who knew him along his route waved and shouted "*Marhaba, Hakeme,*" good morning, doctor.

As he approached the Shatilla refugee camp, Andrew was obliged to dismount from his bike and weave his way through the hordes of people, many of whom were newly-arrived Syrian refugees, literally clogging the road, some buying, others selling vegetables and cheap household goods, all seemingly oblivious to the taxis honking, the air heavy with exhaust fumes, the car radios blaring Arabic music, the planes roaring overhead as they approached the Rafic Hariri International Airport. Even the minaret's call to prayer kicked in. They shouted and haggled in Arabic, a language Andrew now spoke fluently, which gave him a warm sense of belonging. As a foreigner, he had been adopted and loved as one of Lebanon's own, and he had rarely experienced anything more gratifying.

Nor could Andrew have ever imagined anyone living in such horrid conditions. Decrepit buildings and mountains of garbage, the stench akin to a mix of hydrogen sulfate and methane gas, thrown atop piles of rubble lining either side of Rue Sabra, a narrow, scrubby lane that served as the camp's main entrance. Underfoot, anywhere he walked, the ground was damp and reeked of sewage. Corrugated makeshift huts sold everything from refurbished televisions and household appliances to windows, doors and metal sheeting for roofs. A seamstress, seated on a small stool, her back pressed up against a concrete wall in front of her sewing machine, tended to her clients waiting patiently in line to have their tattered clothes mended. Motorcyclists, pulling wide wagons full of water bottles configured on the backside of their bikes, delivered "clean" water à domicile to those who could afford the service. While Andrew was proficient enough in French to use such phrases, he had chosen to concentrate his time on the more challenging Arabic that he needed for his work in the camp.

No matter which route he took, Andrew still had to walk through darkened, fetid, narrow alleyways where beams of sunlight streamed in through the occasional open space and where thousands of wires from makeshift electricity lines dangled haphazardly like slithering snakes across his path. Some walls, covered with graffiti, still bore bullet holes from the 1982 camp massacre that had killed some two thousand; someone had reverently inscribed verses from Mahmoud Darwish, the Palestinian national poet. Andrew continued another half block, along a wider path that saw a bit more sun, past a barbershop and adjacent hair salon squeezed in between dilapidated, three- and four-story cinder block buildings that looked to be on the verge of collapse, until he reached his clinic.

Once just another old house in ruin, its façade painted steel gray, the clinic had been entirely refurbished with large welcoming windows on either side of a wide glass front door. A bright red banner with the words "Medecins Sans Frontieres" (Doctors Without Borders) hung across the front of the building. It was home to a staff of four doctors, each of whom worked twelve-hour shifts, five days a week and every fourth weekend. The clinic employed a secretary officer and four full-time nurses. Medecins San Frontieres operated and funded thirteen medical facilities throughout the country, primarily in the Palestinian refugee camps, but even that was inadequate given the number of patients in desperate need of medical attention. Over the past year, Andrew had treated everything from heart ailments and diabetes to asthma and other lung ailments, with the occasional near-fatal stabbing. He also saw more and more teenagers addicted to drugs, easy prey, sadly, for the worst kind of scum.

Andrew was usually the first to arrive at the clinic and this particular morning was no exception. He closed the door behind him, leaving it unlocked for the others. Wooden benches, hardly adequate for the number of patients who streamed through the door each day, lined either side of a spacious, clean, white-walled waiting room. He walked past his colleagues' offices to his own at the end of the corridor. Leaving the door open so he could hear the others as they arrived, he sat down at his desk and began sorting patient charts.

He heard the front door open and shouted, "good morning," assuming it was one of his staff. He paid scant attention to the lack of reply and only looked up when two men, each with an AK-47 slung over his right shoulder, stood before his desk. Aside from a difference in age, he discerned no physical distinction between the straggly-haired, cigarette-reeking, black-bearded men, each wearing a sweat-stained T-shirt and smelling like rotting cheese.

"*Yallah, Hakeme,* you're coming with us," said the younger of the two, while the older man with a long, jagged scar down his right cheek grabbed hold of Andrew's shoulders and attempted to pull him off his chair.

On more than one occasion, Andrew had come face to face with aggressive camp residents, usually panicked because one of their family members had fallen ill. He learned that if he stayed calm, attempting to impose a bit of civility into the exchange, his aggressor would ultimately do the same.

Andrew looked up at the man strong-arming him. "I'm not going anywhere," he said, wiggling his arm free. "I have twenty-two thousand patients to care for in this camp. I won't be dragged off for one patient, or even two."

The two men exchanged confused glances.

"As I see it, you can either shoot me, or we can sit together and work this out like rational men."

The two apparently saw no need for deliberation. They pulled up two chairs, slipped their weapons off their shoulders, letting them drop to the floor, and promptly sat.

"Thank you," Andrew said, looking at each of them. "I have coffee. Would either of you like a cup?"

The older man nodded. The younger, brows furrowed, shook a defiant no.

Andrew turned to a small table behind his desk where he had just put his thermos. He poured a cup and set it in front of the older man. "Careful, it's quite hot," he said. And turning to the youngster, "It's not Turkish coffee, but it's good. I made it myself. Won't you change your mind?"

He bowed his head and replied cordially, "*Shukraan.*"

"Now then, why don't we start from the beginning," said Andrew. "Tell me who's sick."

"It's my brother," said the older man. "He's very ill."

"What are his symptoms?" asked Andrew, intent on stalling for time until someone from his staff arrives to rescue him.

The young man jumped in. "It started with red spots on his tongue and inside his mouth… but now they've turned into blisters, full of liquid and… they've spread all over his body."

"How long has he been ill?"

"Three days," replied the older man, "and he's getting worse. He has diarrhea now, and he's vomiting, and he's burning up."

"Are any other family members sick?" asked Andrew, trying, in his mind, to run through the list of possible illnesses.

"Two other men fell ill today, same symptoms," said the younger man.

Andrew recognized the young one's accent. "You're American, aren't you?"

"None of your business," he snapped.

"No need to get upset. Curious, that's all. I'm American, and you speak Arabic like me."

"I moved from Iraq to Dearborn with my mother when I was six… after my father was killed."

"I'm sorry… "

The boy shrugged. "It was a long time ago."

"Is this man a relative of yours?" Andrew asked, turning to English.

"No. Why?" he said, responding in kind.

"Because I suspect his brother might have smallpox, even though I know that's not possible. It was eradicated back in the mid-eighties, and yet, the symptoms fit. And if it's smallpox, I can't help you. I don't have the vaccine. I doubt anyone does."

The older man grew agitated and began shouting. "Why are you talking in English? Speak so I can understand."

"*Malishee,*" the young man responded in Arabic, his tone deferential. "Please don't concern yourself. There are certain words the good doctor only knows in English. I hide nothing from you, reverend brother. I ask for your patience. I will explain everything soon."

The older man nodded and settled back in his chair.

"You're right about your diagnosis," said the young man returning to English. "We got hold of some vials of smallpox. One broke. This man doesn't know any of this, and he's worried because it's his brother and... well, he knows something's seriously wrong."

"Did either of you touch the vile when it broke?"

The young man closed his eyes and nodded. "We both did."

Jesus, thought Andrew, and the older man touched me. He took a deep breath.

"How did you get hold of these vials?"

"That's not your business. What's important is that we have plenty of them and plan to use them. Tell that to your bastard American government. Tell the whole fucking world if you want. We don't care. We're ready to die for Allah."

"And the twenty-two thousand people living in this camp? Why come here and involve them? They have nothing to do with your crusade against the infidel. They're Sunnis like you."

Andrew looked up to see, behind the two insurgents, his three colleagues who had stealthily moved in close to his door, along with the clinic's four nurses, all ready to take on these two men. And then he noticed another familiar face snaking her way through the crowded corridor, past the others, until she came to a halt at his door. Aziza, the camp leader, stood there, tall, arms folded across her chest.

"*Marhaba Shabeeb, aibn al kalbiyyun* [Greetings, you sons of dogs], you can choose to leave now, or I can call the camp police and have you arrested. Your choice."

Startled, the two men turned in their chairs. The younger one grabbed his gun from the floor and stood, pointing his AK-47 at the crowd.

"What are you going to do?" asked Aziza. "Kill us all?"

The older man glanced up at his companion, tugged on his arm, and with a tilt of his head said, "*Yallah.*" And as they stood and advanced toward the door, the staff moved to either side of the corridor.

As he passed in front of Aziza, the younger man looked her cold in the eye and said, "*Sharmuta, sayati dawruk* [Bitch, your time will come]."

They were halfway down the hallway when Andrew yelled, "How do I get hold of you if I can find the vaccine?"

"I'll be in touch," said the younger one, not bothering to turn around. "You have two days to find it. Otherwise, I might have to open a few more vials."

"But that's hardly enough time," insisted Andrew, by now on his feet.

"Then I suggest you get to work."

When Andrew heard the clinic door open and close, he collapsed into his chair, threw his head back and let out a huge sigh.

"Thank you all," he said, looking at his colleagues and staff. "You'll never know how grateful I was to see you all standing there. And you, Aziza, I was praying hard you'd show up."

"When I got the call from your secretary, I came running. Are you all right?"

"A bit shook up, I'm afraid."

"I should think so," she said, thanking the staff again before closing the door. "I'm going to call Joe. He's working security in the camp."

"I don't want to see him," Andrew said insistently.

"Isn't it time to forgive past grievances?"

"Not in his case."

Andrew had asked Joe Lavrov to move out of their shared apartment some ten months earlier when he discovered Joe had not shared pertinent information about the kidnapping of his then-fiancée Nadia Khoury.

"Joe knew all along where Nadia was being held and chose not to rescue her, claiming it was a matter of national security."

"Since he works for state security, he must have had a valid reason."

"That's bullshit. He and Fouad were pandering to that dog Jaafar at Nadia's expense."

"Sounds more like your nose got bent out of shape, Andrew. You're bigger than that. Get over it."

"No. Joe knew how I felt about Nadia, and he played me for a fool."

Joe, whose mother was Lebanese, his father a Russian diplomat and probably a spy, had spent twenty-five years as a counterterrorism expert in the CIA before taking a job with Lebanon's State Security. Joe and Aziza worked closely together, and Andrew suspected their relationship went well beyond mere friendship. And why wouldn't it, he thought. With her loose, long, coal-black hair, smoky large dark eyes and high cheekbones, Aziza was a beauty.

"I'm forced to override your personal feelings, Andrew. I'm sorry. Your visitors this morning make this a matter of camp security. Joe needs to be informed."

Andrew acquiesced. "But please call Leila, too. I'd like her here when Joe arrives."

Aziza shook her head. "Thankfully, she wasn't here with you."

"You're thinking the same thing I am?"

"Yes… they would have taken her hostage as a way of coercing you."

"Jesus."

While he had tried to hold onto the memory of Nadia, Leila had walked into his life when he had least expected it. He found himself quite smitten and had asked her to assist him at the clinic since she already had experience working in Shatilla. Not only had he needed help with his heavy patient load, he rather liked the idea of having her by his side, and ever since, they had been partners.

"You know she spent nine years in Khiam prison for attempting to assassinate an Israeli officer?" said Andrew.

"Of course, I know, so does everyone else here. She's a hero not just for her time in that god-awful prison, she also stayed in Shatilla during the '82 Israeli invasion and worked alongside my father, assisting him in surgery."

\*\*\*

Joe and Leila arrived at the same time. Andrew got up from behind his desk and greeted Leila. It was not until he had pulled up a chair and invited her to sit that he finally addressed Joe. "It wasn't my idea to call you," he said, addressing Joe in English.

"I know, Andrew, but I'm awfully glad Aziza did. It's time we cleared the air. Let me start by saying I understand your hurt, and I sincerely apologize. I should never have let Fouad's orders come between our friendship."

"I don't want your apology."

Leila leaned into Andrew's arm. "It's still about Nadia, isn't it?" she said, the hurt swelling in her eyes.

"No, my darling, it's about loyalty and a bond of friendship broken."

A heavy silence hung over the room until Andrew spoke again.

"What's with the long hair and beard?" he finally said. "I hardly recognized you."

"Comes with the job assignment," Joe said, trying to make light of his unkempt appearance.

"I filled Joe in on as much as I knew," Aziza said. "Perhaps you have something more to add, Andrew?"

After describing the men and the probable disease, Andrew said, "Just that they demanded I find them some vaccines... in two days, and that's impossible."

"Deadlines can always be negotiated, Andrew. That's where I come in."

"The last known natural case of smallpox was in Somalia in 1977, and then in 1980, the World Health Organization declared the disease eradicated after they conducted a global immunization campaign. Then, out of nowhere, it turns up here. It makes no sense."

"There's been some chatter across intelligence channels lately," said Joe, "specifically mentioning smallpox as a bioterrorism weapon. And you're right, Andrew. How odd that it would show up in Shatilla."

"*Ya Allah*," said Aziza. "Does this mean this camp is the target of some bioterrorism attack?"

"That's a terrifying thought," said Andrew.

Joe wondered aloud, "How did these bastards get hold of these vials? The US's Center for Disease Control, the Russian State Centre for Research and Biotechnology and Israel are the only three countries that have stockpiles of the virus in their labs. The US and Israel are thought to be the only two with enough vaccines to treat their respective populations if there was an outbreak."

He added, "Maybe they were tasked with transporting the virus to some specific location. They accidently broke one, and now it's become our problem."

Andrew nodded. "But who was the intended target? Surely it wasn't Shatilla."

Joe paced the floor before he spoke again. "Here's what I know. Libya has a booming arms market. It's actually home to the world's largest arms cache. The CIA's been shipping arms to Syria from Benghazi via Turkey. Maybe one of these shipments contained the smallpox virus."

"You work Intelligence. Find out," said Andrew. "Surely you still have contacts with your former employer. And while you're at it, find out if we can get hold of some vaccines."

"I'm on it, Andrew."

"And when these bastards come back in two days demanding a vaccine, you better have some answers for me. And I also want to know where they're hiding."

Joe nodded.

"We know smallpox's highly contagious," said Leila. "What else do we know about it?"

"It's contracted from the variola virus," said Andrew, "and it's fatal in at least 40 percent of cases."

"So, we're talking about a possible epidemic?" asked Aziza.

"If the cases are in the camp, yes," said Andrew. "From onset to wide-spread outbreak, we could be looking at as little as a few days. In a place like Shatilla, probably faster because of the poor sanitary conditions and cramped living quarters. And the only prevention is a vaccine which only three countries have."

"Andrew, can you tell me anything else about these men?" asked Joe. "Anything that could help me track them down?"

"One of them is American. He speaks Arabic with an accent like mine."

"That's odd," said Joe. "I heard a guy speak like that in Daraa recently. It'd be a long shot if it was the same man, but… "

"What were you doing in Daraa?" Andrew asked.

"Fouad asked me to accompany the woman you hate to Daraa, the city where the Syrian uprising began. An old friend of hers, Father Frans, a Jesuit priest, insisted she come. He has a totally different take on what's going on there, and he wants her to expose the truth."

Andrew did hate Sonia Rizk. She planned and helped execute Nadia's kidnapping, an unforgivable act of betrayal from someone who had pretended to be a good friend.

"I'd forgotten Fouad was her newest darling. They deserved each other."

"Was this American young?" asked Joe.

Andrew nodded.

"It could very well be the same man," Joe said. "While in Daraa, I heard a lot of unfamiliar accents—Libyans, Saudi, Iraqi, even, according to Father Frans, Chechen, and then there was this one American."

"Hold on," said Aziza. "You just mentioned Libya again. Maybe it was those Libyans who carried in the smallpox vials."

"Very possibly," said Joe, "Our network was supposed to keep track of weapons being shipped. If you're right, we seriously fucked up."

"Who are these insurgents. Are they part of al Qaeda?" said Andrew.

"Yes, but this group calls itself the al-Nusra Front."

"Fine, we have a name, but who are they?" asked Leila.

"According to their manifesto, they're Syrian mujahedeen. Their aim is to restore God's rule on earth and avenge the Syrian people's violated honor and spilled blood. They refer to themselves as the Muslim nation's weapon."

"The two men who visited Andrew were definitely fanatics," said Aziza. "They could have put a gun to Andrew's head and forced him to go with them or knocked him unconscious and dragged him away. Why didn't they?"

"Two reasons come to mind," said Joe. "The younger one knew he was dealing with smallpox and realized he needed to win Andrew's trust and empathy. Secondly, Andrew had the presence of mind to settle them down. Not sure how he did that, but he did, and that gave staff time to show up."

"I was banking on that," said Andrew, "but Aziza was the real hero in all of this. She stood her ground and insisted they leave," and trying to lighten up the mood a bit, laughed, "I'm surprised they didn't take you with them... a woman giving them orders, that probably never happened before."

Aziza rolled her eyes. "Silly man. Surely their mothers did."

"So, does this mean al-Qaeda has moved into Shatilla?" asked Leila.

"Not sure," said Joe. "My informants in Daraa said only that al-Nusra was freely moving back and forth across the Lebanese-Syrian border."

"I thought the army had secured that area," said Aziza.

"They're doing their best," said Joe, "with Hezbollah's help, but the terrain around Ras Baalbek is mountainous, and there are lots of places to hide."

"They're not just in the Bekaa," said Leila. "Remember the al-Nusra sheikh who stirred up trouble last year in Tripoli? He and his men killed twenty-nine soldiers and wounded another fifty?"

"Yes, an embarrassing security fiasco on our part. And it looks like we now have another one."

"But why come to Shatilla," asked Andrew, "if they have such a strong base in Tripoli?"

"Had," Joe said. "The army undertook a massive clean-up operation there. The sheikh and many of his followers were jailed. We lost track of the others, but not for lack of trying.

"Al-Qaeda also had a stronghold in Nahr al Barad, the Palestinian camp just north of Tripoli, but that, too, was destroyed when the army drove them out," said Joe. "If I were an insurgent looking for a place to hide, recruit followers while planning my next move, I'd think Shatilla the ideal place. It's overcrowded and overrun with desperate Syrian refugees. There's high unemployment and a huge drug problem. Everything points to a fertile recruiting ground, and, as a bonus, they offer a generous monthly salary. Under the current camp conditions, who'd refuse that kind of money?"

"Is Andrew a high-risk target?" asked Leila.

"Yes and no," said Joe, "they won't kill him if that's what you're wondering."

"But you're suggesting they'll return?"

"No doubt about it," Joe replied. "They want Andrew's help, and they need the vaccine. And they'll probably have their eye on you and Aziza, too. Once they settle in, they'll be looking for women to keep them company. In their screwed-up minds, you two would make ideal sex slaves, maybe even kept in a cage so you wouldn't escape."

"That's bullshit," shouted Andrew. "This isn't Iraq or Afghanistan."

"Not yet, it isn't."

"You're a sadistic bastard! Why did you have to say that? You know Leila's history."

"Sorry, I guess I've been in the field too long."

"Come on, Joe," said Aziza. "You're better than that. We don't need this kind of shit thrown in our faces. We know what goes on out there."

Andrew turned and looked at Leila. Tears streamed down her cheeks. He pulled her into his chest, smelling the shampoo in her hair, the fresh scent of her skin. How many nights had he held her in his arms when she was awakened by memories of her rape and torture? And all he could do each time was reassure her she was safe, even though he knew no one was really ever safe in Lebanon.

# CHAPTER FOUR

NADIA LAY IN A LARGE, SOFT BED between freshly laundered satin sheets. The room was dark, and she had no notion of how long she had slept, only that it must by now be late morning. Before leaving for his hastily called appointment with President Assad, Robert had awakened her at an absurdly early hour and quickly made love to her. Though she had laughed at such foolishness, Nadia knew she could hold nothing back if she were to gain Robert's trust and so threw herself into full love-making mode whenever asked.

Thinking she would quietly drift back to sleep after Robert left, she found herself remembering her last encounter with Andrew Sullivan, her then-fiancé, and how rudely she had sent him away. As much as it had hurt, it had been necessary. She had not wanted him involved in her plan to neutralize Robert Jenkins. She would either convince the ambassador to derail his regime change plans or destroy his career. She not only had the evidence to do that, she and Fouad Nasr, deputy head of Lebanon's Internal Security, had drafted a course of action should the latter become necessary.

Nadia finally gave up on sleep. She puffed up the pillows behind her head, folded down the sheets and sat up. She switched on the bedside lamp and looked about the room, hers since she had become a regular visitor, and indulged in the serenity of the bare, pale apricot walls and matching settee and chair. She chuckled when she saw her clothes strewn across the floor, a reminder of how impatient Robert always was to get her into bed. Her plan to lure him into her lair had begun some six months earlier with a kiss of gratitude when he had delivered her safely across the Syrian border. This had led to intimate dinner dates at Beirut restaurants until she had finally agreed to spend time at his official residence in Damascus.

Still feeling the lovemaking, Nadia climbed out of bed and walked into the bathroom. She sat on the stool in front of the sink and, looking in the mirror, saw a woman she hardly recognized. After her first husband Elie died, she had taken for granted that she and Andrew would finally have a life together, only to be abducted by Hassan Jaafar. As soon as he saw her after her release from captivity, wearing heavy make-up and short, tight clothes—changes that occurred during her time with Hassan—she knew Andrew would never want her back since she was no longer the Nadia he had loved. But that was of no concern now, for he was living with Leila and seemingly very much in love with her.

Could she ever go back to being who she had been? In her mind, she had temporarily assumed a role essential to her mission. In wartime, women spies had often used their bodies in the service of their countries. In her mind's eye, she saw herself no differently, nor did she require that anyone other than Fouad know she was trying to avert Syria's destruction. From childhood, her father had instilled in her the importance of maintaining her integrity. It was a burden, and she was learning just how heavy that burden could be and the sacrifices that came with it.

She finally pulled herself up from the stool and ran the water to the right temperature before stepping into the shower. On a molding stood a small bottle of shampoo and a bar of lavender-scented soap. She rubbed it on a wet washcloth and scrubbed her body before folding shampoo into her hair and bringing it to a lather. Finally finished, she wrapped herself in a warm bath towel and dried both her body and hair before slipping into her dress and heels.

When she opened the bathroom door, she was surprised to see Robert pacing the bedroom.

"You're back, finally. That was a long meeting. How did it go?"

He shook his head. "Not well."

She went to him, and wrapping her arms around his neck, pressed his head into her chest. She had known how to calm down Jaafar, too, but she had never had that problem with Andrew. Andrew was not who she would classify as an alpha male. It struck her how as she engaged with Robert, she thought about Andrew. Focus, Nadia!

"Come now, it couldn't have been that bad."

"It was worse than bad. I ruptured what little friendship I had managed to cultivate. Bashar will never agree to see me again."

"You can tell me all about it over lunch in the garden. How does that sound?"

"I'd like nothing better."

"Go and take a shower now," she said, kissing him. "It'll help you relax." And as she was about to leave, added, "And take your time. I'll be busy in the kitchen with Nademe helping her prepare lunch."

"You're a treasure, Nadia."

She smiled as he dropped his clothes on a chair and went into the bathroom. For someone she was scheming to undermine, she couldn't help liking the shape of his buttocks. As she descended the stairs to the kitchen, she admonished herself to be careful. Robert appeared to be easily duped by her beauty, but she knew she must not let her guard down. Her game had only just begun.

While in captivity, she had been played, at least initially, by Jaafar. As a spymaster, he had known every trick of his trade—how to get into the heads of others and how to manipulate and make people do things they did not want to do. And he had known everything about her—her social and intellectual needs, her passions and her weaknesses. What did she know about Robert Jenkins? What were his passions and weaknesses, his vulnerabilities? Surprisingly little, she realized, even after her six month-month long intimacy with him. Once she had made the conscious choice to give in to Hassan, and even though he remained the warden, she the prisoner, she had relied on her shrewdness, her brains and beauty, to successfully exploit his desire for her. Would Robert be so easily fooled? Hassan had understood the threats of the treacherous, fanatic world of which Robert was a part, and he had gone about molding her into an emotionally stronger, more assertive person. Would those skills be enough to bring down the US ambassador?

His official residence, a two-story, white stone mansion on a quiet, palm tree-lined street in the upscale neighborhood of Mouhajreen, had been rented from a prominent Damascene family who resided in the States. A canopy of Mediterranean cypress and Turkish pines, interspersed with apricot and pistachio trees, lined the periphery of the house, hiding the rarest of gardens from the outside world.

Nadia had fond memories of her mother's rose garden, but this was Damascus, home of the famous Rosa Damascene, cultivated for its fragrant, pink flowers, its scent, as best she could discern, a cross between a freesia and a ripe apricot, and used to make the finest perfumes in the world. As she strolled through the garden, she was almost dizzy with excitement, for never before had she seen such a profusion of that most perfect of flowers.

She had Nademe set the table with the fine floral china she found in the dining room along with a matching pale-pink tablecloth from the buffet, and after making sure there were several bottles of wine in the refrigerator, she cut a few roses for the table. Having settled on the menu with Nademe, she took a seat in the garden and waited for Robert to join her.

"Well, well," she said, clapping her hands when he finally appeared, "you look so much more relaxed."

"I am, darling," he said, leaning down to kiss her. "Your suggestion worked wonders."

"And I thank you for inviting me to visit this enchanting house so often, Robert. I'll never tire of saying how much I love it here. It's like a little piece of heaven no one else knows about."

"It's for that very reason I chose this house."

"Indeed," and glancing from the garden to the table in front of her, she marveled at the amazing mezze of stuffed grape leaves, fried kibbeh, the spicy cheese balls and the tabbouleh that Nademe had so expertly prepared.

"And what a feast. Not only do you have splendid taste, Robert. You've gone and hired an excellent cook."

He smiled. "You're pleased. That makes me happy, but I'm afraid I can't take any credit. For my good fortune, Nademe came with the house. Shall I serve you some wine?"

She popped a rice-filled grape leaf into her mouth and nodded, yes.

"It's a Syrian white from Lattakia. I think you'll enjoy it," he said.

Nadia eventually took a sip and said, "I do. Were you always a connoisseur of fine wine and food, Robert?"

"If I am, it's thanks to my doting mother. She called me 'her Robbie.'"

"Robbie? Not a name I'd associate with you now, but… "

"She and her best friend Adele were the only ones who ever called me that, and I'd like to keep it that way, thank you. As for my father, he was always off on some important government business, so I rarely saw him. Strange," he mused, "although I hardly know him, it turns out I'm doing the same thing he spent a career doing. How do you explain that?"

"Maybe your mother instilled in you her sense of pride about her husband's career. It would be only natural that you'd want to live up to their expectations."

"Maybe, but as for fine wines and food, my mother introduced me to a variety of ethnic foods. Lebanese is by far my favorite, probably because we lived there longer than anywhere else."

"What years?"

"1975 to 1983. I attended Louse Wegmann school, and then only on and off because the civil war was in full swing."

"I don't believe it, so did I. What year?"

"I started there in '77."

"I transferred there in the fall of 1982. We had just come off a horrific summer of carpet bombing and camp slaughters. Still, what an amazing coincidence that we'd have gone to the same school. It's strange we never discussed this. Tell me more."

Even though she already knew much of Jenkins' history from Fouad, this was the first time he had opened up to her. Until now, he had been unwilling, or unable, to reveal another side of himself. And maybe that was part of his CIA training, never to reveal things personal, the truth confounded with untruths, not unlike how Jaafar had dealt with people, whether friend or foe.

"I did a stint in the CIA. It wasn't the right fit, and I admit to unapologetically using my father's influence to gain entrance into the diplomatic corps, and here I am."

"What was your major in college?"

"Political Science and Government Policy with a minor in Arabic."

"So, you knew from early on you wanted to go into government."

"Yeah, I did."

"That was still a hefty academic load."

"Both of my parents were top in their class. They expected the same of me, and I didn't want to disappoint." He laughed. "I'm a high achiever, what can I say?"

And why you're an alpha male, she thought.

Robert poured the last of the wine into their glasses and said, "We need another bottle. I'll go fetch it."

Nadia took note of how much wine Robert had already consumed. He was obviously still agitated. Should she be concerned? Was he prone to aggressive behavior when drunk? She knew from Hassan that Robert had defended himself aggressively when a man had tried to rob him, leaving the attacker badly wounded and bleeding to death. She assumed that must have been about the time he had traded in his Intelligence credentials for a career in statecraft.

She tried to match his violent reaction to the charming, smooth-talking diplomat whose company she was beginning to enjoy. And then it hit her. Robert was no different from Hassan, charming when he needed to be, but unlike Jaafar, willing to destroy an entire country.

Standing alongside the table, Robert uncorked the new bottle of wine and served her.

"Thank you, darling," she said, taking a sip. "It's lovely. I'll have to take a few bottles home with me."

"Only a few bottles? That'll never do. You'll take a case."

She acknowledged his generosity with a smile.

"Anything else I should know about you, Mr. Ambassador? Surely, you've had some prestigious assignments, especially with your Arabic language skills."

He shook his head. "Not really. I served in both Algeria and Iraq—not places I'd call prestigious. The world of foreign service has drastically changed over the years, and any glamour once associated with overseas assignments is long gone. The world's a different place today."

"Just different? That's a mild assessment of a world gone mad. It's downright dangerous."

"That's why I'm in Syria… to try and make it better."

Nadia did not trust herself to speak, so she put a cheese ball in her mouth.

Robert placed his hand over hers. "Don't get too full. You saw the fish Nademe was preparing."

"You're right, darling, along with her spicy tahini topping, which I just learned how to prepare, but I haven't tasted everything yet," she said as she served herself some tabbouleh.

When Nademe arrived with the fish, they watched as she removed the skin and expertly deboned it before dividing equal portions to their two plates, then topping each with her sauce.

"*Sahtain*," she said as she served them.

"Thank you, Nademe," said Nadia. "This looks amazing."

After she left, Robert stared at Nadia an awkwardly long time before speaking again.

"What's the matter?" Nadia asked. "You're suddenly very serious. Is something wrong?"

"When were you going to tell me that you'd taken documents from Hassan Jaafar's safe after he was killed?"

She paused a few seconds before responding.

She finally looked up from her plate. "Where is this coming from?" she asked. "Did you ever ask me if I'd taken documents out of his safe? Did we ever even have a conversation about the contents of Hassan's safe?"

"No, but I'm asking you now. Did you, or didn't you?"

"I found a manila envelope and assumed since it was in Hassan's safe that it must have been something important, so yes, I took it, along with the dollars, the euros, the gold bars and his Rolex watch."

"I searched your bag. It wasn't there."

"That's because I hid it. What is this?" she snapped, "some kind of inquisition? Are you accusing me of doing something wrong?"

Keep him on the defensive, Nadia.

"No, I'm not accusing you of wrong-doing, but why did you hide it?"

"Under the circumstances, why wouldn't I have hidden it? I didn't know who you were when you had our car stopped at the barrage. And, as I recall, neither you nor your men ever asked me about an envelope."

"My men searched the car."

He sounds desperate, she thought, and confident of her skills as a lawyer, she continued with her illusory answers, hoping it might confound him even more.

"Did you give them orders to specifically look for a manila envelope?"

"No, but..."

"Did they search the woman seated in the front seat?"

"No... because you claimed she and the man had done nothing wrong, and so I let them go."

"And you were right to do that, and I thank you. Their only crime was getting me safely away from Jaafar's house before the *Mukhabarat* showed up. And for all I knew, when you stopped our car, you could have been one of those dreadful security men about to haul me off to their infamous underground prison in the Syrian desert. So, I was not about to hand over a document I thought might be important to such awful people."

Robert looked at her steadily.

"What's this about anyway? Why are you questioning me like this?"

"As I said, I had a difficult meeting with President Assad this morning."

"And that's my fault?" she snapped again.

"No, it isn't, Nadia. It's just that the president asked about an incriminating document Hassan had on me, and I got put on the spot because I couldn't explain its whereabouts."

"So that made it all right to accuse me of making you uncomfortable?"

Nadia took her time before speaking again, then said, "I'm curious. How did you know Hassan?"

"Years ago, he killed a CIA agent. The man had kidnapped and tortured one of Hassan's best agents, then threw his body along the side of a highway. It was nicely covered up thanks to Hassan's colleagues in Beirut, and I agree the bastard deserved what he got, but he was CIA, and I was charged with finding the culprit. I eventually connected the dots and filled in the blanks and they all led to Hassan. So, I confronted him and offered him a deal, but he refused."

"Yes, and what a deal. You wanted him to help you destroy his country. And when he refused, you had him killed."

"Yes, but with the help of someone inside his compound who owed me a favor. And once he told me where Jaafar would be meeting a former colleague for lunch, the rest was easy."

"That was a messy way to kill someone, Robert. A bullet would have done the job."

Who was the informant, Nadia wondered? Was it Hassan's butler, the one who disliked her? Or was it Moussa, the man who drove her out of the compound and who was now employed by her father? Where were his loyalties? She needed to find out.

"Hassan told me about your regime change plans for Syria. I get that your government doesn't like Assad. Plenty of people in the region don't, for a number of reasons, but why bring down a popular president?"

"We think it's in our strategic interest to have a US-friendly Middle East. Assad, like Saddam, is no longer someone we want on our team."

"But that makes no sense. It was my understanding that post 9/11, Assad handed over al-Qaeda thugs hiding in his country and that he offered full cooperation with Washington. Sounds like a team player to me."

"Let's just say it's time for a change, and we're working with our local allies to make sure everything happens according to plan."

"I assume there was a plan for Iraq. Things didn't go well there, did they?"

"No, they didn't."

"You'll make the same mistakes here. Assad's a leader who's liberal and who supports all minorities. He's also an Arab nationalist, something his people appreciate. There are consequences to such actions."

"I agree, and I'm concerned about what will happen."

"Sounds like I'm hearing some remorse on your part. Are you having second thoughts about carrying out your assignment? If you are, do something to stop it, Robert, before it's too late."

"I can't, my orders come with certain powers, and I'm expected to use them or be replaced by someone who will."

Hassan had said the same thing when she had accused him of abandoning his moral principles.

Robert got out of his chair. "I need a bathroom break. I'll be right back," and as she watched him walk away, shoulders slouched, she saw a man coming undone.

While she finished her fish, she recalled Hassan saying the issue was not Syria per se. It was about dealing a crippling blow to Iran and Hezbollah. To do that, Syria needed to be taken out. Did Robert understand this undercurrent? Did he realize he was initiating what Hassan had described to her as a proxy war with Iran?

When he returned, she asked, "Are you all right, darling? You looked like you were dragging a bit when you left just now."

"I like Bashar, and now he knows what I'm here to do, and it makes me feel like a rat."

"Well, what you're trying to do, Robert, is dirty and cruel and destructive, and you shouldn't be doing it."

Robert starred at her before saying, "He took me by helicopter to Daraa this morning, to the scene of a massacre. Twenty-four young officers, killed. No, they weren't just killed, they were slaughtered, then burned, some beyond recognition. There was one young man whose image I can't get out of my head. He was just a kid. I saw the horror in his eyes, and that look will haunt me for a long time."

"I'm sorry you had to see that. Does that give you some pause about your insurgents? You're basically going to kill tens of thousands, maybe even hundreds of thousands of innocent civilians, then install a puppet regime against the wishes of the Syrian people?"

"I guess it depends on what kind of world you prefer," he said. "The US wants to see a world where terrorists and their backers are defeated. We're just trying to contribute to the greater good of the region."

"How does this make the world right?" she asked. "Isn't it just more of the same madness that keeps repeating itself? Someone in power has to finally steer the boat in the right direction, or we'll continue on a collision course of astronomical proportions. It isn't one country that's evil, Robert. It's we humans who create evil, whether to stay in power or to polish our image. We think we're gods who can do no wrong.

"Look," she said. "I recognize that Syria is hardly a democracy, what country is, but it's the last highly educated, secular, Arab nationalist state in the Middle East. It's religiously ecumenical, and it's been a safe refuge for minorities, particularly Christians. Did you know that Syria opened its doors to at least half a million Chaldean Christians fleeing Iraq? Doesn't that kind of goodwill count?"

"We're not fans of Arab nationalism."

"Radical Islam is far worse than socialism," she said. "I understand that Assad's idea of nationalism isn't for everyone. Like most Lebanese,

I've always tended to look to the West and their form of democracy and culture, but the Syrians have chosen otherwise, and that should be their privilege."

"That's not the view the US government takes."

"What you're really saying then is that in order for a country like Syria to survive, it must fall in line behind US leadership?"

He nodded. "Pretty much."

"That didn't work very well in Iraq, did it?"

"That's why we're still there, trying to fix past mistakes."

"The Iraqi people deserve better than what they've been dealt. Don't you agree?"

"What do you mean? We did them a favor by getting rid of Saddam."

"Have you asked them how they feel about their destroyed country? You've been in the field a long time. What don't you understand about that disaster?"

She thought carefully about how to reach him. Her heart swelled with sympathy for him, and finally said, "It's common knowledge that I was a UN diplomat before Jaafar kidnapped me. My area of expertise is war crimes and human rights. I care too much for you, Robert, to see you mixed up in something as serious as a war crimes indictment."

He stared at her, glassy-eyed.

"Syrians want to lead their lives free of Western domination," she continued. "The CIA and the West have tried for seventy years to make Syria in their image, and they have yet to succeed. You won't win this time, either."

He nodded. "Bashar said the same thing."

Nadia sat back in her chair and looked over at Robert.

"What a mess we've made of things," she sighed. "Just a few hours ago, we were lovers, and now we're bickering like mad dogs."

"That's my fault, Nadia, and I apologize. I was feeling sorry for myself. Bashar reduced me to rubble this morning and sent me packing. He wouldn't even fly back with me, drove himself home instead. That's how bad our meeting went."

She couldn't help feeling sorry for Robert. And for Bashar.

"So, I'd like to ask you again. What have you done with the documents you took from Hassan's safe? It's not information I'm proud of and certainly not something I want anyone to see."

She lied and said, "I burned them."

"Why would you go to such lengths to protect me, Nadia?"

She put her hand on his and squeezed it. "You saved my life, Robert. That's not something easily forgotten. No one else could have gotten me out of Syria without official papers. I'm deeply indebted to you."

# CHAPTER FIVE

SEATED BEHIND HIS DESK, Fouad listened as Odette, his secretary, chatted away with Joe in the reception area. Absent in this amicable exchange was any hint of Andrew's presence. Where the hell was he? Both he and Joe had been summoned to Fouad's office for an urgent two o'clock meeting. He glanced at his watch. Five minutes to the hour. There had been a time when Andrew had respected the American trait of punctuality. Had he lived here so long that he had now taken up the Lebanese habit of being fashionably late? Or worse, cared not a damn that Fouad had asked him to come and therefore did not plan to show up?

This was hardly the time for such games. Fouad was already at the epicenter of multiple firestorms. As deputy director of Lebanon's state security services, he had had a career-long collaboration with his friend and colleague, Hassan Jaafar, a rapport made even more intimate when the bomb that had taken Jaafar's life had almost taken his, too. Robert Jenkins was responsible. Fouad knew it, so did Nadia. Both sought revenge; hers fraught with far more personal risks.

And then there was Sonia, the love of his life, and a seasoned war correspondent, covering a conflict in Homs where Al-Qaeda-affiliated Islamists had just set up their center of operations.

Yet another urgent concern was a possible public health emergency. Until he could evaluate the potential for an actual smallpox epidemic, he had deferred notifying his boss, Abdel Raki, a hawkish Sunni who had the full support of the Western-backed Hariri-led government, the same anti-Syrian coalition colluding with the US to facilitate the entry of al-Qaeda insurgents into Lebanon as a counterbalance to rising Shiite-Hezbollah influence. He understood the Sunni's fear of an upsurge in Shiite power, particularly since they had remained unchallenged and all-powerful for decades, but he refused to excuse their willingness to choose religious affiliation over Lebanon's national security interests. Fouad's check on these opposing forces was Joe Lavrov, and why he had summoned him, along with Andrew, to his office.

Finally, it was only Joe who opened his door and walked in.

"Where the hell's Andrew?"

"Like I predicted yesterday, boss, he won't come. He still hates you for lying about the Nadia business. As it is, he's barely civil to me."

As was the custom whenever he held a meeting in his office, Fouad's secretary brought in a large pot of Arabic coffee and demitasse cups on a brass tray for those attending and placed it on his desk. This day she had added a plate of butter cookies.

"Is there some special occasion I don't know about?" asked Fouad.

"With all you have on your mind, sir, I thought you could use an extra bit of nourishment."

"How thoughtful of you, Odette."

"My pleasure. Anything else, boss?"

"No, thank you, but if Andrew should arrive, please show him in."

"Of course."

Joe poured himself a coffee, as did Fouad, and just as they were about to settle into their meeting, and without so much as a sound of approaching footsteps, Andrew burst into the office. He glanced at his watch, as did Fouad, and saw that it was precisely two o'clock. Fouad stood and held out his hand. Andrew refused it and took a seat.

"Help yourself to coffee and cookies," said Fouad, pointing to the tray.

Andrew nodded and served himself.

Fouad's office on the top floor of state security headquarters overlooked the intersection of Damascus Street and Corniche Mazra, the deadly territorial divide that had separated Muslim West from Christian

East Beirut and determined who lived and who died, according to their religious affiliation, during the fifteen-year-long civil war. He dreaded any such horror happening again. In the current fragile political environment, he feared that a public health issue, were it to reach epidemic proportions, could plunge the country back down into the bowels of hell.

"Thank you for coming, Andrew. I understand how difficult this is, but in a situation as potentially dangerous as this, I think you'd agree we need to put feelings aside."

"I'm here, aren't I?" Andrew replied, dictating, by his response, English over Arabic.

A rebuke on Andrew's part, no doubt, but so be it, thought Fouad. There was no compelling reason to conduct their meeting in Arabic since both he and Joe spoke perfect English.

"If you're looking to me to treat an outbreak of smallpox, I can't. I don't have the vaccine."

"I know. Joe outlined our options… Russia, Israel and the US. None of them realistic. If you have any other ideas, I'd like to hear them."

"Actually, I thought of something on my way here. As you may recall, I befriended Robert Jenkins when I was at the Broumana safe house recovering from my injuries. You'd encouraged me to chat him up, which I did, and we ended our time together on a positive note. We even did a few rounds of boxing in Joe's gym. Any chance you remember that?" Andrew said, inclining his head toward Joe while refusing to make eye contact.

Joe ignored the slight. "Of course, I do, and I can still see the look on his face. He'd let his guard down, and you came at him with two jabs, hitting him in the cheek."

"And boy, did that piss him off," Andrew said, shaking his head as if talking to himself. "And then he thought he could surprise me with a left hook but I saw it coming, and got in another jab.

"So," he continued, "I thought about giving him a call to ask for his help. Even though we had a lively discussion about the US's calamitous role in the region, I think at heart he's a decent guy, just dangerously and naively in love with his country. I should think he'd be amenable to helping us, or at the very least to make a few phone calls. And if the US isn't willing to help, maybe I could convince him to ask the Israelis. They'd have an even greater incentive. Epidemics can cross borders as easily as wildfires."

No one but Fouad knew of Nadia's liaison with Jenkins, and he intended to keep it that way. Now he had to hope Jenkins would make no mention of his involvement with Nadia.

"There's the third source for the vaccine," said Joe. "I'd be willing to contact the Russians if need be. I still maintain cordial relations with my father's former colleagues. The Russians are allies of the Syrian regime, and they may jump at the chance to provide a service for Lebanon in its time of need. It would be an excellent PR move for them. It may even swing Lebanon into their orbit."

"Wouldn't that be bad for this country?" asked Andrew.

Fouad jumped in, "Not in my opinion. Aid from the Americans comes with too many restrictions. The most significant... they'll only deliver military aid to our army if it agrees not to use the weapons against Israel."

"That can't be right. If it came to Lebanon's security concerns, they'd surely allow those weapons to be used in self-defense."

Fouad shook his head. "Not if they were directed against Israel." He let a moment pass before speaking again. "So, would you be willing to call Jenkins now? I have the number of the US Embassy in Syria."

"Of course. I've only been given a few days to get hold of a vaccine. If I don't have something to tell the insurgents when they return, I'm afraid of what they'll do."

"Which is why I'd like to assign bodyguards to you and Leila. I just need Fouad's okay, and I'll arrange it."

"By all means, do whatever it takes to keep Andrew and Leila safe."

Andrew was about to protest, but Joe cut him off. "Don't you dare be so selfish as to refuse. I saw how terrified Leila was. If you don't want to do it for yourself, do it for her."

Andrew nodded. "You're right. We need protection. We're both scared of those men and wonder what will happen when they return."

"When those bastards show up, your clinic will be safe and secure. Your bodyguards won't draw attention to themselves. They'll blend in with the office staff, but unlike the personnel, they'll be fully armed and capable of protecting everyone else there. You'll never be alone, Andrew."

"Okay. Go ahead and arrange it. And when they return, what do I do? Face them and tell them there's no vaccine?"

Fouad heard the fear in Andrew's voice and sympathized. He could barely contain his own anxiety.

"No," said Joe. "You tell them how difficult it is to obtain because there are only three countries who have it, that you're working on getting it, but that it may take longer than a few days. The delay will give us time to find their hiding place. Don't worry, Andrew, just handle them in the same remarkable way you did when they came to your office. Weren't you scared then?"

"Terrified."

"But you handled it like a pro. The next time won't be any different, except you'll have protection waiting in the wings."

Fouad studied Andrew. He so admired this man who had been severely wounded yet had fought back and regained his health. He could have returned to the States but elected to stay and learn Arabic and now has dedicated his life to working with the most disenfranchised people in the world. Fouad was heartbroken that he had lost Andrew's trust. He committed himself to do whatever was needed to gain back his friendship as long as it did not require him to reveal his agreement with Nadia. There I go again, he thought, keeping secrets from Andrew, but it was Nadia who had pushed Andrew aside this time, and it would be up to her, once she had successfully carried out her plan to topple Jenkins, to explain it to him.

"You're ready to make the call?" asked Fouad.

"Right," and Andrew pulled his phone out of his shirt pocket, and handed it to Fouad who was relieved to see that Andrew had finally traded in his old Nokia for an iPhone. He handed it back to Andrew as it rang.

"Office of the Ambassador," responded a woman.

"This is Dr. Andrew Sullivan. I'm a friend of Ambassador Jenkins. If he's free, I'd like a word with him, please."

"Just a minute, Doctor. I'll see if the Ambassador is available."

While waiting, he clicked on the speakerphone and placed it on the desk so Joe and Fouad could hear his conversation.

After a brief delay, Andrew heard Jenkins' voice.

"Andrew Sullivan. What a nice surprise. I hope you're in Damascus. I'd love to see you."

"Afraid not, Robert. I'm calling from Beirut. I have a crisis on my hands, and I'm hoping you can help."

"Sorry to hear that. What's going on?"

"As you may recall, when we met in Broumana, I was studying Arabic so I could join Doctors without Borders and work in the Shatilla Palestinian camp."

"Yes, of course, I remember. I suggested you were wasting your time, but that's only because I thought you were heads above most Americans and selfishly wanted you to come work with me."

Fouad noticed Andrew's face light up.

"I appreciate the compliment. I've been working in the camp now close to a year. I'm one of four doctors taking care of twenty-two thousand people, and that includes the thousands of newly arrived Syrian refugees. It's challenging work and long hours, but I enjoy it."

Jenkins whistled. "That's quite a patient load. Where are you calling from? I hear some noise in the background."

"You remember the corner of Damascus Street and Corniche Mazra, don't you?"

"Of course, yes, you're at the café on the corner."

Fouad was impressed by how skillfully Andrew had handled that question. Had he told Jenkins he was in Fouad's office, the conversation might have taken a different turn. He glanced at Joe, who was smiling, and shook his head, in awe at how Andrew had responded.

"So, here's my dilemma, Robert. A few days ago, some al-Qaeda insurgents walked into my office."

"That must not have been pleasant."

"Indeed not. Apparently, they came across the Syrian border and slipped undetected into the camp. Not sure why they chose Shatilla, but maybe it's because their previous safe havens in the north had been destroyed, and in desperation, they settled on us. They brought vials of smallpox with them, Robert. Somehow one of them broke, and several of their people have come down with the disease."

"Did they say where they got the vials?"

"From Benghazi, but who knows if that's true. This place is full of conspiracy theories."

"Some of those theories are true, Andrew."

Indeed, they are, thought Fouad, as he listened, bewildered, to this bastard who had killed his friend, Jaafar, and who would, no doubt, kill again, chatting up Andrew, the nicest, most gentle of men, as though the two were best friends.

"The vials may very well have come from Benghazi," said Robert. "I'll check it out, but that's neither here nor there right now and doesn't solve your problem."

You are one arrogant bastard, thought Fouad. You were probably in on the CIA operation that had them shipped from Libya via Turkey into Syria.

"They've given me only a few days to get the vaccine, and because they're hiding somewhere inside the camp, I'm worried about a possible epidemic. My research tells me that the US, Russia and Israel are the only countries that have available stockpiles. I'm not sure what the insurgents will do to me or my staff if I can't help them. I'm feeling desperate, Robert. I need your help."

"I can't promise anything, Andrew, but I'll make a few calls. If I feel I've reached a dead-end in Washington, would you mind if I tried Tel Aviv? The Israelis have every reason to want to help, but that'll be their call, not mine. Give me twenty-four hours to get you some answers."

"I don't have twenty-four hours, Robert. I need an answer sooner than that."

"Okay, pardon my ignorance, but what exactly would a smallpox epidemic mean, in terms of deaths?"

"It kills about forty percent of people who get infected. Once the person falls ill, it takes somewhere between five and seven days for it to spread to others."

"Jesus, no wonder you're so worried. I'll get right on it and do what I can to cut through the bureaucracy and get you some answers."

"Thanks, Robert," and Andrew hung up.

This region had seen its share of dead bodies, thought Fouad. The eleventh-century Philistine plague, the Justinian plague in the sixth century that almost brought down the Roman Empire, then the Black Plague in the early 1300s that hit the coastal cities of Ashkelon, Jerusalem, Beirut and Damascus before spreading to Europe. How is it possible that this sort of thing could still be happening in the twenty-first century?

"He didn't sound very encouraging, did he," said Andrew.

"He's a diplomat," said Joe. "They speak in code and double-talk, and half the time, what they say is a lie."

"Look, Andrew," said Fouad, "I've known Robert Jenkins a long time…"

"There you go with your fucking secrets again. You could have been upfront, for once, and told me you knew him. You should have been the one to speak with him, not me."

"But he likes you."

"Don't bullshit me, Fouad."

"I'm serious. You're honest, even if you're still a bit naïve about the world, and you're in his good graces. He's more likely to respond to your request than one coming from me. We trained at the CIA together along with Hassan Jaafar…"

Andrew nodded and rolled his eyes. "Birds of a feather."

"No, Andrew. I lie when necessary, and generally, it's in the service of my country, but I've never squandered my career in skullduggery and subversion like Jenkins has, and he knows that, and he hates me for the ethical principles I never abandoned."

"You only betray friends, is that it?"

"I regret I deceived you, Andrew. Truly, I do, but I still maintain it was for security reasons."

"Whatever…"

"Am I hearing a conciliatory tone?"

Andrew's phone rang. He gave Fouad an anxious look.

"Go ahead. Answer it but put it on speakerphone again."

"Hello?"

"Andrew, I back-channeled this and went right to the person I know in Tel Aviv who isn't afraid to cut through red tape to get things done."

Fouad scribbled something on a piece of paper and slid it in front of Andrew.

"Isn't that a risk since the two countries are enemy nations?"

Robert laughed. "Andrew, you're too honest for your own good. Historically, the two countries have handled delicate matters without any outside interference. With the utmost discretion, my contact is willing to do just that. I thought you'd be relieved I could find help so soon, but I'm hearing you hesitate. Are you interested in his suggestions or not?"

Andrew saw Fouad nodding.

"I apologize if I sound indecisive. It's just that I'm in over my head and nervous about the whole thing. Of course, I want to hear his suggestions."

"Understandable. I'd be nervous, too. This is potentially huge, but you did the right thing by calling me, so relax. Now, my contact wants to know if you have any hazmat wear."

Fouad shook his head and slipped Andrew another note.

"Afraid not, but we do have surgical gowns and gloves and footwear. Will that do?"

"If there's contamination, and you have a lot of people already ill, no. You'll need hazardous material wear. Here's what he's willing to do. Without raising eyebrows, he can get hold of a half dozen hazmat suits and deliver them to the UN headquarters at the Israeli Lebanese border. You'd only have to send someone there to pick them up."

"What about vaccines?" asked Andrew.

"That's a bit more complicated and would take time, which is what you don't have. He'd have to go up the chain of command to the Prime Minister's office for such a request, and he'd like to avoid that if at all possible. He suggests a commando raid. It's expedient and will get the job done quickly. Once you've determined the location, it would be simply a matter of sending in the troops to take them out."

Andrew could not respond.

"Are you still there?" asked Robert.

"I am, just a bit surprised at his suggestion."

"Andrew, there are times when you have to put aside your Hippocratic oath. This is one such occasion."

Joe nodded this time and, with his hand, encouraged Andrew to keep talking.

"Okay, what do we need to do on this end? How long will it take your contact to get the equipment to the border and into the hands of the UN?"

"At most, a couple of hours. I'll call him as soon as we've concluded our business and dial you back with a specific time. Will that work?"

"Yes, thank you, Robert. I'm feeling somewhat relieved already, even if I don't like the idea of killing people."

"These aren't peace-loving people, are they, Andrew."

"No, they aren't."

"Andrew?"

"Yes?"

"Hold onto your integrity. You're the good American. There aren't a lot of your kind left. I should know."

"Thank you, Robert. I'll expect to hear back from you soon," and he hung up.

"Well done, Andrew," said Fouad. "Now, Joe and I'll decide the best plan of action."

"Any idea where they may be holed up?" Andrew asked.

"Pretty much," said Joe. "They'd have wanted to remain inconspicuous, and to do that, they'd have had to take shelter in a remote area of the camp. There aren't many such places, but I remembered the Gaza

Hospital and have sent my men to check it out. It's the only place I can think of."

"Wasn't Aziza's father the hospital's chief surgeon?" asked Andrew.

"Yes," said Fouad. "He ran Gaza Hospital during the Israeli invasion in 1982... and he was quite the hero. While the Israelis were carpet bombing the city, he and his staff carried on, performing surgery under the most deplorable conditions. Your Leila was part of his staff."

Andrew nodded. "Yes, she was... a very brave lady."

"And then in 1984, the camp was savagely attacked by Shiite militiamen," said Joe.

"The infamous war of the camps," said Fouad, shaking his head. "Such a tragic episode in Shiite-Sunni relations. Seventeen hundred people lost their lives."

"My God," whistled Andrew.

"The hospital was badly damaged in the fighting, and the Palestinian Red Crescent Society, which ran the facility, didn't have the money to repair it. Ever since, that ten-story building has been left to fall into disrepair."

"What a waste when we could be using that space."

"Some of the Syrian refugees are living in the upper floors," said Joe. "The basement, that's another matter. That's where the surgical unit and morgue were located. With nowhere to bury the dead, staff had to pile all those bodies there. Imagine the stench that must have permeated the floors and walls. That kind of odor never goes away."

"And that's where you suspect the insurgents are hiding?"

Joe nodded. "Once my team confirms it, we'll finalize our plan."

"What about the residents on the upper floors?" asked Andrew. "Will they be in danger?"

"I don't think so. When al-Qaeda insurgents broke into the Palestinian camp outside Tripoli a few years ago, the residents immediately moved out of their way. These camps are tightly knit communities, and they don't take kindly to strangers worming their way in, especially that kind of vermin. And with the rampant drug problem we have, people are even more leery of outsiders."

"But what if…"

"There won't be any 'what if's,' Andrew. Those sick, regardless of who they are, will be taken out."

"You mean killed?"

"Yes."

Andrew stared hard at Joe.

"Your phone is ringing, Andrew, better answer it."

"Yes, Robert?"

"Your hazmat suits will be at the border within the hour. Keep me posted."

"Will do," replied Andrew. "Thank you for your help, Robert."

After he closed his phone, he looked at Fouad.

"Any idea what the insurgents intended to do with their vials of smallpox?"

"If I had to bet money," said Fouad, "I'd guess these vials were intended for Dahiyah, the Shiite neighborhood. It's the most densely populated suburb of the city, and a smallpox outbreak, with no vaccines, would kill thousands of innocent people."

"Didn't Israel strike that neighborhood during the 2006 war?" asked Andrew.

"Yes, because it's also the Hezbollah stronghold," said Joe. "They destroyed some four hundred buildings and left tens of thousands of people homeless."

"But in this case, it's religion, isn't it," Andrew said, shaking his head. "If they're Shiite, it's all right to expose them to smallpox, but if they're Sunnis, they're safe. This place is an unholy nightmare."

Andrew sat staring out the window behind Fouad's desk until he stood abruptly.

"I must go. I still have patients to see in the clinic."

Joe, seated next to him, also stood and offered Andrew his hand. "I'll see you back at the camp."

Andrew looked at him. "Yeah," and shook his hand.

Fouad came around from his desk, his hand extended too, but by then, Andrew was at the door. He opened it and walked out.

Fouad fell back into his chair. "He's quite a remarkable man, isn't he, Joe. Did you see how he managed not to lie to Jenkins? He should be doing our job. No, he's too nice for our kind of work. We have to protect him. Do whatever it takes. And Joe, I saw how he warmed up to you a bit. Please put in a good word for me when you see him. I love that man, and it breaks my heart to see how much he hates me."

# CHAPTER SIX

SONIA TRIED SEVERAL TIMES from Father Frans' apartment to get a phone connection to Beirut. Homs was only about two hours away, but it may as well have been the other side of the world. It was from the balcony off Frans' living room that she finally got through, and while waiting for Fouad to pick up, glanced out over a city she had not seen in over twenty years.

The Homs skyline, like so many other Syrian cities, was dominated by minarets and church steeples, but the Khalid al Walid mosque, distinctive for its multiple blue domes, stood out from any vantage point as an architectural gem. Unlike Damascus, a bustling traffic-congested city, Homs was clean and orderly; its quiet, tree-lined streets had sidewalks, playgrounds and gardens, and tourists loved its older homes, the ones with prominent Mamluk black and white stone exteriors. Two distinct clock towers still adorned the city center's roundabout, as did a bright blue and white office building, a *veritable* eyesore, Sonia thought, when compared with the French colonial architecture, its stately, sandstone façades dominating the rest of the city center.

"Hi, Fouad, finally. Where were you? The phone rang and rang. I was about to hang up."

"Sorry, darling. I was in a meeting. You're not calling from Homs, I hope."

"Actually, I am. I thought to stay a while longer. I've things I want to check out and…"

"Whatever it is, it's not important enough to risk your life. You need to leave today," he insisted, in an outburst of emotion she had never heard before. "Homs is about to become a war zone—I insist you get out now."

"And you don't think I've ever been in a war zone? I'm a seasoned correspondent, and I won't be told by anyone, least of all by someone's who's never covered a war, what I should or shouldn't do."

"Don't take offense, Sonia. I want you home in one piece, that's all I care about. Besides, I can fill you in on everything you want to know. By the way, thanks to the flash drive you and Joe brought back from Daraa. I now have intel on the insurgents' long-range plans. Trust me, you simply can't stay there."

"What don't you understand, Fouad," by now, her voice so loud that Frans' next-door neighbor rushed onto her balcony.

"Good heavens," the woman said. "Show some civility. We shouldn't be made to listen to such shouting."

Sonia gave her a scornful look, turned her back and continued yelling.

"I'm not a stenographer. I don't take notes from someone dictating to me what's supposedly happening when I can find out myself. Eye-witness events! That's what distinguishes me from ordinary mass-media journalists."

It was Fouad who shouted this time. "I'm not challenging you, so stop being so insolent. I know you're the best at what you do, Sonia. All I'm trying to do is protect you, maybe even save your life. And now, because you're so goddamn stubborn, you're forcing me to give you information I shouldn't be giving you…"

He hesitated a moment, and when he spoke again, he lowered his voice. "An al Qaeda-linked group calling itself al-Nusra will be arriving into the Old City tonight. It won't be pleasant for anyone once they've settled in and set up their headquarters. It'll be very different from anything you've ever covered before."

How would he know, she wondered? She had covered war intimately for years—North Africa, across the Middle East, Central America. Yes, it was a job no sane person would ever want—always the same bombed-out cities with their destroyed buildings, the same wide-eyed faces of terrified children, the same stink of burned, disfigured bodies—but she had come to discover that war was her addiction and her mind was made up. Homs would be her next fix.

"Fine, fine, fine, okay. I'll leave," and she hung up without specifying when, which she knew would infuriate him.

Hot-faced and furious, Sonia stormed back inside the apartment and bumped into Frans, who was standing in front of the balcony door. "You were ripping rather loudly out there, Sonia," he said. "What got into you? Fouad's right. If you had any sense, you'd take his advice and leave. You were very wrong to be so combative. The man obviously loves you and is concerned for your safety."

"Yeah, yeah, I know, I should have been nicer, but my temper flares when someone tells me I can't do something when I know I can. I've covered wars, Fouad hasn't. And I know how to keep out of harm's way. I've been doing it for years."

"Need I remind you that you spent months recovering from the car bomb that was meant to kill you. Thankfully, you only lost an eye. Next time could be way worse. Are you sure you want to risk something like that again?"

"Life is full of risks, Frans. By the way, who's your nosy neighbor next door. She came out on her balcony and gave me a dirty look when I was shouting, and I wasn't very nice."

"Well, you should have been. She just dropped off some freshly baked cookies, and I've a mind not to share any of them with you."

Sonia took Frans' head in her hands and planted a kiss on his bald spot. "Thank you for putting up with me. And despite what you may think, I do have a good reason for staying."

"Is it something I even want to know?" he asked, shaking his head and rolling his eyes.

"There's an American journalist here in Bab Amr by the name of

Mary O'Brien whom I want to meet. She works for multiple media outlets, and I want to ask her why she's embedded with the Western-backed Free Syrian Army, which she describes in her posts as a legitimate Syrian opposition group, except you and I know it isn't. It's a front for al-Qaeda jihadists, and its real name is al-Nusra."

"Her readers don't know that, Sonia, and maybe she doesn't either. From everything I've seen so far, the official narrative of this conflict has been decided, and no one cares if one of the players is called the Free Syrian Army or al-Nusra. What matters is Assad is a brutal dictator, killing his own people, and the protests are peaceful. Anyone questioning that line is marginalized. End of story."

"So, that'll make her a respected journalist because she totes the official line while I'll be maligned if I write what I perceive to be the truth? That's hardly fair. I was taught that a good journalist was supposed to monitor the centers of power."

"It has nothing to do with who's the more respected or who's writing the truth. What's truth anyway? I've been here for fifty-five years, and I still don't know. Is Assad a brutal dictator who should be removed from office, or is he an Arab nationalist trying to protect his country from outside interference? Why can't he be both?"

"Fair enough, but even if I do manage to build a strong case for the latter, special interests will still demonize me."

"Well, that'll be your challenge, won't it? That's what defines a good journalist."

"Such clarity," she said, shaking her head.

"No, I'm just a simple man who tries to be kind to people and show them how to be courteous to others, so they can avoid needless confrontations. Maybe if everyone did that, we wouldn't be in the mess we're in today."

"But you have to admit there's an unprecedented suppression of verifiable facts here, Frans, like the hundred plus dead soldiers over the last six months. Easy enough to verify, yet no one bothers. That's what's different this time."

"No, it's this whole social media thing gone mad. I've watched it raise its ugly head. The lies and half-truths, the misinformation. No one's held accountable. Who knows who and what it will destroy next?"

"This oppressive heat may not destroy me, Frans, but if it continues, I'll wither away. It's the middle of September. Tell me the weather will break soon. No offense, but I'm accustomed to air conditioning, and if I'm going to stay in Homs, I may need to look for a flat that'll provide an occasional breath of air."

Frans' two-bedroom apartment was more spacious than his Daraa flat. It was brighter, too, with a set of large glass doors that led to a balcony that overlooked a garden in a back courtyard five stories below. But it was unbearably hot, and Frans had only a small fan that circulated nothing but hot air.

"I can offer you a stroll through the souk, Sonia. It'll be cooler there."

"A deal, and I'll buy lunch if you find us a nice cafe."

"I know just the place."

"I'm ravenous after all that shouting. Poor Fouad. Was I unbearable?"

"That would be putting it mildly."

As they stepped outside the building, they ran into his neighbor. *"Marhaba,* Madame Chidiac. I'd like you to meet my friend, Sonia Rizk."

"We've already met," the woman replied sharply in Arabic.

Sonia said, "I apologize for shouting and disturbing you earlier, Madame Chidiac. It was very inconsiderate of me."

"Apology accepted, my dear. These are trying times, and it's easy to see how quickly tempers can flare."

"Thank you for understanding and for the cookies," Sonia added. "Frans has promised to share one or two with me, but only if I behave."

"You let me know if he doesn't, and I'll make you some of your very own."

"How kind of you."

"Well, we're off to the souk to escape the heat," said Frans, "and to have lunch. Have a nice rest of your day, Madame Chidiac."

"And to you both," and she walked off, swinging her shopping bag.

As they turned to go in the opposite direction, Sonia slipped her arm under Frans', something she could do in this predominately Christian part of Homs without breaking any taboos. And as they made their way to the souk, people of all persuasions, young and old, whether dressed in chador, hijab, tight jeans or business suits, greeted Frans in their native tongue, wishing him a pleasant day. And it was at this point that Sonia and Frans transitioned to Arabic, too.

"It's heartwarming to see how loved you are by the people here, Frans."

"I minister to all faiths. I don't even like religion."

"But you're a Jesuit priest…"

"And I'm a trained psychotherapist and a student of Zen Buddhism, so what? I believe in the spiritual experience. That's the source of one's faith, and that comes out of the church's teaching of the 1960s, when it still believed in social justice and liberation theology. At least here, I'm far enough away from the rigid hierarchy of the Vatican that I can practice an unorthodox version of what I think it means to be a Catholic priest."

"You're what every priest should be, Frans. And your dedication to special needs people is even more commendable."

"I think it's what I love best. They work on my farm just outside Homs with great pride. The senior Assad gave me a parcel of land years ago, and now, thanks to all my helpers, we have olive groves and vineyards and a large vegetable garden. And each morning, I go around collecting everyone in my old VW van and bring them to the farm."

"You're a regular old hippie, aren't you, Frans."

He laughed out loud. "Why yes, I suppose I am."

"One day, I'll write all about you."

"Oh, no—anything but that."

As they walked, Sonia's mind swirled with the pros and cons of remaining in Homs.

"Frans, do you remember how skeptical I was when you first approached me and asked me to come to Daraa?"

"Yes, but more importantly, I remember how quickly I changed your mind."

"But now I'm feeling a bit intimidated. I'll be going up against powerful forces this time."

"You've never been afraid to take on authority before. You've just been out of the field too long, and jumping back in can seem daunting at first."

Frans was right. Since her injury, she had yet to take on an assignment. Once she took the leap, she would regain her confidence, and the idea of putting herself in danger in order to get the truth would excite her.

As they neared the souk, Sonia marveled at its size; it appeared to span multiple city blocks. And why wouldn't it, she thought. Like all souks across the Middle East, it was the hub of community life and this one in Homs' was no different. Its myriad alleyways bustled with shoppers. Its stall holders shouted out their wares on everything from clothing and textiles to old carpets, gold, silver and spices. One shop boasted more than five thousand types of herbs, plants, spices, oils and perfumes. How could anything better reflect the Middle Eastern merchant, long renowned for his acuity and resourcefulness? With its high rock domes and crowned columns, its huge windows set atop the arches for ventilation, the souk's cylindrical roof was an engineering marvel. Sonia let out a sigh of relief once she breathed in the cool air inside the souk.

"I'm sorry, Frans. I don't mean to always be complaining, but I find the heat unbearable."

"You're spoiled, dear lady."

"Don't I know it."

"If you're going to be staying in Homs, we'll have to do something about that."

"Like what? Have me run laps around the city to build up my tolerance?"

"Something like that."

Fat chance of that happening, she thought.

"How old is this souk, Frans?" she asked as she ran her hand along the stone wall.

"It's thirteenth-century, built by the great Kurdish warrior, Saladin."

"Have you ever wondered what it must have been like to have lived in ancient times?"

"Aside from the few modern conveniences we enjoy today, probably not that different. There have always been the rich and the poor. Those who enjoyed lavish lifestyles and those who labored endless hours, all probably eating the same foods we consume, even using the same spices and condiments, all committing the same scandalous crimes we see played out today all over the world.

"But when the wealthy started to accumulate great wealth and acquire parcels of land and establish borders, and the inequalities became too blatant, the wars began, and the nation-states came crashing down just like we're seeing today."

"Frans, I hope we're going to have lunch before this nation-state comes crumbling down. I'm about to faint from hunger."

"Oh, impatient lady, I've been leading you there all along. It's just inside the next alley." When she saw the crowded restaurant, Sonia let out a cry. "We'll never get a table."

"Don't despair, help is on the way," said Frans, and sure enough, when she looked, she saw a man come rushing toward them.

"*Ahlan, Abouna* [father], *Ahlan*."

"Greetings Joseph, I didn't expect the restaurant to be so crowded."

"It's market day, Father, always my busiest time."

"I'd forgotten the day."

And the reason we saw Madame Chidiac with her shopping basket, thought Sonia.

"Any chance you could find a table for me and my guest?"

"For you, Father, anything. Give me a minute, and I'll get one set for you."

"Joseph's the owner. He'll take care of us."

"I've no doubt," she laughed, shaking her head.

The clean white walls were bare, and a checkered tablecloth and vase of flowers adorned each table.

The owner returned. "I have your table ready, Father."

They followed Joseph, weaving their way through the rows of tightly crammed tables until they reached a quiet corner against the back wall. As they took their seats, both Frans and Sonia noticed the young man at a nearby table. He was talking to a woman seated in front of him.

"Isn't that our Iraqi-American?" Sonia asked.

"I believe it is. And look how he's cleaned himself up."

"Indeed, plaid shirt, khaki pants. Can't get more American-looking than that. Haircut, too, neatly trimmed beard, and now that we can see his face, he's actually quite good looking."

"I wonder what he's doing here."

"On the phone this morning, Fouad mentioned an advance group of Al-Qaeda affiliates moving into Homs. Maybe he's part of that operation."

"Let's find out," said Frans, with a wink, as he stood and walked over to his table, Sonia following close behind. "Greetings, young man, I never did get your name the first time we met. But if we're going to keep bumping into one another, maybe it's time we properly introduced ourselves."

What an amazing person, thought Sonia, as she watched Frans in action. More saint than spy but nonetheless intuitive and intelligent, unpretentious and a keen observer of human behavior, and above all, kind-hearted, forever hoping he can help good prevail over evil.

"My name is Frans, and surely you remember this lady, Sonia Rizk."

The young man gave both of them a hard stare before finally giving his name. "I'm Omar, and this is…"

"Mary O'Brien," said Sonia.

So different from the photos I've seen of her, she thought. In person, she is a beauty, no need for any make-up. Her tan linen blouse and matching slacks, though wrinkled and well-worn, still look so stylish on her that Sonia felt a pang of jealousy.

"And I know you, too," Mary replied, "from your work."

"It looks like you two haven't eaten yet," Frans said.

"We only just arrived," said Mary.

"What do you say we pull our tables together?" said Frans.

And without waiting for a reply, Frans summoned a waiter and asked him to join their tables.

"There," he said, sitting himself in front of Omar while allowing Sonia to be opposite Mary. "First, we see you in Daraa, and now in Homs. What brings you to my city, Omar?"

Sonia was more curious about his appearance. One minute al-Qaeda, now the clean-cut American. Why?

"Mary arrived this morning from Beirut. She'd arranged another interview with the Free Syrian Army, but this time she needed a translator, so I was called in."

That explains his appearance, thought Sonia. First impressions count when you are trying to recruit a journalist to your cause.

"Sonia, you've been quiet since your Hariri work. Is that because you got burned out by your series in *The London Review of Books*? Quite good, by the way, but what a risk you took, calling out Israel the way you did."

"No, it was a car bomb. I lost my eye and sustained other injuries. I spent months between hospital and rehab."

"Sorry, and come to think of it, I did hear about the car bomb. That's when you were due to be in New York for an award. Yeah, it was news for a day or two but then went away."

"Like most stories," Sonia said, pleased to hear Mary mention her award. "I don't know about the rest of you, but I'd like to order. Have you all had a chance to look at the menu?"

"I'm going to defer to you, Frans," said Mary, putting down her menu. "You're from here, and you know the local specials."

Omar and Sonia nodded, and Frans raised his hand to call the waiter.

"We'll each have your spicy kabobs with French fries and baba ghanouj," said Frans, and turning to the others, explained, "It's their very own version. Instead of tahini with the eggplant, they add yogurt, lemon and garlic."

"Any beverages?" asked the waiter.

"I'd like a beer, the coldest you have," said Sonia, looking up at him with a smile. "Anyone care to join me?"

"I'll have one," said Frans.

"So will I," replied Mary. "Omar, what about you?"

"I don't drink," he replied curtly. "Islam forbids it."

"And we all respect that," said Frans, trying to mitigate Omar's harsh tone.

"Sonia, do you think you'll ever get another assignment after attacking Israel?" asked Mary.

"My readership spans all of Asia. No problem with censorship of Israel there. That's more your worry since you report for both US and UK media outlets."

"It is, and you're right, and the rules never change, no matter how outrageous Israel's behavior."

Mary fiddled in her purse before she finally pulled out a pack of cigarettes. "Does anyone mind? I never get to smoke state-side unless I go outdoors."

"Everyone smokes here, go ahead," said Omar, over-riding any possible objection.

"I could lecture you on the hazards to your health," laughed Frans, "but I think you already know that."

"I do, and I appreciate your concern, but when I'm on assignment, smoking relaxes me."

Before Mary had a chance to light up, the waiter brought their food. "I'll have another beer," she said. "Anyone else."

"I'll join you," said Frans. "*Sahtein,* everyone. I hope you enjoy your lunch."

Silence reigned over the table as each of them dove into their food. Sonia let out a sigh of contentedness as she bit into a piece of kebab, chewing it slowing and savoring the spicy flavors.

"What divine food," swooned Mary. "What are the spices I'm tasting?"

"Cumin, cinnamon and a splash of Aleppo pepper," said Frans. "And I hope you like the baba ghanouj."

Everyone looked up from their food and nodded.

Sonia eventually took a break and put down her knife and fork. "Mary, you said you were on assignment. Does this mean you plan to stay in Homs?"

Mary looked at Omar before she answered. "I gathered from my interview this morning that things are about to heat up here. Isn't that right, Omar?"

When he did not respond, she continued. "Not sure why he won't answer," she said, trying to catch his eye, "but yes, I'll be here as long as there's a story to write."

"You do realize your new friends are a front for al-Qaeda, don't you?"

Sonia's comment was directed at Omar, daring him to reveal in front of Mary who he really represented.

"Who says?" scowled Mary.

"Ask Omar. He'll tell you I'm right."

He darted her a menacing look that made the back of her neck tingle.

"Well, whoever they are, the US supports them," said Mary.

"That's hardly a reference. You should have done a bit of research before you agreed to embed with them."

"Regardless of who they represent, we're on the same team. Assad needs to step down. He's a dictator. Obama's been upfront about his position, and that's the storyline I'll follow."

"If that were true, I'd agree, but we're in the Middle East where truth comes in various shades of grey. Whatever the facts, it shouldn't be al-Qaeda or the Free Syrian Army or any foreign power that removes Assad from power. It should be the Syrian people."

"That's your bias," Mary replied. "Anyone care to join me in another beer?" She looked around. "No takers?" She caught the attention of the waiter and showed him her empty beer bottle. "Another, please."

Mary had continued to smoke nonstop, even while eating, and was now on her third beer. Sonia wondered if she wasn't a bit damaged.

She was all too familiar with the signs. She had once been on that same destructive path. Too many wars, too much booze, and far too many men. The average person seldom experienced war. They did not know how it felt to run down a street under mortar fire or dodge a sniper who followed you in his lens as you dashed across a street. What a tremendous toll war eventually takes on one's psyche. Sonia was grateful to Fouad for having helped her recover. She hoped Mary had an anchor somewhere, too.

"Back to your comment about Assad being a dictator, Mary. Saddam Hussein was one, too, but that didn't make what the US did in Iraq right."

"Assad's an Alawite," Omar insisted, "that's the difference."

"God doesn't play favorites, Omar."

He glared across the table at Frans. "By Allah, we shall mince the Alawites in meat grinders and feed their flesh to the dogs."

Brows furrowed, Mary leaned over the table and whispered to Sonia. "What did Omar just say? He sounded angry."

"You don't want to know. You'd get the wrong impression of your new friend if I told you."

"Tell me," she insisted, a bit louder than she should. Annoyed that no one would respond, she stood and announced she needed a bathroom break.

As soon as she left the table, Frans looked across the table at Omar. "What's going on? We know what you believe, who you represent. Why are you in Homs?"

"I'm here to help establish our future caliphate," he responded, far more imperious in his manner than he had been in Daraa.

"How could you even think that a possibility?" asked Sonia. "That sounds so… preposterous. This is the twenty-first century."

"It's you who doesn't understand. There's a new dawn, the beginning of the end for the likes of you, and all Christians in Homs. I've given you fair warning."

"Who's your leader?" asked Frans.

"Abu Bakr Baghdadi. I assume you know who he is."

"Head of the Islamic State of Iraq and the Levant," replied Frans. "Radicalized at Camp Bucca in Iraq."

"I can rationalize Baghdadi's transformation," said Sonia. "He and his fellow Iraqi military officers were tortured in that camp by US soldiers, but how did this happen to you, a nice young man from Dearborn?"

"I told you in Daraa. I answered Allah's call to come kill the infidels."

As he said this, he stared into her eyes with such menace that her mind's eye made a scene of him shooting her in the face.

Frans was about to respond when Sonia put her hand on his arm and motioned toward Mary, zigzagging her way through the rows of tables as she made her way back, meeting anyone's glance with a smile, as she did, and holding her lit cigarette up in the air.

"Did I miss anything important while I was gone?" Mary asked as she sat. When no one answered, she looked at each of them. "Omar, you look like you're madder than hell. Are you all right?"

He forced a laugh and shook his head. "I'm fine."

"If you say so," Mary replied, turning her attention to Sonia. "Tell me why you're such an Assad apologist."

"Maybe it's because I'm Christian and the Assad's have always protected their minorities, or maybe it comes from knowing the region's history and the long list of attempted coups and interventions. But in the end, maybe we just don't like the idea of foreign powers coming in and taking our leaders out."

"Syria's a police state," Mary snapped. "That reason enough."

"That was forced on the Assad's by the Muslim Brotherhood."

"Sonia has a tendency, as you've just heard, to take on a bit of Syrian protectiveness," said Frans. "You can have a police state. Every nation has one. It's necessary to keep law and order, but it doesn't need to be brutal. Bashar isn't holding back when he should."

"You just mentioned the Muslim Brotherhood, Sonia. Tell me about them."

"The Assad's are Alawite, the Muslim Brotherhood are Sunni, and an early version of al-Qaeda," Sonia said. "They declared war on the older Assad when he came to power in 1970, and by 1980, Syria had become the epicenter of Islamic terrorism. The Muslim Brotherhood owned the streets. Their mosque schools were teaching jihad. By 1982, they had seized control of Hama, Syria's fourth-largest city, attacking police stations and murdering party leaders, until every Ba'athist party official had been killed."

"Interesting. I'd only ever heard about the brutality of the Syrian Army in Hama, nothing about the atrocities committed by the Brotherhood."

"That's because it doesn't fit the Western narrative about the Assad's," said Sonia. "If you want to know more about the Brotherhood, ask Omar. By his own admission, he spent months in Saudi Arabia being properly schooled in the region's politics before coming to Syria."

"Isn't that true, Omar?"

Another hard, cold stare but this time, Sonia gave one back.

"Such a pity, all this hatred over religion," said Frans, jumping in. "God gave mankind the ability to choose between good and evil, and here we are thousands of years later still fighting over religion and destroying nation-states."

"Why go back that far? Look at Afghanistan and Iraq," said Sonia. "Omar, you lost your father in Iraq. You know the brutality of war better than any of us."

"It was Shiite brutality that killed my father, not Sunni."

"How sad for all religions that any of this has to happen," said Frans.

"Allah will soon set things right," said Omar. "You'll see. Mary, pay the bill. It's time to go."

"Must we?"

"Mary's right," said Frans. "We haven't had our coffee yet."

"I insist."

"Okay, Omar, but you owe me a coffee later," and she raised her hand, this time to call for the bill. And when the waiter arrived, she asked that it be divided in two.

As Frans and Omar stood and walked toward the door, Sonia held Mary back.

"Your friend Omar is using you as a recruiting tool."

"That's not true."

"Ask him. He interviewed me in Daraa and said as much. Do you speak any Arabic?"

"No."

"Pity, Omar and his pals can feed you any bullshit they want, and you'll be expected to send it off to the States."

"I know bullshit when I hear it."

"Really? Well, good luck."

"There you go with your pro-Assad shit again," Mary snapped.

"It's not so much that I'm pro-Assad as against al-Qaeda. But look at you. You've already bought into the propaganda about Bashar killing his own people when it's his army and security forces who're being slaughtered, not innocent civilians. It isn't Bashar Assad who's doing all the killing. Be careful, Mary. The truth is as clear as day. Open your eyes."

***

"That was a lively afternoon, wasn't it," Frans said as he opened his apartment door to let Sonia in.

"I knew from Mary's posts that she'd been communicating with the Free Syrian Army, but to actually find her here, and with Omar, of all people. Yes, quite unexpected."

"And did you see how Mary gave in to Omar's demand that they leave without their coffee?" asked Frans. "I think he's already claimed her loyalty. Once that happens, it's hard to move away."

"Omar's handlers chose well, especially by insisting he clean himself up. They probably paid him handsomely, too, for successfully hooking her in. She'll be their journalist going forward."

"Maybe. Omar's likely part of the al-Qaeda operation here."

"Why else would he be here if not to recruit their very own journalist."

"Which makes it even more urgent I stay in Homs, but I'll need to find a place to live, Frans. I can't impose on you long term."

"And until you do, you'll stay here with me. I'm happy to have the company."

Sonia pulled her phone from her purse to check her messages. "Oh my God," she said, jumping up from her chair. "Fouad has called me a dozen times since this morning, and here I had my phone turned off. He's going to be furious."

"I suspect you turned it off on purpose," said Frans, shaking his head.

She laughed.

"You're incorrigible, Sonia Rizk."

She punched in Fouad's number as she walked out onto the balcony.

"Hi darling, I'm sorry I…"

"Don't ever hang up on me again, Sonia, and don't, under any circumstances, turn your phone off, especially while you're in Syria. I've been worried all day."

"It won't happen again, darling. I promise. Guess who I met this afternoon… Mary O'Brien."

"I can only guess how she'll turn events around."

"I'm worried about that, too, and tell Joe our young Iraqi-American from Daraa is here as her official escort. Frans and I bumped into them in Bab Amr, and we had lunch together."

"Sonia, that Iraqi is likely the same man who burst into Andrew's office in Shatilla and tried to abduct him."

"What?"

"And now Andrew's gone missing."

"When did this happen?"

"We're not sure. He and Leila had the weekend off. When they didn't show up at the clinic this morning, staff warned Aziza, and she and Joe went to their apartment. There was evidence of a struggle, and some furniture overturned, and the manoushe and the carafe of coffee on the kitchen table were at least a day old."

"What about Andrew's bike. He goes everywhere on that old bike."

"Parked downstairs where he always keeps it."

"And Leila?"

"No sign of her either. Aziza went through their bedroom and found her handbag in the closet. There were traces of blood in the entrance indicating someone may have been injured."

"Poor Leila, as if eight years in Khiam prison weren't enough for that poor woman. Do you think the Iraqi had anything to do with their disappearance?"

"He's the obvious suspect since he's the one who visited Andrew in his clinic."

"If Andrew had already been threatened, why didn't he have a bodyguard?"

"He and Leila each had one, but it appears there was a major fuck-up."

"What do you want me to do from here?" she asked. "Frans and I could scout Bab Amr, ask if anyone's seen a foreigner being brought in…"

"You'll do nothing of the kind, Sonia."

"Fouad, I love Andrew. I ruined his life. I need to make amends somehow."

"We all love Andrew, and we have everyone looking for him. You've already given us our first major lead—finding the Iraqi in Homs. That's a huge help. If authorities in Homs agree, I'll send Joe to help with the search."

"Let me know what you decide to do," she said, turning to see Frans at the balcony door.

"Frans and I will do whatever we can to help," she continued and saw Frans nodding. "And he won't mind if Joe uses his apartment as his base of operation.

"Call me with any updates. I'll keep my phone on at all times. And Fouad, I'm sorry I got so angry this morning. I love you."

"Love you, too," and he hung up.

"I couldn't help but hear most of the conversation," Frans said as Sonia walked back inside and filled him in on the details he had missed.

"Want to tell me how you ruined Andrew's life?" he asked.

"No," she said, shaking her head. "I'm too ashamed."

Frans was about to say something when they heard a knock on the door. Sonia looked at him apprehensively and whispered. "Could it be the Iraqi?"

"He doesn't know where I live."

"You're hilarious, Frans. How hard would it be for him to find out? Everyone here knows you."

Frans shrugged his shoulders, and approaching the door, asked, "Who is it?"

"Father, it's Madame Chidiac. I need to talk to you."

Frans unbolted the door and opened it. "Good evening, Madame, please come in."

"Good evening, Father, and Miss Sonia. I'll only be a moment, but I thought you should know that this afternoon dozens of jihadists drove into Homs."

"Did you see them?" asked Frans.

"No, but my cousin did, and she just called to warn me. She saw them force their way into some houses in the Old City.

"I don't understand," Sonia said. "We were just in the souk, and we didn't detect any unrest."

"Sonia, the souk is massive, and we were only in one small part of it."

"Apparently, this just happened. My cousin said her neighborhood was in complete mayhem. People are worried they'll be thrown out of their homes or taken hostage or used as human shields should the Syrian army move in to attack. My husband and I aren't going to wait around to see what'll happen, so we plan to leave tomorrow morning for Damascus to stay with my sister."

"This is very disturbing news, and we thank you for letting us know," said Frans.

"Madame Chidiac, would you consider letting me stay in your apartment while you're away?" asked Sonia. "I'd take very good care of it."

"Why would you want to do that when you could leave with us. We've plenty of room in our car."

"I'm a journalist, and if there's to be a battle in Homs, I want to be here to write about it." I'll be damned if I'll let Mary O'Brien have the last word about what happens here, she thought.

# CHAPTER SEVEN

ANDREW WOKE DISORIENTED. It was the unfamiliar sounds that confused him. A muezzin calling the faithful to prayer, not the soothing constancy of waves caressing the shoreline in front of his apartment. Men speaking Arabic in accents he had never heard before rather than the quiet slumber of Leila nestled into his underarm. He opened his eyes and reached over to touch her, to assure himself it was nothing more than a bad dream, and when she was not there, he remembered.

The day before, he had gently removed his arm from around Leila's shoulder and slipped out of bed. Hastily dressing in the same pair of khaki pants and linen shirt he had thrown over the bedside chair the night before, he slipped sockless into his soft-leather loafers and, careful not to disturb Leila, had tiptoed down the hallway to the kitchen and closed the door. Ever since his attempted abduction at the hands of the two al-Qaeda insurgents, Leila had grown anxious, a consequence of her brutal treatment in Khiam prison. Even the presence of round-the-clock bodyguards had done little to allay her fears.

He had just put his carafe of coffee and a re-heated day-old *zaatar manoushe* on the tray to carry to the balcony when he heard a knock on the front door. It was their concierge, Andrew assumed, delivering their Sunday newspaper before he left for his day off.

He had no sooner unlatched the chain and opened the door than two men grabbed him, forced him into the hallway and tied his wrists behind his back. There had been a third man, too, a gun conspicuous inside his waistband. When Andrew had tried to turn to see if this man had entered the apartment, someone had gruffly pushed his head into his chest and instructed him to begin walking.

In simulated assault training, Joe had instructed Andrew to maintain an unflappable demeanor. However reasonable that advice had seemed at the time, fear took no time to overmaster Andrew, and his chest began to heave uncontrollably. Despite his desperate attempts to take deep, slow breaths through his nose—another of Joe's debatable pieces of advice—he felt his lungs begin to collapse and gave in without a struggle. The men sent to carry out his abductions were mere foot soldiers, not the mastermind of the operation. They would have panicked had Andrew resisted and might have harmed Leila. He had witnessed Nadia's abduction. When she had flailed about, kicking her assailant in his shins and scratching his face with her nails, he had hit her hard in the face and dazed her. And here he was, feeling far less feisty, except to be grateful that Leila had gone undetected. But how safe was she? Had that other man left and closed the apartment door behind him? What would Leila do when she woke and discovered him missing? Would she call Joe? Would he put out an all-points bulletin? And if he did, would it even matter. By that time, Andrew could be anywhere.

How had it come to this, he wondered, as he was forcibly escorted down the hallway by two petty thugs, their bulging chest and biceps conspicuous in their tight T-shirts. He had made every effort to lead an honest life, to faithfully practice his Hippocratic oath and minister to his patients to the best of his ability. It was not his fault if he had failed to obtain the smallpox vaccine but how to explain that to a bunch of fanatics.

Andrew's kidnapping had been skillfully staged. By taking the back stairwell down the four flights of stairs that led directly to the parking lot behind the building, his abductors had evaded Andrew's bodyguards, who routinely positioned themselves at the front entrance. No sooner had they reached the ground level when Andrew heard the hum of a car engine. Within seconds, a door opened. He was pushed into the back seat, his two abductors jumping in on either side of him, and the nondescript SUV sped off.

Andrew recognized the voice of the man in the front passenger seat as soon as he spoke.

"Your time ran out, doc," said the Iraqi-American. "You left me no choice but to come get you."

"Where's the other man," asked Andrew with some urgency. "I was sure there were three of them."

"That man's already back at headquarters. He was there to make sure you behaved yourself."

"What have you done with Leila? Did that man harm her?"

"Not to worry, doc. She's of no interest to us. We only wanted you."

Joe had also stressed the importance of establishing a rapport with the abductor. This was where it had to begin, Andrew thought, as he nodded, letting the Iraqi think he believed him.

"If I hadn't heard your accent, I wouldn't have known it was you."

Gone was the straggly-haired, cigarette-reeking, long black-bearded man who had burst into his clinic. Instead, he looked like a young computer programmer.

"I can clean up nice," he replied, laughing. "I had a meeting in Homs and needed to make a good impression."

"And did you succeed?" asked Andrew.

"You'll hear all about it soon enough."

"I wasn't able to get hold of the vaccine, so I'm of no use to you anymore. I'd be willing to consider my abduction a complete misunderstanding if you stopped the car right here and let me out. No one would ever know. You have my word."

"No worries about the vaccine. That problem took care of itself. I have a far more important job for you. So, sit back and shut up and no more questions."

So, they're not going to kill me, Andrew thought. He relaxed a little and studied the Iraqi's face. He was probably in his late twenties, high forehead and handsome enough. He was headstrong, yet Andrew saw how skillfully and reverentially he had dealt with the older man in his clinic. He was clever and clearly no one's fool, so Andrew, if he was to survive his ordeal, had to proceed with caution and so focused instead on the rancid odor of body sweat and stale cigarette smoke inside the car, the banged-up plastic seats and their sharp edges, the grimy windows and broken overhead light. When he finally turned his attention to their route, Andrew discovered they had already reached the roundabout, the one he crossed every day on his bike as he made his way to Shatilla. His friend, the policeman, was on duty. Andrew desperately wanted to signal that he was in trouble, but he knew better than to antagonize the Iraqi and let the moment pass.

Instead of heading south off the roundabout toward Shatilla's main entrance, the driver headed east, past the *Stade de Cheila,* the large sports stadium, and continued along the main thoroughfare, a major shopping area. With no warning, the driver made an abrupt right turn into an alleyway, hardly noticeable, between two shops. This had to be some secret back entrance to the camp, thought Andrew, one he had never seen before. The passage was so narrow he wondered how an SUV could pass, but the driver knew his route, taking a sharp left and then a right, coming so close at times to a few shops that the owners had to literally jump out of his way. All this commotion attracted the attention of a gang of boys who began to run behind the SUV, cheering every time the driver managed to maneuver a corner without scrapping something. When he finally brought the car to a halt and the doors flew open and Andrew was pulled out, he realized, from Joe's description, that he was standing in front Sabra Hospital, a ruined building, its entrance staircase crumbling, its front double doors dangling. Some parts of the upper levels resembled the Roman Coliseum, its pillars supporting otherwise deserted floors that stretched back into darkness in haunting symmetry. In spite of the violence and ruination, the building possessed a strange beauty, which spoke of how solidly the building had been constructed.

From a gaping hole on the third floor, Andrew noticed a table and a few chairs. Was there actually a family living there, as Joe had suggested, and did they gather each night to dine with a proper tablecloth and platters of food? On another floor, he looked into a bedroom with a large bed that had seemingly been left unmade for some time, the sheets and blankets lying half on and half off the mattress. He felt like a voyeur peering into someone's private life but marveled at these people's tenacity or was it mere desperation that forced them to exist under such squalid conditions.

In a part of Shatilla that had been one of the frontlines of the 1982 massacre, Andrew recalled the stories of his older colleague who had witnessed the killing rampage. Dead women in their houses, their skirts pulled up to their waists, their legs spread apart; dozens of young men shot after being lined up against an alley wall; children with slit throats, a group of young boys huddled together over a ball, arms linked, shoulders touching, felled together in a pile. A small girl, looking like someone's doll, her dress blotched with blood and dirt, a crimson halo around her head. And then there were the countless babies and toddlers stabbed and ripped apart, their remains thrown atop piles of garbage. All of these mutilated, mangled bodies then bulldozed into mass graves. Destitute families, all of them, descendants of those expelled from their homeland in 1948.

Leila had her stories, too. She had worked as a nurse alongside the surgeons at Sabra Hospital that same summer. It was the startling number of casualties she remembered most, so many they had had to be stacked one on top of the other in the morgue. "We had no choice," she had said. "There were too many of them."

When he reflected on these stories and how brave these people had been, and still were, and what Leila had done to save lives during that horrific summer, he wondered how he could possibly be afraid of what lay ahead or what he would be asked to do.

Andrew, the two men and the driver followed the Iraqi inside the old hospital and down a flight of stairs. At the end of a long corridor, the Iraqi inserted a key and opened a door. Andrew and the others followed him into a large space, where concrete pillars supported the ceiling, but otherwise scant of anything but the most basic of furniture—table, chairs, beds along the back wall, some of them occupied. A blood-blotched floor, walls covered in graffiti and a large double-door off to the left chain-locked shut. Was that where the abandoned morgue and operating rooms had been?

"Whatever happened to the man suspected of contracting small-pox?" Andrew asked in English, sensing he might get more information if the two of them conversed in a language the others did not understand.

"He died."

"And the others?"

"They died, too."

"Died or killed and buried so they wouldn't spread the disease?"

"You cut straight through the bullshit, don't you, doc," the Iraqi said, shaking his head, "I like that. You'll be a useful addition to our team."

"What are you talking about?"

"I'll get to that soon. Please, have a seat," indicating the two chairs around a bare, wooden table. "We have lots to discuss."

Try to keep things amicable, Andrew told himself.

"It might be helpful if we began with names. I'm Andrew."

"You can call me Omar."

"Well, Omar. I was about to have breakfast when your men abducted me. I'm hungry, and I need my coffee. Any chance you can make that happen?"

"*Zaatar manoushe?*" Omar asked.

"My usual," Andrew responded, wondering how long he could keep up this idle chatter.

Omar turned to one of the two abductors sitting nearby. "*Shabab,* two *zaatar manoushe,*" and turning to Andrew, "Would you like yours topped with halloumi cheese?"

Andrew nodded. More filling, he thought. No telling when I will get my next meal.

Omar shouted to the other man, "*Yallah, ithnaan ahweh,*" and turning again to Andrew, "You take your coffee with or without sugar?"

"With, please." He usually drank it black, but the sugar might keep him more alert and give him a few more calories.

"The older man who came to my clinic with you, the one with the long scar down his right cheek. Where is he?"

"You'll be meeting him soon."

"And the vials? What have you done with them?"

"You're full of questions, aren't you?"

"Can't learn anything if I don't ask. It's not as if I don't deserve an answer."

Omar stared at him. This was hardly the typical cat and mouse game, thought Andrew, where two parties engaged in a back-and-forth routine. Andrew was the mouse in this game. What he did not know was how much he was being played. That depended on what his opponent wanted from him.

Omar finally said, "They were given to our brethren here for safekeeping."

"Meaning what? Disposed of? To be used at a later date?"

"Damn, if you're not the curious one," Omar said, throwing his head back and laughing. "That will be for them to decide, doc. It's out of my hands."

"Let's talk straight, Omar. You've gone and spoiled my day by bringing me here. You obviously have a reason. You have my undivided attention so go ahead. Tell me. What's going on. Who are you? Are you part of al Qaeda?"

Andrew felt he had nothing to lose by being so assertive. Omar wanted something from him, so why not press him for answers. Either he would respond and shed light on his plans, or he wouldn't.

Without a word, Omar handed Andrew a *manoushe* wrapped in a newspaper and a carafe of coffee. Omar looked on, barely touching his food, and what was left, he passed on to one of his men. When he finished eating, Andrew thanked Omar for his hospitality.

"My pleasure, doc," he said, still staring at him.

"Are you going to answer my question or not?" asked Andrew.

"Do you know what a caliphate is?"

"A general idea," Andrew said, wondering where this was headed. "An Islamic state with a chosen leader."

"Yes, and that leader is called a caliph. During the Ottoman Empire, the title of caliph was used as a political rather than symbolic religious title."

"Wasn't that a good thing?"

"Yes and no. The Caliph was supposed to be both the head of state and the top divine representative on earth, sort of like a Roman emperor and pope rolled into one. He lowered taxes, provided autonomy to the regional governors, granted religious freedom for Jews and Christians, and brought peace to a people disaffected by decades of warfare."

"The bit about equality and freedom sounds reasonable, and the rest, no different than today with people tired of wars and religious strife."

"The last caliphate was abolished in 1925 by Turkey's first president, Ataturk, a secular nationalist like Assad, and it's been dormant ever since."

"Maybe it should have stuck around. Too many Muslims today have turned to a more fanatic form of Islam, one very different from the ancient caliphs' ideas on religion."

"When I answered Allah's call, I was selected to study in Saudi Arabia in one of their madrassas."

"Which means you were tutored in Wahhabism and to my point. There are more benevolent forms of Islam. Why didn't you study one of them?"

From discussions he had had with Aziza, Andrew knew it was the most austere form of Islam that insisted on a literal interpretation of the Koran. Strict Wahhabis believed that those who did not practice Wahhabism were heathens and enemies of Allah.

"I learned in medical school that a lot of our early knowledge of science and math comes from some of those ancient caliphates. Islam has a long history of brilliant minds. Why don't you try to emulate them? Wahhabism's nothing more than an oppressive, intolerant form of religion that stifles progress."

"But those old ideas don't address the carnage and humiliation we're subjected to by foreigner invaders today or the economic and social challenges from outside influence."

"But you'll never be able to address these challenges or establish a successful caliphate by rejecting science and math and making your biggest priorities persecuting women and minorities. What you want is unattainable. You can't reclaim lost dignity and glory. You have to build on it, and you're doing just the opposite."

"You're a learned man, Andrew. I respect you. I ask that you respect my beliefs, too."

"I'll work on it, Omar," he replied courteously, careful not to incur his wrath. "Does your group have a name?"

"We call ourselves al-Nusra Front. We're the Syrian people's weapon against the Assad regime."

How presumptuous, thought Andrew.

"I saw you earlier glancing at the men in the beds at the back of the room, said Omar. "I'd like you to examine them. I want to know if they can travel or if I need to leave them behind."

To be shot and buried, wondered Andrew, like the others?

"I don't have my stethoscope or any medical supplies with me."

"I think you do," Omar replied in Arabic, giving an order to one of his men who produced Andrew's backpack and dropped it on the table.

"I believe you now have everything you need," said Omar, with a look that indicated he was losing patience with Andrew.

"*Yallah,* now go check on your patients like I asked you to do."

Did this mean that if he cooperated, he would be released? Feeling somewhat relieved, Andrew reached into his backpack, retrieved his stethoscope, wrapped it around his neck, and stood. The room, essentially the basement of the hospital, was vast, some forty or fifty feet square. As he turned his back on Omar, he could feel his cold, piercing eyes on him. Careful, Andrew, no foolishness.

He began by asking the men to take off their shirts. With their chests bare, he listened to their lungs, then asked how long they had been ill. How long had they been coughing? Had they run a fever? Any other symptoms? When he had determined their illness was lung-related and most likely bacterial pneumonia, he had them dress again. And by then, Omar had crossed the room and stood, waiting for Andrew to turn around.

"Well?" he asked impatiently.

"I suspect they both have pneumonia, but since I can't run lab tests, I can't be more specific," said Andrew, continuing in Arabic so the others could understand. "So, I'm going to recommend a treatment of antibiotics."

"How soon can they travel?"

"That depends on how well they respond to treatment. Obviously, the sooner they start, the better. I have a prescription pad in my backpack. You can send one of your men to the pharmacy here in the camp to get it filled."

In the back of his mind, he reasoned that if the pharmacist, whom he knew, had something in writing that indicated Andrew had been in the camp on that day, at that hour, it might facilitate the search for his whereabouts.

"*Yallah*," Omar shouted to one of his men, "you're going to take this prescription to the pharmacy."

Andrew got out his pad. "What's your name," he asked.

"Mohammad Osman," the man responded, and Andrew wrote an order for antibiotics, and as he was handing Mohammad the prescription, he noticed the gun inside his waistband. *So, there was a third man at my door after all.*

As Mohammad was about to leave, Omar said, "Shoot the pharmacist if he doesn't fill the prescription."

"What?" Andrew shouted. "There's no need for such talk."

"Did you hear that? We're not allowed to talk like that in the doctor's presence," Omar said, in a particularly foul manner that even his men appeared to find grossly offensive.

Rather than add to the uneasiness, Andrew sat quietly until Mohammad returned from the pharmacy.

"When the pharmacist asked me what was wrong, I told him I had an infected toe."

When everyone laughed, it struck Andrew that these were young men bantering among themselves. They were human beings, not monsters, caught up in something they probably did not fully understand.

"But it's true," insisted Mohammad. "I do have a toe that hurts."

"Let me look," said Andrew.

When Andrew touched Mohammad's toe, the man flinched and cried out. "That really hurts, doc. I think I need some of those antibiotics, too."

"I agree. Take two twice a day for five days and *Inchallah*, your toe will heal." Andrew suspected the man was diabetic, the coloration suggesting the toe had already gone gangrenous. Had this patient come into a hospital in the states, he would have been referred to surgery for removal of the toe. Andrew had no access to such treatment, so he prescribed the only thing he could.

"Omar, this man needs bed rest until his toe heals."

Omar nodded. "Mohammad, you heard the doctor. You'll join us when you're feeling better." And turning back to Andrew, "Now give the antibiotics to the others. I need them well as quickly as possible."

After he had administered the medicine and returned to his seat, Omar said, "I'm very pleased with you, doc. You're going to be a valuable asset."

"What are you talking about? I'm not an acquisition. I've done what you asked. Now, let me go."

"Sorry, doc. We need you. We're taking you with us."

"Where?"

"Homs, Syria."

"I don't have my passport," he said, hoping Omar had not discovered it in an inside compartment of his backpack. "I'm not going anywhere with you. I've already told you I'm responsible for thousands of patients. My presence in the camp is indispensable. As it is, we're already short-staffed."

"That's their loss, I'm afraid. We need you more… and by the way," showing Andrew his passport, "I'll be holding it for safekeeping."

"What the hell are you talking about?" shouted Andrew, desperate, his head spinning.

"I've been asked to set up a medical clinic in Homs. You're going to run it."

"I'll do nothing of the kind," Andrew shot back. "I'm a reasonable man. You said so yourself. Why would you ever think I'd agree to such a preposterous idea?"

"If you like your Leila, who you're living in sin with, then you'll agree to help us. If not, we can take care of her anytime we want."

Joe's training manual stressed that any sign of vulnerability was a weakness and a weapon that could be used against him. And while Andrew's heart ached for what could happen to Leila, he refrained from betraying any emotion. Such a display would have been a win for Omar, and he refused to grant him that victory.

# CHAPTER EIGHT

NADIA WAS RELIEVED TO BE BACK at her parents' home. The peacefulness of the compound, with its arched rosemary bushes and overgrown olive trees that lined the long driveway sheltering it from the outside world, enchanted her. The house itself, with its high open ceilings, plush chairs and long inviting sofas, its large windows looking out across the pool to the gardens and the city beyond, made her feel free in time and safe again. Memories of Andrew invariably snuck up on her, too—the two of them in her bedroom after everyone else had gone to bed, taking each other's clothes off and making love.

Nadia had called home the day before to announce she was coming. When she heard that her mother had gone to London with friends and would regret having missed her visit, she was selfishly relieved. She wanted her father all to herself.

Nadia had known from an early age that she had been born into a privileged world where education, a successful career and the right socially connected marriage were all that mattered, but that was before the civil war had gone and shattered that utopian dream for her and her peers. While her father had been quick to adapt to the societal changes, Nadia's mother had continued on in her role as the ever-gracious hostess, entertaining Beirut's high society. She had been part of that social stratum long before she married Victor Helou, the only son of a wealthy Greek Orthodox family and head of one of Lebanon's most prestigious law firms.

To the horror of her parents, Nadia, during her early years at the American University of Beirut, had a brief liaison with Hassan Jaafar, Syria's Intelligence Czar. When he proposed marriage, she considered saying yes until her father had urged her to end the affair, citing that she should not become the wife of the most feared man in Lebanon. To the relief of her parents, she ended the relationship but then married Elie Khoury, her college professor, a man of questionable character. Whether she wedded him to get away from Jaafar, who continued to pursue her, she refused to say, but two years into their marriage, after speaking openly against the Syrian government, her husband disappeared and, as was later revealed, left to rot in a Syrian dungeon. After thirteen years and no sign of him, Nadia assumed he had died. Had Jaafar arranged his abduction to punish her? At the time, she had not been sure. It had been a very confusing period politically when Elie was taken away. There had been widespread anger at the Syrians for ruling every aspect of their lives. Elie had ignited that anger and made himself a prime target. After his abduction, Nadia had left Lebanon to continue her studies. She received her law degree from Boston University and a PhD in International Law and Human Rights from the London School of Economics. Shortly after, she was appointed to the UN High Commission on Human Rights.

Her parents were delighted when she announced her plans to marry Andrew Sullivan, an American physician. And who could have blamed them? They had waited thirteen years to see their daughter so joyously happy again. Her father had declared Elie officially dead, a recent decree by the Lebanese government that anyone missing more than four years making that possible. But then, Elie was mysteriously found alive and Nadia had felt obliged to rescue him. Throughout those turbulent years, Victor had been Nadia's rock, never critical, always ready to help. And now, more than ever, she needed his wise counsel.

Nadia had already begun to question the muddled entanglement she had gotten herself into with Robert Jenkins, but then came Fouad's frantic call. Andrew had gone missing and, in all likelihood, had voluntarily accompanied the insurgents to Syria. Days earlier, he had sat in on a meeting with Fouad and Joe where they discussed the possibility of a commando raid on the old hospital to eliminate the smallpox victims in an effort to avoid a camp epidemic. Andrew had been incensed at such an idea. Even if she had felt somewhat reassured that Andrew had simply gone off being a hero again, taking care of sick people he did not want to see killed, and presumably not in danger, the news had been the jolt she had needed. Jenkins, her current lover, the US ambassador to Syria, the same man who had been using these insurgents to carry out his regime change plans could, if Nadia asked, help find Andrew. Andrew was the most important person in her life, the only man she had ever truly loved, even if she had had to compromise herself with both Hassan Jaafar and Robert Jenkins, the former to survive her four-year captivity, the latter to avenge the death of the man who had etched his way into her heart. All of these things she wanted to tell her father.

Her parents' home in Hazmieh, an upscale neighborhood minutes from the city center, dominated all of Beirut from the hills of Achrafieh and its public gardens, past the newly rebuilt downtown—with its waterfront skyscrapers, luxury hotels and boutiques—to the Rafic Hariri International Airport and points south. Victor had suggested they talk in the library. The sun-drenched room was Nadia's favorite. It was quiet and private and smelled of cigars and fine leather. A large Persian carpet with its cardinal reds, burgundies and shades of blue, covered most of the parquet floor. Aside from a large window that overlooked her mother's gardens, thousands of shelved books reached the ceiling on three sides. Father and daughter sat in their usual plush leather chairs, she in front of his desk, he behind. He had called it his listening chair, for as a child, Nadia had forever asked him questions, and sensing a budding lawyer and careful not to disappoint, had answered as well as he could everything she asked.

"You're looking like my beautiful Nadia this morning," Victor said, pleasure sparkling in his eyes. "You don't know how happy that makes me."

"Thank you, Papa. How lovely that you noticed. I'm beginning to feel like my old self again, and it's a welcome change."

She had dressed for their talk in a white silk blouse, knee-length black skirt and matching heels, a simple yet elegant outfit she would have worn while attending graduate school or out on a date with Andrew, or even at work in her UN office. She had forgone make-up, too, and had softly brushed her unruly auburn hair back into a ponytail. She had examined herself in the full-length mirror and smiled, pleased at how lovely she looked and at how easy it had been to slip back into her old self. She had gone on a shopping spree with her mother shortly after Jenkins had brought her home, and now wondered what she could have been thinking, all those short, tight, low cleavage dresses, clothes she knew she would never wear again, and it dawned on her that she had two lives living in her closet, from two different times in her life. It was as if she was recovering from a long illness, and getting back to her parent's home had been the best way to make that happen.

"I heard you talking to Fouad just now. You mentioned Andrew. Did something happen to him?"

"He didn't show up at the clinic this morning. Fouad thinks he may have accompanied some insurgents to Syria to care for their sick."

Victor shook his head. "That wasn't a very wise thing to do. Poor Andrew. Ever the caregiver. I hope we'll discover that he and Leila simply left town for the weekend and decided on an extra day off and that no harm has come to him. I love that man like my own son."

"I know, Papa. We all love him. Fouad and Joe have the entire camp looking for him, any clues as to his whereabouts. He'll call us as soon as he knows something."

"How can you say you love him when you didn't even want to see him when you got home from Syria?"

"I love Andrew with all my heart, Papa, but there was a reason I broke off with him. That's part of what I wanted to tell you, some pretty shocking things, in fact, and I hope you won't think the lesser of me."

"*Wallow.* What could shock a seventy-five-year-old man? Besides, you're an adult. You're responsible for your own actions. Do I get confused at times by what you do?" he laughed. "Yes, but I've never been unduly judgmental."

"Well then, let's begin with the day Hassan Jaafar was assassinated. When I heard the news on television, Ani, then my maid, now yours, insisted I pack my belongings and leave the house before the *Mukhabarat* arrived, but how was I to go anywhere without a car? That was when she suggested Moussa, her friend and one of Jaafar's chauffeurs, might be of use."

"This was four years into your abduction," said Victor. "You might think this an insensitive question but, since we're talking adult to adult, how did you feel when you heard that Jaafar had been killed."

"Good question, Papa, and one that gets right to the point. I actually felt quite numb. It was hard not to be. I had Ani beside me, sobbing hysterically. She had worked for him, and before that, for his wife in Damascus for several years and had become attached to the Jaafar family. Once the shock wore off, I was very sad. In his own misguided way, Jaafar deeply loved me. And I remember thinking, I'm now a free woman, but I still can't go anywhere. I didn't have any ID papers. It was only thanks to Jenkins and his diplomatic status that I was able to cross the Lebanese border."

"And I assume all your documents have been reissued? Passport, Lebanese ID?"

"Yes, Papa, everything's in order, including my diplomatic passport from the UN."

Victor nodded and then cleared his throat nervously before asking, "Did you love Jaafar?"

"He eventually worked his way into my heart. Was that love? Let's just say I grew to be very fond of him. He never forced me to do anything I didn't want to do and," putting her hands over her eyes, and looking down at the carpet, and knowing how difficult it would be for her father to hear, said as delicately as she could, "it was two years before we became intimate."

"Well, you warned me we'd be having an adult conversation."

Nadia felt grateful for the absence of her mother.

"As awful as that sounds, Papa, I allowed myself to get closer to him because I came to discover there was a real man in him who was actually fun to be with. Imagine my surprise when I learned he was an excellent chef and loved fine wines. After completing his studies at the University of Damascus, he earned a master's from L'Ecole Polytechnique in Paris before deciding finally to join the CIA. He was a good conversationalist and well-read, and his library was as impressive as yours. And the more our relationship thrived, the more he interacted with his staff. He let them take books from his library, and the most amazing thing happened. Everyone started going around with a book in their pocket and every free moment they were reading, and those who couldn't, were being taught. And it was Jaafar who had transformed all these people into avid readers. One day he came home from a trip with a book in Armenian for Ani that he'd found in a bookstore. A thoughtful gift for a woman who'd served his family for so long. It's one of Ani's prized possessions. So, you see, Papa, there is sometimes kindness and love and generosity in the most ruthless of men."

"I may not have killed anyone, Nadia, but I'm not perfect either. In my long career, I've done things I wish I hadn't done, things I've never dared tell anyone."

"Regrets are reminders we're human, Papa. Regardless of what you may or may not have done, you've always been my hero. You listened when I needed an ear. You spoke the truth to me, whether I wanted to hear it or not. My accomplishments are an extension of you and your influence on my life.

"And as much as I adore, Mama, how many times over the years have you saved me from attending one of her frivolous social events. You made this library of yours my refuge any number of times and even sat me in this very chair and walked me through the ramifications of some silliness I'd just gone and done."

Victor laughed at such talk but then turned back to Jaafar.

"How did you reconcile what Jaafar did as Intelligence Czar?"

"I didn't. When I called him on it, he said he was simply following orders. He thought of himself as a Syrian patriot, no different from any other man who pledged allegiance to his government. When I accused him of being a war criminal, he said that if he was, then so was every man who had ever served his country in time of war. Like it or not, he had a point. I heard the same thing from Robert Jenkins, only he was far more cynical. He was training death squads in Iraq and gearing up to do the same thing in Syria, and he felt his actions justified."

"That nice American diplomat who brought you home?"

"The very same."

"If you know that, why do you spend so much time with him in Syria?"

"I'll get to that, but first, let me finish the bit about Jaafar. I needed cash in case I had to pay my way out of Syria, so I visited Jaafar's bedroom. I found the key to his safe. He'd been in a hurry to leave for a meeting in Lattakia with Fouad that morning and had forgotten to put it and its chain back around his neck. You saw all the stuff I brought out. Most of it's still in your safe here in this room."

"You also asked me to keep a manila envelope. What was that?"

"The most important part of the whole story. As we drove away from Jaafar's compound, a car met us on the road. It was Robert Jenkins making his way to Jaafar's hoping to find that manila envelope."

"Why was that so important to him?"

"It was an official document compiled by Jaafar highlighting myriad bits of incriminating evidence of crimes committed by Jenkins. Attempted murder of an important Shiite cleric, the assassination of a high-level Hezbollah operative in early 2004, and much more. We can go over it together later if you'd like, but if made public, it would surely get Jenkins thrown out of Syria and cause embarrassment for the US government."

"Why are you so sure that's what Jenkins was after?"

"Two reasons. Years ago, Jaafar killed a CIA agent in Beirut. Jenkins discovered it was Jaafar and threatened to expose him if Jaafar didn't help him bring down Assad. He refused, and Jenkins promised he'd crush him along with Assad. And then, there was the manila envelope which Jenkins knew Jaafar had and, for obvious reasons, wanted back. Jenkins thought by killing Jaafar, he could go straight to his safe and retrieve the document. Eventually, he realized I had it and questioned me about it. I admitted I had had it but had since burned it to save his reputation. For whatever reason, he believes me—or pretends to."

"How did you pull that off?"

"I can be persuasive when necessary, but back to the assassination, I've lots more to tell you."

"All right."

"When I saw Jenkins making his way to Jaafar's villa, I handed Ani the envelope, wrote your phone number on it and asked her to hide it. She did a good job because when Jenkins' goons searched both she and Moussa they found nothing and let them go. And that's how Jenkins ended up bringing me home. He sweet-talked me the entire way with his politeness and concern for my well-being. That's when I made the decision to lay a trap for the man who had killed Jaafar—and destroy him. And why I ended up going back and forth to Syria so many times. I knew the closer I got to him, the easier it would be to bring him down, and I had the evidence to do that."

"I never imagined you such a brave woman, Nadia. What you're trying to do takes courage."

"No, Papa, my conduct has nothing to do with bravery. When you've been someone's prisoner, you learn quickly how to appease that person, even if he's become a genuine human being, and do whatever makes your captivity more bearable. To his credit, Jaafar also helped mold me into the more assertive person I am today, but don't think I'm out there doing all this on my own. I'm working with Fouad. I send him regular reports on Jenkins' activities, and collectively we're doing whatever we can to disrupt his regime change plans.

"Jaafar prided himself on being a Syrian patriot, doing whatever Hafez Assad asked of him. He was very loyal to that man, less so to Bashar. That doesn't mean what he did during his tenure was anything less than evil. Jenkins, on the other hand, is someone who touts his patriotism as a legitimate reason to destroy a country. He claims that it's in the national security interest of the US to initiate regime change in Syria, destroy the country, even if it kills hundreds of thousands of people, and install someone friendlier to the US. God save us from patriots, Papa. They'll get us all killed."

"Impressive! My daughter the spy."

Nadia smiled, got up from her chair, approached her father and gave him a hug. "You always were my cheerleader, Papa, whether I deserved it or not."

From behind his desk, she glanced out at the garden. "What do you say we have lunch on the terrace today? I think you'd agree we need a bit of fresh air after all this business of assassination and betrayal."

"A lovely idea. I'll ring for Ani."

Within minutes, Ani knocked on the library door, entered, and said, "Yes, Mr. Victor?"

"How close are you to having lunch prepared?"

"Everything's ready, sir. I just need to set the dining room table."

"We've decided to have lunch on the terrace in this nice weather," said Nadia, "so please set that table instead. And could you also open a bottle of *Blanc de Blanc.*"

Ani left the library, shutting the door behind her, and they both listened to her shuffle in her slippers back to the kitchen.

"I'm delighted we have this time together, Nadia. Your mother would have made a fuss and insisted on setting a formal table."

"Are you and mother happy with Ani?"

"We are. She's a hard worker, polite and discreet, and she's an excellent cook," and he chuckled, patting his stomach, "I've even put on an extra pound or two since she began working here."

"What about Moussa?"

"Of course, he isn't Samir, but then no one will ever be as faithful and as devoted to our family. I think about him every day and the horrific way he died, and it breaks my heart."

"Mine, too, Papa," reaching across the desk to squeeze his hand, remembering how the airstrike had severed Samir's head. "What have you been able to learn about Moussa?"

"Only what he's told me… he worked for Jaafar for some ten years. He's Sunni and swears he's not part of the Muslim Brotherhood."

"You actually asked him that?"

"Why not! I want no fanatic in my house. Given what's happening, can you blame me for being cautious?"

"Of course not. I'm glad you're satisfied with his work."

Some minutes later, Ani tapped on the door, then opened it. "*Fadallouh*," she said, inviting them to lunch.

The last time sat on the terrace was when Andrew had been due to fly into Beirut to celebrate their engagement party. She had arrived a few days ahead of him and, still a bit jet-lagged, slept late that morning. When she finally joined her family, her father had stood and opened his arms, and she had stepped into them, smelling his cologne and starched shirt. She had felt like such a lucky woman that day, her family so loving and tender, respectful, as happy as she was and eager to meet Andrew. And then Sonia went and spoiled the day with her dreadful news that her husband Elie might still be alive in a Syrian prison. Papa, remember how you cautioned me not to meet with Hassan Jaafar? You were sure it was a trap, and you were so right."

"And now we know Sonia set you up, aware all along that Jaafar wanted to get his hands on you."

"And had I listened to you, I'd be happily married to Andrew now and living back in the States. Could I have made a bigger mess of my life?"

"What happened, happened, Nadia. You're wiser now, and probably better placed to tackle the challenges ahead, and, of course, I'll help in any way I can."

Ani had set a lovely lunch on the terrace, and as a good student of her mistress, had draped the table with a floor-length tablecloth and matching napkins. Nadia served the wine, lifted her glass and offered a toast to her father. "To the wisest, kindest, and most open-minded gentleman I have ever had the pleasure of knowing."

"*Merci, cherie*," his reply, his voice barely audible as he had already stuffed a piece of grilled shrimp into his mouth. "Delicious…and so sweet, cooked to perfection."

"Be sure to save room, Papa. Ani has also prepared *Sultan Brahim*, fried like you like them."

"Not to worry, I'm feeling ravenous… must be all your stories," he winked as he lifted the bottle from the cooler to serve himself again. "Shall I serve you another glass?"

"Yes, Papa."

"Can we get back to Andrew? I'm curious why you sent him away."

"In spite of everything he'd gone through, he managed to hold onto his inner goodness. By the nature of what I had to do, I'd lost mine, and he saw that when we met. Hassan had remolded me into his image of a woman with the makeup and tight clothes, and even if I didn't notice the changes, Andrew did as soon as he saw me. He was all about simplicity and natural beauty, and he saw none of that in me when we met."

"You're back to your beautiful self now," Victor said, smiling at her.

"Yes, I am, but I said my good-bye and wished him well with his lovely Leila, and if Andrew were with anyone, I would want it to be someone like her. Do I still love him? With all my heart, but I can't go back to being his old Nadia, at least not yet. In order to bring down Jenkins and avenge Jaafar's death, I need to be the Nadia of lost innocence, the woman with the scarlet letter on her chest. Does that make sense?"

"Strangely, it does."

Nadia sat back in her chair. "All the way back to Elie's disappearance, and his thirteen years in prison, I had never lost my inner innocence, and now look what I've done. Between Jaafar and Jenkins, I'm nothing to be proud of."

"You're being too hard on yourself, Nadia."

"No, and don't for one second think I don't feel guilty for having brought Andrew to this crazy country. What was I thinking when I abandoned him and went looking for Elie? And then, the endless mounds of mess I got him into, poor man."

"He might have some regrets, but just look at what's he's gone and done with his life. It's remarkable."

"Is it true he learned Arabic and started working in Shatilla to make me proud?"

"Yes, it is. Who told you?"

"Jenkins. He met Andrew in the rehab center when he was recovering from his injuries. Lauded a lot of praise on him."

"At least Jenkins recognized an honorable man when he saw one. And yes, Andrew did say that. Fouad, Sonia and I spent our days and nights at his bedside, praying he'd recover. We didn't think he'd make it. Emergency surgery for a ruptured spleen. According to his doctor, his assailant, or assailants, used a heavy metal bar on him, tore open his side and almost severed his spine."

Just then, Ani arrived to clear the first course dishes. "Thank you, Ani, no need. We'll continue with the same plates. And I'll take care of serving the fish when you bring it out. Tell me more about Andrew," she said, turning her attention back to her father.

"I had just dropped him off on the Corniche. I had some errands to run, and he wanted to watch the sunset. Sometime during his walk, two men grabbed hold of him and pushed him into a car parked alongside the curb. He was blindfolded, and his hands tied and driven to some deserted beach. When they arrived, he was taken from the car and told to walk. Without warning, one of the men pulled off his blindfold and yelled, "Mr. Jaafar didn't like your interview on CNN," and the beating began until he was on the sand fighting for his life. Luckily, two security guards who worked in a nearby factory were on their cigarette break. When they saw Andrew on the ground and the men beating him, they fired their guns in the air and scared off his attackers. They're the ones who called an ambulance and saved Andrew's life."

"When Jenkins told me about his beating, I immediately connected it to his TV interview..."

"You saw it?"

"Yes and, unfortunately, so did Jaafar. I didn't link the dots together until Jenkins told me about the attack, and then I realized it was Jaafar who had given the orders."

"When Andrew recovered, we all encouraged him to leave Lebanon," Victor said. "He refused. As long as you were being held hostage, he insisted he wouldn't abandon you, and he shut down any further discussion on the matter."

Nadia pulled a tissue from her pocket and wiped away her tears just as Ani arrived back at the table.

"Thank you, Ani," she said, taking the cutlery and platter from her and serving her father a generous plateful of the tiny fish, fried to perfection.

"*Merci, cherie.*" He took a mouthful, savoring it, before continuing. "As soon as his doctor deemed him sufficiently recovered, Fouad had him transferred to a private clinic in Broumana for rehab and training to regain his strength, and that's when Joe became part of Andrew's care team. It was Fouad who had insisted he learn Arabic. And, I hate to bring up her name, but it was Sonia who suggested he work with Doctors without Borders in Shatilla."

"Now I understand how all of this fell into place, even the bitch Sonia's role. When we discovered it was Sonia who had arranged my kidnapping, I told Andrew I wanted her tortured to death, an indication of how much I hate her for ruining our lives, but you know what Andrew said? 'My Nadia would never have gone to that extreme.' I remember stomping my foot and yelling, 'Your old Nadia doesn't exist anymore,' and then, I went and accused him of being too goddamned righteous, but not before adding, 'And that's another reason I fell in love with you,'" and she paused, reaching for another Kleenex.

Nadia shook her head. "I finally had to back down and say, 'Okay, maybe it's enough that Sonia knows we know,' and we both agreed to leave it at that."

"Had you met Leila?" Victor asked.

"Yes, a beautiful woman, inside and out. Andrew, me, Sonia, Samir, we all stayed at her uncle Camille's house during the 2006 war, and she left with us in the UN caravan out of Marjeyoun."

"Yes, of course. I'd forgotten that detail."

"At the time, I didn't know much more about her until Fouad mentioned she'd spent all those years imprisoned in Khiam. She's the brave and courageous one, Papa, not me."

Nadia put down her knife and fork. "I just remembered something, maybe it's nothing... it's about the two men who attacked Andrew. Shortly after the CNN interview, I heard Jaafar shouting orders at someone... most probably, it was to those two men. And now I wonder if one of them could have been Moussa. Why do I think that? When Andrew climbed into your car the day I picked him up to go walking along the Corniche, he stared hard and long at Moussa as if he'd seen him before. Had Andrew recognize him as one of his attackers?"

"Why wouldn't he have said something if he had?"

"I'm not sure. Ours was a pretty intense meeting. Neither of us knew what we were doing. He was nervous, so was I. Maybe he thought to mention it later to you privately, didn't want to bring it up with me. I don't know."

"We'll need to talk with Moussa."

"We will, Papa, in due time."

"The fish is delicious. I'll have another serving." Victor said, "but please don't tell your mother. She'd disapprove if she thought I'd overindulged. She's overly cautious about my health."

"It's our secret, Papa. Jaafar had two chauffeurs, the other one was Khalid. He's the one who died with Jaafar in the explosion. We had a mutual dislike for one another, he and I. He didn't like that I was friendly with Ani, and anytime he could, he tried to take her away from me. The few times I mentioned his conduct toward me, she defended him, saying he was a decent man and respectful to staff, particularly to the women. Khalid was also Jaafar's personal butler. If he traveled from Slunfeh, which was where I was held, to Damascus or anywhere else in Syria, it was Khalid who drove him. Moussa was pretty much left to run errands."

"How strange after all this time," Victor said, "that we never thought to ask where you'd been held. I know the area well. It's beautiful but very remote."

"Yes, I used to compare it to Saladin's impenetrable castle, which was close by."

"We took you there as a child. Did you get along with the rest of the staff?"

"Yes, except for Khalid, I was well respected, and after Jaafar was killed, I found everyone's ID card in his safe and gave them all back, along with wads of cash which made them love me even more."

No sooner had Ani cleared the table and returned to the kitchen to prepare coffee when the phone rang. She answered and then came running back outside.

"It's for you, *Sitt* Nadia. It's Mr. Fouad. I told him you were still dining, but he said it was urgent."

"Thank you, Ani," as she wiped her hands on her napkin before taking the phone. "*Bonjour,* Fouad, any news?"

"There are things I need to talk to you and your father about. I should be there in about five minutes. Please have Moussa open the gate."

"Just in time for coffee. We're on the terrace. Join us there."

Nadia rang for both Moussa and Ani and gave them their orders.

"And Ani, Mr. Fouad and his driver will be joining us for coffee. Serve them some baklava, too."

Moments later, they heard the crunch of car wheels on the gravel driveway, then doors open and close. They both turned to watch a glum-faced Fouad walk toward them while his driver stayed behind. He kissed Nadia on the cheek and shook Victor's hand before collapsing into the chair between the two.

"You must not have good news," Nadia said.

Fouad exhaled deeply and shook his head.

"When Andrew didn't show up at the clinic this morning, we assumed, as I said earlier, that he'd gone with the insurgents, but then Joe and Aziza went to his apartment and discovered there'd been a scuffle, a chair overturned and dried blood in the foyer."

"I thought Andrew and Leila had been assigned bodyguards?" said Nadia. "Where were they?"

"Parked in front of the building, never saw a damn thing. Back at Shatilla, Joe and his team went to the old Sabra Hospital. After the insurgents had come to Andrew's office, we'd discussed the possibility that they could have been hiding there. The ideal place. Abandoned since '82, except for some desperate Syrian refugees who'd recently moved into the upper floors. They found a man in the basement, his foot bandaged, barely able to walk. Joe relieved him of his revolver and started questioning him. When he refused to speak, Joe threatened to use the man's gun to blow his head off if he didn't cooperate. He said his name was Mohammad Osman, and yes, the American doctor had been there. He'd been the one who'd examined his foot, put him on antibiotics, and prescribed bedrest, and that's why he was still there. When asked specifically about the Iraqi-American, the man got confused. 'The man with the funny accent,' Joe finally said. 'Oh yeah, the leader. He's the one who forced the doctor to go with him to Homs.' This is significant because when Sonia was in Daraa about six months ago, she interviewed this Iraqi-American, who identified himself as al-Nusra. He's also the same man who visited Andrew in his clinic recently and tried to kidnap him."

"What was Sonia doing in Daraa?" asked Nadia. "That would have been about the time of the uprising."

Nadia remembered that Jenkins had been there at the same time, and when she had asked why, he had given her some nonsense about monitoring the uprising.

"Actually, the initial phase had just ended a month or so earlier. She had received a call from her good friend Father Frans, a Jesuit who's lived in Syria for the last fifty-plus years. He's based in Homs but was in Daraa at the time of the uprising and saw first-hand what had happened."

"I've heard a lot about him," Victor said. "He's a remarkable man, has a big farm just outside Homs, hires all the local disabled people."

"That's right, and according to Frans, it was the insurgents in Daraa who carried out the killings… the usual mode of operation when an outside force wants to initiate an overthrow. Frans insisted Sonia come see for herself. That's when she met the Iraqi-American, and at Frans' urging, he gave her an interview.

"Joe had Mohammad Osman taken in for further questioning, and I sat in on that session. According to Osman, four men went to Andrew's apartment. Two took Andrew down the back stairs to the waiting car, he and another man stayed behind in the apartment."

"Did they know Leila was there?" asked Nadia.

"Yes… their orders were to leave her alone."

"But they stayed," she said, the blood already pounding in her ears.

"Yes… and they found Leila… and she was still in bed, and naked and, as the bastard said, 'we just wanted to have a little fun,' but when she started screaming and kicking, they stuffed a sock they found on the floor in her mouth and…"

Nadia's brain shut down, unable to bear the image of these two animals on top of Leila, repeatedly violating her, and focused instead on a red-headed goldfinch flying about in the garden. Her pain turned quickly to rage, and she cried, "And this savage just sat there and gave you all the details?"

Fouad nodded as he retrieved a handkerchief from his pants pocket and blew his nose. "I'm sorry. I'm supposed to be immune from this kind of crime, but I love Leila and Andrew like my own family."

"I know," she said, crying openly.

"Do you want me to continue?"

"Yes," Victor wailed, unable to contain his sobbing. "I want to know what …"

"So, after they raped her, they were going to tie her up and leave her there, but somehow, she wrestled herself free and went charging down the corridor. She had almost reached the front door when Osman tackled her from behind. As she fell, she hit her head against the edge of a marble table in the entrance. In all likelihood, she died before she even hit the floor."

"What did they do with Leila's body?" Nadia asked.

"They pulled up one of the carpets from the living room floor, laid her on it, rolled it up and tied it shut. They carried her body down the back steps and threw it in the dumpster just outside the entrance to the parking lot, then took off and headed back to Sabra hospital."

"Between Andrew's kidnapping and the discovery of Leila's body, we're talking a good twenty-four hours," said Victor. "During all that time, no one in that building threw anything in that dumpster?"

"Those garbage bins are huge, Victor. Usually, people open just one side and only enough to throw something in, and her body wasn't that obvious."

Numbed by what she was hearing, Nadia looked across the pool at Ani and Moussa talking to Fouad's driver. Though out of earshot, she knew when she saw Ani put her hands up to her face that she had just learned what had happened to Leila, and there was Moussa, standing alongside her, tenderly putting his hand on her shoulder.

"What will you do with those useless bodyguards?" asked Victor angrily.

"They'll be dealt with."

"And no witnesses either to these outrageous crimes? Incredible."

"It was a Sunday morning, and, as you know, the weather's still warm. People either head to the beach or to the mountains, and all their neighbors confirmed they had done one or the other, so these bastards literally had the building to themselves."

Victor shook his head and, leaning on the table for support, wearily pulled himself up. "I'm sorry," he said, his face wet with tears. "I need to lie down."

"Shall I have Moussa help you to your room, Papa?"

"No, that won't be necessary."

His shoulders slumped, his gait unsteady, he appeared to Nadia a shriveled form of himself. She waited until he had entered the house and disappeared from view before turning her attention back to Fouad.

"Did Osman tell the Iraqi what he'd done?"

"No, neither of them did… apparently, they were too frightened to say anything to anyone."

"Where's the other man?"

"He left for Homs with the Iraqi and Andrew, along with a third man."

"Andrew must never know what happened," cried Nadia.

"He won't. You have my word."

"Come, walk with me," Nadia said as she stood, and taking Fouad's arm, led him across the terrace, down the stone steps, past the pool to the edge of her mother's rose gardens. She stood there a few moments before speaking.

"I'm overwhelmed with remorse for the way I so cruelly treated Andrew when I got back from Syria. When I turned him away, I lost the better part of myself."

"Why'd you do it?"

"I had no choice. I'd sullied myself with Jaafar… and then he was already in a wonderful relationship with Leila. If he'd been involved with any other woman, I might have been jealous, but I loved that he was with someone as wonderful as her."

"He was willing to give her up to come back to you."

"Yes, to the old Nadia, not the one who'd gone and done some immoral things."

Fouad put his arm around her shoulder, pulled her into his chest and let her cry.

Eventually, Nadia pulled herself out of his embrace, and together they walked back to the terrace and sat again. "So, now what?" she asked. "We assume Andrew's been taken to Homs. How do we get him back?"

"Joe's on his way there now, left about half an hour ago. In the meantime, Sonia and Father Frans are looking for the Iraqi. Talk about a coincidence. They had just had lunch with him two days before all this happened."

"What?" asked Nadia. "You never mentioned that. Homs one day, Beirut the next? This Iraqi sure gets around. Did he say why he was in Homs?"

"According to Sonia, he'd been asked to translate for an American journalist who'd scheduled a meeting with reps from al-Nusra."

"So, we just sit back and wait to hear from Joe?"

"Pretty much."

"There's got to be something we can do."

Nadia paced back and forth across the terrace before grabbing her mobile from the table and clicking a number. She showed Fouad whose number she had dialed, and he nodded. While waiting for him to answer, she hit speakerphone. On the second ring, Robert Jenkins picked up.

"Robert, darling, something dreadful has happened. Andrew's been kidnapped by al-Qaeda insurgents and taken to Homs."

"Where are you?"

"I'm sitting on my father's terrace."

"Are you alone?"

"Yes," she said, looking at Fouad, who nodded.

"I'd heard that Andrew had been taken, such sad news."

"You have to do something."

"What makes you think I can?"

Nadia wondered how he already knew. "Because you're an ambassador, darling," she said. "And you know important people."

"Thanks for the compliment, but…"

"You saved my life, Robert, and now I'm asking you to save Andrew's. I know you're very fond of him, as am I, and such an honorable man doesn't deserve to end up in the hands of Al-Qaeda."

"I agree, but what makes you think I have anything to do with insurgents in Homs?"

"I think no such thing, Robert, but since you told me you'd recently visited Homs, I assumed you might have contacts there."

"I'll make a few phone calls, Nadia, and see what I can find out. No promises."

"I understand but imagine the coup for your career if you were able to rescue a fellow American from the clutches of al-Qaeda. It would be viewed favorably by many."

"I'll do what I can, Nadia. When are you coming back to Damascus? I miss you."

"I miss you, too, darling," and she hung up.

"Well done, Nadia," said Fouad. "You called him on his lie. Let's see what he does."

"I no longer like that I've committed to this relationship with Jenkins, but I'm willing to stay with it because he needs to be stopped. I did suggest that his plans equated to war crimes and that he should think hard and long about carrying out his orders."

"Well, then, let's see what choices he decides to make."

They heard someone come up behind them and turned to see Moussa, tears streaming down his cheeks.

"Mr. Fouad, I'm from Homs. I would like to offer my services. I have amends to make to Mr. Andrew."

# CHAPTER NINE

JENKINS CURSED HIMSELF. Nadia had just caught him lying, and it had been his own fault. He had had no business telling her about his recent trip to Homs, yet he had, and worse, he might have to reveal his lapse in judgment to his guest. Against protocol, he had interrupted a late afternoon meeting with an important visitor to take Nadia's call. What could he say in his defense, if asked, other than he was worse than a love-struck schoolboy? All it took, anytime they were together, was some erotic nonsense whispered in his ear, and she could ask of him anything she wanted. But then, why was he so worried? He had not crossed the reddest of lines like his visitor, David Peters, both a retired four-star US general and former CIA director who, through his own indiscretions, had incurred not only misdemeanor charges but a $100,000 fine for sharing top secret information with his mistress, yet, was still somehow entrenched inside the DC Beltway power circle and advising the White House in its war against Bashar Assad.

Jenkins knew that despite his apparent stellar diplomatic career, he would get no such sweetheart deal for his part in arming members of the Syrian al-Nusra group, an off-shoot of Al-Qaeda, and a US-designated terrorist organization, should he ever be accused of war crimes. Nadia had been the one to warn him about the possibility of just such an investigation. "Don't trust anyone," she had said. At this stage of the operation, he had no choice, at least for now, but to obey his marching orders and proceed with regime change. His hope was that he could also find a way to rescue Andrew. What troubled him was the insolence of that Iraqi American, who seemingly now only took orders from al-Nusra.

"Sorry, sir, for the interruption, but the call was important," said Jenkins, as he rejoined his guest. "It would appear al-Nusra has kidnapped an American doctor from Beirut and taken him to Homs."

"Not our concern, Robert. The poor bastard was probably in the wrong place at the wrong time."

Robert hated that he was expected not only to pander to his wretched comments but to his inflated ego. Peters was a slight man with a wide forehead, sharp nose and protruding teeth, not someone who would necessarily attract the attention of any woman. On the other hand, with his sandy hair, intense blue eyes, fit physique and playful smile, Jenkins had no trouble attracting women, but, after years of playing that game, he was willing to abandon his philandering ways for Nadia.

"I beg to differ, sir. This doctor, Andrew Sullivan, works with Doctors without Borders in the Shatilla refugee camp in Beirut, and the man who kidnapped him, a young Iraqi American, is one of ours. He also helped himself to some of the smallpox vials from the Benghazi shipment and took them to Beirut to distribute in Hezbollah's Dahiyah neighborhood, only one broke, and some of his men contracted smallpox. He expedited their demise and buried their bodies which, given the circumstances, was probably the only thing he could have done, but he's proven himself a loose cannon, and I wonder if he shouldn't be taken out before he causes us more headaches."

"Robert, our mission here is to create havoc, and it sounds like he's doing just what we want our recruits to do."

"Constructive chaos is one thing. Unintended consequences are something else, and we already have a dismal history of that sort of failure. The year 1985 comes to mind, sir, when then CIA Director Casey ordered US Special Forces to teach state-of-the-art sabotage techniques to Pakistani Intelligence, who then trained thousands of Afghans and foreign mujahedin, most of them Saudis, to kill Soviet troops in Afghanistan."

"That was the greatest transfer of terrorist techniques in military history and, thanks to that operation, the mujahedin forced the Soviets to withdraw their troops."

"Yes, and we assumed those Saudi-backed Sunni mujahedin would crawl back into the woodwork once their work was done, but they didn't, did they, sir? Instead, they and their progeny went on to become al-Qaeda."

"Yes, that was an unintended consequence. On the other hand, look what 9-11 gave us. An opportunity to go after the Taliban in Afghanistan and Saddam in Iraq."

"I'd hardly call those achievements, sir. Since 2001, we've only gained control of 10 percent of Afghanistan and reduced Iraq to failed-state-status, with no exit strategy for either operation."

"Hardly a problem. Short-term goals rarely meet expectations, Robert. That's what those morons in Congress expect, but that's just not realistic. The military characterizes its military objectives across the Middle East in terms of successful sectarian divisions, and that's working well for us in Iraq. Just look at the turmoil there and, if properly carried out, we could see the same process unfold across Syria."

"Sir, my father was also a diplomat and believed firmly in the power of diplomacy. His career spanned a time when enemy nations still spoke to one another and, in so doing, accomplished a great many things. There's a quote from former Secretary of State James Baker he liked. 'Negotiations are not a reward, nor are they a gift. They are rather a process in which two adversaries, or enemies, engage as a means to end the conflict between them.'"

"I couldn't agree more, Robert, and I say that as a military man who's judged by the wars he commands and wins. However, if I'm not mistaken, Baker also suggested a phased withdrawal of troops from Iraq. I questioned the wisdom of such a move then and still do."

"We invaded falsely claiming that Saddam had weapons of mass destruction, so why not offer war reparations and withdraw our troops?"

"What are you, Robert, some kind of anti-war lefty?"

Jenkins raised his arms in the air and said, "Me, a lefty? Hardly, sir. I just like a stimulating conversation, especially when I get to probe the mind of an intelligent man. And I promise, sir, nothing we say will ever leave this room."

"And no secret recording devices?" Peters asked, glancing around the room.

Jenkins laughed. "No sir, my word on that, too. May I also be so bold as to suggest that this occasion calls for a bottle of fine whiskey? What do you think?"

"By all means, my boy. A splendid idea. Bring it out."

Jenkins rang for his maid. When Nademe opened the door and entered, he asked her to bring not only whiskey and ice but a little *mezee* for them to snack on.

"As to your suggestion we pack up and leave Iraq, Robert, that can't be allowed to happen. We've invested too much in this enterprise, and any withdrawal goes against our national interests. We're simply going to need substantial, residual troop levels in Iraq for a long time to come."

"Baker had also suggested we offer an incentive to Syria and Iran to enter into some kind of negotiations," said Jenkins.

"Yes, but such suggestions come with too high a price tag. Iran will ask, in return, that Israel dismantle its nuclear warheads, which they will never do. Syria will be asked to stop supporting Hezbollah, which they won't do unless Israel stops its repeated threats to continue invading Lebanon.

"I have a little insider story to add here," Peters continued. "Early in 2003, Iran asked the US to end its hostile behavior, lift economic sanctions and guarantee Iran access to peaceful nuclear technology. In exchange, Iran offered to accept full transparency in its nuclear program and end any material support for militant groups in the Middle

East, specifically Hezbollah and Hamas. This was the boldest gesture from Iran in a quarter-century."

"So, the rumors were true," Jenkins said. "I'd heard bits and pieces of this proposal. What happened to it?"

"Not a goddamn thing. Bush junior and his hardliners not only refused to reply to Tehran's proposal, but they also reprimanded the Swiss ambassador for having the temerity to deliver it."

Jenkins whistled. "Bold gestures need to be met with a willingness to make deals."

"And in this instance, a moot point because this president doesn't want to give up anything either. Doesn't think he needs to."

Nademe knocked on the door and entered with a platter of finger food and placed it along with napkins and plates on the table between the two men. She returned a second time to bring in the whiskey and ice.

"Thank you, Nademe. That will be all for the evening. Feel free to retire."

She nodded and left the room.

"Help yourself to the whiskey, sir, and may I recommend the kibbeh. They're filled with ground lamb and pomegranate syrup and are dangerously addictive. So are the spinach turnovers and sambousek. Those are meat-filled, too."

"Thank you, don't mind if I do," he said, popping a kibbeh in his mouth. "Delicious! The whiskey's excellent, too. My compliments. And I assume if I overindulge, I need only walk up a flight of stairs to your guest bedroom, which I presume is ready."

"Of course. It's ready when you are."

They clinked glasses.

"Now, sir, I'd like to hear more about your plan to convince some al-Nusra fighters to join a much weaker rebel group so we can arm them. Even your own CIA has concluded that arming any rebel force, whether they be a notorious terrorist group or not, is generally a very bad idea, and I have to agree."

As preposterous as it sounded, his plan called Timber Sycamore was gaining traction in Washington. A one billion dollar classified weapons supply and training program run by the CIA, in partnership with the UK, so the White House could claim exemption from notifying Congress, and supported by Qatar, Saudi Arabia and Israel, all supplying money, weaponry and training to a siphoned-off portion of al-Qaeda fighters to take on Bashar Assad.

"Sir, I was one of the frontmen who trained death squads in Iraq, but we never used rebels, moderate or otherwise. Our initial plan had been to undermine Assad's ability to govern the country without physically removing him from office, essentially rendering him irrelevant, so the US could then deploy jihadists to capture and hold large sections of the country and make it impossible for the central government to control the state."

"Robert, you talk as if you're the only one who's ever trained murderers. I've trained my share, too."

"Of course, sir."

"In Iraq," said Peters, "we convinced some Sunni tribes to switch sides temporarily and work with the US military..."

"Excuse me, sir, but there were tens of thousands of US troops on the ground who made that happen, and even then, it didn't work."

"But if we can co-opt rank-and-file members of al-Nusra, particularly those who don't share the hardcore al Qaeda Islamist philosophy, it could work."

"Your plan is not only strategically risky, but also flawed. How do you determine who's more fanatic? Subject them to some litmus test?"

"There are always risks, Robert."

"Yes, and oftentimes they end very differently from our own expectations. The moment we decide who the good guys are and who the evil monsters are, we revert to our old mistakes."

"You're quite the philosopher, Robert. I'm impressed."

"Thank you, sir. Allow me to serve you more whiskey, if I may. I've another bottle close by should we run out."

"Very generous of you."

"About old mistakes that keep repeating themselves, sir. Not too many years ago, in Gaza, we encouraged the Israelis to support the formation of Hamas as a counterbalance to Fatah in the West Bank. In Lebanon, shortly after the 2006 war, we promoted the inflow of Fatah al Islam, a radical Islamic group, as a counterbalance to Hezbollah, with catastrophic results. What's to happen when we learn that your 'moderate rebels' are nothing more than an apocalyptic killing machine for the Islamic State?"

"That's a possible outcome in some future scenario, but in the present time, these elements share our goal of bringing Assad down, so why not use them?"

"Even when you know full well that groups vetted as 'relatively moderate' are highly vulnerable to be taken over by al-Qaeda affiliates?"

"Do I detect a reluctance on your part to carry out your duties, Robert? If so, I know any number of qualified men who could step in and take over your responsibilities."

"No, sir, I'm committed to fulfilling my mission. I just worry that any kind of blowback could jeopardize our plans going forward."

"You leave those worries to the experts. We can handle any blowback that comes our way."

Right. Just like you handled the bombing of the American Embassy in Beirut in 1983 and the killing of 241 US Marines in their barracks that same year.

"What about our European allies?" Robert asked. "They aren't equipped to cope with any blowback. They're already being hit with terrorist attacks, not to mention the political fallout from the refugee crisis."

"There's fallout from any war, Robert. We absorbed tens of thousands of refugees after the Viet Nam war. Europe will have to do the same this time."

"I understand the West's fear of a nuclearized Iran and the need to find a solution, but in diplomatic negotiations, you approach it slowly, gradually establishing confidence-building measures. Isn't that an approach worth taking?"

"In the case of Iran, it's far from certain negotiations could produce a new security arc across the Middle East."

"But not making an all-out effort plays into the hands of those who want to intensify regional tensions. Sure, negotiations could fail, but the stakes are so high that refusal to even try is pure folly." Jenkins paused. "Do you think people realize what's at stake here? Do they understand this regime change plan has nothing to do with protecting the Syrian people from a brutal dictator, that it's a proxy war against Iran, and that we've chosen Syria to be the battleground?"

"Very few people understand the conflict here, which works to our advantage. Average Americans believe what they read, and as long as mass media promotes the 'Assad is a brutal dictator' line, we needn't worry. To those who're smart enough to ask, I tell them the truth. Yes, this is a proxy war against Iran, and if we don't destroy Syria, how else are we going to hurt Iran, and by extension, Hezbollah in Lebanon. Syria is Iran's only Arab ally. It's crucial we hurt them in as many ways as possible. If we destroy Syria, we also limit Russia's impact across the Middle East, and if we succeed in putting a puppet regime in place here, we will also have limited Russia's access to its Mediterranean seaport. All valid reasons to continue this war to the end, regardless of consequences. Look, I'm not in favor of a shock and awe campaign like we conducted in Iraq. If Assad agrees to step down, and we can install a government of our choosing, there'll be no need to destroy his country. The choice is his."

"I'm going to play the devil's advocate here and suggest that's wishful thinking. The majority of Syrians support Assad. And it isn't just the Alawites. He also protects the interests of the Christians and Druze. His army supports him, too, even though a large percentage of his troops are Sunni. There's also a strong sense of nationalism. Syrians are proud people who love their country. So, if our goal is to render Assad irrelevant, it's not going to happen."

"Be they right or wrong, there are those in this administration who think that if we push Assad hard enough, his people will revolt and demand his departure."

Robert shook his head. "People might react negatively to some of the things their government does, but they'll come together and resist if they fear their country is going to be attacked, or occupied, or otherwise humiliated. It's called nationalism, and Syrians are fiercely loyal."

Jenkins served himself a few sambousek.

"You haven't tried these yet, sir. You should." And as he helped himself again, he recalled a story he had heard from Nadia.

"In the 2006 war in south Lebanon, Israel and the US felt certain the Lebanese would revolt against Hezbollah's actions. The opposite happened. They overwhelmingly supported Hezbollah's actions and still feel that Hezbollah's Lebanon's only deterrent against another Israeli attack."

Jenkins had felt it important to hear stories like this from a Lebanese who knew the local culture and understood the mentality. The US was unschooled in the political underpinnings of the Middle East. It had tried repeatedly and unsuccessfully to deal with the region and its different ideologies without a well-grounded understanding of what motivated and inspired the people and their leaders. Blinded by distrust of the unknown and unwilling to reverse their flawed thinking, the US had let itself sink into willful ignorance, and by extension, so had the American people.

"I understand the Lebanese," said Peters. "They've been invaded five times by Israel, but Israel's our major regional ally, and we're wedded to a mutual military partnership. We've no choice, just as we had no choice but to appease them by designating Hezbollah a terrorist organization. It's a conundrum, Robert. Hezbollah is just as big a threat to Israel as Israel is to the Lebanese. How do we strike a balance in that kind of equation?"

"Maybe we can't, sir."

"In this nasty Syria business," said Peters, "our job is to keep Americans on our side, and that'll only happen if our mass media continues to promote the 'Assad is a brutal dictator killing his own people' theme."

"How do you see that playing out, sir?"

"It depends on how we manipulate the media. If we put ourselves in the 'savior role of a missionary,' our liberal media will jump on board. President Reagan successfully coined the phrase 'freedom fighters' when he covertly supported the Contras in Nicaragua, and the mujahedin in their fight against the Soviet Union, so we've already set a precedent with the appropriate use of certain phrases. It's just a matter of humanizing the freedom fighters we now call rebels and demonizing any dissenters as unpatriotic. It's really not that difficult to control press coverage, or for that matter, the masses."

What the fuck, thought Jenkins. Whether it was the sterile thinking of the man sitting in front of him, or Nadia's admonition, or Andrew's abduction, he felt an inescapable moral burden weighing him down and decided then and there to do something about it.

"Okay, let me play devil's advocate again, sir. Right now, we have Sunni extremism funded by the West and its regional allies with the goal of crippling Iran's growing influence in the region, and by extension, dismantling Syria and Hezbollah. What if amassing jihadist armies isn't enough, and those Shiite entities prevail, and they pool their resources, and create a central command, and share intelligence and coordinate military operations? What if you've miscalculated Russia and China and their influence on the U.N. Security Council? All of these entities are heavily invested in the outcome of the Syrian conflict, each for their own reasons. What if we had understood this at the outset? Would we have been so willing to push this crisis to the brink?"

"You ply me with whiskey and good food, and then you ask questions I can't answer, Robert. I don't disagree with anything you've said. In fact, I think we've had a brilliant conversation, but my brain's had enough stimulation for one day, so I'm going to retire."

"Very well, let me show you to your room, sir. Do you wish to be awakened at a certain hour in the morning?"

"Hell no, I'll wake up when I wake up."

"Anything, in particular, you'd like for breakfast?"

"After all that whiskey? Coffee. Lots of it."

Jenkins accompanied the general to the second floor and showed him his room. "Good night, sir. Sleep well," said Robert, closing the general's door.

Back downstairs, Robert shut himself off in his library and called Nadia.

"Sorry, darling. I know it's late, but I wondered if you had any news on Andrew?"

"None, I'm afraid, other than he's somewhere in Homs. It's all rather discouraging. As for the Iraqi-American, who calls himself Omar, he met a few days ago in Homs with an American journalist by the name of Mary O'Brien. I'm not sure where she is now, but she may be able to give you a lead on his whereabouts."

"How do you know all this?"

"From Fouad Nasr."

"Fouad?" What the hell is going on? he wondered. Had Nadia been manipulating him all along?

"Are you there, darling?" Nadia asked. "Fouad says he knows you from your time together in the CIA. He's spoken very highly of you. Apparently, he and Andrew developed a close friendship while I was being held by Jaafar, and now he wants to do whatever he can to find him. I'm sure he'll be relieved when I tell him you're willing to help."

A plausible explanation thought Jenkins, and even if it wasn't, and he was being played, and if Nadia had piled on him a lot more propaganda than the State Department had ever been able to do, that was all right, too. It was time he pushed his moral compass forward. A virtue never tested was no virtue at all, he thought, and those who deserve repute are those who make amends for their mistakes.

"I'll get right on it, Nadia. I'll try to contact this journalist in the morning and take it from there."

"This's such good news, darling. I can't thank you enough. Miss you and look forward to being with you very soon."

He laid on the couch, closed his eyes and contemplated everything that had happened, both past and present. None of this regime-change business was new. As far back as 1996, diplomatic cables suggested that Netanyahu, in his first term as Israel's prime minister, had hatched a plan to overthrow Assad by engineering sectarian strife in his country and isolating Syria from its strongest regional ally, Iran. And yet, despite this, he, Robert Jenkins, had continued to play his role as a dutiful servant and follow orders. How refreshing, he thought, to finally see himself become so rationally sensible and able to examine, however painful, who he really was. A man capable of beating a robber and leaving him to die, then using his father's influence to escape criminal charges and worm his way into the diplomatic core, then working alongside a man infamous for turning El Salvador and Guatemala into killing fields. By association, Jenkins had earned his disreputable reputation as the man who showed up in countries about to burn. It had not just been Nadia who had prompted his self-reflection; it was the small-brained dinosaur sleeping upstairs in his guest bedroom who, despite repeated strategic military mistakes, refused to change his trajectory because of so little vision, and Jenkins wanted no part of it anymore.

He promised himself that as soon as Peters left in the morning, he would make some calls; and, satisfied he had made the right decision, closed his eyes. The next thing he knew, it was morning, and Nademe was tapping him on his shoulder.

Jenkins opened his eyes and sat up. "Is our guest still asleep?"

"I believe so, sir. He hasn't come down yet."

"Good, set the table for breakfast and have plenty of coffee on hand. The general's going to need it."

Before he showered and shaved, Jenkins called his secretary at the embassy and asked her to track down Mary O'Brien. "She's a well-known journalist and shouldn't be that difficult to find."

Before Jenkins had time to leave his library, his secretary called back. "Ambassador, that was an easy hunt. Ms. O'Brien is here in Damascus."

"Good. Please invite her to come to my residence as soon as possible. Send her a car if necessary."

After Jenkins showered and dressed, he read up on Mary O'Brien: A reliable, independent-minded Western journalist. While she presented both sides of a story, she knew, in the end, to come down on the right side. Satisfied, Jenkins closed his computer and went to breakfast.

"Good morning, sir," Jenkins said when Peters finally joined him in the dining room. "I trust you slept soundly with no disturbances."

"It was still dark when one of those infernal *muezzins* woke me."

"Sorry to hear that," Jenkins replied, repressing a smile, knowing that particular guest bedroom directly faced the *muezzin* who did, indeed, call his faithful to prayer much too early.

"Shall I make arrangements for you to travel back to Beirut?"

"That won't be necessary. I've already called my driver," and looking at his watch, added, "he should be here in about half an hour."

"Then you have time for breakfast, sir. Nademe makes a fine omelette..."

"No, coffee will do. I've had time to reflect on our conversation last night, Robert, and I think we set the record straight. Quite pleased we did. We're a team, but we need everyone to do their part, and that includes you."

"Yes, sir."

Jenkins accompanied General Peters to the front door just as Nademe was greeting Mary O'Brien.

Peters had obviously been as taken aback by Mary O'Brien's ivory skin and bright hazel eyes and loose shoulder-length black hair as had Jenkins because it had taken the general a few seconds to react and extend his hand.

"How do you do, Ms. O'Brien, I'm General David Peters. It's a pleasure to finally meet you. I follow your work and commend you. Well-balanced, accurate reporting, that's what we expect from our journalists, and you deliver. Keep up the good work."

Peters turned as he exited and waved to Jenkins. "Appreciate the hospitality."

Finally, Jenkins stepped forward and introduced himself to Mary. "And thank you for coming on such short notice."

"My pleasure, sir." And he led her into his study and closed the door.

"May I offer you coffee or tea?" he asked.

"I never refuse an Arabic coffee."

He nodded. "Nothing epitomizes the social graces of the Levant better than their coffee rituals."

"It's one of the things I love about my Middle East assignments. It's also the people, and their hospitality, and in the poorest of places, their selfless generosity."

"Yes," replied Jenkins as he rang for Nademe and asked her to bring them coffee, "and a plate of Arabic sweets, too, please."

"Mary, before we begin, I have to insist that this meeting be completely off the books. No recording, no mention whatsoever of anything we discuss. Can I have your word on that?"

"Certainly, Ambassador."

"You've covered enough crises across this region to know that sometimes a single word can make a difference. An illegal settlement in East Jerusalem described as a neighborhood, or a military checkpoint in the West Bank referred to as a patrol. A fence that is in fact not a fence but a ten-foot-high separation wall, the Palestinian territory, omitting the qualifier 'occupied.' You get my drift."

"I do, indeed, sir. It's a huge challenge for us as reporters on the front lines. We witness those things. We report it accurately only to see those defining words changed by our news editor to reflect something less offensive."

"Which brings me to a recent interview you conducted with the Free Syrian Army in Homs and the Iraqi-American who acted as your translator."

"How did you know about that?" Mary asked, a bit taken back.

"The Syrian government has its *Mukhabarat,* and we have ours, especially when young American women go off on their own. Never know what kind of trouble they'll find themselves in. Tell me about the Iraqi."

"I was a bit surprised by his appearance, especially since almost everyone here has a beard, but there he was, clean shaved, nicely dressed and quite good looking."

That is not the image of the young man I know, Jenkins thought. He had obviously cleaned himself up to impress her.

"He's fanatic in his views," Mary said, "and hot-headed when he doesn't get his way. We had lunch together after the interview, and when I didn't want to leave the restaurant, he got unreasonably upset."

"You were in Homs when the Syrian Army put the city on lockdown. How did you get out?"

"There's an underground tunnel, clean enough, that we crawled through. Not something I'd want to do for every story, but..."

"If it was that hard to get in, why did you leave?"

"I'm only as good as the stories I write, and things were quiet, nothing to report. If things flare-up, I'll go back."

"Tell me more about your meeting with the Free Syrian Army."

"They've set up their own media center in the Old City, adjacent to Bab Amr, the Christian neighborhood, and it was obvious they were looking for favorable coverage. Why else would they have invited me?"

"I'm glad you recognize that. How many were they?"

"In total, I'm not sure. Two men talked to me."

Nademe knocked on the door and entered with a tray of coffee and sweets.

"Thank you, Nademe," Jenkins said. "I'll serve the coffee."

And before he turned his attention back to Mary, he filled the two demitasses and handed her a cup.

"Please, help yourself to the sweets. You were essentially being recruited to be their mouthpiece to the Western world."

She shrugged. "And why isn't their message important? They're fighting Assad like our government is, so they deserve to have their side aired."

"What do you know about the Free Syrian Army?"

"They're defectors from Assad's army and want to see him toppled."

"That may be true of some, but they're also a front for al-Nusra, an affiliate of al-Qaeda. They were recently labeled a US-designated terrorist group."

"I wasn't aware of that. It's hard to come into a conflict like this and know all the players, especially when they're constantly changing their names. I'm also at a disadvantage because I don't speak Arabic."

"This goes back to what we were saying earlier about the use of language. Our government calls them 'rebels,' which has the same connotation as Ronald Reagan's 'freedom fighters' did in the 1980s when they were actually members of death squads. I have the utmost respect for journalists who make every attempt to present the truth, but when it comes down to it, we're all vulnerable to our own country's national interests, aren't we? We say we're the good guys fighting a brutal dictator, but are we? Is there such a thing as black and white when it comes to wars, particularly Middle East conflicts? Is there ever a wrong or right side? Isn't everyone involved in conflict just looking out for their own self-interests?"

Mary looked at him with curiosity and asked, "Do you agree, or not, that Bashar Assad should be taken down, Mr. Ambassador?"

"Remember—we're off the record. That's a decision for the Syrian people, not the US government. You've been in the field long enough to know we support many a brutal dictator. Saddam was one of ours for decades until his usefulness was no longer needed. Yemen's president just last week killed one hundred people. By all accounts, it was a massacre, yet our government didn't call him a 'monster killing his own people.' Why? Because Yemen's a client state located on a strategic waterway and has large quantities of oil. As for Bashar, yes, he's a dictator, but we're targeting him because he isn't one of ours. He's a nationalist who puts the wellbeing of his country before the interests of other nations."

Jenkins saw the look of surprise on Mary's face.

"These are things I never expected to hear from an American ambassador, but I get it. I, too, have my own ideas about Bashar. Maybe it's his British accent and the fact that he's a doctor, but he seems out of place in Syria. He should be back in London practicing medicine."

Jenkins nodded.

"I've been in the diplomacy business a long time, Mary. In the end, I'd like to see international law applied not just to a few powerless nations but to all countries."

"A refreshing idea, Mr. Ambassador."

Jenkins was impressed by Mary's uprightness, a quality he hoped she would retain throughout her career.

"We all strive to serve our country in the most honorable way possible. You try to write a balanced narrative giving both sides of an issue. My job is more nuanced. I'm the face of my country, and as such, I'm expected to show unwavering patriotism, yet, at the moment, I think it more urgent I help restore its lost moral compass."

"An admirable goal, Mr. Ambassador. I wish you luck."

"I'll need it," he replied, smiling wearily, knowing he would first have to overcome his own streak of moral blindness.

"There's another reporter in Homs. She's Lebanese. Her name's Sonia Rizk. She's hanging out with a Jesuit priest, a Father Frans…"

"I know who he is."

"Well, you might want to get in touch with her. She and her friend joined the Iraqi and me for lunch a few days ago. She knew him from an interview they did together in Daraa. She may be able to give you more information."

Jenkins stood. "That's very helpful. Thank you, Ms. O'Brien," he said, offering her his hand. "I trust I have your word that nothing we've said will be repeated."

"My reputation is solid. You can count on it, Mr. Ambassador."

I know I can, he thought, as he bid her goodbye.

"Thanks. And do be careful. The situation across the country is about to get much worse."

"So, I've heard," she said as the door closed behind her.

# CHAPTER TEN

YET AGAIN, SONIA WOKE EXHAUSTED, the nape of her neck moist, her scalp clammy, her underarms stinky, the lethargic heat unabating, and Frans' fan worthless. She longed for her air-conditioned Beirut apartment and hoped when she finally moved next door to Madame Chidiac's, which had better cross-ventilation, that she would finally be able to get a decent night's sleep. She dragged herself out of bed and into the bathroom. A cold shower usually roused her.

Once she had dressed, she joined Frans at a tiny table on the balcony.

"I just made this," he said, lifting the *finjan* by its long handle and pouring her a cup. "You look like you need it."

"I do," she smiled wearily, bringing the demitasse to her nose and smelling the rich, thick black cardamom-spiced coffee. "I can't abide this heat."

"Even by Homs standards, this is unusual for late October."

"Like everything else going on here," she said, looking out over the city.

In lockdown for only two days, Sonia was taken aback by how quickly the city had transformed itself into a war zone. Seemingly overnight, the Syrian military had set up its command center along the northern quadrant of the Old City in the Kahlidiya neighborhood. Russian-made T-90 tanks had been positioned at intersections. Sol-

diers manned checkpoints and verified IDs at every entrance to the
Old City. From their balcony in Bab Amr, the adjacent Christian quarter, she saw shoppers wishing to enter the market already standing in
long lines, waiting to be vetted.

During Lebanon's civil war, most Lebanese had considered both
the Israeli and Syrian armies hostile occupying forces. How ironic, she
thought, that now, as she faced al-Nusra, she would take solace in the
presence of a former foe poised to protect her and the residents of the
Old City and its immediate quarters. While reassuring, the sight of
forty-eight-ton T-90s catapulted her back to the dreadful summer of
1982 when Israel's Merkava tanks had rolled onto the streets of Beirut. She had been at her grandmother's apartment in Achrafieh for
lunch when she heard the deafening, metallic sound of wheels rolling
over asphalt, its sound like steel blades clashing against one another, vibrating the French glass doors that led from the dining room to
the balcony. Sonia had been drawn outside by the noise, just as every
Lebanese had for any explosion, any air raid, any incoming mortar
round or suspicious sound. The sixty-five-ton Israeli-made Merkava
had meant to intimidate, to instill fear into the hearts of the Lebanese
and, in some neighborhoods, extort unconditional surrender. Sonia
had watched, fascinated, as the tank had slithered its way down the
boulevard, spewing blue-gray fumes out its rear, ripping up the hot
summer asphalt like it had been sticky glue, engraving the road with a
reminder of its passage, in case the Lebanese might one day forget to
be thankful for its arrival. Daunting, and with no regard for anything
in its path, the tank had continued along its route, crushing two cars,
a large garbage container and a stop sign before it had come to a halt
and parked itself in a nearby field to 'protect the neighborhood' against
opposing militias.

It had been even more intimidating, days later, when she found
herself standing alongside a Merkava while refueling her car. Her five-
foot-six-inch frame had come nowhere near the top of its wheels, and
it had not just been the enormous height that she found so unnerving,
but the dark dome of its turret looming over her, watching her every

move, turning with her as she moved. It had been spooky as if no human had been inside.

"Frans, in relation to us, where are the other Christian quarters?"

"There are two," he said, pointing east toward the souks. "We're standing on the southwest edge of the Old City. Hamidiyah, the closest, is just inside the old wall, and Bustan al-Diwan is off to its right."

Frans shook his head. "There was a time in Homs when the two faiths were so intertwined it was impossible to find a street that was solely Muslim or Christian. If there was a church on a street, there was a mosque. If there was a minaret, there was also a bell tower. Shiite shops in predominately Sunni neighborhoods, residents at peace with one another, and now look at us. We're targeted for our religious beliefs."

"What's the population of Homs?" Sonia asked as she pulled her notepad and pen from her shirt pocket and began taking notes.

"About eight hundred thousand, maybe the total's closer to a million by now."

"Total population in Syria?"

"Eighteen million."

"How many are Sunni?" she asked.

"Seventy percent of Syrians are Sunni."

"Alawites?"

"Twelve percent."

"What about the Christians?"

"Only 10 percent."

"What's the breakdown in Homs?"

"Seventy-five percent are Sunni, 15 percent Alawite and 10 percent Christian or about one hundred thousand. Kurds represent 10 percent of the population, with a smattering of Assyrians, Turkmen and Circassians, all in the 1 to 5 percent range.

"Pretty much mirrors the national statistics. What's the Christian breakdown according to rites?"

"Mostly Eastern or Syriac Orthodox, with some Protestants thrown into the mix."

"Were there always Christians in Homs?"

"They've been here since the middle of the second century, which makes them one of the world's oldest Christian populations. In the middle of the fifth century, an important relic was discovered here—the head of St. John the Baptist—and that instantly made Homs a popular tourist destination."

Sonia laughed. "Incredible to think that a tourist destination existed that long ago."

Frans nodded. "Indeed, it did."

"Were there ever any Armenians here?"

"Of the one hundred thousand or so in Syria, about 60 percent of them live in Aleppo. Here there's only a scattering. After the Armenian genocide, those who didn't settle in Aleppo moved to Lebanon."

"What's the socio-economic status of the Christians in Homs?"

"Like in any religious sect, there are wealthy Christian families, but the majority here are middle class, like Madame Chidiac, who owns a car and is able to leave to stay with family elsewhere. The rest are either too poor to leave or have nowhere else to go, and they're the ones down there in those lines, preparing for what they see as a double whammy, an attack by al-Nusra because they're Christian, and then the inevitable military assault to rout al-Nusra out. Not an enviable position to be in."

"Won't we face the same problem here in Bab Amr?"

"Oh, indeed we will, maybe more so," he said, looking at her. "And why I didn't want you to stay."

Sonia ignored his remark.

"Doesn't this rebellion also put the Alawites in a delicate situation?"

"Doubly so. Not only are they considered infidels like us Christians, but they're also employed in many of the state-run industries and military institutions located around Homs. In a region that's suffered economically, this self-identifies a privileged group of people, loyal to the regime because of their economic dependence, who would otherwise be inclined to hide their religious identity."

"And their other problem?" she asked, taking shorthand notes as quickly as she could.

"The infamous *Mukhabarat*, run by Bashar's brother Mahar, is a predominately Alawite organization, and so the regime has unwittingly implicated them in the conflict and made them, in the eyes of the insurgents, not only infidels but legitimate targets."

"Damn wars and all religions," Sonia said.

On a macroscopic level, Sonia could understand the Sunni's fear of a rising regional Shiite power, but she could not understand the willingness of some in Homs to side with these insurgents. Yet this was what she saw as she looked out—a divided city and a shift in the balance of power.

If rumors were correct, the wealthier Sunnis had already fled the city while a minority of those who had stayed did so out of a conviction that Bashar would be forced to step down, or they had harbored long-standing grievances against his government and hoped an insurgent-led rebellion would restore justice, and if successful, they would lend a hand. There were those, too, who, because of the prolonged drought, had been unemployed and unable to provide for their families and simply yearned for a change in the power structure, whatever the cost. Those were all legitimate grievances that needed to be addressed, thought Sonia, but they were not going to be resolved by yielding authority to madmen insurgents. Why did people not recognize that? Or, was that the same kind of illogical thinking that had led many Lebanese to ignore the signs of their own civil war?

When Sonia decided to remain in Homs to witness what she had assumed would be an inevitable clash between al-Nusra and the Syrian Army with the Christians and Alawites in the mix fighting for their survival, she had given little thought to the possible personal ramifications. Yes, she had not wanted Mary O'Brien to have the final word on what eventually played out in Homs, but had such a cut-throat attitude portended senseless danger? She had covered many wars, but reporting on a conflict was not the same as actually hunkering down and surviving it day in and day out. Front line reporting, with rare exceptions, had more to do with extreme adrenalin highs while sneaking

in and out of hot spots, often accompanied by military or opposition forces, who wanted their side of the story told, then getting
the hell out.

She was a young child when the Lebanese civil war began and
didn't remember much about how her parents had initially prepared.
Who had known anything about war back in 1975, she wondered?
The notion that one could ready oneself for something so cataclys-
mic had seemed preposterous at the time. To Sonia's parents, it had
been unimaginable that life, as they had known and enjoyed, could
suddenly come undone. But as she grew older and the war dragged
on, she learned for herself just how short-sighted that kind of thinking had been. At the onset of the war, newspaper articles reported on
civil unrest in Sidon, along with mass demonstrations throughout the
country. Tens of thousands of refugees from the south began pouring
into Beirut because Israel had routinely bombarded their villages, and
with that influx came a sharp rise in unemployment. Yet, no one paid
attention to these telltale signs. Looking back, Sonia realized that Lebanon's leaders—through personal greed, political inflexibility or sheer
ineptitude—failed to save a nation they had been trusted to preserve.
Lebanon had always been a nation of tribes, each person loyal to a
particular religious sect or political leader, with little loyalty to the collective well-being of their country. During its fifteen-year civil war, was
it any wonder, then, that Lebanon had fallen victim to such intense
sectarian divide lines that the various communities had yet to heal their
wounds?

In Sonia's opinion, Syria was different. Syrians were proud people,
loyal to their country in spite of the stranglehold the Assad family has
had on their country for decade. Yes, there was rampant corruption
in the halls of power and a rising level of poverty due to years of extreme drought. Still, Syrians had been encouraged by Bashar's recently
announced reform package and his promise to clean house and relax
martial law. All of which portended a brighter future, particularly because such reforms excluded the interests and dictates of other nations.
Syrians were well aware of the CIA's seventy years of interference in

their affairs and its blatant attempts, at least since the early 2000s, to carry out regime change to topple the Assad government, and they took pride in their leader's refusal, despite the pressure, to bend to outside interference.

What, in Sonia's opinion, had been the difference between Lebanon's unrest and that which the Syrians were about to face? Lebanese leaders had had the power to put an end to its civil war. Bashar Assad had been powerless to stop the West's regime change plans. This was evidenced by the 2006 WikiLeaks revelation of a deliberate plan, hatched years prior, by the West to trigger social chaos, discredit the Syrian government of Bashar Assad, and ultimately destabilize Syria as a nation-state.

So, had Sonia made the right decision to stay in Homs? Had she—in her haste to compete with Mary O'Brien—put herself in physical danger? Fouad had said as much when he insisted she leave. And if she thought she could self-isolate in Frans' or Madame Chidiac's apartment to prevent such a possibility, would she not then be defeating the whole purpose of staying in Homs and covering the war?

"Frans, like it or not, it's time we prepare for the worst. Let's start by making a list of things we'll need to buy."

"I'll let you take charge of that, Sonia. My job will be to counsel and comfort people."

"As best I can tell, we'll need to stock up on staples like sugar, rice, lentils, nonperishable vegetables, and maybe a few extra gas canisters for cooking. Do you have enough matches and candles? What about buckets? If there's a water shortage, we'll need more than one to store extra water."

Frans shrugged his shoulders. "You've been through this before. I haven't." She shook her head and laughed. "Okay, I'll work on the list while you get breakfast, and then we'll go shopping."

"There's a problem," Frans said. "I haven't the money to buy large quantities of anything."

"I'll take care of buying the provisions."

"But I can't..."

"You can't what?" Sonia interrupted. "You're going to be putting up with me, maybe for a long time, so this is the least I can do. And if this drags on, you'll surely have people coming to you for help. And then there's Joe, who's about to arrive to search for Andrew, and we may have to lodge him, too. So, stop arguing and let me get on with the list so we can get to market before all of Homs decides to do the same."

They waited in a long line to have their IDs checked, and, as was Frans' habit, he began chatting with those, mostly women, in line.

"So, you're staying in Homs, Father Frans?" asked a lady behind them.

"Of course, where else would I go? This is my home."

"I'm relieved, Father. I'm afraid we're going to need many prayers in the days ahead."

"Have a lot of people already left?" he asked.

"I've been told that most of the Sunni in the wealthier neighborhoods have fled and that some of those remaining have already moved into their apartments. A smart move, if you ask me."

A lady in front of her spoke up. "Can't blame them for grabbing an empty apartment when a refugee camp might eventually be their only other alternative. Even if things get really bad, there's no chance on earth I'd take my children to sink in mud in some god-forsaken camp. I'm staying in my own house, no matter how hard it gets, even if we only have bread to eat."

"No need to worry about food," Frans said, addressing the woman. "We'll help each other. No one will go without food in the Old City."

There he goes, thought Sonia, giving away food when we have not even bought it. And shaking her head, she grabbed hold of his arm and moved him forward in the line.

Behind them, Sonia heard a lady pick up on someone's comment about leaving their home. "If I were an Alawite, I'd be long gone, too. Why would I wait around to have my head chopped off?"

"Is it true some Alawites have started wearing crosses?" another woman asked.

"A lot of good that would do them if they're stopped at an insurgent's roadblock. All any insurgent need do is look at their ID, and they'll know they aren't Sunnis. Names like Hussein or Hassan or Ghazi, or even Hafez, can't be anything but Shiite."

"Why's the army asking for IDs?" someone in line asked.

"Not sure," said another. "Maybe they're making sure the person actually lives here and isn't an insurgent."

"How will they determine that?" asked another. "Sunnis have names like Omar and Mahmoud and Bassam, just like the insurgents."

"How sad it's come to this. We've never had to think about IDs identifying us as Christian or Muslim. It's never been an issue."

"You're right, but Christian names like Thomma and Mariam won't save us, either. Al-Nusra considers us infidels like the Shiites."

"I had a cousin in Beirut during their civil war who told me that if you happened to land at a checkpoint with the wrong last name, you were taken out of your car and shot dead."

"That would never happen here," someone said. "We may have a ruthless government, but our army would never allow such a thing."

"It has nothing to do with our government or our army. It's the insurgents. It's the local thugs who some say belong to the Assad government, each protecting their own turf. Goddamn all religions, they're going to get us killed."

"Amen," said Sonia, hoping Frans had not heard that last remark.

To Sonia, the sea of agitated people inside the souk felt like a powerful wave crushing her. Shoulder to shoulder, shouting at vendors, haggling over prices, they pushed and shoved to get ahead of the others, a mother clinging desperately to her young child. Sonia wondered why a mother would even bring a child into such mayhem. There came a sudden thunderous sound from somewhere deep inside the souk, bouncing off the high domed roof and crashing back down, causing panic. A cacophony of screams echoed through the souk's stifling air. She caught a glimpse of Frans, looking despairing at her, and grabbed hold of his hand.

"We can do this. Just stay close to me."

Together, they forged into the crowd, jostling for a space of their own, weaving in and around groups to reach the head of the line and come face to face with a vendor, and when Sonia felt she was being swindled she haggled as hard as anyone else over the price. "What do you mean a hundred and fifty Syrian pounds for a kilo of rice? That's absurd when you know it isn't worth more than fifty. Give me ten kilos."

And when the merchant knew he had not only an intelligent shopper but one who wanted to buy in large quantities, he lowered his prices and, in the end, gave her a discount. She handed off each purchase to Frans, who put it in a large cloth bag slung over his shoulder.

As they searched for the last items on their list, they noticed some areas of the adjacent shopping mall had already been claimed by refugees, presumably Alawites, who had felt their lives in danger elsewhere. A blanket strung from one corner to another was enough to assure that family's privacy, and everyone respected that, hoping they would not have to do the same.

They left the souk late afternoon, and since they had only shared a *manoushe* while shopping, they both felt hungry. Frans' drawn face showed that the outing had been too much for him. On several occasions, Sonia offered to help him carry the heavy bag, but he would not hear of it.

When they returned to Frans' apartment, she fixed him a lebneh sandwich—he wanted nothing more—and put him down for a nap. While putting the provisions away, she munched on a ham and cheese sandwich. Her task completed, she peeked in to find Frans fast asleep. She tiptoed into his room, covered him with a light blanket, and with house key in hand, left again, this time to explore the area around the Old City. If she was to cover events as they unfolded, she needed to have a good grasp of the city's layout.

The nearby streets were practically deserted of locals, but she saw a group of soldiers standing on a nearby corner. If anyone knew what was going on, they would, so she headed in their direction. Along her route, she noticed large quantities of munitions stored inside the alleyways. Was it solace or dismay to know such weaponry was at the ready? She was not sure.

Sonia walked up to an officer among the soldiers and introduced herself.

"*Ahlan,* Colonel Yakob Asali. A pleasure to meet you," he said, shaking her hand. "You're the reporter who covered the Hariri assassination. Even if you hadn't said your name, I'd have recognized you by your..."

"My eyepatch?" she laughed. "Yeah, it's become my trademark."

"Did you ever find out who planted the car bomb?" he asked.

"The same people I accused of the Hariri murder."

"Of course," he said. "I never did think Bashar was involved. He had too much to lose."

"Would you mind if I asked you some questions?" Sonia asked.

"Not at all. Why don't we sit somewhere and have a coffee."

"Thank you. I'd like that very much."

Yakub turned to his men. "Carry on. I'm going to have coffee with Madame Rizk."

Sonia followed Yakob along the western parameter of the Old City toward the Khalidiya quarter, where they found a quiet café.

"Are you here to cover the siege?" he asked, once they were seated and he had ordered their coffee.

"I came at the request of a friend, Father Frans."

"I know Father Frans very well. He baptized my two children. A great man."

"He's convinced there's a lot of misinformation about what's actually happening in the country. He insisted I come see for myself."

When they were served their coffee, Yakob asked Sonia if she would like something else. "A cake or perhaps some knafeh? We're famous for that dessert here."

"And one I'd never refuse. Thank you," she replied, remembering her hastily eaten sandwich that had done little to alleviate her hunger.

"And now, a few questions if I may?"

"Of course."

"From your perspective, what's going on here exactly? Has al-Nusra moved in? Have they seized houses and taken hostages as some have suggested, or are those just rumors?"

"Unfortunately, they're true."

"The army's put the city in lockdown. A good first step, but what's next. Are you prepared to…"?

"Attack? Hardly. Our hold on the Old City is tenuous at best. It's a huge area to cover, and to do it as it should be done, we'd need three times the military support we currently have. As for securing all the quarters in and around the Old City? We don't even dare go into the Sunni quarters, most of which have been vacated. When the insurgents moved in there, they laid booby traps and mines, and they're well-armed with grenade launchers, AK 47s, the works."

"Is there a plan of any kind in place?"

He laughed. "Our orders are to drive the insurgents out of their strongholds. That's unlikely to happen. Why would they surrender or allow themselves to be driven out? We'd have to flatten large swaths of the Old City to make that happen. Some parts of the Christian area have already been mined, and that includes parts of Bab Amr, by the way. Imagine the cost to my men. I'd literally be sending them into an ambush, and they'd all be killed."

"So, what's the alternative? Bomb the rebel areas from the outside and hope your men hit their targets?"

"Pretty much."

"Do you have any idea how many insurgents there are?"

"At least five thousand, some say closer to a thousand, maybe more. I've not seen any official figures. Out of the million inhabitants here, and if half have already fled, that still leaves a hell of a lot of people to protect from a band of fanatics."

"What about defectors? Western media reports high numbers."

"Since Daraa, seven months ago, there've been some, very few in fact, when you consider the overall size of the army, and the defectors are either non-commissioned officers or conscripts. Out of approximately two hundred twenty thousand soldiers, the majority of whom are Sunni, plus an additional eighty thousand Republican Guard troops, plus reservists, the vast majority have remained loyal to the Assad regime."

"That's quite significant."

"Indeed, it is, and it makes me proud. Our problem isn't defectors, it's the pro-Assad militiamen literally acting as bandits, going around robbing vacant houses."

"Those are the *shabbiba* everyone's talking about?" asked Sonia.

Yakob nodded. "Petty gangsters, that's what they are."

"We had the same problem in Beirut during the civil war."

"You lived through that hell? Yes, of course, you did."

"And it was terrible, and some of our militias did the same thing, particularly the Christian ones. They even went so far as to set up a market to sell their stolen goods. And worse, people came and bought whatever they could find, claiming they were the spoils of war and their right to take. Wars are bad enough without seeing young men turn into petty thieves. Our militia also used massive amounts of drugs. How else could they have committed the atrocities like the Sabra-Shatilla massacre if they hadn't been completely stoned? At least you don't have that problem here."

"Al-Nusra's drug is fanaticism. That's worse. Just the other day, I saw a severed head lying in the dirt like it was some worthless rock, with hordes of flies on it and maggots eating away at its flesh. Did you know maggots could consume 60 percent of a human body in just seven days? It's the stuff of nightmares. I haven't had a decent night's sleep since. And now, today, on top of everything else, I get a call that my sister's son is now a *shabbiba*. I hate that these boys do such things. It brings shame on our families, on all of us who are trying to fight a vicious enemy."

"What do you know about the media center al-Nusra has set up. I don't know its location, only that it's somewhere in the Old City."

"It was set up a few days ago in the northern quarter near Kahlidiya."

"Would it be easy to access? Could I just walk in there and ask them for an interview?"

"Not if you value your life. They've placed mines around its entrance. You'd have to be accompanied by them to get in and out safely. There's also a tunnel they use to access the center."

"Why don't you bomb it, so they can't use it?"

"Easier said than done. How many of my men would I have to sacrifice just to get close enough to do that?"

Sonia nodded. "Have you heard anything about a possible field hospital the insurgents might have set up and where that might be? If not an actual hospital, maybe a clinic to take care of their wounded?"

"I'm not aware of one. Why do you ask?"

"A few days ago, al-Nusra kidnapped an American doctor who was working at the Shatilla refugee camp with Doctors without Borders. I believe he's here somewhere, being kept against his will."

"In Daraa, I know the insurgents had medical personnel who took care of their wounded, so it wouldn't surprise me if they hadn't made similar arrangements. There'll be a far higher level of casualties here once the fighting starts, and they won't be able to get their wounded out, so it would make sense to have someone on the inside."

"Any chance you could snoop around, see what you could find out? I realize you don't have a minute to yourself, but should you discover something, I'd appreciate knowing. This doctor's a good friend of mine."

"I'll do my best."

They exchanged cell phone numbers, each adding the other to their contact list.

"Don't hesitate to call me if you need anything," Yakob said. Sonia stood and shook his hand. "Thank you for taking the time to speak with me. And good luck in the days ahead. Father and I will be praying for your well-being."

"It was my pleasure, Madame Rizk."

"If I want to walk around by myself, will I be safe? I'd like to get a lay of the land, so to speak, before any battle begins. Learn where all the different quarters are in relation to Father Frans' house."

"If you stick to the main walkways and don't venture off into alleys, you should be safe."

Sonia watched the Colonel walk away before turning and heading in the opposite direction. From Frans' balcony in Bab Amr, she had identified the parameters of the Old City. The area included some six neighborhoods, covering an area equal in circumference to about a mile with, in some places, four- and five-story buildings lining the outside parameter, which contained the vast interior of the Old City, with its ancient dwellings, souks and malls.

Sonia walked along the southwest quadrant until she reached the northern Kahlidiya neighborhood. In spite of the late hour, there were crowds of people—parents with children, elderly couples, teenage girls and boys hovering around the fast-food joints that sold falafels and meat pizzas, everyone jostling for a spot on the sidewalk. And up ahead, a short distance away, over the heads of those leisurely strolling, four men caught Sonia's eye. The one in the middle was taller than the others and lighter-skinned. When he turned to get into the van, she saw it was Andrew. She shouted out his name and began to run, pushing her way through the crowd, only to get close enough to bang on the back window of the van before it pulled away from the curb. Andrew turned and scanned the crowd. She was not sure he saw her, and then there was that brief second when their eyes met, and he recognized her.

# CHAPTER ELEVEN

Two months had already passed since Sonia Rizk had banged on the back window of the SUV in which Andrew was being spirited away by his handlers. They had just escorted him out of the Kahlidiya neighborhood of the Old City where they had set up his clinic that day, and in a rush to reach the curb, had had to push and shove their way through the crowd to get him into the waiting vehicle. As it pulled away, he heard someone repeatedly pound on the glass, but precious seconds had passed before he was able to discreetly turn his head and scan the crowd, finally making eye contact with a face he knew so well yet hardly recognized. He had not seen Sonia in almost two years and was struck by how much she had aged. She wore no makeup, which could have explained her exhausted appearance, and her hair had turned more salt than pepper, and then there was her distinguishing eyepatch, but she must have thought the same of him with his gray streaked hair and the beginnings of an insurgent beard. In those brief seconds, had she seen the relief in his eyes, he wondered, the comfort it had given his hopeless grief to know that someone had finally discovered his whereabouts? To survive the inhumanness of his captivity, he had had to suck himself dry of emotion, but in that fleeting moment, when their eyes had met, he dared imagine some sort of rescue. He felt confident Sonia would move mountains to free him from Omar and al-Nusra Front.

Omar had coerced Andrew into leaving Sabra Hospital, making it perfectly clear he had no other choice if he wanted Leila kept safe. He, Omar and two other men had then driven out of Beirut in the same stale, cigarette-smelling SUV up through the mountain village of Alley until they had reached *Dahr al Baidar,* the summit of the Beirut-Damascus highway, before descending into the Bekaa Valley, once part of the Fertile Crescent, now infamous as the insurgent's key supply route and, because of its proximity to Damascus—a mere fifteen miles—the backyard of the Syrian capital.

In 2006, he had traveled through this region with Victor Helou's trusted chauffeur, Samir. A native of the area, Samir had explained the sordid reputation of the valley as a lawless haven for smugglers, weapons dealers and hashish farmers. Decades of unhindered passage and close tribal and familial ties had rendered the official Masnaa and Qaa border crossings all but meaningless. Divisions in the valley over the war in Syria had fallen along the usual sectarian lines, Sunni versus Shiite, and emboldened the disenfranchised Sunni population in the otherwise Shiite-dominated Bekaa, to offer any insurgents on their way to Syria the help they needed to cross the border.

The official demarcation between the two countries' nearly two-hundred and twenty-five-mile border was murky at best, as Andrew had discovered when he and Nadia, along with her then-husband Elie, without ID after his thirteen years in a Syrian prison and unable officially to cross into Lebanon, had had to traverse the rugged Syrian border by foot, a perilous journey Andrew hoped never to repeat. This time Omar had arranged transport in a modified 4 x 4 truck, its bed and chassis reinforced with welded steel, strong enough to endure the arduous journey, yet not impervious to snipers, patrols and land mines, not to mention frequent forays by Syrian army gunships.

As a courtesy, Omar had invited Andrew to join him inside the cabin while the others, seated in the cargo bed, were left to hang on as best they could as they traversed the rugged terrain. Andrew assumed this gesture to be Omar's attempt at establishing a better rapport between them. However farcical any notion of amicability, particularly when one was the jailer, the other his slave, Andrew nevertheless appreciated the favor of a comfortable seat in an air-conditioned portion of the truck.

"Were you born in Baghdad, Omar?" Andrew asked in English, hoping he would open up and speak more freely since their driver did not understand their common language.

"Yes, but I left when I was six."

"Because of the US invasion?"

He nodded. "And then when Baghdad fell, and Shiite militiamen killed my father, my mother saw no reason to stay and moved us back to Dearborn where she had family."

"I'm sorry for your loss, Omar. I'm fortunate to still have both my parents."

"Where do they live?"

"In Pennsylvania, in a small rustic community outside Philadelphia. My father's a physician serving the rural poor there."

"And you've followed in his footsteps, working in Shatilla."

"Thank you for recognizing that. You must also know how devastated they'll be when they learn I've been taken against my will."

"You have a higher mission now, Andrew."

"By definition, one takes on a higher mission voluntarily. It's never imposed."

Omar ignored Andrew's remark and continued, "My father was an engineer. Perhaps I would've followed in his footsteps if we'd stayed in Baghdad."

"But you were in the US with even more opportunities. Why didn't you pursue any of them?"

"You think it's easy being a poor, young Arab immigrant in the US? The sigma never goes away. Any attack anywhere in the world and you suddenly become a suspect."

"So, instead, you answered Allah's call and came here."

"Yes. To fulfill His will."

"Where does that leave me? The unwilling participant in Allah's plan?"

"That's your choice, to be unwilling. Back in Beirut, I had asked that you respect my beliefs."

"Yes, Omar, I remember, but respect works both ways. Why hasn't my wish to remain in Beirut been respected?"

Omar stared at the road ahead and refused to respond.

They reached Syrian soil at dusk and were met by a driver in a mud-splattered white van. From there, they drove due north some two and a half hours. It was nightfall when they finally reached Homs. Squeezed as he was between two men in the front and winding in and out of unfamiliar neighborhoods, Andrew had difficulty visualizing the city's layout.

He knew a bit about Homs but had never actually visited it. The closest he had gotten was a restaurant on the city's southern edge. He and Nadia had stopped there on their way from Damascus, where they had liberated her husband Elie from prison, to Tel Kalakh, a small Christian village southwest of Homs. It was Elie, a former history professor at the American University of Beirut, who had shed some light on Homs' four-thousand-year-old history. The greatest chariot battle, involving some five to six thousand chariots, had been fought in Homs in 1274 BCE between the Egyptians under Rasmus II and the Hittites, not forgetting, at the end of his lesson, to add a bit of trivia about its trees, most of which bent sideways because of a strong wind that blew through what he called the Homs Gap, an opening that extended from the Lebanese shore of the Mediterranean, through the mountain range that divided Lebanon from Syria, to Homs' Orontes River Valley.

When they reached the Old City, Andrew was escorted from the van down a dimly lit alleyway to a three-story building. Taken aback by the enthusiasm his arrival caused, he quickly discovered that those assembled were al-Nusra family members or new recruits, many of whom needed medical attention. It had never been the practice of the

US military to allow its soldiers to bring their families with them into battle, but when al Qaeda had asked its adherents worldwide to join its jihad, both men and women had answered the call, some bringing their families, others marrying, giving birth and building families on-site.

Once Omar had introduced him to the others, Andrew was shown his private living quarters—a minimally furnished bedroom with a private bath on the second floor—but only after seeing his new clinic on the main level, which he found surprisingly well-equipped with everything from multiple examining tables to stethoscopes, blood pressure monitors and pulse oximeters. There were lab diagnostic tools for urine and glucose analysis, even an EKG machine. As Andrew soon discovered, this clinic would be the only bearable part of being an al-Nusra slave while the rest was barbaric and depraved, the stuff of enduring nightmares and the horrors had begun that day after his brief encounter with Sonia outside the Old City.

Her nearness that day had so heartened Andrew that he found it impossible to concentrate on where he was being taken, yet it behooved him, on his first trip outside the Old City, to pay attention should there be a time when he might find a way to escape. As best he could determine, the city center was dominated on one end by Clock Square with its two distinct clock towers and the other by the three-domed Khalid Bin al Walid mosque, named, according to Omar, after an Arab military commander who led the Muslim Conquest of Syria in the seventh century, ending Byzantine rule. Syria was 75 percent arid or semi-arid desert, so once they left Homs, their vista was pretty much an open stretch of land, parts laid long fallow because of Syria's worst drought in nine hundred years.

When their van stopped alongside an otherwise unidentifiable expanse of barren landscape, Andrew was instructed to follow Omar and the other two men as they walked toward a group already assembled. As they drew near, Andrew noticed a lone woman surrounded by a half dozen men. According to Omar, she had been accused by her husband of committing adultery. One man, older than the rest and seemingly in charge, stood apart. Andrew recognized the elder with the long scar

down his cheek. He had accompanied Omar that first time they tried
to kidnap him. When the elder saw Andrew, he nodded, not so much
out of a position of power, or so Andrew assumed, but out of respect
for his status as a physician. Andrew did the same, remembering one of
Joe's monitions, to never antagonize your captor. Behind him, Andrew
noticed the freshly dug hole; the dirt removed as dry and as barren as
its topsoil. The woman, angelic in her beauty and stature, and amaz-
ingly serene, given her circumstances, was made to kneel alongside the
hole. She wore a long black *abaya*; her black hair loose down her chest,
her hands bound behind her back. When the elder gave the signal, two
of the men lifted her to her feet and lowered her into a hole, deep and
wide enough to hide all but the tips of her shoulders and head. They
then returned the unearthed dirt back into the hole to prevent the
woman from moving. The elder came forward, picked up a cement
block and handed it to the husband. In that brief pause before her
death, when her world held still, the woman bowed her head and, in
a voice barely above a whisper, recited a verse from the Qur'an: "I seek
forgiveness from Allah. There is no deity but Him, the Living, the
Eternal. And I repent unto Him."

When she fell silent, her husband then lifted the block over his
head and hurled it as his wife's head. Andrew turned away. The husband then stepped back, allowing the other men to throw a succession
of smaller rocks until there were no recognizable signs of her face, her
eye sockets empty holes, her neck broken, her nose torn off, her brain
matter spewed across the cracked earth.

"*Ya Hakeme*," shouted Omar, his voice bellowing in Arabic off the
emptiness of the land. "Make sure the woman's dead."

Andrew did not move. Whatever Joe's monition would have been
under such circumstances, he refused to budge.

"Need I remind you that you were living in sin with a woman,"
Omar said. "A word from me and the same thing will be done to her."

Andrew stepped forward and knelt beside the woman's body. Mercifully, she was dead, and he pronounced her so. Standing alongside
her, the unbearable heat weighing on him, choking his lungs, he of-

fered a silent prayer for the woman's soul that she might have finally found peace and forgiveness.

He stood, and without looking at the others, began to walk back toward the van. Out of the noticeable silence that had befallen the gathering, Omar shouted out his name.

"*Hakeme*, where are you going? We're not finished."

From another van, parked alongside the murder scene, a man slid open its side door and pulled out a long wooden post. He dragged it to a spot alongside the woman's remains. His accomplice pulled a hammer from his pocket and, lifting it above his head, pounded the stake repeatedly until it was sufficiently anchored into the dry earth. The elder stepped forward, tested its steadiness, then gave the order to bring forward the man who had been waiting in the van. Whether drugged beforehand or delirious from the stifling heat, his withered body was dragged along the ground, leaving in its wake a cloud of powdery earth, and dumped at the base of the post. His shirt was torn off before he was lifted up, his hands and ankles then tied to the post.

The elder stepped forward. "For your crime of adultery, one hundred lashes."

Everyone around Andrew stood breathlessly silent as the whip hissed through the dry air, its wiry sound meeting human flesh, tearing long, blood-gushing slashes the length of his back. How could he be the only one sickened by such barbarity, Andrew wondered. Finally, after one hundred lashes, the man's body was untied and left to fall to the ground.

"*Hakeme*," said Omar, "I'll have him sent to your clinic so you can heal him."

"Heal him?" Andrew shouted. "And leave the woman to be eaten by vultures? If Allah says both are guilty, why must only the woman die?"

Andrew had long ago understood the status of women in certain societies in the Middle East. Honor killings were still permitted to preserve the family's "honor" when a woman was sexually assaulted or accused, guilty or not, of adultery, so why should he be surprised that they would kill the woman but allow the man to live.

The elder approached Andrew and took him aside. "You were polite and received us honorably when we visited your clinic, and for that, I am willing to forgive your outburst."

"How is this barbarity still permissible? This isn't the twelfth century."

"Our laws are Allah's laws."

"The Qur'an says to give those who commit adultery, men and women, each a hundred lashes."

"Our laws are not to be questioned by an infidel, even if he can recite a few verses from the Qur'an. Do you understand?"

Andrew nodded.

You use your extremist al Qaeda beliefs to make a mockery of Allah's laws, he thought. Damn you and your so-called religious laws. They have nothing to do with any god, he thought.

"I am glad," said the elder. "Now go."

And Andrew joined the others already in the van.

\*\*\*

Since that day, Andrew had not left the Old City and when permitted the occasional stroll within those confines, had been accompanied by one of Omar's men. Mercifully, at least, the days had grown cooler, but what did it matter if, as reported in the nightly news, Homs was about to descend into chaos with the army poised to flush out the insurgents, and he desperate and depressed, with no choice but to stay. At least for the moment, they had sufficient food, and even though Andrew had grown tired of shawarma noon and night, with only lebneh and bread with his morning coffee, he was aware there would come a time when food would become scarce or simply unavailable.

Proper nourishment was not the only thing that concerned Andrew. In a normal physician-patient relationship, his work would have ended when the patient had been treated and sent home. Not so in a war zone and under captivity. Initially, with the severely wounded, those necessitating amputations or spinal cord injuries or requiring blood transfusions, he had performed what he called "damage control," then sent the patient to a nearby hospital, but with the Old City now encircled, he had nowhere to send the critically ill. Did it even matter, wondered Andrew, for when the army began its all-out assault, who among any of them would be spared?

He lived through the 2006 war in south Lebanon and should have already known how to manage this current crisis, but did anyone ever truly acquire that skill? And with everyone around him glued to the television, watching RT, Iran's Press TV, Syria's SANA, al Jazeera or CNN International, the incessant "live" updates on the army poised to enter the Old City and take out the insurgents, Andrew found it nearly impossible to concentrate, or even fall asleep. As if the news and threat of impending death wasn't enough, he had to contend with the incessant hum of generators, the burst of machine gunfire outside his bedroom, the airburst grenade launcher exploding in midair, shattering any remaining windows in the building, and the eerie whistling sound of an incoming rocket, trajectory unknown, until it landed, one night, somewhere on the top floor of his building. The dead? Discreetly removed and buried, he knew not where. His job was to tend to those still living—the shrapnel or embedded bullet wounds, the occasional fractured jaw, splattered knee or gangrenous foot. Those gravely wounded he made as comfortable as possible, then left them to die.

The continuous shelling, the rise in the number of wounded and dead, the lack of electricity, the ever-increasing scarcity of water, the screams of children terrified by the unfamiliarity of war, the deafening, rumbling metallic sound of tanks along the cobblestone streets tightening their circle, and snipers preventing anyone from safely venturing out, had forced the elder and Omar to take the decision to move Andrew's clinic from ground level to the basement. They had also decided that, since the transfer of critically wounded patients to other hospitals was no longer an option, Andrew would have to take on the task of performing any needed surgery.

"That's not a decision you take without consulting me," protested Andrew. "I'm a cardiologist, not a surgeon. I barely have the necessary equipment as it is. I'm desperate for more bandages and antiseptics, a better sterilization machine. I don't even have a goddamn ventilator. To perform surgery, I'd need special instruments and a lot more morphine for pain and sedation since I've no anesthesia meds to put a patient under."

"What you can do for our wounded will be better than nothing," said the elder.

"And if one of them dies?"

"He dies. You won't be held responsible."

Andrew had no way to gauge the number or kinds of severe injuries he would continue to treat in his clinic. What he had seen in the preceding days and weeks had already been horrific. A fifteen-year-old recruit, brought in unresponsive, with severe bleeding from head and chest injuries. Andrew had tried to resuscitate him, but without a blood bank and the proper drugs, the kid died.

Andrew assumed the Christians and Alawites would suffer the most casualties since, as infidels, they would be the insurgent's primary targets. But according to some of the wounded who now flowed into his clinic, their injuries had been inflicted not by the Syrian army but by the *shabbiha,* an irregular mostly Alawite paramilitary group, dressed in civilian clothes. Apparently, they had set up a detention center with judges and prosecution officers designated to carry out interrogations, and worse. One of their victims came to Andrew, his hands cut off and his tongue severed. He wrapped the victim's stumps in gauze and applied pressure, hoping the blood would clot, but what could he do to stop the man from choking on his own blood except to try and aspirate. Neither of those measures saved the patient, and he died.

He wondered where Sonia was in all this mess, presumably in one of the Christian quarters. Alone or with friends? Was she here to cover the siege, or was she working with Fouad and Joe to free him? How ironic, he thought. Sonia, Fouad, Joe—all people he hated, and now he prayed they would save him.

As the days wore on, his challenges mounted. To a man whose jaw had been destroyed by a sniper bullet, he could do nothing but suture him up. After being hit by an incendiary device, a woman came in with her clothes still smoldering. Unable to treat burns, Andrew could only give her a dose of morphine and hope it would alleviate her agony.

Andrew spent a lot of energy establishing amicable relationships with the insurgents and their families and this only enhanced his Arabic skills. He lived with them in close quarters. He took his meals with them, watched television with them, listened to their stories, their secrets and fears. Many of them were also his patients. Some had volunteered with only the vaguest notion of what they had signed up for, while others adhered to firm religious ideology like Omar and were prepared to die as martyrs. And then there was a particular group of men whom Andrew classified as psychologically unfit to be members of society. He had taken care of such patients during his medical rotation in psychiatry and discovered that such men had had either an unfavorable experience in childhood or had been taught the ways of sadism—the tendency to derive pleasure, especially sexual gratification, from inflicting pain, suffering, or humiliation on others. In the case of these insurgents, they boasted shamelessly over meals, in idle chitchat, about their role as al-Nusra's "video team." It was their job to stage and carry out mass murders, film them, then distribute the videos of the "massacres" to embedded journalists or social media outlets as evidence of Assad's brutal regime.

In one such video, a hundred and thirty bodies had been lined up on the floor of a "rebel mosque" inside the Old City—men, women and children, draped in white burial cloths, all victims, all previously taken hostage, all purported to have been tortured by Mahar Assad's elite Fourth Armored Division. The bodies were then carried in a "procession" to a mass grave supposedly in the Old City and buried *en masse*. Among these videos was one sensational story of Syrian security forces supposedly firing on a car, killing two women, a child and his father. The rebels "recuperated" the body of the small child, draped it in white and placed it in the van of an international observer, knowing it would be photographed and circulated as proof that Assad was killing his own people.

One night, Andrew was called out of bed to examine the elder who had complained of severe chest pain and shortness of breath. An EKG detected a myocardial infarction, but Andrew also suspected severe blockage of his coronary artery. In a normal hospital setting, Andrew would have prescribed a clot-dissolving drug and possibly a balloon angioplasty. Without treatment, it was unlikely the elder would survive. Rather than leave him alone, Andrew helped him undress and made him as comfortable as possible in one of the beds in his makeshift hospital. He then dimmed the lights, hoping his patient would fall asleep.

"You're a good doctor, Andrew. *Shoukrin.*"

"*Afwan,*" Andrew replied. "We've never been introduced, so I don't know what to call you."

"I'm called Mahmoud, and I am fifty-two years old."

"A man of your age shouldn't have such serious health issues unless you were a heavy smoker or had a bad diet. Your heart blockage worries me because I have no way to adequately treat you."

"If it is Allah's will, I will survive. I put myself in his hands."

"Would you like to try and sleep, or shall we talk a while?"

"I would enjoy talking to you, but with less passion this time."

A clear reference to Andrew's outburst after the stoning.

"Yes, of course. I have a few questions. May I?" Andrew asked as he pulled up a chair.

"Certainly."

"I envy anyone who believes in a God. Tell me why you pray to Allah."

"Allah has opened direct access for us to call Him anytime we want. This is an invitation to pray, so I accept."

"Does the Qur'an condone war?"

"The Qur'an does not promote fighting for the purpose of religious coercion. Others take this further and regard non-Muslims, and Muslims who don't conform rigorously to the Islamic code, as enemies of God against whom it is legitimate to use violence, but the idea of unrestricted conflict is completely un-Islamic."

Mahmoud recited a verse from the Qur'an, "Fight in the cause of God against those who fight you but do not transgress limits. God does not love aggressors."

"Let me understand. You're saying that Islam favors peace over violence?"

"Yes, murdering the innocent leads to punishment in hell. If anyone kills a person, it is as if he has killed all people."

The elder fell silent. Andrew wondered if he had finally drifted off to sleep, but then he spoke again.

"The Qur'an says, "Those who readily fight in the cause of God are those who forsake this world in favor of the Hereafter and shall be granted a great recompense.'"

"Is the cause ever defined?"

"Yes, Islam sets down guidelines as to when war is ethically right, with clear rules as to how such a war should be conducted."

"What are those guidelines?"

"War is permitted in self-defense, or when other nations attack an Islamic state, or if another state oppresses its own Muslims."

"And is there a certain way war should be conducted?"

"Yes, in a disciplined way, so as to avoid injuring non-combatants and with the use of minimum force. You seem very interested in Islam, Andrew."

"I've lived here quite a few years and have been studying your religion. The Islam I know is beautiful. It doesn't advocate killing. If it occurs, it's the work of a few misguided individuals on the fringes of society. Islam, as I understand it, denounces all violence. Islam literally means peace and tolerance."

"I'm impressed, Andrew."

Well, he thought, you won't be when you hear what else I have to say.

"You give me too much credit, Mahmoud. I don't practice any form of religion. I'm shaken by the constant talk here of sectarian violence. I thought Lebanon and Syria were a holy nightmare, but it's the entire Middle East with some of its people still believing in gods sitting on clouds while others spew fanaticism and exceptionalism. This is the twenty-first century, not the twelfth."

The elder nodded and closed his eyes.

"Shall I let you sleep?" Andrew asked.

"No, no, I'm just trying to absorb everything you've said."

"So, you give me permission to continue?"

"Yes, by all means."

"If you agree with me that Islam means peace and tolerance, tell me why you're here waging war and killing innocent civilians when two tenants of a religion you claim to practice forbid it?"

"There are verses in the Qur'an called 'sword verses' that justify war against unbelievers."

"But, as I understand it, that's a radical interpretation, not espoused by most Muslims. Zealots do the same thing when they distort Biblical verses to expel entire indigenous populations from their land, just as misguided Christians believe they're fighting a holy Crusade and carve crosses on their AK47s on their way to the Middle East. In your case, you're using your own interpretation of the Qur'an to kill those you call infidels, whether Christian or Alawite, and you're being paid to do it."

"Now you're misinterpreting our mission."

"How is that? Someone's funding your war on infidels. When you and your followers answered Allah's call, you were given arms and training and a salary. Am I right?"

"Yes, just like any other army in the world."

"But yours is not a regular army, Mahmoud. Soldiers defend their country and, when asked, fight wars. You're a religious mercenary, and like all mercenaries, you get paid to take on a job wherever and whatever it is. In fact, unlike a soldier defending his country, you leave and return home once your job is done until the next call comes to do Allah's work."

"You seem to have spent a lot of time studying all of this, Andrew."

"As you know, I work in a Palestinian camp with wonderful people, all of whom are Sunni. We exchange views. I talk to them about Islam. They ask me about my beliefs. It's my way of better understanding the world in which I've chosen to live."

"Mercenaries have been a part of warfare for centuries," said Mahmoud, "and like any army, they're paid to be warriors."

"But the irony is that you're taking money from the very same government your leaders claim to hate."

"Historically, mercenaries answered the call to war, regardless of whether they liked that leader or not. They were warriors, oftentimes poor. They took work wherever they found it."

"So, am I correct in calling you a mercenary?"

"If you insist on using that word, then yes, I'm part of Allah's mercenary army."

"War is never the solution to disagreements, whether over border disputes or religion. And in war, both sides commit atrocities. The Syrian Army will be wrong if it starts to bomb innocent people living in the Old City, just as you and your fellow jihadists are wrong to take those same people as hostages and expose them to the mercy of an army trying to oust you and your men."

"I find fault with your argument," insisted Mahmoud. "What if each side thinks they're right. There can be two rights, just as there can be two wrongs."

"Surely, your Allah sees the better solution, that men lead a life of peace and harmony, just as the Qur'an says. Why can't that happen? Will religion continue to be the cause of all wars across the Middle East? If so, damn them all."

When the elder did not answer, Andrew sat quietly, assuming he might have finally fallen asleep.

"That was quite a discussion you two were having."

Startled, Andrew turned to find Omar standing behind him.

"I was told the elder had taken ill, and I came to pay my respects to the man who has been my mentor."

When the elder did not react to Omar's voice, Andrew bent over Mahmoud and checked his pulse. "You've come too late, Omar. Your mentor has gone to meet his Maker." After a pause, Andrew continued. "Will his maker welcome him into Paradise after all the awful things he's done in his life?"

"That will be for Allah to decide."

"Mahmoud was stuck in twelfth-century thinking and could be excused for some of his beliefs but, you, Omar, you grew up in Dearborn. You've lived most of your life in the twenty-first century. You have a mother who loves you, who worries about your well-being. How can you justify what you're doing here? I've read the Qur'an. It's contradictory in parts, I agree, but it clearly states you should love one another, not kill one another."

Andrew fell silent before speaking again. "Sorry, I meant no offense. You're mourning a loss, and I've unfairly attacked you in a moment of vulnerability. I'm tired and in need of sleep."

Omar stepped forward and placed his hand on the elder's forehead. "May Allah have mercy on you, Mahmoud." And turning to Andrew said, "Right or wrong, he was like a father to me. I'll miss him," and he pulled up a chair and sat.

"With death comes decorum. It's our custom to not leave a body alone as it makes its journey back to Allah."

"We have a similar custom, especially in Irish families like mine. We call it a wake, and we, too, keep vigil on the body of the deceased. I'll be happy to sit with you. I'm not much for prayers but would certainly respect your need to say some for Mahmoud."

Head bowed, Omar sat quietly beside the old man's body for some time before he spoke again. "Shall we continue the discussion you were having with the elder?"

"We were discussing the absurdity of war."

"Yes, I caught most of that. Go on."

"We sit here in this building in the Old City surrounded by the Syrian army, essentially targets, like ducks sitting on a fence post waiting to be picked off. Am I right or wrong?"

Omar nodded. "You're right. Going forward, the battle will be very difficult."

"So far, all you and your men have been able to do is kill some innocent people and blame the killings on the Assad regime. In my opinion, that's neither honorable nor heroic."

Omar did not answer.

"In the end, will your paymaster consider your job well done? Or was your job all along to play the role of sitting ducks, about to be slaughtered by the Syrian army, so the West could blame Assad for trying to kill the 'moderate rebels' whom they back in their bid to get rid of him?"

"As I said before, Andrew, you're a very smart man."

Omar looked at his watch. "A few hours still remain before dawn. Why don't you try to get some sleep?"

"Yes, thank you. I will. I'm exhausted."

As Andrew was about to leave, Omar said, "I almost forgot. We have a new recruit who says he's had some medical training. I thought you could use some extra help. I'll have him check in with you later."

"Thanks, Omar, I'm grateful for any help."

"Now go… and thank you for taking such good care of Mahmoud."

***

Andrew managed to get a few hours' sleep before returning to his clinic. There he saw a man examining the equipment, his back turned. "You're to be my new aide?" Andrew asked.

"Yes," said the man as he turned. "Good morning, doctor."

It took a few minutes before Andrew recognized him. It had been about two years, the last time he and Nadia had met. He had been behind the wheel of her car that day. When Nadia had introduced him as Moussa, the person who had driven her out of Jaafar's compound, he had politely nodded, tipped his cap, but had not turned to introduce himself. They had also met on a separate occasion. That time, this man had grabbed him off the Corniche, pushed him into a waiting car, taken him to a deserted beach, and beaten him senseless.

"I'm here to make amends, Mr. Andrew, and to ask your forgiveness. I'm originally from Homs, and I know the city, and *Sitt* Nadia thought I might help get you out."

"*Sitt* Nadia?"

After their last meeting, he remembered waving goodbye as he had exited the car, but Nadia had not bothered to turn her head to watch him walk away. This had been the final crushing blow from the woman he had so deeply loved but who had just betrayed him.

"She's been working with Fouad, and when I heard about your kidnapping, I offered to help, especially since I was a medic in the army. I'm a bit rusty. It's been years…"

"Part of me wonders why I would want anything to do with a man who tried to kill me…"

"I understand, Mr. Andrew. I'm not a killer, but I was given orders by Mr. Jaafar to do a job."

"You could have said no."

"I know, sir. I'm truly sorry for what I did. And if you don't want me in your clinic, I will understand, but please don't blow my cover with Omar. He'll have me taken outside and shot."

"Okay, I understand. Now tell me, have you any news of Leila?"

Moussa diverted his eyes away from Andrew's and stared at the floor.

"Moussa?"

When he looked up, Andrew saw the tears in his eyes.

"What is it?"

"She's…" Moussa stopped, unable to continue.

"She's what?"

"She's dead, Mr. Andrew. It was Mr. Joe who found her. He thinks she was being chased by some of Omar's men and somehow fell. She hit her head and died instantly."

Andrew collapsed on the bed and began to cry.

"I'm so sorry. I didn't want to tell you. We were all so profoundly sorry when we learned of her death. *Sitt* Nadia arranged a beautiful funeral for her in Marjeyoun with her uncle Camille and his friend, Yousef. Mr. Fouad, Mr. Joe, Nadia and her father and me, we were all present. Camille had her buried near her family home. There's a cluster of red poppies along the terrace below her house. I don't know if you remember the spot, but Mr. Camille said she loved it there, and that's where she rests in peace. My deepest condolences, Mr. Andrew."

"No lies, Moussa. The truth. Did Omar have her killed?"

"No, I swear. He doesn't know she's dead. It was one of his men who chased after her. He confessed under interrogation, according to Mr. Fouad, and said he'd been too afraid to tell Omar what had happened."

Andrew lifted himself off the bed. "I'm going to my room for a while, Moussa. I'll leave you to tend to any patients who come in."

"Very well," Moussa replied, but when he saw Andrew unsteady on his feet, he rushed to his side. "Let me help you to your room."

"No, I can manage. If Omar asks for me, tell him I needed a bit more time to rest."

"Yes, of course."

Andrew climbed the two flights of stairs to his room. He closed the door behind him and fell on his bed. As he lay, eyes closed, the sound of mortar fire overhead, he thought of how little anyone mattered, not him, not his lovely Leila, and how quickly and senselessly and randomly death came.

# CHAPTER TWELVE

ROBERT JENKINS KNEW THE THIN LINE between patriotism and nationalism had been crossed. He was one of the professionals whose job it had been to advance the interests of his country to the detriment of another sovereign nation. What could he do to rectify such wrongdoing? Possibly nothing. So much damage had already been done, yet an idea, however uncertain its outcome, began to crystalize after a conversation he had with a man he hardly knew. His father had been an obscure figure in his life. In fact, until a day ago, Robert would have unequivocally said that he knew very little about his father or his career, or even if he liked him. The surprise, when he finally learned the facts, was not so much that his father had had a distinguished career, the usual approbation for a retiring diplomat, but that much of it had been spent performing what Robert was now doing—his government's dirty work.

A day after he had promised to do what he could to rescue Andrew, Robert received a call from Adele, his mother's sister-in-law, informing him that his mother Frances had suffered a stroke. A year earlier, she had suffered a heart attack but had since assured Robert that she had fully recovered. Whether or not that was true, that was how Frances dealt with life. New England stoic to the core with a constancy, given her lonely marriage, that Robert never understood. His father was no damn use either, but then he was part of the problem, wasn't he? He never even felt it necessary to return any of Robert's phone calls.

"How bad is it?" Robert asked.

"She's had a massive cerebral bleed and is on a ventilator. Her doctors say she could hang on another day or two, maybe longer, but there's no guarantee. I'm so sorry, Robbie."

His brain spun inside his head, and all he could say was, "I'll catch an early flight out of Damascus. Which hospital, Adele?"

"Massachusetts General."

He shared the news with Nadia and left for Boston the following morning.

No matter where he had lived in the world, Robert had always made it a priority to visit his mother once a year, but with the turmoil in Syria, a year had turned into eighteen months, and now with her stroke, he was stricken with remorse. At least, in a recent phone call, he had promised to come for Christmas and hopefully bring the woman he had fallen in love with and hoped to marry. She had laughed with delight at such wonderful news, and that brought him some small comfort. How often had she reminded him that at forty-six years of age it was long past time he settled down and started a family. Robert wondered what Nadia would think of such an idea.

*** 

En route from the airport to the hospital, he called Adele.

"How's my mother today?"

"When I told her you were coming, her eyes flickered. She's holding on for you, Robbie. Come directly to ICU, second floor. I'll be on the lookout for you."

Robbie—his mother had given him that nickname as a small child and Adele was the only other family member who called him that.

With its 999-bed capacity in multiple interconnected buildings, the Massachusetts General Hospital complex literally dominated Boston's West End neighborhood. The taxi dropped Robert off at the hospital's main entrance, and he had only to walk the length of the lobby and take the elevator to the second floor. When the door opened, Adele, as promised, was there waiting for him. She kissed him and fussed over his pallor, forgetting he had just spent twenty-plus hours between layovers and flights.

"You just missed your father. Poor dear, he's been here since early morning and needed to rest."

"Poor dear, indeed."

"Robbie, don't judge what you don't know. After you've seen your mother, we'll have a little chat."

He gave her a curious look.

"Go on, now. The nurse is expecting you. She'll escort you into ICU."

Robert stood at his mother's bedside. Even at seventy-two, Frances was still a head-turning beauty, and for a son who had only known his mother as a vibrant, self-sufficient woman, deeply passionate about her likes and dislikes, it was hard to see her so delicate and vulnerable. Eyes flooding with tears, he bent over and kissed her forehead.

"Mother, it's Robbie. I love you, and I'm here for you," and as he took her hand in his and squeezed it, she opened her eyes. Unable to speak, her gaze told him everything she could not say—my son, my greatest joy, the light of my life, take care of yourself—and he understood. Unaware of time passing, he remained at his mother's bedside until the nurse suggested he leave. He found Adele waiting for him in the family area. He pulled up a chair and sat next to her.

"Why does it have to be my mother dying, Adele? Why couldn't it be..."

"Your father? Oh, Robbie," Adelle said, wiping her eyes with a tissue and frowning.

"How can I say this? Frances and I have been best friends since college, and I never wanted to be put in this position. Frances had always wanted to tell you things about her life but never found the appropriate moment. And now..."

"She wanted to tell me what things?"

"Things you may not want to hear."

"But I do want to hear them," he insisted.

"You've known your mother as an intelligent, inquisitive, cultured woman who loved art, opera, classical music…"

"Everything my father wasn't."

"Don't judge, Robbie," cautioned Adele. "Hear me out, please. To the envy of her girlfriends, including me, your mother also had a recklessly bold side to her which she wasn't afraid to explore. She was beautiful, and men courted her, and she loved the attention. And then she met your father, a quiet, handsome man who didn't fawn over her like the others and, well, that attracted her to him even more, and she persisted until he finally asked her out, and one date led to another until she found herself pregnant."

"I never knew this," Robert said, aghast.

"Of course, you didn't. Children aren't meant to know everything about their parents. And because this is your mother we're talking about, wouldn't it have been better if you'd never known this?"

"No." He thought for a few seconds and then said, "Because I guess knowing this makes me feel differently toward my father since he did the honorable thing and married her."

"Only after your maternal grandfather offered him an incentive he couldn't refuse. Your father came from a wealthy family but nowhere near as successful as your mother's father, a man of extreme wealth with considerable influence in both financial and political circles, and he made a proposition to your father. If he agreed to marry Frances, your grandfather would assure him a successful and prosperous career, and your father agreed, which got him to where he is today."

Robert laughed. "Nothing's simple, is it. I wish I could have heard this from mother."

"Oh Robbie," said Adele, hugging him. "She was a great storyteller, and you'd have been properly entertained."

"After I was born, she could have divorced my father. Why didn't she?"

"By that time, your parents had established a mutually respectful relationship. Your mother was a realist. She knew she'd married a man of remarkable talent, that he'd do great things, and she signed on for the ride, with no regrets, and she remained loyal to your father. That's not to say she didn't have the occasional discreet affair, but that's how their marriage survived."

"She never gave the impression she was unhappy."

"Because she wasn't, Robbie. She loved her life. She traveled. She lived in exotic places, met interesting people, and that occasional affair added the extra spark she didn't get from your father who, by the way, was rarely home, and yet another reason she was able to stay married to him."

"Did he intentionally stay away?"

"No, he had huge responsibilities placed on his shoulders, while on the home front, your mother—beautiful, articulate, steeped in social etiquette, the portrait of a loving wife and mother—was the perfect partner to a man who aspired to ever higher and more prestigious positions, and he appreciated her for those qualities.

"Robbie, you were your mother's greatest joy. She adored you and was so proud of your accomplishments. She and I were friends since college, so imagine how happy she was when her brother Michael and I fell in love and married. We tried for years to start a family, but it never happened, and when your mother chose us to be your godparents, you became the son we never had. You even look a bit like your Uncle Michael.

"Now, go home. Visit with your father, then get some sleep. You must be terribly jet-lagged. I'll keep an eye on your mother, and unless something happens during the night, I'll see you back here tomorrow morning."

\*\*\*

It was Robert's mother who had chosen their Victorian red-brick row house in Boston's Beacon Hill neighborhood with its cobblestone streets, boutiques and trendy restaurants. And why not? During her forty-seven-year marriage to William J. Jenkins, her husband had rarely spent more than a few weeks at a time at any of their homes, so she had every right to choose a neighborhood where she had many close friends.

Both of Robert's parents had gone to the proper boarding schools and colleges—William Yale, Frances Radcliffe. After Harvard Law, his father, unbeknownst to Robert at the time, had worked for the CIA before transitioning to other government positions. Frances hailed from a long line of women accustomed to privilege but understood it also came with solo-child-rearing responsibilities when married to a man asked to serve his country. She had nurtured Robert and overseen his studies. A linguist in her own right, she had insisted, wherever they lived, that Robert learn that country's language, its culture and traditional norms. If Frances had thought an occasion important enough, she insisted her husband make an appearance or send his son a congratulatory note for some scholastic achievement, but then Robert could go months, sometimes a year without ever seeing or hearing from his father, and then suddenly, that changed.

Robert used his key to open the front door. From the foyer, he called out to his father.

"I'm in the kitchen, Robert. Come join me."

From the doorway, Robert saw his father's shining, well-trimmed head barely visible above the back of the chair. Had he shrunk?

"I've just come from the hospital," Robert said as he walked across the room. More inclined after his conversation with Adele to show some compassion for his father, Robert wrapped his arms around William's shoulders and gave him a hug. His father patted the chair next to him. As Robert sat, he noticed the untouched plate of food on his father's plate.

William J. Jenkins looked every bit his seventy-seven years with his back slightly hunched, his worn face, its multiple worry lines imprinted across his forehead and under his puffy eyes. He had been crying.

William saw his son staring at him. "What?" he asked. "You're surprised to see me grieving? I may have been absent for most of your life, but that doesn't mean I didn't love your mother very much."

"Did you ever tell her, Dad?"

"Never enough, I'm afraid."

And when William saw the tears streaming down Robert's cheeks, he took hold of his son's hand and squeezed it. "I love you, too, Robert, and deeply regret never having told you how much."

Robert pulled a handkerchief from his pants pocket and blew his nose.

"Your mother and I got off to a bad start in our marriage. I wasn't ready to assume the responsibilities of either husband or fatherhood, especially when I was expected to focus on an important new job. It was a lot to throw at an immature thirty-year-old at the time, and yes, we had our tragedies along the way, too, which made certain moments in our marriage very difficult. I lost my brother in a boating accident."

"Yes, I was quite young when that happened, but I remember how sad it made Mother."

"Thankfully, the pain has eased...it's been many years."

Robert was surprised to see his father dissolve into unexpected emotions. A man, seemingly aloof and insensitive, suddenly admitting his vulnerabilities brought tears to Robert's eyes again.

"Your mother and I had other tragedies, too."

"Her affairs?"

William nodded. "I got hurt plenty by them, but I was partly to blame. Your mother was an ardent and passionate woman, and I wasn't always there to give her what she needed."

Could William's brother have been one of his mother's lovers, Robert wondered?

His father pointed to the fridge. "If you're hungry, Adele left us plenty of food. Help yourself."

"I'm not hungry just yet. Apparently, you aren't either. You haven't touched anything on your plate. I could do with a whiskey, though. Will you join me?"

"I was hoping you'd ask. I don't like to drink alone. I'll take mine neat, no ice, please."

"The way I like mine, too, Dad."

Robert took a bottle from his mother's liquor cabinet and poured two fingers into each glass.

"To your health, Dad."

"And to yours, Robert."

"Did you know Mother was ill? Did she mention anything to you?"

"No," William said, "but then she never spoke of herself, did she, even after her heart attack last year. It was always how I was doing."

Robert nodded. "And her answer was always the same. 'I'm fine, darling. Don't worry about me.'"

"When the inevitable happens, Dad, there'll be funeral arrangements."

"Adele will take care of everything…but then, all she'll have to do is follow your mother's written instructions. Her funeral will be held at Cathedral Church of St. Paul, just across the Commons, then burial in the family crypt at King's Chapel."

"Did Adele know she was ill? Had Mother asked her not to tell us?"

"No, no one knew. Your mother never troubled us with what she considered trifling matters. She planned her own funeral, for heaven's sake. That's how she did things…alone and always one step ahead of everyone else. She was an exceptional woman."

William swallowed the last of his whiskey, then stood. "I'm off to bed, Son. You must be jet-lagged, so I wish you a good night's sleep. We'll leave for the hospital right after breakfast."

Robert stood and gave his father a hug. "Good night, Dad."

"Good night, Son. I'd like it if you could arrange to stay on for a while. We have a lot of years to catch up on."

"I plan to, Dad."

Robert had always known his family was a mess, but it had been easy enough to overlook because he had focused his attention on his mother. He wanted to love his father, but how was he supposed to love a man he barely knew? The moment of truth had come, and Robert knew he had this one opportunity to open his heart.

***

Adele and her husband Michael were already at the hospital when Robert and his father arrived the following morning.

"How is she today?" Robert asked. "Any change in her condition?"

"This morning, she took a turn for the worse."

"I want to see her," said William.

Adele nodded. "The nurse is expecting both of you."

The nurse met them at the door and walked with them to Frances' bed.

"Her condition has dramatically changed since you saw her yesterday. This morning she suffered a second stroke. Her neurological signs have worsened, and she's nonresponsive. We'd like permission to take her off the ventilator."

"What will happen if we agree?" asked Robert.

"She'll pass peacefully with no suffering."

Robert felt a wrench in his heart as he observed his frail father, so beaten up by the horror that had been visited on his wife of forty-seven years. William closed his eyes and nodded.

"You have our permission," said Robert, as he pulled his father into his arms and hugged him.

"May we stay with her?" William asked, his voice barely audible above the sound of beeping machinery.

"Yes, of course," said the nurse.

Robert and William sat on either side of Frances and held her hands as she took her last breaths.

\*\*\*

"It was a beautiful funeral, don't you agree, Dad?" Robert whispered to his father.

"Yes, it was," his father replied, his voice heavy. "It was just as she'd planned, but her death came too soon. I'd hoped we'd have had more years together."

"Would it have made a difference in your lives?"

"I'd like to think so, Son. I'm retired now, and I would've had the time to devote to her and hopefully make up for all those years I was absent."

Robert wondered how would his mother have felt about that as he watched his father stand and exit the pew.

Robert had particularly appreciated the grandeur of the Episcopalian funeral—the historically significant cathedral dating from 1891, the massive pipe organ, its bell-like sounds echoing into the vast reaches of the church's interior, the profusion of white lilies, his mother's favorite, the high Mass in full attendance—the ceremony, a tribute to a great lady. He could not remember the last time he had visited a place of worship or said a prayer, or even thought about God. And yet, when the organist played Bach's *Toccata & Fugue,* one of his mother's favorite pieces, a sound so mighty it made the very air vibrate—the hair on his arms stood up, and his spine tingled, and he thought he could imagine what it would be like to be in the presence of God. Was this simply the sense of loss he carried in his heart, or was it the deep shame he felt in his soul for what he had been doing with his life, and if it was the latter, was it too late to correct those wrongs or even re-establish a relationship with God? And did it even need to be a relationship with God? Could he not change his life and correct his wrongs with no credit due to anyone but himself? Robert would have been content to ponder this question a bit longer, but he felt someone gently tugging on his arm. He turned to see an elderly man who wanted to thank him for the beautiful service. In fact, there had been many single old men in attendance, and Robert wondered whimsically if any of them had been his mother's lovers. Wouldn't she have been pleased if they had come to pay their final respects? He promised himself he would revisit his connection with God and left the pew to join his father, receiving condolences at the church door.

When the mourners had left, Robert invited his aunt and uncle back to the house, but they declined.

"You and your father need some time together, Robbie. We'll come around five o'clock tomorrow evening for cocktails and dinner."

"Even better," said Robert, kissing Adele and thanking her for all she and Michael had done.

Finally, Robert and his father took the funeral home's limousine back to the house.

"Would Mother have been embarrassed by the accolades," asked Robert, glancing at his father, seated beside him.

"No," William said, laughing softly.

"Surely you're not suggesting she was vain."

"Certainly not, but who among us doesn't enjoy compliments, especially if they're heartfelt."

When they arrived home, William suggested they have tea in the garden.

Robert said, "I'll prepare everything and bring it out. You go ahead and relax. It's been a long day."

It was a warm day for February, and Frances' garden was beginning to show a little spring green. He knew that soon there would be a profusion of blooming purple and pink rhododendrons, peonies and roses. He longed to see that again and thought about how Nadia would love it here. He placed his mother's silver tea service on the small round table between him and his father and let the tea steep before pouring.

"Well, where shall we begin?"

"From the beginning, Dad. I feel like I know precious little about your career. Since I was born in Istanbul, why not start there."

"That would have been 1967, the year you were born."

Robert laughed. "You actually remember the year?"

"You're serious, aren't you, Robert?"

He nodded. "I'm afraid so."

"And you think I'm a failure as a father, don't you?"

"I don't know you, Dad, but I hope we can change that."

"I hope so, too. All right, then…I was CIA Chief of Station at that time. We were scrambling to monitor the Arab-Israeli Six-Day-War, which had just ended on June 10, the day you were born."

William smiled at his son and nodded as if to say, *I remembered the day, too.*

Robert smiled back.

"I didn't make it to the hospital for your birth, but I was able to see you and your mother a short time later and hold you in my arms for the first time. I was terrified. What did I know about becoming a father? I made all sorts of promises, too..."

"Did you keep any of them?" asked Robert.

"I meant to, Son."

"During my early childhood, you were rarely home, and when you did show up, I remember asking Mother who you were."

"Hmmm... that's rather embarrassing. It was a tumultuous time across the Middle East, Robert. Israel had grabbed the Golan Heights in Syria, the Sinai Peninsula from Egypt and the rest of what had been historic Palestine. No sooner had things settled down a bit when in October 1973, we had to contend with the Yom Kippur War, Syria trying to retake the Golan, Egypt, the Sinai, and almost succeeding. We were already in Beirut by then. I was Chief of Station there, too, with tremendous responsibilities. You've been sitting in Damascus long enough to know what that feels like, the pressure, the day-to-day crises."

"When I got that assignment to Damascus, I hoped you'd reach out, or at least send a congratulatory note."

"Surely you're past the age where you expect compliments."

Robert laughed. "You don't suffer from an excess of parental pride, do you, Dad?"

"Oh, come now, Robert. I knew you were up to the task. Otherwise, you wouldn't have been given such a prestigious posting."

"You talk as if you were responsible for my assignment."

"We'll get to that."

What the hell did he mean by that, Robert wondered.

"But back to the early years. By 1975, civil war had begun in Beirut. You may or may not remember."

"I was six by then. Of course, I remember. What kid ever forgets being part of a war, and much to my delight, Louise Wegmann canceled classes, and then mother went and spoiled my time off by hiring a tutor who came every day."

"That wasn't your mother's idea, Robert. I'm the one who wanted your mind kept usefully occupied."

"And then she went and insisted I learn all those languages. Oh, did I complain, but she knew what she was doing. They've served me well in my career."

"Arabic, Turkish, Spanish, Latin and French—an impressive list, Robert. Sadly, I only speak English."

"I consistently ranked first in my class, too."

"I know. Your mother kept me abreast of everything you did."

"So, the war continued. School was on and off. Then came the summer of '82. when Israel invaded. Pick it up from there, Dad."

"You and your mother, along with all non-essential embassy personnel, were evacuated to Cypress. I didn't bring you back to Beirut until the following spring, in time to pack up the house for our move back to the States. You may remember that's when your mother decided to buy this house."

Robert nodded.

"A week after we left Beirut, jihadists drove a two-thousand-pound car bomb into the American Embassy and killed sixty-three people, seventeen of them American. I had just assembled a new group of station chiefs before leaving, and they, in turn, called a meeting of all CIA station chiefs across the Middle East. Many of those seventeen killed were CIA. It was a devastating loss for the agency."

"So, Mother and I are back in Boston, and you were off to where? Central America?"

"Eventually, yes."

"But not before you insisted I attend Exeter and then Yale, no choice in the matter."

"Proud family tradition, my boy. A son follows in his father's footsteps."

Robert lifted the teapot and deemed it ready to pour. "Shall I serve you, Dad?"

"No, Robert, I'd like to serve you," and holding the lid tight, he poured the tea and handed a cup to Robert. They took a small break in their discussion, each holding their cup to their nose, inhaling the mild citrus scent of the bergamot tea.

"In some ways, my career has mirrored yours, Dad. I'm referring to your mission in Honduras and mine in Iraq. Was it your idea to have me posted in Iraq?"

"Quite the contrary. When your name was put forward, I voted against your nomination."

Robert looked surprised. "Why?"

"I'd come to hate what we did in Honduras, and since we had planned to use the same model in Iraq, I didn't want your name associated with such abhorrent behavior. I've spent my entire career doing my government's dirty work. I see myself in you, Robert. I didn't want you making the same mistakes."

"Who overrode your objection?"

"I'm not sure, possibly the man you served under in Iraq."

"Why?"

"Several reasons. Your unflinching support of your government's policies, your willingness, when needed, to operate on the fringes of the Intelligence world, and your Arabic skills."

"Some of that doesn't sound very creditable, does it?"

William shrugged. "Foreign service assignments are never without fault, are they?"

"You mentioned a second possible reason."

"I voiced my concerns not only about my government's actions but also about Negroponte's."

Robert nodded.

"The Pentagon's Salvador Option for Iraq, the one used in Honduras," said Robert, nodding. "The background. Some of it I knew, a lot of it I still don't. From what I could tell at the time, it was pretty much kept under wraps."

"Details on such assignments were, as you know, on a 'need to know' basis. It was only because of a rare 1997 report by the CIA inspector general that what happened in Honduras ever came to light. The embassy under Negroponte had routinely suppressed inconvenient information."

"The Salvador Option."

"El Salvador, 1980, civil war between leftist guerillas and a fascist US-backed military government and its right-wing paramilitary forces that included death squads. A year earlier, Nicaragua's US-backed dictator was deposed and replaced by the Sandinista government. The Sandinistas were opposed by a coalition of counterrevolutionaries known as the Contras. The action played out in Nicaragua and El Salvador, but Honduras, with its powerful military, became the training ground and headquarters for the Contras and other right-wing forces that were sent to wreak havoc across Nicaragua and El Salvador. Negroponte headed the operation. He got US military aid to Honduras increased from four million to two hundred million dollars. President Reagan insisted on a steady stream of obfuscation from the Honduran Embassy, and Negroponte obliged. He whitewashed the atrocities and sanitized any reports sent to Congress."

Robert nodded. "I remember his 2001 confirmation hearing to be Bush's ambassador to the United Nations. He insisted he never saw any convincing evidence of death-squad activity even when the Honduran press was putting out hundreds of stories about military abuses, tortures, corpses beheaded, throats cut, bodies dismembered or impaled on fences, decapitated heads hanging from trees, the full gambit of atrocities."

"Even by my standards, it became too much in the end," said William.

"In the end? Did the atrocities ever stop?"

"Not really, they eventually just bleed themselves out. Look at those same countries thirty-five plus years later—extreme poverty, unemployment, corrupt leaders, brutal military, many of them trained at our School of the Americas—and you have your answer."

Robert nodded. "Numbers of deaths in Central America?"

"Astronomical. Guatemala 200,000; San Salvador 75,000; Nicaragua 43,000. And our methods used there are still considered a success by Pentagon officials."

"What was your job in all of this?"

"I was the Pentagon's point person. I oversaw Negroponte's work and made sure the lid stayed covered on our activities."

"And you're the person who coined the phrase 'Salvador Option'?"

"The same. In Central America, the objective had been to eliminate opponents but also through torture and gruesome crimes, to terrorize the population. That was the key objective for the Salvador Option in Iraq, too. Because those who sympathized and supported the resistance were less easily identified than Iraqis who joined the US puppet regime and its security forces, it became necessary to carry out collective punishment on the entire population."

"Which ensured a full-scale civil war between Iraq's Shiites and Sunnis, and the same thing I'm dealing with in Syria, made worse by our affiliation with al Qaeda."

"I know this will sound macabre, but when the American public learned we were fighting the spread of communism throughout our hemisphere, they were totally on board. Obviously, that would never have been the case had they been made aware of the atrocities committed or the final death tolls."

"Yes, our never-ending list of 'ism's.' Patriotism, nationalism, communism and our newest one, fundamentalism, whether Christian or Muslim. We'll always be in search of good catchphrases or enemies to test our loyalty and justify our wars."

"We have to manufacture our wars somehow, Robert, and then leave it to our politicians sell them to the public. Most Americans see patriotism and nationalism as dual duties to support whatever we do abroad, even if it's to the detriment of another nation," said William. "I was just as much an idealist in the '80s as you were when you went to Iraq. I could have warned you, but would you have listened?"

"Probably not," answered Robert. "I was still the person who saw things as I thought they should be, that it was in our national and strategic interest to have a friendly Middle East, rather than what they actually were, destroying yet another country for our own reasons. There's a man I know. His name is Andrew Sullivan. When he knew I had worked with Negroponte in Iraq, he immediately made the connection to Central America and asked if what we were doing in Iraq was any different than what we had done in Central America. A damn smart man, far brighter than I was at the time."

"They were few and far between, I'm afraid."

"You held a civilian position in the Pentagon and could have stayed on. My guess is that you retired because you didn't want to see the Middle East turned into another Central America."

When his father did not answer, Robert joked, "No need to worry. There're no hidden recorders anywhere in the garden."

They both laughed.

"When will all this madness end, Dad?"

"When the politicians tell us to stop."

"No, it'll stop when enough people like me refuse to carry out their wars. I consider myself an intelligent man. How is it that it's taken me so long to figure all of this out?"

"The important thing is that you have and that you're willing to make the necessary changes in your life. It took me a lot longer and all those years doing God-awful things I'm not proud of."

"Unlike you, Father, I'm still young enough to try to make some changes. Will I be able to dismantle the entire structure of lying at the national and international level all by myself? Of course not. It would be incredibly naïve of me to think so but…"

"Robert, I've decided to write a book about my career, about all the lying that's been going on, all our unnecessary wars, our failed policies. It would be infinitely more interesting if you'd agree to co-author the book with me. Between us, we have a lot to say about diplomacy, or the lack thereof, about international affairs, human rights, abuse of power and the lies that go into manufacturing senseless wars, regime changes and assassinations. I believe it could be a tremendous contribution to academia and maybe even reshape government policy for the younger generation of diplomats and make our world a better place. Will you join me?"

"It would be my honor, Dad."

William lifted the teapot to pour Robert another cup.

"None for me, thanks, Dad. I need to stretch my legs and clear my head," he said, standing. "Would you like to come for a walk with me?"

"I walk too slowly. I'd only hold you back. I had to stand a long time today. Maybe tomorrow when I'm more rested."

"I'll hold you to it. I won't be long, just a brisk walk around the Commons. We'll have our whiskies when I return, and there's plenty of food in the fridge."

"Thank you, Son."

\*\*\*

After Robert undressed and lay on his bed, he called Nadia.

"I was hoping you'd call," she said. "I knew you wanted time with your father and didn't want to intrude. I'm so, so sorry about your mother, Robert. Had circumstances been different, I would have been there with you."

"I know, darling. I was able to see her, talk to her before she died, and that brought me some comfort. And she had a grand funeral, and that helped, too. I've changed my travel plans, though. I've decided to stay on in Boston a few extra days. I want to spend more time with my father, take him for walks and get to know him better."

"I thought you didn't get on with him."

"I've had my first real conversation with him, Nadia, and I've changed my mind. He opened up, and so did I, and we had a very pleasant time of it."

"This often happens," she said. "His wife is gone, and you're all he has left in the world. And it's always a beautiful thing when it does. I'm happy for you."

"You deserve some of the credit, Nadia. You opened my mind to a lot of things about what's going on in Syria and my role in it, and

I think this made me more receptive to what my father had to say. I discovered I knew precious little about my parents, too. It's all been quite remarkable. I only regret my mother wasn't able to be part of it."

"The reconciliation with your father might not have happened had she still been alive, Robert. She was the dominant figure in your life. Perhaps she had to step aside for you to know and appreciate your father. As sad as your mother's death is, she's given you and your father a great gift."

"I feel a bit like Saul. I came to Damascus blind. My eyes were opened when I realized I hadn't been living in good faith with the world, and I want to change that."

"And how do you plan to do that, darling?"

"Be the good American I should have been all along."

"I'm very pleased, Robert."

"Anything I need to know about Syria that isn't in the news?" he asked.

"The same hot spots. The siege in Homs is still going on."

"What about Andrew, anything to report?"

"Not yet. It's very worrisome not knowing if he's all right."

"I'm going to do everything I can to get him out of there, but I don't want him to get out and for you to run straight into his arms."

"Darling, Andrew and I have moved on, each with our own lives. Let me know when you plan to be back in Damascus. I'll be there waiting for you. I miss you, Robert. Take good care of yourself and enjoy your father. You two have a lot of catching up to do."

"Thank you, darling."

# CHAPTER THIRTEEN

RUMORS OF AN IMMINENT ASSAULT had persisted for months, but when negotiations finally broke down and the insurgents refused the government's offer of safe passage to an enclave in northwest Syria, Sonia realized the dreaded ground attack was about to begin. What she never imagined was the toll it would take. Finally, when six Syrian soldiers had died at the hands of al-Nusra and their armored vehicles destroyed, four thousand soldiers surrounded the district and prepared to attack.

When the army launched its assault, the residents of Bab Amr re-arranged their lives to coincide with the few pre-dawn hours when shelling momentarily paused. For Sonia, this meant a race to the souk in search of increasingly scarce fresh produce and other necessities, but before venturing out, she inspected Frans' apartment, taking notes and recording any new damage, relieved this particular morning to find only some additional bits of shattered mortar scattered across his balcony. Just hours earlier, an adjacent building had taken a direct hit. Once the shelling had stopped, she was in the street, videotaping the destruction on her phone. The bomb had fallen through the roof, gutted all three floors, sending most of the red tiles flying off the roof, its green shutters hanging perilously askew, its balconies demolished. As she made her way across Bab Amr, Sonia took note of the newly collapsed roofs, the sheared-off walls, the blackened hollow skeletons of buildings, the broken water mains and open sewers. Streets were strewn with burnt-out shells of cars, sadly Frans' vintage VW Wagon among them. Abandoned dogs and cats were now forced to share their meager existence with city rats, all scavenging for whatever scraps of food they could find.

Sonia had spent the last three months researching Bashar Assad, his family and inner circle. She studied the regime's history with the Muslim Brotherhood, CIA interference, its regional allies and foes. But now that the battles were raging, she turned her attention, camera and notebook in hand, to write down everything she saw, every bit of gossip she heard, every neighbor lost or disappeared, the massacres, the decapitated heads and mutilated bodies, determined to put it all into a book.

Once the hub of community life, with its myriad cobblestone alleyways, usually bustling with shoppers, the souk now rang strangely silent, its ancient stone walls cast in pre-dawn dimness, its cylindrical roof with its high rock domes and crowned columns, shattered on the ground. Gone were the merchants shouting out their wares. Gone, too, was the sea of people, moving like waves, shoulder to shoulder, the cacophony of their voices shouting as they pushed and shoved to get ahead of a line. It was the amazing olfactory experience of shopping the souks that Sonia missed the most—the mouth-watering smell of flat bread dusted with zaatar and olive oil baking in an open-fire oven, the rich aroma of Lattakia pipe tobacco, roasting coffee beans and the whiff of spit-roasted chicken smothered in aioli and spicy meat kabobs on skewers cooking over charcoal. There was no need to haggle over prices either. The exotic fruits like red pomegranates, yellow quinces, burnt-orange persimmons, and wrinkly-skinned pomelos were no longer available. The few merchants who did show up every morning were grateful for any customers willing to buy their meager offerings—zucchini, carrots, eggplants, along with the usual abundance of onions, garlic and potatoes. No meat or fish was to be found anywhere.

While encounters in the souk with insurgents were uneasy, since Christians were generally regarded as pro-government, Sonia felt them less threatening because of her modest attire and hijab. There was even the occasional "good morning" or "good afternoon." By contrast, if Sonia came face to face with a Syrian soldier, he might, because of her attire, consider her an insurgent sympathizer because she had stayed in Bab Amr and not fled. When she decided to remain in Homs to cover the siege three months earlier, she had assumed al-Nusra would determine her fate. Instead, it would, in all probability, be the Syrian army, indiscriminately shelling Bab Amr to flush out the insurgents, unable to distinguish innocent civilians from legitimate military targets.

As Sonia made a final run through the souks searching for a bakery, she spotted Mary O'Brien in the distance. She was leaning against a wall, jotting down something in her notebook.

"Mary," she shouted, walking toward her. "What are you doing here?"

"Sonia! Hello! I got word that the assault was on, so I slipped in a few hours ago."

"How? I thought the army had dug trenches around the perimeter."

"They did. I snuck in through the same tunnel I used last time, but I'm filthy and in need of a shower and…"

"Where are you staying?"

"Omar got me a room near al-Nusra's media center, but I just checked it out. It's disgusting, full of cockroaches and rats."

"Could you get out of that living arrangement without causing suspicion?"

"I don't see why not. Contrary to what you thought last time we met, they don't own me. After everything I've learned since my last visit here, they're lucky I'm willing to even listen to their side of the story."

"Good. Then, come stay with Frans and me. I have access to an apartment adjoining ours, and there's an empty bedroom. A counter-terrorism expert from Lebanese security is using the other room. Joe's a good friend, and he won't bother you, and you'll have your own key, so you can come and go as you please. So far, we still have water for showers and, if you're lucky, it may even be hot."

"Much appreciated. I gladly accept."

"I was just on my way to find some bread. If you don't mind, come with me and stand in line while I try to find the last few things on my list."

"I'd be happy to."

Sonia and Mary made their way back to Frans' apartment with a dozen freshly baked pita breads wrapped in day-old newspaper and the last of the groceries equally distributed between two cloth bags. As they turned a corner from one alleyway to the next, they encountered a mass of people hoarded together.

"What's going on?" asked Mary.

"Quick. We don't want to be here," Sonia said, grabbing Mary's hand and turning around. "Let's backtrack."

As they reversed course, they encountered even more people coming toward them. They pushed their way into the oncoming traffic until they reached the end of the pack, where they found themselves face to face with armed insurgents.

"Turn around and follow the crowd," one of them ordered.

"But we have errands to run in another district," Sonia insisted, realizing, too late, her distinguishable eye patch and insolence could, in the future, target her for some form of violent denunciation.

The insurgent slid his AK-47 off his shoulder and pointed it at Sonia's chest. She raised her hands in surrender, and without another word, she and Mary turned around and followed the crowd into an enclosed courtyard where they were ordered to form a circle around an elevated platform.

A collective hush fell over the crowd when, from a corner of the yard, two men dragged a young boy along the ground, his body badly mutilated, a cross carved into his bare chest, his hands amputated, his eyes gouged out, and mercifully already dead. His body was hauled onto the stage, then tied to a cross.

The woman next to Sonia gasped, "Oh my God. It's my neighbor's son. He's just a simple-minded coffee seller."

"How old is he?" asked Mary.

"No more than twelve," she said, her lips trembling.

Mary turned to Sonia and asked, "What the hell's going on here?"

Before Sonia could answer, a bearded man walked into the center of the crowd and spoke, "This is what it is like to be tortured and killed by al-Nusra. Let this boy's death be a warning to all of you."

As soon as the al-Nusra men walked away, Mary asked, "What could that boy have possibly done?"

Sonia shook her head. "Whatever it was, he didn't deserve to die like that."

"And there were young kids here, Sonia. They saw it all. Imagine the nightmares they'll have."

"I assume this is a side of al-Nusra you've not seen before?"

"In Iraq, yes, but I'd no idea this kind of thing was already happening here."

"They're the same fucking fanatics, aren't they?"

Mary met Sonia's glance and nodded. "How the hell am I supposed to write their side of the conflict after seeing this?"

"Stick around," Sonia said as they made their way out of the souk, "and you'll get even more visuals. Decapitations, impaled bodies on fence posts, women kept in cages. It's my lucky day when I can run errands without seeing these kinds of horrors."

"Have you been taking pics?"

"Of course. Last week, I was on my way home from the market, and like today, I got caught in a roundup. That day the victim was an old man. He was blindfolded and whimpering, aware, no doubt, what was about to happen. Two men dragged him to a table set up in the middle of the circle, then forced him to his knees. A third man grabbed his right arm, stretched it over a large wooden board and tied it down. A fourth man standing alongside the table pulled out a saw from a bag he had over his shoulder and proceeded to cut off the man's hand. Why the insurgent chose a saw instead of a hatchet, I don't know, but the butchery took a god-awful long time and the poor man's mournful walling so painful I actually vomited. Me, war correspondent, who has supposedly seen every possible atrocity man can inflict on man. I still hear that poor man screaming."

"Did you get video?"

"Yes, as much as I could without being noticed. Seems like that's all I do these days."

"Who are you reporting for?" Mary asked.

"No one. This is all for a book I intend to write."

"Good for you. A historical record of atrocities, certainly more powerful than any newspaper article."

"That's if anyone reads anymore. We're not far from the apartment. We'll have a nice verbena tea to calm us down when we get there."

"The hell with tea, Sonia. I'll need whiskey—straight."

"Then that's what you'll have," laughed Sonia, shaking her head as they walked. "We're supposed to be immune to this sort of thing, aren't we, but in the end, it just gets to be too much. Recently, a nineteen-year-old university student committed suicide because her parents had forced her to marry a member of al-Nusra. He divorced her a short time later and passed her along to other members of his unit until, finally, after repeated rapes, she ended her life."

"I saw that happen in Iraq," said Mary. "Poor women."

"Fucking male warriors. They're all the same. They use women like they're disposable rags. Journalists aren't immune, either, Mary. Several have already been killed by the insurgents, so while you're here, be careful who you meet with."

"You'd think after all these years in the field, I'd finally give it up and try my hand at something else," said Mary, "but I'm addicted to this kind of macabre adventure. Hell, I'll likely die on the job."

"Not you, Mary," she laughed. "You're tough. You'll live to a ripe old age."

When they reached the building, they walked up the five flights of stairs, and stopping on the last landing, Sonia said, "Give me a minute, I'll just drop off the groceries and grab the key to your apartment."

"Will your friend be there?"

"Joe? I don't know. He pretty much comes and goes as he pleases."

"Here we are," she said, opening the door, and as they walked past Joe's bedroom, he walked out blurry-eyed. "Oh, sorry," he said, looking at Mary, "I didn't know anyone was here."

"Joe, I'd like you to meet Mary O'Brien. She's a journalist here to cover the assault. She'll be staying in the other bedroom. I didn't think you'd mind."

"Quite the contrary," he said, giving Mary a big smile and reminding Sonia of the first time she had met him when he had lifted her hand to his mouth and kissed it. Still quite the charmer, she thought.

And as he extended his hand to shake Mary's, it was evident to Sonia there was an immediate attraction on both sides, and why wouldn't there be. Joe, with his thick, wavy hair and beard, was unquestionably handsome, and then there was Mary with her beautiful smile and hazel eyes, warm and inviting.

"Welcome to crazy Bab Amr," he said, holding onto her hand longer than was necessary.

Mary smiled. "Sonia told me you're here to rescue your friend Andrew. I've had several meetings with al-Nusra, so if I can help in any way, don't hesitate to ask. I understand you also brought sad news about Andrew's lady friend. I'm sorry for his loss. He must be devastated."

"We don't think he knows yet," said Sonia.

\*\*\*

On those evenings when neither Sonia nor Frans had to leave the apartment, they looked forward to settling back and enjoying a glass of whiskey from their stash of Johnnie Walker Black Label. Their evenings eventually expanded to include Joe and Mary, their arrival proving even more appreciated because each of them had brought their own supply of scotch. On the occasional quiet night, Sonia invited Colonel Yakob to join them. In charge of the Syrian army's assault on Bab Amr, he was the ideal person to not only give Mary the information she needed for her story but to plead his case to an American journalist.

"I hope you don't mind," Yakob said, "but I asked Yousef to come along. He's a fine officer with an excellent command of English, and since he's originally from Homs, he might be able to find your friend Andrew."

"Welcome, Yousef," said Frans.

"How thoughtful of you, Yakob, in light of all the other things you have to worry about."

"Yakob," said Mary. "Do you mind if I jump right in? I've some questions about your assault on defenseless civilians."

"I know our operations haven't been the most accurate, but…"

"That's a bit of an understatement, isn't it? I mean no offense, but some of my colleagues have accused your army of carrying out a scorched-earth campaign on Bab Amr."

"We're doing no such thing, Mary. Admittedly some rules of engagement regarding civilian safety are being violated, but we're taking every possible precaution. We use drones when we can. Unfortunately, they're not sophisticated enough to do a decent job, leaving me with few other options. It might be helpful if you understood what's really going on here."

"I agree," Sonia muttered.

"Al-Nusra has taken this district and claimed it as their liberated zone, something no government would tolerate. It'll be a God-awful bloody and costly battle, no matter how careful we are, to get them out."

"I'm just thinking about the civilians caught in the cross-fire. It isn't fair to them."

"They were offered safe passage out. Those who have chosen to stay are well aware their decision could kill them. Look, I dislike what I'm obliged to do, but I think you'll find that this campaign is consistent with western standards, although your government would be loath to admit any such thing."

"Will your tanks be entering Bab Amr?" asked Frans.

"No, it's too risky. We'll remain on the perimeter and attack from there."

"God help us," Frans said, shaking his head.

Yakob nodded. "We'll definitely need His help, but again I ask, what am I to do?"

"Give the insurgents safe passage out of Bab Amr," said Mary.

"We offered them this option, but they refused."

Yakob paused and took a long sip of his whiskey.

"Let me give you the full picture, Mary. Not only has al-Nusra taken over all of Bab Amr, they've attacked and killed our soldiers and our security forces. They blew up a pipeline to Homs' oil refinery. They bombed a civilian bus, killing eight people and wounding a dozen more, and then destroyed a train carrying diesel oil. A police bus was blown up, killing several officers. Bridges were bombed, and just two weeks ago, they attacked one of our checkpoints. They killed ten of my soldiers and took an additional nineteen prisoner. That was the last straw. Just imagining what they'll do to those poor men gives me nightmares."

"You're in a tough position," Mary said. "There's no easy, clear-cut decision. The number of wounded and dead will be high, not to mention the backlash you'll get. You face a no-win situation."

"Exactly."

"Christians and Muslims share a common heritage here," said Frans. "We, who have chosen to stay, understand the predicament Yakob faces. You must at least recognize that covert outside support is fostering this sectarian violence, and it's directed primarily against us. If not reigned in, al-Nusra or any of their affiliates will take over the government and cause us even greater harm. Look at what their death squads did to the Chaldean Christians in Iraq. And yes, Mary, I'm well aware the Syrian government bears a burden of responsibility for the often brutal way it has responded to the insurgency, but to argue that the West's idea of regime change, using al-Nusra to do their dirty work as the better alternative, is preposterous."

"I understand all of that, Frans, and I agree, but it's my job as a journalist to criticize, to ask questions. That's all I'm doing here, looking for clarity, but I also have to tell both sides of the story."

"Provided you do it in an unbiased manner," insisted Frans. "It's not true that the Syrian government has only bad sides and the opposition only good ones. The objective of this armed insurrection is to trigger the response of the military to justify a humanitarian intervention, like what the West just did in Libya. We don't want that kind of armed interference here, so I find your claim that the other side has a right to be heard discourteous to those of us who are here. Al-Nusra has taken over our Christian neighborhoods and turned them into a battleground against the Syrian army. How is that justifiable?"

"I hear what you're saying, Frans, but it can't change what I'm asked to do. Good journalism is supposed to flush out both sides. I also have a certain political agenda problem to contend with, so I walk a very fine line. If I want any of my reporting to appear in print, I have to carefully craft my stories. That's just the way things are in this war."

"In any war, Mary. There'll always be bias no matter whose war it is."

Mary nodded. "That's the nature of man, isn't it? He creates wars and then manufactures his own narrative." She turned to Joe and said, "I understand you want to find al-Nusra's medical clinic. If it's anywhere near their media center, I can get you in there."

"But the area's not safe," said Yakob, "Parts of it are mined."

"You're right, but I still think I could get Joe inside without getting us blown up. I was there just yesterday."

"Was Omar there?" asked Sonia.

"Yes, he acts as my translator whenever I meet with the higher-ups."

"Could you ask Omar to give you a tour of their medical clinic?" asked Joe. "You might suggest it would look good to your American readers if they saw how well their government-supported rebels were being treated."

"And I assume Omar runs that operation, too," said Sonia, "so, you shouldn't need to do a lot of convincing."

"A brilliant idea, and it may just work. I'll try to arrange it."

"That would be very helpful," said Joe. "I'd volunteer to come as your assistant, but Omar might remember me from my visit to Daraa last March. If so, my presence would not only put your life at risk but compromise my attempt to rescue Andrew."

"But if Mary knew ahead of time, she could notify you, and you could follow her," said Sonia.

"That would work unless Omar played extra cautious and had his men accompany us."

"It's a chance I'll take if the opportunity arises," said Joe.

"If I can play any part, I'd be happy to," added Frans. "I've had a few meetings with Omar, as you know, Mary, so he'd consider me non-threatening if I were to accompany you."

"Another good idea," she said. "I'll consider these options before approaching Omar."

When Mary finished, Sonia turned to Yakob.

"How safe are journalists here?"

"They're certainly not targeted by us, I assure you. We tried to intercede with western journalists, many of whom were embedded with the Syrian army, to leave before this offensive was launched. I understand you snuck in under our radar, Mary, so you may not know we offered the others safe passage out to Lebanon. I could arrange the same for you. We even opened a dialogue with the insurgents suggesting the ramifications, publicity-wise, should their embedded western journalists be killed."

"I have a lot of respect for any correspondent working in a war zone, Yakob," Sonia said, "but I'm particularly concerned for Mary's safety since she's working directly with al-Nusra. Call her decision unwise, she's nevertheless part of a brave pack of international journalists who dare to venture into war zones. I was once part of that pack, so I know what I'm talking about. We do the world a service by providing eyewitness reporting but often at the cost of our lives."

"Yes, but bear in mind," said Yakob, turning to Mary, "you voluntarily agreed to enter this war zone, so when one of you gets killed while covering the story, it shouldn't come as a shock."

"Shit happens, I know that," said Mary. "I also know that journalists are generally not targeted killings, and I appreciate your effort to keep us safe, Yakob. Thank you."

The four of them fell awkwardly silent for a moment.

"Sonia," said Joe, "I don't know if Fouad told you that he managed to get Moussa inside Andrew's clinic as a nurse's aide."

"No, he didn't tell me, probably because I don't know who Moussa is."

"He was one of the men who beat Andrew almost to death. Odd as it may sound, he also helped Nadia escape Jaafar's compound after he was killed."

Sonia felt a cold tingle down her spine at the mention of Nadia. She may end up playing some small part in rescuing Andrew, but Nadia would still hate her and wish her dead, and for good reason.

"Why would he now be helping Andrew?"

"When he heard about his kidnapping, he came forward and told Fouad he wanted to make amends."

"Good, that means we have an ally inside the clinic."

Yakob stood and excused himself, "I wish I could stay longer, but I need to get back to my men."

"Can I tag along?" asked Joe. "I'd like to acquaint myself with Bab Amr."

"I'd like to come, too, if I may," said Mary.

"I've duties to attend to, but Yousef can give you a walking tour."

"It would be my honor," the young Yousef replied.

"Can I have a minute to change clothes?" asked Mary.

"Me, too," said Joe.

"Of course," said Yakob, and biding Sonia and Frans good night, added, "I hope we can do this more often. A bit of socializing is good for everyone's morale."

"I agree," Sonia said, walking him and Yousef to the door.

"I appreciated the opportunity to speak with Mary," Yakob said. "It's important she hear our side of the story."

"I agree," and when Sonia opened the front door, she found Joe and Mary, their clothes already changed, waiting for Yakob.

*** 

Sonia was still awake when Joe and Mary returned to Madame Chidiac's apartment. The walls were thin enough that she could hear their voices but not their actual words, and after a fashion, she realized they were not speaking at all but had moved to Joe's bed, which wall-to-wall was closest to hers. It had not been her intention to listen to their lovemaking, but she was happy for both of them. It was not easy or sustainable to cover a war zone without the occasional pleasure. And how wonderful that the most natural thing between two people had happened, which only made her long even more for Fouad and their own moments of pleasure.

Sonia spent the rest of the night contemplating what role she would play in rescuing Andrew when, over breakfast, an opportunity presented itself. Joe planned to accompany Mary that night to the media center. Why shouldn't she tag along?

"Fouad would never forgive me if I let you come," Joe insisted. "Be reasonable, Sonia. You've only got one eye. Your night vision is limited and… well, you haven't been back in the field since the car bomb. What if…"

"Are you suggesting I'm no longer fit for this kind of work?"

"*Ya Allah*. Not at all. I just don't want to go behind Fouad's back. Part of my mission here is to protect you, not put your life in danger."

"He doesn't need to know."

"And if you get injured?"

"I could just as easily get hurt or killed running errands."

Joe sat silent for a few minutes, then finally said, "I'm meeting Mary at midnight. She's going to show me the media center, but from there, I'll go on to the clinic alone. No need to endanger anyone else. Is that understood?"

"Yes," Sonia said, knowing full well she was not going to let him leave her behind. "Frans likes to go to sleep early, so he won't even know I'm gone."

"He'd object?"

"Didn't you?"

Joe laughed. "And a lot of good that did."

"Yousef has agreed to accompany us. He knows where the insurgents and their snipers are posted."

"Then we have a good chance."

\*\*\*

The moonless night worked in their favor as the three of them entered the maze of Bab Amr's narrow streets and alleyways. Yousef, in an insurgent-style black cap and black T-shirt, waited for them in front of the café where Yakob and Sonia had met. Usually, the army's cannons fell silent between midnight and pre-dawn hours, but that was not the case this night.

"What's going on, Yousef?" Sonia asked. "I assumed we'd have a quiet night."

"So did Yakob, but a short while ago, we received word that dozens more insurgents were moving in with additional weaponry. We had no choice but try and stop them."

"Not our lucky night then, is it? Should we call off our mission?"

"No, we'll just have to be careful. Yakob knows we're out and where we're headed."

"And you know where the mines have been laid?"

"Yes, I've patrolled this route many times."

The three of them fell in line behind Yousef, only walking where he walked. A short while later, it was Mary who spoke. "We're nearing the media center," she said, pointing. "Just ahead, on the left, about fifty meters."

"How can you see that far in the dark?" asked Sonia.

"I recognized that storefront and its outdoor stand," Mary said, pointing to an object on the ground next to her, "and if you look carefully, you can see the center up ahead. There's a light spilling into the street. Their front door must be open, which tells me there's a lot going on."

They heard a loud shrill, the sound of an incoming shell.

"Take cover," shouted Yousef. And as they pressed their bodies against the wall of the nearest building, they heard a loud, wailing scream, possibly that of a small child, then glass shattering and heavy chunks of mortar crashing to the ground.

"That was close," said Mary.

"If you hear the shrill of an approaching rocket, you won't die because you'll have time to take cover," Sonia said.

"How reassuring," Mary laughed.

They stayed in place until Yousef determined it safe to advance, then followed him up the cobblestone street until they were close enough to the media center to see for themselves the flurry of activity. A man shouted orders while others ran in and out, trying perhaps, to pinpoint the targeted building and rescue the wounded.

Suddenly, Mary stopped and pointed. "There's Omar. He just walked out of the center. This could be our lucky night. He's likely heading to the clinic."

"What are we waiting for?" Sonia asked. "Let's follow him."

"Okay, but at a distance," cautioned Yousef.

"Shouldn't we be worried about mines?" Joe asked.

"Walk where he walks," Yousef replied. "He knows where they've been laid."

By the time they reached the entrance to the clinic, it hardly mattered that they had lost their cover. There was mass confusion. The bomb had ignited a massive fire in a nearby building. People, frantic, ran out of the clinic screaming for volunteers to search for any survivors. Sonia saw a desperate young couple arrive, a small child in their arms. A man covered in blood, his right arm dangling, walked unsteadily down the street only to collapse on the ground outside the clinic.

Sonia turned to Yousef. "This is our chance. We walk in with everyone else. We find our friend and get him out. *Yallah.*"

The rocket arrived with no warning and exploded so close the four of them were thrown to the ground. It took Sonia a minute to focus on what had just happened. Her ears rang. She saw people up ahead moving their mouths, but she could not hear anything. She looked to her right. Joe, on the ground next to her in a pool of blood. To her left, Mary unconscious. She felt a tug on her leg and turned to see Yousef crawling up toward her.

"Stay put, don't move."

"What?" she shouted, realizing she must have spoken louder than necessary and pointed to her ear. "I can't hear you."

She struggled to regain her hearing.

"Are you hurt?" he shouted.

"No, but Joe is, and so is Mary. They're not moving."

Yousef crawled over to Joe, and as he gently tried to turn him, Sonia saw the open wound in his left side.

"Yousef, do something. Call Yakob. They need help."

He pulled out his phone and punched in Yakob's number. When he had given their precise location, Sonia grabbed the phone.

"Yakob," she cried. "Joe and Mary are seriously wounded. *Saeidni.*"

"He'll get an ambulance in as close as he can," said Yousef, trying to reassure her, "then walk in the stretchers."

"That'll take too long," she cried. "Why can't we take them to the clinic here. We just need to call for help like the others are doing. I know the doctor here. His name is Andrew. He's the man we're looking for. He'll take care of them."

When Sonia tried to get up from the ground, Yousef pushed her back down.

"No, *Sitt,* you can't take them in there. This clinic isn't equipped for the seriously wounded. Your friends need a proper hospital. Yakob will have them taken to the one in Homs' city center."

"Okay," she sighed. "While I check on Joe, you see about Mary," and she crawled on the ground until she lay alongside Joe. "Talk to me, friend. Can you hear me? Open your eyes, Joe. Stay with me. Speak to me, Joe…Joe?" His eyes flickered and finally opened. "Good, hang in there. The ambulance is on its way. You're going to be all right." And when he closed his eyes again, she pleaded. "No, Joe. Stay with me. Open your eyes."

As Sonia looked up to speak to Yousef, she saw Andrew rush out of the clinic, no doubt running toward the bodies lying in the street. Could one of them be Omar, she wondered? Wasn't he just ahead of them when the rocket exploded?

"Andrew," she cried, as loud as she could. In the commotion, he did not hear her. She yelled again, this time louder. "Andrew," repeating his name until he finally turned his head in her direction. "Over here, please come. It's Joe. He's seriously wounded."

Andrew rushed toward her and fell to his knees.

"He came to rescue you, Andrew. We can't let him die," and as she spoke, two pairs of soldiers arrived with stretchers. Joe was lifted onto one and Mary the other, and as they raised Joe, his body limp and unresponsive, she saw the open, bleeding wound.

"*Hakeme*," said Yousef, "we're taking them to the hospital in Homs. It's better for them, don't you agree? Please explain that to your friend."

"At a proper hospital, they stand a chance of surviving, Sonia. I can't do anything for them here. I haven't the equipment. I can't even do basic surgery."

"*Hakeme, Hakeme*," someone behind them shouted. "*Saadounie*."

Andrew turned his head and answered, "Yallah, I'm coming," and as he stood to leave, he explained, "We have a lot of wounded. They need my help. I have to go," and he hurried away.

# CHAPTER FOURTEEN

WHEN ROBERT EXPLAINED what he intended to do, Nadia thought he had gone mad. Had he carefully considered the consequences? Could he be accused of betrayal and face possible charges of traitorous behavior? Was he prepared for the political fallout that would surely follow? What were his odds of successfully creating a new career path? When her counterarguments had failed to dissuade him, Nadia applauded his boldness and pledged to support his career move.

Robert had thought to bring her to his meeting with Bashar Assad, but in the end, decided it best if he muddled through the encounter alone. These were his misdeeds, no one else's. His mission had been to bring about the dismantlement of the Syrian state. His new goal going forward would be to mitigate any further damage. He had requested that their meeting be private, removed from all embassy protocol—no military *attaché* or official car, his arrival and departure by taxi—and to his surprise, Bashar had agreed and kept Robert's visit off his official schedule. When he arrived at the presidential palace, he was escorted into Bashar's elegant wood-paneled sitting room and told that the president would be with him shortly. The lingering smell of Nadia's perfume on his neck and the promise she had made helped ease his anxiety as he paced back and forth across the white marble floor. His last encounter with Bashar, a helicopter ride to Daraa, had been a demeaning experience. Though humiliated, he realized Bashar's mild rebuke had been an unstintingly generous gesture given that he could just as easily have had Robert arrested, thrown in prison and tried for masterminding an insurrection. Robert had further exasperated their tenuous relationship when, a few months later, he made another public visit, this time to Homs, to lend his support to the uprising. It was a credit to Bashar's astuteness that he had even agreed to meet with Robert again.

"Mr. Ambassador," Bashar said, again foregoing first-name greetings, thus setting the tone for their meeting as soon as he walked into the room.

"Mr. President, thank you for agreeing to see me on such short notice."

With a wave of his hand, Bashar directed Robert to two chairs in front of double French doors that overlooked the palace courtyard.

"You've just returned from the States. What? Two days ago?"

"Yes," Robert replied carefully. "You're well informed, Mr. President."

"Why wouldn't I be? Our *Mukhabarat* is just as good as your FBI when it comes to keeping track of people, especially those who go around my country inciting violence. And let me clearly state that it wasn't in deference to your diplomatic credentials that I agreed to grant you this meeting. It was purely to satisfy my curiosity. You made an openly provocative visit to Homs in support of the insurgents when you were already on very shaky ground. Yet, you took the risk when you knew I could have had you arrested."

"Congressional pressure was of greater concern to me, Mr. President. In their eyes, I wasn't a harsh enough critic of you when it was my job to work with the rebels to overthrow your government. Mine had been a recess appointment, as you may recall. From the beginning, Congress had frowned on the idea of sending an ambassador to Syria, thinking it gave you unnecessary credence, so, to appease them, my president insisted I visit the rebels in Homs."

"Your president's an unprincipled weasel. He throws out words like 'rebels' and 'moderates' as if they ranked alongside Ghandi or Mandela. Who does he think he's fooling?"

"The American people, sir. If they knew their president was in league with al-Qaeda insurgents, there'd be open rebellion across America."

"And if I'd listened to my security team and expelled you after that stunt, I wouldn't have to sit here and listen to such drivel." Bashar stood. "I had an early meeting and missed my morning stroll. If you've anything else you insist you need to tell me, you'll have to tag along," and with that, he opened the French doors and walked out.

When Robert caught up with him, he said, "I've written my letter of resignation, Mr. President. I wanted you to know before I sent it off."

Bashar stopped in his tracks. "You know me well enough, Robert. I'm not the asshole your press makes me out to be. What kind of nonsensical bullshit is this?"

Notwithstanding the seriousness of the matter, Robert was amused to hear Bashar, with his excellent British accent, using expletives.

"I've been doing some soul-searching and…"

"Damn it, Robert, you don't have a soul."

"I didn't, but I've had a change of heart."

Bashar pulled sunglasses from his breast pocket. "Here," he said, handing his jacket off to Robert and rolling up his sleeves before taking back his jacket and slinging it over his shoulder. "Thanks."

"What's really going on, Robert? You didn't just suddenly wake up and discover God and decide on a career change."

"Are you a religious man, Bashar?"

"I believe in God, if that's what you're asking."

"On the occasion of my mother's funeral, I had to enter a church, something I hadn't done in years. This particular cathedral is quite famous in Boston for its magnificent pipe organ. I don't know if you've ever heard the sound it makes, but it's loud and powerful and uplifting in a spiritual way. Obviously, I went into that space with a sense of being wrong about everything I do, and that organ struck as some sort of higher power shouting at me. And with my magnificent mother being honored, I felt like a traitor to her and how she had raised me. The experience got me questioning what I'd been doing with my life and the answer, as you well know, is nothing good. After the funeral, I stayed on a few extra days at my father's request. Whether it was the emotion of my mother's death or the organ bellowing out that magnificent Bach cantata, I can't say, but I came away from Boston with a great appreciation for a father I'd hardly known."

"How was it that you didn't know your father?"

"He was always off on some government assignment, and when he was home, it was for short periods of time, and seemingly uninterested in me or what I was doing with my life. How well did you know your father?"

"As president, my father's first obligation was to his country, but he also loved his family. My mother, like yours, assumed the day-to-day activities of me, my two brothers, and sister, but my father was present in a kind and thoughtful way. I remember telling him I wanted to be a doctor and work for Doctors without Borders. He said he would support anything I chose to do as long as I did it well and was successful. That was a gift my father gave me, the choice to make my own decision about my future. Of course, I never wanted to be president, but you already knew that."

"It was my father, in part, who influenced my decision to leave government and concentrate my energy and skills on something more meaningful than destroying countries. That's what he'd spent his career doing, I discovered. Only his assignments were in Central America, not the Middle East. He deeply regrets what he's done and doesn't want to see me make the same mistakes. What I found so striking in our discussions was how similar our jobs were. Pretty horrifying, actually. We've decided to collaborate on a book about our respective assignments."

"Do you have other siblings, Robert?"

"No, I'm an only child. I grew up spoiled and privileged, as you've already surmised, no doubt, and been pretty much an arrogant bastard most of my life."

"Arrogant doesn't begin to describe you. You're a war criminal, and you'll burn in hell for what you've done to my country, and I shouldn't care what happens to you, yet I feel compelled to offer you a piece of advice. Watch your back. You're a CIA puppet. You won't be allowed to walk away from the family without some form of reprisal. In their eyes, you'll be betraying your country, and you'll pay dearly. Hell, even I don't have full authority to do anything I want. I certainly couldn't just abandon my post and walk away. I wouldn't get any farther than the front door before I'd be detained and whisked off to prison. If you think your CIA's any different, you're fooling yourself."

"I won't be the first person to resign my post and become a private citizen."

"Maybe you're right, but it's a cowardly act when you could stay on here and do something meaningful, maybe even reverse the course of this war. If you decide to do that, I'll do everything in my power to help."

"How would you do that, Bashar? The world's against you."

"That's absolute balls, Robert. That's what your government wants its people to think. Syria has trusted allies. They're waiting in the wings for an invitation from me to come in and help me save my country. I'm referring to Russia, of course. From my father's time in power, Syria has maintained strong military and strategic ties with that country."

The two walked on in silence for a few minutes until Bashar spoke again.

"Remind me what you did in Iraq before being assigned here?"

"The backstory began in 2003 when President Bush assigned Paul Bremer as Proconsul of Iraq. Keeping the Iraqi army intact had always been part of the Pentagon's strategy, but unbeknownst to them, Bush and his vice president ordered Bremer to disband the military. Since the US had illegally invaded Iraq, the administration knew it would come up against staunch resistance, so it was Bremer's job to re-organize the country along ethno-sectarian lines to encourage its citizens to vie among themselves rather than to unite in opposition to the US. Under secular nationalist rule, Iraq's politics were organized around Iraqi nationalism and the political independence of its people."

"Not just identity," Bashar explained, "but unity and freedom from foreign domination, and control of their economy, exactly what my father had proscribed for Syria—formal political divisions based on rifts that worked against an oppressed people uniting against foreign interference."

"Bremer resolved that Iraqis shouldn't view the most significant opposition in their political lives as a conflict between nations but in terms of conflicting polarities within Iraq—Shiite versus Sunni, Arab versus Kurd, and my job was a continuation of the same policies, only it got more lethal when we formed death squads whose job it was to hunt down Sunni jihadists."

"And now, you son of a bitch, it's Syria's turn."

"Only here, we reversed the process. Sunni death squads going after Alawite infidels and other minorities. But none of this could have come as a surprise to you."

"Of course not, I've known for years that Syria's been in the crosshairs of multiple American administrations, but what could I have done to halt their agenda?"

"Not a damn thing. By 2007, the Iran-Syria-Hezbollah strategic alliance had strengthened and your fate sealed. Saudi Arabia was convinced the best way to fight Shia ideological fervor was with Sunni ideological fervor, and the Iraqi death squad strategy was transported here to contain Iran and Shia influence across the region. This war isn't about you or Syria per se. It's a proxy war about Iran. The US and its allies think that by undermining you, they can inflict a damaging blow to Iran's regional position."

"That belief's incredibly naïve and very Western, I might add. Iran's been around as a regional power for about 2,700 years. And Shia Islam isn't going away either. There's no reason to defeat Iran. And the Israeli right-wingers who are also pushing for Iran's demise are deeply ignorant of history. If everyone is so hell-bent on destroying Iran, why not attack it directly and spare my country?"

"That's what the Saudis wanted the Americans to do, but such an attack would have set off a chain reaction with regional and global consequences the US wouldn't have been able to control. In lieu of direct conflict, they and their regional allies are using economic warfare, targeted assassinations of Iran's nuclear scientists and cyber warfare against its nuclear program."

"None of these actions have been very successful, have they, and they've done nothing to hamper Iran's long-term ambitions."

Robert nodded. "And that's why my government finally decided their only other option was to destabilize Syria."

"And you'd done it in Iraq, so you already had the blueprint for sectarian warfare here."

"That's right, and the Saudis provided two billion dollars in seed money for the operation so the Obama administration wouldn't have to go before Congress to explain their actions."

"And my demonization began."

"Hell, that part was easy. There was already legitimate opposition to your government's policies. You'd pledged long-overdue reforms but never carried through with them."

"I'd written them, even signed off on them, but you're right, I never implemented them. I never got the chance, and I had to contend with lots of opposition from my inner circle, some of whom I inherited from my father's time in power. And when it came time to actually enact the political and economic reforms, the Daraa uprising began. By the way, my reforms included some pretty ground-breaking changes for Syria I'm proud of, like the suspension of five decades of emergency law that had prohibited public gatherings, the formation of political parties, the lifting of press censorship, limits on the role of the Mukhabarat and finally, prisoner releases."

"An impressive list of to-dos, Bashar, but events were all perfectly timed. You were never going to be allowed to institute your reforms, and if you had succeeded, your enemies would have called them too little, too late or simply window-dressing to hide your brutal regime."

Robert observed Bashar as he looked forlornly out at the horizon. What was going through his head? Anger, regret, fear of what the future held for him, his family, his country? Robert wondered if he had gone too far in exposing the raw realities on the ground. No, he concluded, it was best Bashar knew everything. The question now was how he was going to ameliorate the situation.

"Even before Daraa, we had already begun to train activists in the use of videos and social media for propaganda purposes. We provided the necessary communications equipment, including a mobile phone with its own virtual country code. We brought in the *agents provocateurs*. Snipers killed the demonstrators in Daraa using the same guns and ammunition as the police and army so the state would be blamed. Our agents burned the Ba'ath Party offices and other public buildings in Daraa, everything underwritten by Saudi Arabia in order to make an end-run around Congress and the American public, keeping both in the dark. Americans don't like to think poorly of their government, and aside from some critical thinkers, they are generally content not to know the dirty details."

"And all the while, your president claimed he was willing to work with me to resolve the conflict. If he'd been serious about normal relations and gotten rid of those awful war hawks who'd wiggled their way into his administration, I think we could have had a decent, honest discussion and avoided a lot of pain and suffering for my people."

"Unfortunately, war hawks manage to exert pressure on every administration. They're influential people with powerful backers who have a vested interest in promoting wars. You have your own share of war hawks, Bashar. Isn't your brother Mahar one of them?"

"In his defense, he doesn't go looking for wars, but he'll defend Damascus to his last man if he has to."

"And the shabbiha, your low-life gangsters?"

"In war, some levels of society break down, and the crazies creep out in the open. They're hoodlums, and I condemn their actions, and if I had my way, they'd all be rotting in prison. And to be perfectly honest, my control over my own security apparatus is fairly limited. I have to contend with competing security actors, and it isn't always an easy road to navigate.

"But back to the reforms for a minute, most Syrians agree with the legitimate, peaceful protesters demanding reform. I certainly get that.

Thankfully, only a minority are willing to risk destabilizing their country. We're not a wealthy nation, but we do provide basic services like free education, healthcare and food staples for the poor. I think that's why such a small percentage of people have actually joined in the protests, even if your media uses terms like 'the Syrian people,' implying the uprising has the support of the entire Syrian population. How do you think the pro-stability Syrians feel when Western officials and their media imply that all Syrians are on the side of regime change?"

"Lies are useful, Bashar. That's how successful regime changes happen. Manipulation of the masses. Such CIA-led policies are so deeply enmeshed as a normal instrument of US foreign policy that they go unnoticed."

"So, where do I go from here, Robert? What must I do to stop the bloodshed and destruction and save my country?"

"I have a few ideas."

"They better be quick and easy fixes if you plan to retire."

"It may not be enough, but I'll try to mitigate some of this."

"*Fadel*," said Bashar, inviting Robert to join him on a bench overlooking Damascus, some five thousand feet below. Though it was late February, there was a hint of spring in the air, and it felt good to sit in the warm morning sun.

"Legend has it that between 661 and 750, this area was inhabited by Yemini migrants."

Robert shook his head and smiled. "I love the history of this region. It's endlessly fascinating."

"Speaking of fascinating history, there's a cave just below us. It's said to have been inhabited by Adam, the first human being. There are various other stories, too, which I love. There's one about Ibrahim and another about Jesus, both of whom supposedly prayed in the cave. It's also mentioned in the medieval Arab history books as the place where prayers were immediately answered, a place where, during droughts, the rulers of Damascus prayed for rain."

"Your country's suffering its worst drought in nine hundred years. Have you gone there to pray for rain?"

"No," he replied, a bit embarrassed. "But I should, shouldn't I, and while I'm at it, pray for an end to all hostilities. Maybe we should go there together, Robert."

"Do you fear your government's days might be numbered?"

"If I listened to your government, yes. Your political pundits claim that even if I manage to weather the storm, the country's economic woes are a ticking time bomb and that eventually, even the middle class will abandon me."

"Do you believe these so-called pundits?"

"This isn't the first time Syria's economy is predicted to be near collapse. My father passed through several crises, and here I am three decades later, facing a similar one. The West has been sending me messages through their Gulf Arab allies that suggest I'm in real trouble if I don't play by their rules and terminate relations with Iran and disarm Hezbollah. And if I cooperate with them, they claim they'll help me stay in power and turn a blind eye to the mass killings I supposedly carry out on my people, like they do for Saudi Arabia and Bahrain. I'm not intentionally killing my own people, Robert."

"I know that, and so do they, but they've a point about brutality. Your government has a reputation for extreme violence. Syria's the CIA's favorite rendition site. They know your security personnel will torture their victims to extract any truth they want. According to one former CIA official, 'if you want your victims tortured, you send them to Syria. If you want them disappeared, you send them to Egypt.'"

"I'm not proud of that reputation, Robert. It's a stain on my government, but it's a legacy handed down from my father that I need to erase, though I might make an exception when it comes to the Muslim Brotherhood. They plagued my father and now me, especially with their recent move to cozy up to the al Qaeda-linked insurgents."

"How many children do you have, Bashar?"

"Three, the oldest Hafez, is eight."

"I should think you'd want that reputation long gone by the time your son is old enough to assume power if he chooses to enter government service."

"A worthy goal, Robert, and one I'll readily commit to."

"If you'll permit me to suggest… another thing you should do is communicate more with your people. Give regular press conferences, assemble Syrian journalists who are more apt to report your words accurately, not distort them the way some foreign journalists do."

"I've not been a great communicator, you're right."

"Well, that needs to change. Your people want to hear a convincing and accurate account of what's happening. If you don't start doing that, you'll lose your supporters. Right now, the vast majority of Syrians stand behind you, so does your army. They want the war to stop. They want to give you time to initiate your promised reforms. Every few days, they go through the painful exercise of waiting to hear more bad news. Give them accurate numbers of dead. The opposition claims all the dead are peaceful protestors. According to your government, the dead are armed men who attacked the army or police. You've lost a good many soldiers and security officers. I've seen the numbers. I know they're accurate. Tell your people that, and more importantly, be honest. Admit mistakes. That's what I'm going to have to do going forward if I'm to foster changes in my government's foreign policy."

"I get bad press no matter what I say. Why aren't journalists asking who's killing and who's dying?"

"Because, for the most part, they're reporting from Beirut and getting their stories from social media."

"If they'd been here, on the ground, getting first-hand, accurate information, I think this conflict would have been presented to the world very differently. My figures show there was parity in the killing which means my government's response to the opposition hasn't been unreasonable."

"The opposition's engaged in serious, organized propaganda. All the more reason not to stay silent. And they do post annoying stories about regime brutality, not that some of that doesn't happen, right?"

"We've already agreed on that point."

"Just remember, the vast majority of Syrians are genuinely supportive, or at least tolerant, of your government, so be honest and upfront with them, and give them the reforms they demand and deserve, so they won't go elsewhere looking for leadership. Syria also has a problem with corruption. It needs to be cleaned up. I'm not singling your country out. God knows, there's no country worse than Lebanon, but…"

"It's a difficult problem to control. Those who have the most to lose resist the most. They're entrenched in the system and won't let go. They're also easy opposition targets, so I do owe it to my people to try, and I will, although it'll be one of my most difficult challenges. A lot of those in power have inherited their positions from their fathers and, in some cases, their grandfathers. It will take a lot to overcome those legacies."

"But not impossible."

"No, you're right, but the Alawites and, to a lesser degree, the other minorities won't let me sweep away the current system without putting into place reforms that guarantee their rights. The Alawites view Syria in much the same way as the Jews view Israel, the Kurds, Kurdistan and the Maronites, Lebanon. This is one country in the world where the Alawites can dictate their own affairs and not have to worry about being repressed as a minority. If I'm to bring democracy to Syria, it has to happen gradually and in a region that's not boiling in sectarian anger. In the end, the main players in the region have no long-term interest in trying to destabilize my country. Even if they hate to admit it, they know Syria plays a stabilizing role across the region."

"Or at least it used to."

"Robert, one final question. What's the best-case scenario for Syria?"

"It's a lot of things we've already discussed, Bashar. You need to reassure your people you're committed to the reforms you put forth in this most recent referendum. You loaded it with a lot of things—freedom laws, political party laws, decentralization, handing over more power to the provinces, gradually undoing the Ba'ath party's monopoly on power and a limit of two-seven-year terms for future presidents. Eighty-nine percent of your people supported your proposed measures, which is an enviable number. In the States, we're lucky if we get forty percent voter turnout. I also understand you're about to sign onto a comprehensive five-year plan as you move toward a democratic system, while still maintaining control of an army. That's not only smart, it reassures stability. In the end, I think your greatest achievement will be regional peace. The status quo isn't sustainable. In fact, I believe history will prove that the US, using regional adversaries to effect regime change, was a colossal mistake. Syria could trigger a global reshuffle. Look at all the players involved so far, and Russia, a staunch ally of Syria, hasn't even played its cards yet. Bashar, your government has decades of intense and extensive experience in the region. Make good use of that asset and then, once you've contributed to peace, retire from office with a fine legacy to hand off to your children."

"Do you really think any of this can actually happen?"

"The reforms, yes. You're quite capable of seeing them through. As for the rest, I'm not sure. This is the Middle East, after all. Look, it's hard not to be pessimistic, especially with such intransigent regional players, but you've got to take a crack at it, and if you're lucky, you'll at least get credit for trying. The wrenches Israel and Saudi Arabia are currently throwing into the mix aren't sustainable in the long run. Your effort at peace will eventually resonate across the region." Robert looked over at him. "We can dream, can't we?"

"And you, Robert, what are you going to do to help the region? You said you had a retirement plan. What is it?"

"I've already told you about my book project. It's time someone with first-hand experience exposed my government's flawed Middle East policies. Five years out, I plan to be Massachusetts' newest Senator. I have the finances and backing to make it happen. I've already initiated talks with people who'll support my run. Once in Congress, I'll push for a reversal of our endless wars and a reduction in military spending and…"

Bashar laughed out loud.

"What's so funny?"

"You have about as much chance of changing the world as I do, Robert."

"We'll each give ourselves five years. I'm optimistic we can accomplish at least some of the things we've set out to do. It's the right time in history, Bashar. People are restless. They want change. They're tired of perpetual wars. In the meantime, I propose a joint venture that will have an immediate impact and improve your standing in the world."

"Go on."

"It has to do with the ceasefire plan Kofi Annan has just proposed. It has the backing of both the Arab League and the UN."

"I'm one step ahead of you. I've already spoken with Secretary Annan. I've agreed not only to the ceasefire but full withdrawal of troops from Homs, and I've committed to setting up a protective corridor so anyone wanting to leave Homs can do so safely. In exchange for these concessions, al-Nusra was to agree to leave both Bab Amr and the Old City and relocate to the northwest."

"Where's the problem?"

"Al-Nusra has refused the proposal."

"In the end, they'll agree. I'll see that it happens, but you'll get credit for changing their mind. Aside from the Christians and Alawites, you'll be liberating in Homs, you'll also be freeing an American doctor who's been held captive there for the last seven months. He was working with Doctors without Borders in the Shatilla refugee camp in Beirut when al-Nusra kidnapped him and brought him to Homs to run their medical clinic. Bashar, when he walks out with the others, you'll come out of this looking like a true statesman."

"How are you going to pull that off, Robert? You're about to resign your post."

"Two reasons. One, I'll hang on for another week or so before officially resigning so I can help carry this off, and two, I have a president who needs a bit of glory at the moment. Word has gotten out that he's working with al Qaeda-linked insurgents, and he needs some good press. 'President saves American doctor from the clutches of al Qaeda.' As an extra bonus, maybe I can get him to pull the plug on insurgent funding and weaponry. At a time when the world has been focused on the siege of Bab Amr, he'll welcome both the coverage and the chance to withdraw from Syria."

Robert stood. "We'll work out the details over the next few days. In the meantime, I'll take my leave. I've already consumed most of your morning."

"Thank you, Robert. This has been a productive meeting. Why don't you let my chauffeur drive you home?"

"I think it best if we kept this visit private. But thanks anyway."

"As you wish. I'll have my secretary call you a taxi."

As Bashar walked away, he stopped and turned. "Robert, whatever happened to the extra copy of the dossier Hassan Jaafar had on you?"

"It was destroyed. The woman who took it from Jaafar's safe burned it. And the copy you have?"

"Insurance, Robert. You help me, I might be persuaded to help you."

\*\*\*

Nadia had been waiting by the window, so when the taxi pulled up outside, she opened the door and rushed out to greet Robert. He took her in his arms and swung her around. "I'm the happiest man in the world," he said. "I'm about to resign my job, I have you, and I have a decent man's future to look forward to."

"I want to hear all about it. Lunch is almost ready. You must be famished. In the meantime, why don't you change out of those hot clothes."

"I have a much better idea," he said and hurried her upstairs.

Once in the bedroom, he pushed her onto the bed and, without taking the time to arouse her, took her. In that instance, he was the all-powerful, overly confident alpha male, and she hated him. After he left to shower, she lay on the bed trying to compose herself, before fleeing the room.

She was seated in the living room when he eventually joined her.

"You've kept me in suspense long enough, Robert. Tell me about your meeting with Bashar, every little detail."

"It went surprisingly well, although he thought my resignation was a mistake. What he really wants is for me to stay on a while and help him reverse the course of the war."

"That may not be a bad idea. You'd be leaving on a good note."

"And if I help, he may be persuaded to destroy the dossier he has on me. For now, I gave him some ideas."

And he left it at that while he uncorked the wine she had placed on the coffee table in front of them. "In the end, we restored our friendship for which I'm grateful, but more importantly, he's willing to help free Andrew."

"That's such a relief. Thank you for helping make that possible, darling."

He poured wine into two glasses and handed her one. He was examining her face closely, and she felt she could track his thoughts. He would be worried about losing her to Andrew. They clinked glasses, and she tasted the wine, which, somewhere amongst its fruity complexity, produced a strong hint of blood. He sat opposite her, crossed his legs and said, "It'll be a matter of days, maybe even weeks before the ceasefire actually takes hold, but it'll happen. Bashar will get credit for Andrew's release, and he'll have me to thank for that."

"Now tell me more about your visit with your father. You were happy to have finally gotten to know him and..."

"And oddly enough, I discovered my career has mirrored his."

"In what way?"

"The Iran Contra scandal, rebels in Nicaragua, death squads."

"The Central America atrocities."

"Yes, what came to be called the Salvador Option. In Iraq, I was basically carrying out the same kind of abhorrent behavior, but when I heard the numbers, the hundreds of thousands of deaths across Central America, I realized I'd be just as guilty of the same numbers if I continued my job as ambassador. Not even counting what I'd already done in Iraq, and as you alluded to a while back, a possible war crimes indictment."

"What was your father's job in Honduras?"

"He oversaw the slaughter and covered it up."

"Did the atrocities in Central America ever stop?"

"To some extent, but we left those countries impoverished and with brutal military dictatorships. Sickened by what he'd seen and done, my father retired from government service. He admitted he didn't want to see what happened in Central America happen across the Middle East, and that's when I had my moment of clarity and why I decided I should resign my post. My father and I are going to write a book together. We want this madness to stop and aren't willing to wait for the politicians and the military to come to their senses."

"That won't happen."

"No, and why we need to sound the red alert, although this time it isn't an imminent attack from a foreign nation. It's our own government. And in all of this, I discovered I knew precious little about my parents. It's all been quite remarkable." Robert laughed, "I only wish my mother was still here."

"As I think I said on the phone, reconciliation with your father might not have happened had she still been alive."

"And I told you I feel a bit like Saul on the road to Damascus. That feeling's even stronger now. I was blind, and now I see what must be done."

"And that is?"

"Be a good American."

"You might have to change your name, darling."

They both laughed and drank wine, eyes on each other.

"My dad encouraged me to run for the Senate. Massachusetts will see one of its senior senators retire in a few years. He thinks I have a good chance of winning the seat, Nadia, and I'd like you to be part of that dream. I hope that's something you'll consider. I don't expect an answer right away but promise me you'll at least give it some thought. I love you, Nadia. Surely you know that by now. I want to spend the rest of my life with you and possibly start a family. How I wish my mother could have hung on so she could have met you. I'd planned to ask you to accompany me to Boston for Christmas. I even told her I planned to propose to you. You'd love the garden my mother planted. I know I'm rattling on, and maybe not making much sense, but I hope I can eventually win your heart."

"I care deeply for you, Robert, and I'm relieved you don't expect a definitive answer right away. I feel as though I've only just gotten over my four-year captivity, and I'm not ready to commit to any long-term relationship. Give me time, darling."

"Is it Andrew?"

"No, it's an overload of too many emotional entanglements, from an abducted husband to finding him alive in a Syrian prison after thirteen years, then losing him to an Israeli bomb. There was my engagement to Andrew, which Jaafar deprived me of when he kidnapped me and held me prisoner for four years. You're the only good thing that's happened to me in recent memory, Robert, but my soul still needs mending, and if I'm going to dedicate myself to you and your ambitions, I need time to fall truly, deeply in love with you."

"So, I still have a chance of completely winning over your heart?"

"Yes, you do, Robert."

# CHAPTER FIFTEEN

IT HAD BEEN TWO WEEKS since Joe's death, and Sonia still found it difficult to square Yakob's platitude, however sincere, with the loss of her friend. The fact remained that a Syrian army shell had killed Joe, and he had bled to death on the pavement outside Omar's media center. When Yousef arranged to have Mary transferred to a hospital outside the Old City, Sonia had insisted Joe's body be taken there too, and placed in the morgue until she and Frans could arrange a proper burial.

At Frans's suggestion, they visited an old Jesuit Church in the Christian Bustan al-Diwan neighborhood of the Old City. The church itself was in ruins, its walls crumbling, its furnishings long since looted or vandalized, its ornately-carved wooden ceiling and wall panels thrown into a nearby heap of garbage, the fate of eleven other churches in the Old City, but behind the church, enclosed within a stone wall, was a garden, or what Sonia assumed had at one time been a garden. It was February, not only the shortest month of the year but one of the darkest, with no sign of plant life except for a singular terebinth tree with oblong leathery, bright green leaves, particular to the Homs region, which according to Frans would bloom reddish-purple flowers come mid-March. A perfect place to lay Joe to rest, she thought, though she and Frans would need help. Neither was physically capable of digging a grave in the rock-like earth. Once again, Sonia prevailed upon Yakob, who sent a few soldiers to do the job while she and Frans went back to the morgue and prepared Joe for burial. In the absence of a coffin, something difficult to come by in a war zone with so many dead, they wrapped his body in a white cloth and, again with Yakob's help, had him transferred to the church garden. He was lowered into the grave, his body covered with earth, and in an ecumenical spirit becoming the community of Homs, Christians, Alawites and Sunni soldiers joined Frans and Sonia to pray for the repose of Joe's soul and lay him to rest, placing a wooden cross on top of his grave to mark the spot.

One hundred and fifty thousand civilians had died during the Lebanese civil war. In the aftermath of wars, other countries had built monuments to commemorate their dead, places where bereaved families could come to remember and honor their loved ones. Lebanon had built no such monument. Sonia was not sure Syria would either. It was important Joe not be erased from memory and why she felt it urgent they mark his grave.

While Joe had been mortally wounded by the Syrian army shelling, Mary had suffered what her doctor had described as a coup-countercoup injury, her brain slamming against one portion of the skull when she was thrown to the ground by the explosion, then bouncing against the opposite side of her head, causing significant swelling. After a three-week stay in the hospital, she was once again alert and sharp-witted. Since the swelling was sufficiently reduced, her doctor allowed her to be discharged into Sonia's care until she could arrange Mary's evacuation to a rehab center in Beirut. When Mary learned that Sonia had asked Fouad to facilitate the transfer, she put her foot down. She intended to stay and cover the war, whatever the cost to her health. Sonia understood her fervor and was amenable to letting Mary be the journalist. She, by contrast, had already turned her full attention to writing her book, amassing copious notes, conducting dozens of interviews and cataloging a computer file of photos.

From her hospital bed, Mary had confessed to Sonia that she had hardly expected to lose Joe so quickly and in such a tragic way. She knew the risks, of course. She had been in the field long enough to know that people died. By the very nature of her profession, she had struggled with meaningful relationships until she met Joe and was angry and hurt that her lovely Joe had been taken from her.

Joe's death hit Fouad very hard. The two men had worked alongside one another for years. Fouad held the powerful position of Lebanon's deputy director of state security services. Still, he was only as good as the men he put in the field, and Joe, his counterterrorism expert, had been his eyes and ears in the back alleyways of the city's worst neighborhoods. Like Fouad, Joe had spent many years in the service of the CIA before returning to his mother's native Lebanon. Ever the affable sophisticate with a lingering hint of his father's proper Russian breeding, not to mention a smile that lit fires in women's hearts, Joe had come to be Fouad's best and most trusted friend. It would be a long while before he made peace with Joe's death. Fouad had sent Joe to Homs to rescue Andrew, and, however irrational, he felt responsible for his death. Sonia had decided against telling Fouad that Andrew had refused to abandon his patients when given the chance. She still had not reconciled herself to his decision that night. She was not sure Fouad would either.

Visits to Mary at the hospital were not as frequent as Sonia would have liked. Yakub made that decision, depending on whether or not it was safe to cross from the Old City into Homs' city center, the part of Homs untouched by the conflict. Even then, Yakub insisted that a soldier accompany her for her own safety. It felt surreal to be able to step out of a war zone and into a normal life situation simply by traversing a few city blocks. It had been no different in Beirut during its war, she remembered, when, on a mortar and sniper-free day, one could cross the infamous Green Line—the deadly territorial divide that separated East from West Beirut—and resurface on the other side of the same city into a completely normal place untouched by war, where life was normal, and people visited cafes and where shops were open and flush with customers, and traffic was so congested a policeman was needed to direct it. With each hospital visit, Sonia took advantage of her brief respite. She sat in a café and ordered a coffee and drank it lavishly. She conversed with other patrons questioning them about their perception of what was happening in Bab Amr and the Old City, and notebook in hand, took detailed notes. It was no surprise to her that when asked, they said the same things people in Beirut had said when the bombs were not falling on their heads, "Thank God it isn't us. We know what's going on, and we're grateful we live where we live."

Each time she left Bab Amr, Sonia took a wad of her remaining cash and stocked up on fresh and dried foods, candles, medicine, batteries, another bottle of Johnnie Walker Black Label—anything she thought they might need—before heading back into the war zone. On any one of those visits outside Bab Amr, Sonia could have made the decision not to return. No one would have blamed her, and yet it was not an option Sonia ever considered. It was essential for her to remain in close proximity to Andrew in order to help free him from al-Nusra, something Joe had lost his life trying to do. Had Sonia walked away, she would have rendered Joe's death meaningless. Unlike most people, Sonia already had the necessary skills to survive the absurd dysfunction of war. She could do it again in Homs. And now that she was writing what she hoped would be a critically acclaimed book about the travesty of Syria's dirty war, she also wanted to explore the psychology of war, the toll it took, the reasons people chose to stay in war zones. Did people actually become acclimated to the habit of war, and if so, did that emotional adjustment become their new norm? Why did people risk injury and even death to protect their homes? Nadia's parents, with whom Sonia had sheltered, had refused to leave, insisting they needed to stay and protect their home and possessions and for their morale remain in the community of family and friends, rather than become refugees in some foreign country.

Sonia, the soon-to-be author, found it stimulating to write alongside Mary, the journalist, even though they each had their own way of working. Sonia liked the peacefulness of her bedroom, door closed. Mary brought a table from Madame Chidiac's apartment and set it up in a corner of the living room, preferring the noise from the open balcony door, the idle chitchat she overheard from neighbors, the food vendor shouting out his wares as he pushed his cart through the neighborhood, or digging stories out of Frans about Syria's history. It was either instant gratification for having written an unbiased account of a particular battle or, as was often the case when she reported on a massacre committed by the rebels, replete with irrefutable evidence, a letdown because her editor had chosen to rewrite her story to reflect another angle, usually something anti-Assad.

Unlike Mary, who wrote synoptically about events on the ground, Sonia was writing from inside the situation and explaining, in great detail, what happened when a mortar shell hit a wall, or an RPG blew out an entire floor in a building, or what remained of a head once a sniper bullet had shattered it, or how a mother dealt with the death of her small child. And in the evening, even if it was by candlelight, they often read their work to each other and offered feedback.

Mary: "Today, the Syrian army laid siege on Bab Amr. They are preparing an imminent all-out-attack…"

Sonia: "No, Mary, the army didn't just decide on a siege. Give the history, the events that led up to it. How many Syrian soldiers have already been killed by the rebels? Was that the motivating factor that led to the assault? If not, what was?"

The month of March, traditionally the advent of spring, brought not only calmer, warmer weather but news of a possible UN pause in hostilities. In one of her dispatches, Mary had been one of the first to report from a credible diplomatic source that a ceasefire was imminent, that Bashar had agreed to the terms and the American ambassador was working with the US-supported rebels to do the same. If negotiations were in the works, why was it taking so long, Sonia wondered? Would Homs be like Beirut when a credible rumor or a visit from some foreign dignitary repeatedly lulled Beirutiis into the false hope that the horrors would stop? With only the occasional cessation of hostilities, the residents of Homs had otherwise suffered seven months of tit-for-tat between the rebels and the Syrian army, the insurgents indiscriminately car-bombing Bab Amar neighborhoods, the army responding with ever-increasing rocket attacks.

Aside from the glass or two of whiskey in the evening, and the occasional card game in the company of Yakob and Yousef, sometimes their only entertainment in weeks, they otherwise carefully rationed their food and lost weight and impaired their health. Sonia had yet to confront Frans about his boundless generosity when it came to food, but one night when she realized their supply was quite literally evaporating, she finally said something.

"Where has our food gone, Frans? For three weeks, I put my life on the line to visit Mary in the hospital and bring back whatever I could find. I probably hauled back more than you and I originally bought at the beginning of the siege, and when my back is turned, you give it away?"

"Are you suggesting I deny food to the hungry?"

"Yes, Frans," she said, arms extended, eyes wide, "that's exactly what I'm suggesting. If the rumors are true, it won't be safe for me to go anywhere anymore, and I want to be able to feed my hunger."

In fact, rumors had begun circulating that al-Nusra had joined forces with the Islamic State of Iraq and Syria, a group infamous for its beheadings, mutilations and crucifixions. Wasn't the Islamic State, or some version of it, already in Homs? Weren't they the crazies she and Mary had encountered in the souks, brutally killing young boys and chopping off heads and carving crosses on bare chests? Were they the reason negotiations had broken down? Residents were justifiably terrified. They were desperate, too. Vendors rarely had something to sell. Even the ubiquitous potato, a staple found historically in the worst of famines, was hard to find. Bakeries had closed, too. They had no flour to make bread.

The insurgents had become desperate, too. They broke into people's houses and robbed them of food, jewelry, money, anything they found of value. This had yet to happen to Frans and Sonia, but they knew their double-bolted door could not stop desperate people.

Sonia also worried about the sudden lack of water. A dependable flow from the faucet had gone from sixteen hours a day down to a few. Even electricity, once a reliable twelve hours, had dropped to two. Although both she and Mary could still use their iPhones while charging to check news outlets, write emails, and in Mary's case, send dispatches to her editors in London and New York, there was the constant worry that the electricity would suddenly disappear and they would be left rudderless. Mercifully, the sewage system still worked, but Sonia had to anticipate a misdirected cannon shell that could destroy it, and those precious bottles of water she had so carefully carried from a nearby well would be all she had to cook, do dishes, flush toilets and wash clothes.

At least throughout the winter months, they had had the luxury of a heated apartment. In the early days of the siege, Frans had put his handyman talents to work and installed a wood-burning sobia. He also had the foresight to purchase a significant supply of chopped wood, which was stored on the balcony. Even with that heating device, Sonia constantly felt the need for an extra layer of clothing, a wool hat and socks, a shawl thrown over her shoulders to ward off the dampness that penetrated to her bones. Sonia had stocked up on an adequate supply of candles and batteries when she had visited Mary at the hospital. She felt confident that, even with an eventual electricity blackout, they would not only have light, however inadequate, but voltage to run Frans' transistor radio.

One night as Frans, Sonia and Mary sat at the kitchen table playing cards, someone knocked on the front door. At first, Sonia insisted they not respond, thinking it was someone looking for a food handout. When a knock turned into a banging on the door, Frans finally went to the door and asked who it was.

"It's Omar, open up."

Frans glanced at Sonia and Mary, and they both nodded. "Let him in."

Frans unbolted the door and opened it.

"Good evening, Omar. This is a surprise. How did you find me?"

Omar gave out a laugh. "Are you kidding? Everyone in Homs knows where you live."

"Well then, what do you want?"

"Food. My men and I have run out of food."

"Hasn't everyone?" said Mary, getting up from the table and walking toward Omar.

"I wondered where you'd gone," he said, glancing at her scornfully. "You were supposed to be reporting for us."

"She was," insisted Sonia, "until she was almost killed by army shelling. She spent three weeks in the hospital recovering from a serious brain injury. When she was discharged, we took her in knowing you wouldn't have time to take proper care of her."

"We have a clinic with our own doctor. We could have taken her in."

"And given her your undivided attention? I don't think so. Anyway, she's here now, and here's where she'll stay until she has completely recovered."

While she and Mary were talking to Omar, Sonia caught a glimpse of Frans going into the kitchen and filling a plate with food. He put it on the kitchen table.

"Come and have a bite to eat," and as he looked over at Sonia, said, "it isn't much, but it should help stave off your hunger."

They watched Omar as he began to eat, at first taking tiny bites, then stuffing the food into his mouth as quickly as he could.

He looked up at Frans. "Thank you. That's the first food I've had in two days."

Frans caught Sonia's grimace but turned his attention back to Omar and said, "You're welcome."

"Frans, I want you to make a video appeal to your pope for food that we'll post on the Internet."

"Where did you ever come up with such a crazy idea? I can't just call on the pope and ask him to do something like that. Who am I, anyway, to ask anyone to send in food?"

"Your pope will listen if you ask on behalf of the Christians."

"Why should Frans use Christian suffering to score you favors with your starving men?" asked Sonia. "You have your al Qaeda affiliates around the country. Ask them for help."

"We have. They refused. They have their own problems."

"Doesn't that make you wonder why you're associated with such people if they can't help their brothers-in-arms?" Sonia said.

"Ask your real boss, the big guys," Mary suggested, "the ones who train you, supply you with arms and pay your salaries."

"We did," his voice reflecting his letdown. "We're still waiting for a reply."

"What don't you understand about that relationship, Omar?" asked Sonia. "You're fodder to your CIA bosses. You were taught how to lead the charge. You created the desired level of havoc, killed a lot of people, and carried it off brilliantly, probably beyond their wildest expectations. You've done their dirty work, and now you've been discarded."

"Shut up, bitch. I'm not waiting any longer for anyone's help because Frans is going to do what I ask," Omar said, pulling his gun from his pocket and pointing it at Frans' head.

"Oh, bad move, Omar," said Mary. "How do you think that story will look on the front page of the *New York Times*. 'CIA trained and funded rebel kills local priest for food.'"

"Your handlers wouldn't be too happy with that kind of publicity," said Sonia. "I have a mind to call your mother, so we can tell her what you're doing here. You two could have a nice little chat."

"Leave my mother out of this," Omar yelled.

"Omar, put away the gun," said Frans. "I get that you're desperate. We're all desperate, but no one's going to kill anyone for food. I'll make the video appeal to Pope Francis for all the good it will do. Apparently, the UN has a warehouse nearby with ample food supplies."

"You're a fucking liar, Frans. You claimed there was no food, and all along, it was just a few kilometers away."

"The army has been blocking any food delivery to Bab Amr, fearing it would only go to your men. Now, if the pope is amenable to my request, and he asks the UN to release the food, they might agree to deliver as soon as tomorrow but, and this is the stipulation I insist upon, that any food delivered will be equally distributed. Everyone will get their fair share, and that means everyone in Bab Amr and the Old City, but on one condition. You and your men agree to the UN ceasefire proposal and leave the Old City."

Omar took the gun away from Frans' head. "What the hell are you talking about? I know nothing about a ceasefire."

"The American ambassador is working on it, and a Syrian officer confirmed it to us," said Sonia.

"I don't give a shit what some diplomat is doing or isn't doing. I'll wait for confirmation from the Syrian government before I make any decision."

"You mean you'll consult with ISIS," said Sonia. "They're the big guys in town now, aren't they?"

"We work together, bitch. Our goal is the same, the establishment of a caliphate like the one that existed one thousand four hundred years ago, and no one will be able to stop us."

He was probably right, thought Sonia.

Mary got out her iPhone, brought up one of her online articles and showed him. "See, a ceasefire plan is in the works. I have a quote here from both the US ambassador and the UN. They're working with Assad to make this happen."

"Frans," Sonia said, "You can't make any appeal, any video to the pope until Omar agrees to one more demand," and turning to Omar, she said, "You free Dr. Andrew."

"Who are you to make demands of me?" Omar shouted.

"We're three people who insist Andrew be set free. We'll accept nothing less."

Omar stared at them. "I can't do that. We need him."

"No," Sonia said, glaring at him. "You owe him."

"What do you mean?"

"After you kidnapped him, two of your men stayed on in his apartment, raped his lady friend and killed her. You need to let him go so he can return to Beirut and properly mourn his loss. You bloody well owe him that, Omar."

"How do you know all this?"

"I have my contacts in Beirut. An investigation was carried out. The man you left behind in Shatilla, the one with the infected foot, confessed that he and one of your other men had carried out the crime but had been too afraid to tell you."

Omar shook his head and, like a wild animal, began pacing back and forth across the room, chanting a dull and monotonous *Ya Allah*.

And then suddenly, he stopped. "Does Andrew know any of this?"

"No, how could he?" replied Sonia, wondering as she said that if Moussa had already told him.

"And you didn't know?"

"I swear to you on Allah I didn't know. I made a promise that his woman would be safe as long as he cooperated with us."

"Whether you did or didn't, I'd advise you not to bring it up. He deeply loved that woman. Imagine how devastated he'd be if he knew, and he'd blame you, and for good reason."

"I won't. I'm heartbroken for Andrew, and I regret this happened."

"When the ceasefire is finalized and you and your men prepare to leave Homs, I want you to tell Andrew that he is free to return to his patients in Shatilla."

Omar nodded. "Of course."

"Good," said Frans, dialing a number and handing the phone to Omar. "Then tell Colonel Yakub when he answers who you are and that you agree to a ceasefire. And when you've done that, I will make your video appeal."

Sonia envisioned a day soon when she and Andrew would walk out of Homs, but with it came a feeling of dread. Would it be enough to wash away her sin of betrayal? And if Andrew did, by chance, count it as reparation for her egregious crime, would Nadia?

# CHAPTER SIXTEEN

ANDREW LAY IN BED in a room full of books, their corners worn with use, three floors above his clinic, unable to sleep for the incessant explosions, some close enough to literally shake the walls around him, wondering why he hadn't insisted on moving to his basement clinic, a far safer place, even if it meant sleeping on an uncomfortable cot? Was this sorry plight any different from the wildly outlandish unpredictables that had befallen him the last seven years? How had it all happened, he wondered? Had it been his fate, his destiny, as the Arabic word *Maktoub* suggested, or had it just been a bizarre combination of unforeseen circumstances that began innocently enough when he took time off from his cardiology practice in Washington, DC, to travel to Beirut to celebrate his betrothal to Nadia Khoury. Though it had taken Andrew those many years and myriad adventures to deduce some pretty profound insights, his education from unschooled ignorance to a higher form of political savviness began with what should have been, had he been paying closer attention, a warning or at least a preparedness of what was to come.

To celebrate their engagement, Nadia's mother had planned a lavish garden party in the presence of family and friends, but while Andrew was in route to Beirut, Nadia had discovered her legally declared dead and disappeared husband of thirteen years alive in a Syrian prison and off she had gone to rescue him. Instead of biding his time in Beirut awaiting her return, Andrew found himself chasing after Nadia in

Damascus and helping her not only free her husband from prison but illegally smuggling him out of Syria back into Lebanon. He shook his head at the folly of it all, the sheer stupidity and arrogant disregard for his personal safety, and yet there he had been, not only freeing but transporting a wanted man across an international border. That should have been enough, he mused, to recognize that life in the Middle East was dangerously unpredictable, yet a few days later, and quite without his consent, he found himself in South Lebanon in the middle of a nasty Israeli-Hezbollah war. Within an hour of their safe return to Beirut, Nadia was kidnapped by Hassan Jaafar. Then when Jaafar discovered Andrew was Nadia's fiancé, he had him beaten and left for dead.

Who made him Jaafar's prey? The same woman who had "discovered" Nadia's husband alive in a Syrian jail to coincide with Andrew's arrival in Beirut and the cancellation of their engagement party. The same person who had orchestrated Nadia's kidnapping, who had feigned tears at his bedside while nursing him through his recovery, then claiming it would make Nadia proud if he learned Arabic and worked in the refugee camp. The same woman who, after a stressful journey in a UN convoy out of South Lebanon, had notified Jaafar of their arrival back in Beirut and when the requisite time had elapsed, had sent Nadia out to her car to fetch a computer, knowing Jaafar and his men would be there waiting to snatch her up and whisk her away. The same woman who, when Nadia did not return, tried to prevent him, literally blocking his way, from running outside to find out why. The despicable Sonia Rizk, the ultimate snake in the grass who deserved, as Nadia had suggested, to be tortured and bled to death, or even strangled with his bare hands as Andrew had often imagined doing. Losing an eye was not enough of a punishment for her. And now the shameless betrayer had turned up in Homs. What the hell was she doing here? Writing a book about the conflict? Maybe, but she probably also wants me to forgive her for ruining my life. Not a goddamn chance!

Resentful indignation and months of wrongful enslavement had made Andrew despondent. Leila was gone. He had lost a lot of weight.

He felt his strength waning, and he looked as bad as any al-Nusra fighter with his long, straggly hair and beard. He smelt as bad, too, and for lack of water, could not remember the last time he had taken a shower or washed his clothes. He did not know how much longer he could keep up his twelve-to-fourteen-hour shifts in the clinic. Thankfully, he now had Moussa on whom he increasingly relied, but as the battles intensified, the patient load had increased and their wounds grew more severe. All he could do was keep them comfortably sedated until they died. No matter what he did or who he treated, or didn't, he was haunted by something far more profound than hopelessness—a deep and painful remorse for his abandonment of Joe on the pavement outside the media center. Given the severity of his wounds and the loss of blood, Andrew could not have saved Joe, but he should at least have stayed with him, cradled him in his arms, told him he loved him and, more importantly, asked Joe to forgive him for doubting his friendship. He did not do any of those things, and he would carry that deep and painful guilt with him for the rest of his life. And lovely Leila was gone. How much more pain could he absorb, how many more senseless deaths would he have to endure before he became completely undone?

Andrew lacked a deep belief in God or any firm conviction that might have sustained him in his daily trials. He had grown up Catholic but felt let down by his religious education. His Protestant friends knew all about this area of the Middle East from reading the Bible. He knew the Galilee was where Jesus Christ had performed the miracle of a few loaves and Cana where he had turned water into wine, but not much else. And he supposed that someday he would finally have to break down and read the damn book, but in the meantime, his minimal sensitivities to religion had been severely damaged by the incessant talk of religious revenge and sectarian fighting.

Omar had talked about his religious beliefs, about his eagerness to see the establishment of a caliphate, an Islamic state under the leadership of a person considered a politico-religious successor to the prophet Muhammad. Thus a leader of the entire Muslim community, akin to the pope overseeing worldwide Catholicism—all pretty far-fetched stuff, or so Andrew thought. As a prisoner, Andrew had not been allowed access to a computer, but he was curious to know more about what Omar was part of, and so had memorized the access code to the computer and, in the dead of night when everyone had gone to bed, he perused the internet looking for anything he could find on ISIS, particularly how and why it had proliferated so rapidly.

Syria was not only the first war to unfold on social media; it was also the first war where fighters documented their experiences in real-time, these virtual diaries catching the imagination of jihadists worldwide. The lure of ISIS with its caliph and caliphate among young Muslims from the margins of society was strong, as was the pull of the *ummah*, the notion of an Islamic community uniting Muslims worldwide. According to reports Andrew read, more than 30,000 foreign fighters had already answered the call and made their way to Syria.

One such youth, a slight, bearded, nineteen-year-old Somali kid from Minneapolis named Hassan, came to Andrew's attention when he sought treatment for diarrhea, a common affliction for newcomers not used to drinking unfiltered water and unwashed raw food. After a few visits to the clinic, it became apparent to Andrew that this teenager, with his Midwestern English, did not fit the mold of an ISIS fighter.

"How did you end up here, Hassan?" Andrew asked.

"Facebook, that's how I was recruited. I felt a disconnect from the real world. When I failed eleven subjects in my last exam at the engineering college, my father began beating me for my poor grades. I hated school and resented my father. I felt trapped, but online I found freedom and Facebook became my life. I spent entire days consuming real-time information about the war in Syria, surfing page after page. The more pages I marked as liked, the more I commented, the more information I craved."

"Did you ever think about verifying the information you read online?" asked Andrew.

"No. I don't read newspapers. I don't watch TV news. I believed what I saw online. It all made sense and felt very real. I discovered and immediately identified with a group of people involved with ISIS in Syria. I began making comments, which were liked, and when I made a friend request to someone named Abou Aziz, he responded and pretty soon he was sending me messages, said he was a sniper and sent photos of himself with his assault rifle. It looked exciting. He shared stories from the battlefields, talked about their victories, about the comrades who had died. Pretty soon, I was being shown the location of the last round of fighting, the weapons used, the kind of assault the Syrian army had launched. I felt like I was there, alongside this sniper. He asked me to pray for him and his buddies because their losses were great. He said the *ummah* needed all the help it could get.

"I told him I was not tall or particularly strong and would be of no use in battle. He said a Muslim needed not be any of those things. He just had to be a well-rounded believer. He encouraged me to join the fight in whatever capacity I could. He presented me with verses from the Quran that suggested the Caliph had arrived and that the Caliphate was legitimate."

"You don't appear to come from a wealthy family, Hassan. Where did you get the money to travel, or for that matter, a passport?"

"When I admitted I had no money, I was put in contact with a man who arranged everything. We met, and a few days later, when I saw him again, he handed me cash and a passport. From the time I left Minnesota, I was told where to go, eventually meeting up with other recruits on the Turkish-Syrian border."

"When you arrived here in Homs, did you meet your recruiter Abou Aziz?"

"No, Omar received us, and when I asked about the man, Omar said he'd never heard of him."

It dawned on Andrew that by the time this young man arrived in Syria, he had been properly vetted and mentored. He had up-to-date information on the day-to-day skirmishes. He was essentially battle-ready, with very little training required. An overall, well-perfected recruitment technique from one of the world's wealthiest militant groups, their war chest estimated at two billion dollars, and in control of a landmass between Iraq and Syria, equivalent to the distance between Washington, DC and Cleveland, Ohio.

"What did it mean to you to become a member of a caliphate and fight the infidels?"

"The Quran says, 'Those who readily fight in the cause of God are those who forsake this world in favor of the Hereafter and shall be granted a great recompense.'"

Andrew knew the quote. He had heard it from Mahmoud, Omar's elderly mentor.

"Even though Islam denounces violence and states you should love one another, not kill one another?" asked Andrew.

"According to the Quran, those who fight God and his Messenger Muhammad, and fail to repent are to be killed, crucified, have their hands and feet cut off or be banished from the land."

"You don't strike me as someone who could actually carry out such atrocities."

"On our first day in the field, I was handed a knife and told to cut off the ears and noses of the dead Syrian soldiers. I couldn't do it."

"Did you want to leave and go back to Minneapolis?"

"That would not have been possible. Once we enter the land of Islam, we are prohibited from returning to the land of the infidels."

"Were you reprimanded?"

"Omar explained there were many ways to spread God's word. I'm now part of the recruitment team."

Andrew understood that ISIS used atrocities not just to demonstrate power but as a means of controlling the local population, both of which were vital to establishing legitimacy as a state. To establish statehood, ISIS needed recognition and sovereignty. Media created awareness of its existence, but that was not enough. ISIS needed men to carry out its agenda.

Andrew had not had any one-on-one time with Omar in a long time, and a catch-up chat was long overdue, especially in light of what

Andrew had learned about ISIS, the newest insurgent group to muscle
its way into Syria. He found Omar alone one night and invited him to
his clinic. The two of them pulled up the only two chairs, moved them
to the back of the room and sat.

"I had a chance to speak with Hassan—one of the guys on your
new recruitment team. I knew you used your media center to communicate with the press but tell me about this new department."

"It's pretty straightforward. ISIS commits atrocities for both practi-
cal and spiritual reasons. The graver the atrocities, the greater the head-
line news, the greater the influx of new followers, not to mention an
increase in financial resources. Atrocities demonstrate not only power
but fear which enables ISIS to control the local population and acquire
additional territory which a califate needs to establish its state."

"You've memorized your lines well, Omar. Now let me see if I understand it in real terms. ISIS maintains a state of strife and conflict to
assure its control over the local population. It then uses those atrocities
to establish legitimacy as a state."

"That's right."

"Whatever happened to al-Nusra's idea of winning the hearts and
minds of the locals?"

"Here in Homs, we haven't given up on that idea, and to be honest,
that idea better suits my personality, but ISIS sees things differently,
and in the long run, who's to say they're wrong?"

"Better be feared than loved, is that it?"

Omar nodded. "In the end, it comes down to a black or white
choice. You are either with us or against us."

Andrew remembered the last time he had heard those very same
words. George W. Bush, after 9/11, had said it to the American people.
"You are either with me or against me in this 'crusade.'" That word is
a reminder to Muslims of a series of religious wars between Christians
and Muslims that had begun in the late eleventh century. Was it any
wonder then, in the twenty-first century, that those same words would
not only spur on some Muslims to resort to specific "sword verses"

from the Quran to justify their war against the infidels, but to some Christian Evangelical pastors who would use it to propagate the perception that Islam was not only spiritually evil, but promoted violence, and therefore had to be defeated.

"Let me tell you something, Andrew. ISIS's current scale of recruitment, and its use of social media to create agents and supporters, is so successful it will literally outlive itself, regardless of what the West does."

"Explain."

"Even if the current caliph, Abu Bakr al Baghdadi, were to die, ISIS as an idea and an organization will outlive him because even in death, the caliph lives on as a martyr, especially if he's been killed. Either way, his death, were that to happen, would be the ultimate recruitment tool."

"If you're suggesting that radical ideas outlive a movement and the people who create them, it's not true. They eventually die to the point of being consigned to the dustbin of history."

While Andrew had clandestine access to a computer, he also read Arabic and had borrowed any books the new recruits had brought with them. From his readings, Andrew learned that Muhammad's earliest conquests had not been tidy affairs. The laws passed down in the Quran and in the narrations of the Prophet's rule were calibrated to fit a turbulent and violent time, not unlike the Old Testament and its atrocities. However, that did not mean those horrific practices should be cherry-picked from medieval tradition and applied to the twenty-first century. Political discontent, instability, ignorance and poverty all had a tendency to create conditions ripe for both extremism and recruitment. Without those essential parts, Sunni extremists would not have had the desired power over their disciples, but then wasn't that the goal of all religions?

Andrew wondered if it was not permissible, at least on some level, to compare Opus Dei, the secretive, ultra-conservative, cult-like movement within the Catholic Church that sought ever-more influence and control over the Vatican hierarchy, and forbade adherents any deviation from its core beliefs. Maybe that was a preposterous analogy, particularly since they did not chop off heads, but then Andrew did not think much of any religion, much less ones that suppressed open-mindedness.

"If ISIS claims to be so pure, why do they abduct women and use them as sex slaves?"

"In their eyes, it's not only remuneration for long-serving fighters but bait for younger recruits."

Andrew shook his head. "Do what I say, not what I do."

"ISIS runs slave markets where they sell and buy women. It's common practice. They also take young boys and train them in weapons and warfare and call them Cubs of the Caliphate. Young boys are also praised in Islamic erotic poetry. It's considered on a par with praising God, although I have to admit some of those poems are so bold they make me blush."

Andrew was surprised at his stark openness and wondered if Omar might be gay. He had never married, never mentioned any woman in his life, aside from his mother.

"Can you give me an example?"

Omar hesitated, embarrassed, but then recited a verse, "My heart is passionately in love with a goldsmith fawn. My love for him has taken firm root in the bottom of my heart. Oh, what would that I were the bellows at his mouth, so that I could kiss his lips every time he blows."

Omar quickly changed the subject. "ISIS is a well-organized group. It presents itself as the only Islamic entity willing to spread God's word and revive Islam's golden age, but it's also good at advertising. On their webcasts, on Facebook and in their Twitter feeds, they explicitly mention the end times, and when they do, their recruits multiply a hundred-fold."

"Tell me about this end times business."

"These beliefs aren't mere superstitions. They began when the US invaded Iraq, and they've affected huge parts of ISIS's operations, from its recruitment strategy to its military operations. In early Islam, there were a series of civil wars mostly centered around who would be the caliph after Muhammad's death. Each side invented prophecies and attributed them to Muhammad, whether or not they were his actual words. It's a bit like your Christian evangelicals reviving the Book of Revelations and claiming it to be the word of God."

"How do you know all these things, Omar?"

"I told you already. I was chosen to study in Saudi Arabia because I was smarter than a lot of the young men my age who answered the call. Had I stayed in the States and not had the stigma of being an Arab from Dearborn, I probably could have gotten into a very good college. In Saudi Arabia, I studied to impress my teachers, and the more I excelled, the more they threw at me, the more I learned. Recently, when we discovered how important it was to recruit new followers, I had no problem working with Hassan and developing a recruitment program.

"But getting back to your question about the end times as a recruitment tool, those ancient civil wars took place in what is now Iraq and Syria. The civil wars evaporated, but the residue remained. With the US invasion of Iraq and the war in Syria, these prophesies gained a lot of currency and a lackluster interest in the end times suddenly turned into a hot topic and ISIS jumped on the wagon and brought it all back. Imagine the appeal to a downtrodden youth from Minneapolis to travel to a land where the final battles of the apocalypse would take place."

"Has ISIS already established itself in Homs?"

"Not yet, at least not officially. They're still primarily in eastern Syria in the desert, near the Iraqi border. A few cells are operating in the souks here, but so far, al-Nusra's been able to quell their activities. And until such time as ISIS makes its entrance here, we will still keep trying to win the hearts and minds of the locals by acting less savagely."

"Is Islam an inherently violent religion?" Andrew asked.

"If you look at early Islamic scripture, you'll find passages that promote violence. There's the Quran, the word of God as spoken to Muhammad, and then there are hundreds of volumes of literature attributed to Muhammad, some of which promote violence. Did it all come from Muhammad? It's similar to the Old Testament, works attributed to God that also promote violence. Do we know for sure it was the word of God? No, but Muslims, like Christians, must make sense of these contradictions."

"So, ISIS goes and looks for the violent passages to justify its actions," said Andrew.

"And to assure its grip on local populations. Do you remember when ISIS burned a Jordanian pilot, set him on fire, claiming he was an infidel even though the poor man was a Sunni? Islamic scripture forbids this kind of thing. No two ways about it. Only God can carry out such an act. Scripture also says you can't kill women and children. If you're looking for rough passages that promote this kind of violence, they're there, and ISIS finds them and uses them to justify what they're doing."

"What you're essentially saying is that you shouldn't paint an entire religion with one brush. It's a small minority who cherry-picks passages that end up denigrating a religion."

"That's right."

"You mentioned earlier that ISIS had been hugely successful recruiting new adherents. Was it the end times that boosted the numbers?"

"Yes, especially with foreigners. They don't have family or tribal ties, so they make better shock troops. They're not only willing to be brutal, but they're also prepared to die."

"Do you agree with all the savagery?"

"There are many ways to serve Allah."

"I find everything about ISIS unsettling. Suppose ISIS visits my clinic one day. What will happen to me? In their eyes, I'm Christian. I mean no offense, but face it, you and your men are a ragtag, disorganized operation with little or no support from the Westerners who put you on the ground and told you to fight to the death. You wouldn't be able to offer me much protection."

"Supposedly, Christians who don't resist the caliphate and who acknowledge their subjugation are spared. I suspect that would be open to interpretation, depending on who you come before."

"Not very reassuring. However glorious early Islam sounded, Omar, it had its critics. Did you ever hear of Richard Dawkins? He's an evolutionary biologist and professed atheist who famously said, "Do not suppose the statements of the prophets to be true. The sacred books are only a set of idle tales as any age could have, and indeed did produce."

"Andrew, every religion including Christianity has its critics, you among them. Do you believe every word of the Bible? Surely, that text, like the Quran, also has some idle tales, many of them concocted hundreds of years after the supposed events took place. That doesn't mean you throw the entire text out the window."

"Was Muhammad tolerant of other religions?"

"He believed that Jesus was born to the Virgin Mary and therefore a human prophet, just not the Son of God. He also believed Jesus was a Messiah and one of the most important prophets of God. He wrote a surprisingly secular document called the Constitution of Medina in which he stipulated that Muslims, Christians, Jews and even pagans should have equal political and cultural rights. There's one passage in the Quran that says Christians and Jewish believers share in God's favors. The passage goes something like this: 'Be they Muslim, Jews or Christians, those who believe in God and the Last Day and who do well will have their reward with their Lord. They have nothing to fear, and they will not sorrow.'"

Omar went on. "There's another of the most often quoted revelations of the Quran that says 'If God had so willed, He would have made all of you one community, but he had not done so in order that he may test you according to what he has given you. To God shall you all return, and He will tell you the truth about what you have been disputing.'"

"It heartens me to know that you don't fully support ISIS, Omar. That shows a lot of maturity on your part."

"Islam is a beautiful religion. Parts of it have been hijacked and turned into something ugly and vile."

"Do you ever think about going back to Dearborn?"

"That's out of the question. I can never go home. In the eyes of the

American government, I'm a terrorist. I'm here to stay. I'm now part of ISIS, although I haven't yet pledged my allegiance, but once they arrive here, I'll be made to do so. I may not be able to cut off limbs, but that's why there's a media and a recruitment center for men like me. We're all needed."

"Could you put a gun to a man's head and kill him?"

"If asked, yes, I could do that. All that requires is pulling a trigger."

"Then I misjudged you, Omar. You'll make a good ISIS fighter."

"I have no choice."

"And your men, what about them?"

"Why would they be any different? We've all answered the call. If we initially had confidence that al-Nusra could win over the majority of locals, it hasn't been as successful as we'd hoped. ISIS has it right. Muslims need to unite and reject Western ideas and organize a community around conservative interpretations of Islam as a way of reviving and reclaiming the old caliphates' greatness, and if it has to use atrocities to establish legitimacy as a state, then so be it."

From all his reading, Andrew came to realize how difficult it would be to reconcile the region's long history of former greatness with its more recent history of colonialism and subjugation by Western powers. What has ravaged the Middle East goes far deeper than ISIS. It began in 1916, post-World War I, when the British and French diplomats Mark Sykes and Francois George-Picot divided up the Middle East. The artificial lines those two men drew in the sand have since been blown away. In their full arrogance, the Western powers have failed to recognize that ISIS, and al Qaeda and the Afghan mujahedeen before them, have taken those egregious acts of divide and conquer and used them as a way to subjugate local populations and establish their caliphate.

Andrew thought ISIS deviously clever for both its combined Islamic piety and reverence for the prophet and its modern social media platforms and encryption schemes. Andrew had not seen them, but apparently, their videos blended the raw pornographic violence of a snuff film with the pious chanting of religious warriors, and the group had the discipline of hard-core followers to carry it off. had been The American military imprisoned Many ISIS founding members in Iraq and, because of torture, became radicalized beyond redemption. Andrew, the once naïve American, knew enough now to feel sorry for his country. The US would never change countries like Iraq or Syria into their image. Rather, these countries would change America because it would become inextricably enmeshed in those countries' bloodied histories.

ISIS was essentially an anti-colonial religious movement yet psychological and technical in scope, taking, as its reference point, Islam's pre-colonial power as a Sunni, Islamic caliphate. Andrew knew, too, from listening to the men around him who were well versed in both religion and regional history, that the Syrian conflict, of which he was now an integral part, was not only a civil war of people against its government, but a religious war pitting Assad's minority Alawite sect, aligned with Shiite fighters from Iran and Hezbollah fighters from Lebanon, against Sunni-led rebel groups and the US's regional allies, all working to curtail Iran's influence across the region.

While in Broumana together, Andrew remembered asking Robert Jenkins why Syria was interested in the American government.

"We think it's in our national and strategic interest to have a US-friendly Middle East. Assad, like Saddam, is no longer someone we want on our team."

Even back then, Andrew knew Jenkins' comment did not ring true. Camille, Andrew's friend and Leila's uncle, had taught him a great deal about Middle East politics, and one of the things he remembered clearly was that the issue had not been Syria, per se. It had been about dealing a crippling blow to Iran and Hezbollah, and Syria, as their lynchpin, needed to be taken out. At the time, Andrew pegged Jenkins as an arrogant bastard. He assumed he still was. Hadn't he heard that Jenkins was now the US Ambassador to Syria? Did this mean Jenkins was responsible for the Homs hellhole he found himself in? Had he been the one who trained Omar and his men? If so, he had done a poor job.

Andrew knew, too, from personal experience that the Lebanese lived by the simple fact that their history was imbued in a culture of violence. They had seen civil war. They had experienced five Israeli invasions, seen their capital Beirut carpet-bombed, their bridges and infrastructure destroyed and witnessed too many political assassinations. Syrians had lived vicariously through Lebanon's experiences. Now, they were being subjected to their own blood bath. Did Middle East wars ever end with outright victory and permanent stability? In his limited experience, Andrew did not think so. At best, it meant stable ceasefire lines, reduced bloodshed, fewer refugees and less terrorism. Each sect had what amounted to a safe zone in a deconstructed state that functioned under the umbrella of an old broken system. It may be too late for the Iraqis to improve their calamitous situation, but he hoped that would not be the case for Syria.

# CHAPTER SEVENTEEN

THERE HAD BEEN SIGNIFICANT TALK of a pause in hostilities, a quasi-ceasefire, in fact, and people let their hopes soar after a few days of relative calm, thinking it could actually happen. They dared to venture out to visit family and friends they had not seen in eight months. They allowed their children to play outdoors and soak in the sun and breathe in fresh air after the long, dreary months of winter. Mary, too, was busy typing up her dispatches, eager to announce the news to the world. As excited as everyone else to be out and about, Sonia and Mary visited the souk one morning in search of provisions while Frans, exhausted from his efforts with his shrinking congregation, slept in.

The rocket attacks came suddenly and from all directions, deafening and deadly. They were a block away from home when they saw a bomb slam into the upper floor of their building. It appeared to be a direct hit, and Sonia assumed from the sound that it was probably a 150-mm mortar shell and that it must have gutted their apartment. The explosion had unhinged the tiles on the roof and sent them, along with huge chunks of broken mortar, flying into the street. The third floor, also hit, now resembled an unfinished construction site, pillars the only thing seemingly holding up the ceiling, while the building itself, as if staggering from the hits, seemed uncertain whether to crumble or resist and stay standing. The green decorative shutters adorning each street-facing window hung askew, and the balconies, every last one of them, broken and felled, and all Sonia could think of was Frans under all that rubble. She started to make a dash for the entrance when Mary grabbed hold of her wrist, spun her around and together they fell to the ground and crawled under a burned-out Mercedes. From her pocket, Mary pulled out two pairs of earplugs and handed one to Sonia, who promptly pushed them into her ears. She had forgotten how useful these were in muting out sounds and wondered when she saw Mary pick up a supply in the souk why she had not done the same. And while earplugs somewhat stifled the shrill noises that caused the inside of heads to ache and ears to ring, they did not absorb the vibrations or the thud Sonia felt inside her head when a bomb fell nearby and exploded. The car next to the Mercedes they were under caught fire, the heat eventually hot enough to blow its tires and push the hot blast in their direction. They covered their exposed cheeks and pressed their faces to the ground, and hoped they would not be burned to death.

As quickly as it began, everything went quiet. There was something very welcome in the unexpected abruptness of guns going silent after so much noise. Sonia's ribs hurt from being thrown to the ground, her head ached and she had dust and grime up her nose, but she was otherwise intact and grateful to be alive. She removed her earplugs, and as she edged her body out from under the car, a piece of metal caught hold of her eye patch and tore it off but, unable to do anything about it, she continued until she was able to get on her knees and finally to her feet. She lent Mary a hand and helped her out only to discover tears streaming down her cheeks. It seemed the clear-headed, fast-thinking woman who had saved her life was not so resilient after all. How long had it been, Sonia wondered, since her brain injury? Two months, a bit more? Maybe she had not fully recovered. In extremes of desperation, one tried to clutch hope, however futile, but that required more than Mary was apparently able to give at the moment, and Sonia had only just realized this. But then, Mary must have been just as surprised. Sonia knew the stomach-churning, shock factor of seeing an oval-shaped slab of slimy, red, raw meat where an eye should have been. Without a word, Mary pulled out a bandana from her purse and fashioned an eye patch for Sonia.

Nearby, a dozen people stood around three dead bodies. A man lying face down, his legs completely unspoiled down to the crease in his trousers, his head a mangled mess. Next to him was a woman, her legs blown off. Sonia stared at the third, a young boy, about seven or eight years old. He looked merely asleep. A man, perhaps his father, pushed his way through the crowd as he walked toward the child and fell to his knees beside the body. He lifted the boy into his arms. Two men nearby helped him to his feet. He pressed the child to his chest and kissed his forehead. As the man moved away, carrying the small body, the boy's head bobbed and his thin arms dangled. The crowd parted, and Sonia and Mary watched in silence as he walked away.

"This is going to give me more fucking nightmares," Mary said.

Sonia glanced over at Mary and, wrapping her arm around her shoulder, said, "We're all having nightmares."

Not only had it been a challenge to suffer through the stifling heat of summer in Homs without air conditioning, but the ultimate privation was living on the top floor of a five-story walk-up. The sidewalk outside the building's entrance had erupted during one of the explosions and heaped a mound of chiseled stone in the entryway. Sonia and Mary waded their way through the mass of pulverized dust and grime before beginning their gradual ascent, grateful, at least, for the sunlight that played patterns on the steps through the broken windows along the stairwell. On prior outings, Sonia had had the occasional run-in with rats, their intelligent, piercing black eyes and pointed noses almost human in their boldness, and was grateful she had no such encounter this day as she climbed what already felt like an impossible race to the top, touching the dirty walls just enough to steady herself and watching where she put her feet, with Mary close behind.

When they reached the fifth floor in its full openness, Sonia could hear the anguish of grieving voices and the sorrowful dong of church bells playing across Bab Amr. She felt the wind and welcomed its freshness as it brushed her face. And then she heard what sounded like words being whispered in a muffled voice and turned to Mary.

"It's Frans. He's alive."

"Impossible. Look at this place," Mary said, as they made their way through the rubble, conscious of the sky above them, the wind rushing through the open space, the interior wall that their kitchen shared with Madame Chidiac's apartment, the only one still standing. The living room wall was gone, that entire side of the apartment sheared off, the few pieces of furniture, either blown out the open wall or crushed by debris and fallen glass.

Sonia shouted Frans' name and once again heard, as if in response, someone moaning.

"It's Frans. I told you he was alive," and they frantically made their way through the rubble, following the prolonged, low, inarticulate sound of someone in pain, until they reached what had been the door to Frans' bedroom and saw him on his bed, one arm pinned down by a large piece of fallen wall, the rest of his body covered in shattered glass and the exterior wall blown out. Sonia glanced at Mary, and together they made their way over the cluttered floor.

"Frans, you're a goddamned miracle."

"I don't feel much like a miracle," he whispered, his voice barely audible.

"We'll get you up and out of here in no time," Sonia said, as she and Mary tossed off the clutter and gingerly brushed off the shards of glass from his hair and clothing.

"There, up you go," she said, trying to pull him to his feet, all ninety pounds of him.

"Not so fast," he yelled when Sonia attempted to lift him up. "My chest hurts... and so does my right arm."

Aside from a bloodied face from the cut glass, a possible broken rib or two and maybe a broken arm, those appeared to be the only things wrong. "You're one tough fellow, Frans. Your wounds could have been a hell of a lot worse."

When he tried to laugh, he winced. "That was a close call, wasn't it?"

Sonia, holding back tears, smiled back. "Yes, Frans, it was, but you pulled it off. You must have been praying awfully hard."

He smiled. "I was."

Taking hold of his left arm, Sonia brushed off more glass and helped him to a sitting position while Mary guided his feet into his slippers.

"Let me see that arm," Sonia said. The area between the wrist and elbow was swollen and possibly broken. "I can try to make a sling…"

"Let me do that, I know how," said Mary, and she took one of Frans' shirts and fashioned a sling, just as expertly as she had created an eye patch out of her bandana, and gently wrapped it around his arm and shoulder. "That should make you a bit more comfortable until we can get you to a doctor."

"It already feels better," Frans said, trying to smile.

"You don't have to play martyr for us. If it hurts, say do."

"Okay," he shouted. "It hurts like hell."

"Mary, maybe we'd better bind his chest, too, in case his ribs are broken."

When they finally got him up and back to what had been the living room, Mary brought over one of the remaining kitchen chairs.

"Have a seat, Frans, so we can clean the cuts on your face."

"I need to pee."

"There's still a toilet, Frans," Sonia announced, "but no wall."

"That's all I need, thank you," and they turned their backs and waited for him to do his business.

"How is he going to do that with one hand?" Mary whispered.

"He'll figure it out."

"I'm going to try to get to Madame Chidiac's apartment to see if hers is as badly damaged," said Mary. "Be right back."

While waiting for Frans to finish, Sonia walked through the rubble to the edge where there had been a wall, a large double glass door and a balcony. She peered down the five stories to the rubble-strewn alleyway between theirs and the adjacent building. A group of people huddled over a body, lying face down in a pool of blood. Whether from shrapnel or falling mortar, in the already hot sun, the woman looked like a swollen, pulpy slab of slaughtered beef still oozing blood. She had on a black skirt, and when she fell, the skirt rose up her thighs to reveal her panty line. A woman standing nearby took off her jacket and delicately covered the victim's legs so she would not look so naked.

Sonia turned back to see Frans making his way into the living room. "Looks like you may have lost your neighbor on the first floor, Frans. *Nushkur Allah,* we're very fortunate. We still have you. Now come and sit while I patch up your face. You're a bloodied mess at the moment."

"Where's Mary?" he asked.

"Gone to check on Madame Chidiac's apartment."

"If it isn't as damaged, we could move there," Frans said. "But there's also the rectory alongside the church in Bustan al Diwan where we buried Joe. I checked it out when we were there."

"I remember, but it has no electricity. Mary and I need to keep our cell phones charged."

"True, but we haven't any electricity here now, either. At least there, the walls are still standing and the roof's intact. Compared to this place, it's going to look luxurious."

"Doubtful," scoffed Sonia, "but we would be closer to Andrew, and that would be a plus. I'm worried Omar will renege on his promise and force Andrew to leave with them. I want to make sure I'm there to convince him otherwise when the ceasefire takes hold."

"Madame Chidiac's apartment is unlivable," said Mary, returning with some of her clothes and personal items. "And look, my computer still works. I'd slid it under my mattress when we left for the souk. Good thing I did."

"Christ, I didn't even think to look at my things," Sonia said as she dashed off.

"And where do you think you're going?" Mary asked when she saw Frans stand.

"To find my transistor radio. It's somewhere near my bed. We need to know what's going on."

"Sit down. We don't need you falling over debris," ordered Mary. "I'll look for it."

Sonia returned, looking forlorn. "I have about as much left as Mary," Sonia said, holding up her few pieces of clothing, "but I can't find my pile of hand-written notes. Damn it! All that work."

"And your computer?" asked Mary.

"Intact, *nushkur Allah,* but my charger is missing."

"Never mind. You can use mine."

"Ladies, I can't stand it any longer. My arm's throbbing. I need a shot of whiskey. I hope we still have a bottle."

"You're in luck," said Sonia, holding up the bottle as she walked back into the living room from the kitchen, such as it was. "And, miracle of miracles, we still have most of our food and one glass that didn't break."

Frans took the glass and looked up at Sonia. "A large, long shot, please."

"I'll have one, too," Mary said, returning with the transistor radio and handing it to Frans.

"Thanks, Mary, just put it on the floor." And after drinking his whiskey, Mary poured herself a shot. She slugged it down and, much to Sonia's surprise, poured another.

"Want one, Sonia?" Mary asked.

She shook her head. "No, thanks. I'd be done for the day if I did."

Suddenly, out of a relative calm that had finally settled over Bab Amr came men's voices, seemingly a large number of them, chanting in the street below, "Come out Christians so we can slit your throats," and promising to fill Bab Amr, Zahara, the Alawite quarter and the Christian Bustan al-Diwan neighborhood with their blood.

"Isn't Bustan al-Diwan where you want us to go, Frans?" asked Mary anxiously, and when he did not respond, she turned and saw him, transistor to his ear.

When he finally put down the radio, Mary asked, "Did you hear what those men were yelling?"

He nodded.

"Bustan al-Diwan's more dangerous than here."

"We've no choice, Mary," said Frans. "I've just listened to the news. The army's urging Christians to leave Bab Amr. ISIS has pledged it will come through here and kill every last one of us. As for you two ladies, well, I've heard what ISIS does to women. I wouldn't want to see that happen to you."

"Nor would we, Frans," Sonia said. "How much time do we have?"

"We should try to hold out until nightfall if possible. It'd be safer as we make our way to the Old City."

"Maybe we should ask Yakob for his advice," Mary suggested.

"I tried calling, but he isn't answering. I'll try again later. In the meantime, let's get some breakfast, it may be our last meal for a while. I'll put water on for tea, if we have a teapot left."

"We do," said Sonia. "I checked."

When Frans stood up, Mary took the chair, put it at the kitchen table and sat. Sonia saw her bent over the page and peered over her shoulder. On an otherwise blank piece of white paper she had torn out of her notebook, Mary drew a small square cage in the far right-hand bottom corner of the page. Next to it, she printed the word 'Me.'"

"Is that how you see yourself?" Sonia asked.

Mary nodded. "Something's not right with my head, Sonia. I get these awful headaches. They make me feel like I'm in that cage. I can't even clear my mind enough to write my dispatches."

"You were quick to act when you threw me to the ground and saved my life."

"That was sheer gut instinct."

"What about all the aspirin I got you? Doesn't that help with your headaches?"

"They're all gone, took them all."

That was boxes and boxes, thought Sonia. What the hell was going on with her?

"It won't be long now. As soon as the ceasefire takes hold, I'll get you out of here and have you examined by a doctor in Beirut. As for your dispatches, just tell me what you need done. Going forward, that may not even be an issue if we don't find electricity to recharge our phones."

"Don't get me wrong, I'm not hanging this up, Sonia. I'll come back…"

"We'll come back together. There's a story here that needs to be told, and we'll do it, together."

Out of the blue, they heard someone shout, "Hello?"

They all turned to see a soldier standing at what had been the front door.

"I have a message from Colonel Yakob."

"Yes? What is it?" asked Frans.

"He insists you leave Bab Amr immediately. The army expects an imminent attack, and he wants all Christians out. We've moved our tanks inside Bab Amr, and once the fighting begins, you'll have no way of getting out."

Frans, frail and in pain, with his right arm in a sling and his ribs tightly wrapped, was of no use to Mary and Sonia as they hurriedly threw their meager belongings, the remaining food and whiskey into plastic bags and prepared to make their desperate escape to Bustan al Diwan. They divided the load, and with Frans cushioned in between them, they gradually made their way down the five flights of stairs, careful that Frans not slip or stumble over the debris in the stairwell. Their move was not supposed to happen like this. They had planned to slip away under cover of night, but there they were. It was midday, the temperature unusually warm for the middle of March with swarms of people flocking into the streets all at the same time, all desperate to escape ISIS. As she got closer to ground level, Sonia heard the commotion from the street and panicked, her mind full of random thoughts she could not control. Why had they not decided instead to seek shelter in the basement of the building? Why had Frans not thought of it, or maybe he had and decided it offered no protection from ISIS fighters on the prowl for men's throats to slit and women to capture. On the other hand, could anything be worse than a crowd of crazed, unreasonable, overwrought people all frantically running in the same direction, everyone for himself, indifferent to the needs of others? Such thoughts were pointless, Sonia concluded. The attack had begun, and they were already in the street and fair game to either the helicopter gunship overhead, unable to determine if they were friend or foe, or the sniper hiding on the top floor of the opposite building who assumed anyone walking in the streets to be live fodder.

The apartment buildings in Bab Amr in the southwest quadrant adjacent to the Old City sat one right next to the other, not in any way resembling a slum like Bombay with open sewage, but clean and orderly, but now badly damaged or destroyed, their streets cluttered with fallen debris and chunks of broken matter and sandbags scattered close to holes gouged in walls, possibly former ground-level sniper positions. Fires still smoldered in some apartments, billows of smoke in others, all rendering habitation impossible. Women, dazed and weeping, walked through the wreckage of their neighborhoods searching for some keepsake from their former lives—wedding photos, toys, student textbooks, baby strollers, clothes, stuffed animals, bedding, cooking utensils, pages from the Quran—all of these things once their families' precious possessions. One dress shop owner pushed a cart full of mannequins looking eerily like humans. What was she thinking, wondered Sonia? At one particularly dangerous intersection, the army had erected a ten-foot wall of mortar blocks so residents could safely cross what they called sniper's alley. No matter where Sonia looked, everything looked gray, the color of war—the unrecognizable streets she had recently walked on her way to the souk, now choked with blocks of cement, twisted metal, splintered door fronts, skeletons of severely damaged cars, some thrown blocks away by the bombs, dead body parts not yet discovered poking through the rubble, the stench in the heat unbearable. Metal shutters ripped from hundreds of shops, their wooden shelves stripped for firewood, their safes blown open and looted and merchants, owners of those shops, sitting despondent on sidewalks, or what was left of them, selling whatever they had salvaged. Great hulks of sheered-off and collapsed buildings scarred with bullet holes, the all, resembling some dismal imaginary place. Even the min-

arets and domes of churches visible in the distance, a testament to a
time when Homs had been a place where a Sunni Muslim majority had
lived in peace with Christians and other minorities, seemed an epoch
long gone. And everywhere, on the faces of the residents, a deep pen-
etrable wound, all of them unable to come to terms with the calamity
that had befallen their city. How could they, wondered Sonia.

Though she had been through wars before, she had forgotten its
physical energy, its slow, cancerous spread, the encroaching enemy
coming at them from all sides, the street to street combat in the alleyways behind buildings, the 150-mm mortar shells fired back and forth
over their heads, the incessant, deafening explosions, the dreaded power outages leaving them without cell phone service, that extraordinary
device they had come to rely on. And when they could no longer plug
theirs in and have instant access to the outside world, or Mary could
no longer send out her dispatches, or Sonia communicate with Fouad,
what then? Or, when they ran out of batteries for Frans' transistor radio
and could no longer get the local news, and they had to ration their
food, or go without, then what? She had never experienced starvation.
How long could one survive without food?

With helicopter gunships overhead and snipers hungry for a fresh
kill and mortar shells whizzing in all directions, and unsure which
alleyway to traverse or avoid, turning around in some cases and attempting other routes, Sonia, Frans and Mary slowly made their way
through the streets of Bab Amr, hugging the facades of buildings, their
backs to the walls at times, avoiding as much as possible the attention
of their two enemies, both of which considered them fair game. They
were about to leave Bab Amr, traverse an unprotected intersection before reaching Bustan al Diwan, just inside the southwest wall of the
Old City. Sonia motioned to Mary and Frans to lag behind while she
peered out from behind a corner store to see if it was safe to cross. A
bullet brushed past her face, so close the fuzz on her cheek stood on
edge. She pulled back and pressed herself against the wall, but just
as she tried to move closer to Mary and Frans, the first bomb fell,
then the second, so powerful it knocked Sonia off her feet. Before she

could regain her footing, the glass on the storefront shattered, and a large razor-sharp shard penetrated her right shoulder pinning her to the ground. Mary left Frans and crawled to Sonia's side. While she was able to pull out the chunk of glass, she could do nothing to stop the bleeding and so tore off part of her shirt and pressed it into the laceration, trying to clot the wound. And there they sat for the symphony had, by that time, begun in full force, the artillery fire and the RPGs in a vile cacophony of outlandish sounds.

"We have to get you out of here," Mary shouted, "I'm worried the bleeding won't stop."

"Unless we can find an alternate route, we're stuck here until nightfall. No way we can dash across that intersection now," and with that, Mary left them, retracing their steps. She was familiar with the area. The media center was a short five-minute walk from the Bustan al-Diwan district, even if it was across the dangerous divide. Before she left, Sonia asked Mary to help her to her feet.

"Fine pair we are," Sonia said as she dropped back to the ground alongside Frans. "And fair warning. There'll be stiff competition for that bottle of whiskey once we get to the rectory," and they both laughed.

By Sonia's watch, Mary had been gone half an hour when finally, she saw her, in the distance, returning in the company of a Syrian army officer.

"Look who I found," Mary said as she got close enough.

"Yousef, oh my God, aren't you a welcome sight," Frans said, and Yousef helped him to his feet while Mary helped Sonia.

"He knows a way across the intersection, but it's a bit of a walk from here," Mary said.

"As long as it's safe, we don't care," Sonia said.

"Feeling better?" Mary asked.

"I'll be better when we're inside the rectory and can enjoy some slugs of whiskey."

"I'm with you there."

Yousef led them back almost to the middle of Bab Amr before heading north this time instead of due east, their original route, finally reaching the Old City then turning southwest until they arrived in

Bustan al-Diwan. And all the while, behind them, the bombs continued to fall, and buildings hit and huge chunks tumbling to the ground; gravel and particles spewing into the air like an erupting volcano and shaking the ground beneath them as they hurriedly made their way to the rectory.

Weary and distraught, Sonia was confused and a bit ashamed of herself for thinking ill of the number of families already settled into the rectory's reception hall, each having secured a section and cordoned it off with bedsheets, just as she had seen refugees do in the empty alcoves throughout the old souks. In one corner, a young Muslim girl tended to an elderly woman who appeared to be quite ill. In another, young parents, the woman in chador, trying to calm two cranky toddlers, and then there was the elderly man with a drooping gray mustache who, when he heard the commotion of new arrivals, poked his head out from behind his privacy curtain. When he saw it was Father Frans, he shouted loud enough for the others to hear, and they followed him to the corner when Frans, Sonia and Mary were busy claiming the last remaining space as their own.

"*Ahlan*, Father Frans, *Ahlan*," he said, wasting no time rummaging through the bags Sonia and Mary had hauled over from Bab Amr.

"*Al Hamdalillah,* you brought us food."

Annoyed that this man of somewhat dignified bearing would assume such a thing, Sonia approached him and said, "This is what remains of our food and..."

"And we'll be happy to share it with you," said Frans, ignoring the nasty glance Sonia had shot his way.

"ISIS is always showing up here and threatening us and insisting we give them food. When they come next time, and we don't have anything to give them, I'm afraid of what they'll do to us."

An old woman whom Sonia assumed was the man's wife popped her head out from behind the same curtain.

"We've a little rice and cracked wheat and some beans left, but that's all."

"And the others?" asked Frans.

"We're all hungry, especially that young family with the two little ones. It's one thing for us to go hungry but imagine how hard it must be for that mother to tell her children she has no food to give them. *Haram.*"

Based on common basic needs, Christians and Muslims had become each other's new families, and those who had taken refuge in the rectory were a perfect example, thought Sonia, of how the lines that had once defined religion and sect had become blurred. Along with everyone still in the Old City, these people, now shared a new identity—besieged—and with that came the now familiar sounds of shelling and suicide bombings, the absence of water, food, power and dignity.

"I was assured this morning that we'd be getting humanitarian assistance," Frans said.

"But Father, it was just on the radio. That aid convoy headed to the Old City came under attack. Apparently, mortar fire landed close to the convoy and wounded the driver, and the truck was turned around."

"But I don't understand," Frans insisted. "At al-Nusra's insistence, I'm the one who helped arrange it. Why would they have attacked the truck?"

"It wasn't al-Nusra, at least according to the radio. They gave another name, an al Qaeda affiliate group I'd never heard of before. Apparently, they control the area where the warehouse is located, and they're the ones who fired on the convoy."

"What are we supposed to do?" the old lady asked. "We can't go on like this."

"Maybe you should do what I do," said a ghostly figure of a woman with hollowed-out eyes, clothes drooping from a body shrunken from insufficient calories, who had just entered the rectory. "Every morning, I scan for shoots of green anywhere I can find them. Look at this one," she said, opening one hand and fingering a clump of basil-like leaves. "It's good with a bit of oil, and this one," opening her other hand and showing them some spiky purple and pale green sprigs that reminded Sonia of chicory. "These you can chop into little pieces, add a dash of salt and they become quite tasty."

Humbled and in awe of such tenacity, Sonia could only reply, "You're quite the proficient forager. How remarkable."

She winked at Sonia and said, "You should see what the rebels did around the corner. They planted a garden with tomatoes and herbs for themselves and their families. If I had access to such seeds and plants, I could feed the whole lot of you."

"How do you manage to walk around this neighborhood and not get shot by a sniper?" asked Frans.

"God watches over me."

"How could I not have known that," he replied, shaking his head.

When they had finally arranged their own space and unpacked their meager belongings, Mary examined Sonia's shoulder wound.

"You need stitches, no way it's going to heal otherwise. It'll get infected if we leave it like this."

"What do you propose we do, Mary? It isn't as if we could walk out of here and go to a hospital."

"I could try and stitch it," Mary said.

Sonia laughed. "Aren't you the Florence Nightingale, and it's not just slings and eye patches. You're now going to magically pull out thread and needle?"

"I am," Mary said, smiling. "I knew I was coming to a war zone and packed accordingly."

"I'm impressed," she said as she watched Mary thread the needle. "No offense, but I'll need a shot of whiskey before you begin."

It took seven stitches to close the gash. Every time Mary's needle pierced skin and weaved its way through muscle and tendon, Frans gave Sonia, in between her grimaces, a sip of whiskey. When the wound had been closed, however crudely, Mary pulled out a half-dozen band-aids from her bag and covered the wound.

When Sonia had sufficiently recovered, Frans suggested they show Mary where Joe was buried. Since their last visit, the winter-stunted little garden to which they had entrusted Joe's body had transformed itself into a resplendent carpet of green. Even the terebinth tree was in full bloom. Ahead of the others, Sonia stopped at the edge of the garden and stared.

"Where exactly did we bury Joe?" she asked.

"I thought it was there," Frans said, pointing, "just below the tree. We put a cross on top of his grave… and now it isn't here."

"It's not as if his body has disappeared," Mary said. "This garden isn't that big. Surely, we're in the approximate vicinity of Joe's grave."

"That's not the point, Mary. This is how bodies get lost over time. When we couldn't even find a coffin to bury Joe in, we had to do with putting him in the ground with only a cloth to ward off the usual elements that infest a buried body. It's the same in any war, I guess, where mass burial is the only option, but we erase that person's identity, and now, we don't even have a proper grave marker. It's only been three months, and we don't know where we buried his body. Even the bloody cross is gone. Okay, some poor old soul probably needed it for firewood, but the tragedy is that even a cross is no longer sacred."

"No sense bemoaning what we can't change," Frans said. "And if you two ladies don't mind, it's time I had a shot of whiskey to dull the pain in my arm."

"I could do with another one, too," Sonia said.

"I'll fetch the bottle, and then we'll offer a toast to Joe," Mary said. "Give me a minute," and she ran back into the rectory.

"Here we go," she said a few minutes later, holding up the bottle. "But we've no glasses."

"Not a problem," Frans said, grabbing the bottle and taking the long drink.

"Your turn, Sonia," Frans said, passing her the bottle, and then it was Mary's turn, and the two others watched as she took a long slug, then another and another.

"And now, if you two don't mind, I'd like some private time with Joe," Mary said. "I'd appreciate it if you went back inside and left me alone."

"Of course," Sonia said, aware the whiskey had already gone to Mary's head. As she lagged behind Frans, she could hear Mary talking to Joe, mentioning his lovely cock frozen in the ground and how much she missed the way he had touched her body and set it on fire and what a good match they'd made until he'd gone and gotten himself killed. Damn you for dying, Joe," she shouted. "I miss you so much."

"What's that she's mumbling?" asked Frans.

"Nothing you need to be concerned about," Sonia said, and she took hold of his good arm and led him inside.

When they had settled back into their private space, Sonia surprised Frans by bringing out a second bottle of whiskey. "Our reserve, your medicine and mine, Frans. It's here whenever you need it. I picked it up on one of my trips to visit Mary in the hospital."

"Bless you, dear lady."

"I'm a bit worried," Sonia said.

"About Mary?" asked Frans. "She's been acting a bit weird."

"That too, but about the aborted aid delivery. Do you think it will affect Omar's decision to leave the Old City?"

"Why would it? I did my part. I recorded the video in front of him. If he's mad, he should take it up with his ISIS buddies. I say we wait for the announced evacuation, then make contact with Andrew."

"And with Fouad," Sonia said, "since he's the one who'll be coordinating with the ambassador on his end."

Frans lifted the whiskey bottle and offered a toast. "To your health and safety, Sonia. Thank you for being here. It's made this tragedy a bit more bearable."

She smiled, took the bottle from Frans, and lifting her left arm, took a long sip.

"You know," said Frans, "you've never told me why it was so important you help Andrew."

"That's because I've done terrible things."

He thought for a moment, and a little drunkenly, said, "Are you confessing, Sonia?"

And when Frans said that, she realized she was talking not to her friend but to a Catholic priest.

"Yes, I guess I am. Bless me, Father, for I have sinned."

"When was your last confession?"

"I haven't been a practicing Catholic for years," she admitted in a hushed voice. "I betrayed Andrew and set up his fiancée, Nadia, to be kidnapped by Hassan Jaafar, who held her captive four years. I did this to get a scoop on the Rafic Hariri assassination."

"At the time, did you feel justified in doing this?" Frans asked.

"I knew when I agreed to set Nadia up, I was doing something terribly wrong, but I did it anyway. Getting a scoop for my story was more important to me than her well-being."

"I don't need to remind you how wrong that was, Sonia."

"I know, Father, and I also realize there's nothing I can ever do to make amends."

"You're trying to free Andrew, that's part of making reparations, and God will see that and forgive you, but don't expect those whom you've hurt to be so forgiving, although Andrew will surely be grateful."

"Being grateful isn't the same thing as forgiving."

"While certain things aren't forgivable, that doesn't mean we shouldn't forgive the wrongs of others, even though it's oftentimes the hardest thing in life to do. Hatred is self-destructive, and it's a heavy burden to carry. I hope Andrew and Nadia will come to realize that. That wasn't an easy thing to confess, Sonia," as he made the sign of the cross and gave her absolution for her sins. Sonia knew even a priest like Frans was capable of carrying her confession around in his head, and she wondered if, despite everything he said, he could forgive her treachery.

\*\*\*

After a week in the rectory, their food rations almost gone, and everyone afraid to step outside for the ISIS patrols eager to chop off heads and snatch up women, Sonia had never gone so long with barely enough to eat, and hunger, true physical hunger, brought out the worst in her. She was angry, mostly at Frans because unbeknownst to her, he had given away most of what they had left, and it was not just the people in the rectory he had shared their food with, it was any beggar who showed up at the rectory door.

"You simply can't give away our food, Frans. If you want to deprive yourself, that's one thing, but Mary and I have a right to that food, too."

Sonia glanced over at Frans sitting on the floor next to her, seeming oblivious to what she had just said. "Did you hear me, Frans? I said I was hungry, and you're the reason why."

At the seventy-two-hour mark, Sonia had felt her body begin to cannibalize itself. Depleted of sugar and fat, it had sought energy from other sources and turned to her protein reserves. And now, a week without food and no vitamin or mineral intact, her body's immune system began to shut down. Sonia had covered enough wars to know that people did crazy things when they were hungry. They resorted to eating rats and, in extreme cases, dug up and ate human remains. To prevent anything like that happening to Joe, Sonia went around the church grounds in search of and found a large piece of discarded mortar which she laid across his grave.

"God never refused the hungry beggar," Frans said.

"You're God-like, Frans, but you're not God, so you have no right to give away our food. If the ceasefire doesn't happen, what are we going to do?"

Frans finally looked at her and sheepishly raised his eyebrows.

"Exactly," she said. "And look at poor Mary, in her hunger she can hardly open her eyes her headaches are so severe. You'd better start doing some powerful praying, Frans."

Fouad's call came before dawn, waking Sonia from a severe hunger hangover. "It's official, darling."

"What is," she asked, her voice slurred.

"What's the matter, are you sick?"

"I'm hungry, Fouad. I haven't eaten in days."

"You'll be able to eat soon. The evacuation's just been announced, and you'll be coming home, and I'll be waiting for you with open arms."

With tears streaming down her cheeks, Sonia momentarily forgot her hunger, shook both Mary and Frans awake, grabbed his radio, stepped outside their curtain and turned up the volume for everyone in the rectory to hear.

"Thousands of Syrians trapped in the Old City of Homs without aid for the last eight months will be evacuated today in what is being described as a three-day humanitarian pause. The United Nations Emergency Relief Coordinator called today's operation a breakthrough and a small but important step toward compliance with international humanitarian law. Those evacuated today will be taken to the places of their choice, escorted by UN and Syrian Arab Red Crescent staff."

The firing had stopped. The silence felt eerie.

The medical clinic was a five-minute walk from the rectory and, with the announcement, Sonia thought it urgent she find Omar.

"Frans, we'll all go together. I want Andrew to have a look at your arm and ribs."

"I'd like that, too," he said.

"Good, we'll leave in five minutes."

With Mary leading the way, they arrived at the media center to find Omar talking to several of his men. When he saw the three of them, he broke away and joined them.

"The ceasefire's been announced. Have you told Andrew he's free to leave?" Sonia asked.

"No, but..."

"Why Omar?" asked Frans. "Is there some untoward behavior going on here, some reason you don't want to let Andrew go?"

Before Omar could say anything, Moussa, standing nearby, stepped forward when he heard the tone of the conversation. He knows something, Sonia thought. She picked that up from his facial expression and assumed from the way Omar and Moussa exchanged glances that Omar realized Moussa knew there had been something inappropriate in his behavior.

"I suggest you take us to him right now and tell him, in front of us, that you insist he return to Beirut where he belongs."

Omar stared at Sonia.

"Do it," she said, speaking in English so Mary would understand, "or I will make bloody sure you're handed over to the Syrian *Mukhabarat.*"

He gave Hassan, the new recruit, some instructions about how to download a new computer program and then led Sonia and the others out of the building and up the street to the medical clinic, the one Sonia had seen the night Joe had been mortally wounded and Mary brain-injured, and from where Andrew had refused to leave. What would he do this time, she wondered?

Sonia felt the nervous energy, the chaos, as soon as she stepped inside the building, the medical clinic in the basement, the families living quarters on the upper stories. In the lobby, she saw men, women, even children wandering around, seemingly in a daze about what was going on. Apparently, they, too, had just heard of the ceasefire but had no idea how or if it would affect them. She tried to put herself in their mindset. Most of them had come to Homs from other countries to support their Sunni brethren in their struggle against the Alawite infidel. Many of them would have lost loved ones. If given the opportunity, would any of them choose to leave, she wondered.

Sonia left them to ponder their plight while she and the others followed Omar down a long flight of stairs, shuffling from one side of the steps to the other to accommodate the occasional worker carrying up boxes until she reached the ground level. The clinic, off to her left, was brightly lit, and aside from a shelf full of instruments and medical supplies, there were but two examining tables and two chairs. There was a young man, badly wounded by the amount of blood Sonia saw, lying on one of them, and there was Andrew with a long straggly beard partially hiding his hollowed-out cheeks and slouching shoulders, manifestly oblivious to anything other than his patient, unaware of the flurry of activity around him. When he glanced up and saw Sonia, he did a double-take.

"What are you doing here?"

"I've come with good news, Andrew. The United Nations has arranged an evacuation. We're free to leave Homs, and I'd like you to walk out with me."

Andrew glanced at Omar.

"Yes, my friend," Omar said, his emotions clearly on display. "It's time you got back to your patients in Beirut. I've kept you here long enough. You're free to leave."

"Are you and your men leaving?" Andrew asked.

"No, this ceasefire agreement is a goodwill gesture on our part. If ISIS had already moved in, this would not be happening, but at least for now, we're still al-Nusra, and we believe in trying to win the hearts and minds of the locals and recruiting those who want to defeat the Syrian regime."

Mary raised her eyes to Heaven, and Omar frowned at her.

"We saw some pretty gruesome things in the souks, chopping off of hands, brutal treatment of children, torture. Those were ISIS atrocities. How can you say they aren't here yet?"

"What you saw were rogue units belonging to ISIS. They're the taste of what's to come. Consider yourself lucky you're getting out now."

Omar walked over to Andrew and gave him a bear hug. "You've been loyal to our cause. You're a great man, Andrew, with a kind heart, and I'm grateful to have known you. I'll miss you." And then, he pulled out Andrew's passport from his pocket and handed it back to him. "You won't get very far without this."

Sonia was taken aback. Even if she thought there was something nefarious going on, she did not expect Omar to exhibit his emotions so overtly.

"Omar, I'd like it if Moussa could come with me to Beirut," Andrew said. "We need someone like him in our Shatilla clinic," and Moussa, who had followed them down to the clinic, came forward to face Omar.

"Who am I to deny you this simple request, Andrew."

Sonia suspected his magnanimous gesture had little to do with Andrew. Omar was likely relieved to be rid of Moussa.

Fouad had told Sonia about Moussa and was both amazed and grateful at how diplomatically Andrew had handled that situation, for obviously Moussa had told him who he was and who had sent him. And then she wondered if Moussa had told him about Leila.

"Andrew, by the way, this is Mary O'Brien. She was Joe's girlfriend. She's a journalist, too, and she'll be recording this historic day for the world."

"And this is Father Frans, a Jesuit priest who has spent the last fifty-five years working with Christian communities throughout Syria. He's also the one who insisted I be here to cover this war. He was injured a week ago and has a very sore arm. Could you please check to see if it's broken? Mary made him a sling, but he may need something more stable."

"Why don't you hop on the table so I can have a look," Andrew said, as he carefully removed the sling and began to move Frans' arm. "Does this hurt?"

"Yes," he said, jumping, "but not as much as it did initially."

"It's not broken, just a bad sprain which, unfortunately at your age, will take a while to heal. I'd encourage you to gradually begin to move it. Keeping it stiff and in one place isn't a good idea."

"Do you have any meds you could give him?" asked Sonia. "He won't admit it, but he's still in quite a bit of pain."

"Certainly," and he went to his medicine cabinet and pulled out a box. "Here you go, Frans. Take one every four hours or as needed."

Frans nodded, then said, "Sonia, let Andrew look at your injury. A large piece of glass fell and embedded in her shoulder. Mary sewed her up, but I'm afraid it might be infected."

"If it isn't bothering you…"

Sensing his unwillingness to treat her, she said, "It can wait until I see a doctor in Beirut."

She saw Moussa go to the medicine cabinet and take something out.

"It'll be some hours before you reach Beirut. In case there's an infection, I suggest you rub some of this antibiotic ointment on the wound."

"Thank you, Moussa."

She suspected it was already infected. It was hot to the touch, and the slightest movement of her arm hurt.

"*Hakeme*," said Moussa, "why don't you go and pack. I'll take care of your patient, then join you upstairs."

Andrew nodded, left the room and climbed the stairs. Omar, Sonia and the others followed close behind.

When Sonia saw Andrew in better lighting, she was shocked by how frail he looked, how much weight he had lost, glaringly evident by the way his shirt and pants hung on him.

"I see you looking at me," Andrew said, "I can only imagine how bad I look, probably as bad as you, Sonia, especially with that silly bandana over your eye," and she laughed because she knew it was true. "And how badly we both smell and need a bath."

Given the gravity of the moment, Andrew had little to say, but then, quite unexpectedly, he broke down and cried. "I'm grateful for the rescue. Thank you."

Unsure how to respond, Sonia asked, "Would you like to visit Joe's grave?"

Without a moment's hesitation, he said, "I'd like that very much."

"You two go alone," Mary said. "I'm going to stick around here. I have some questions for Omar."

***

"I want you to know I still think you're a goddamn bitch, Sonia Rizk," Andrew began when they were alone in the street, "and just because I thanked you for freeing me doesn't mean I forgive you. You're single-handedly responsible for everything that's gone wrong in my life. I lost Nadia because of you. I'm here in large part because you set me up to work in Shatilla. I've repeatedly thought of strangling you, and believe me when I say I gave it serious consideration, but that won't happen. You deserve to die, but I won't be the one who kills you. I'll leave that to someone else. I can't speak for Nadia, but I'll never forgive you for what you've done. I've held those words inside my heart for a very long time. I'm glad I finally got them off my chest, and don't think I don't mean every word. I do."

Sonia nodded. "I understand, Andrew. I'm truly sorry, and I know better than to expect forgiveness. That would be too much to ask."

"Indeed, it would."

She knew those words sounded petty, but what else would he have been prepared to hear?

When they arrived at the rectory, Andrew followed Sonia to the garden where she invited him in.

"It was the most peaceful place we could find to lay him to rest. Just this week, I threw that piece of mortar over the grave to protect it. People were beginning to starve, and I was afraid of what they might do if they got hungry and desperate enough. I'll leave you alone for a few minutes," and she stepped outside the garden and watched as Andrew knelt in front of Joe's grave. She hoped he was asking Joe to forgive him for doubting his friendship. If he did, Joe would be pleased. He so loved Andrew.

Just then, Mary arrived with Moussa. "It's time to go."

"Where's Frans?" Sonia asked.

"He felt he'd already said his goodbye and asked that you didn't go looking for him. I think it would be too emotional for him."

Or maybe he was so disturbed by her confession he could not bear to see her.

Sonia, Andrew, Mary and Moussa were among the last of the twelve hundred, eight hundred of whom were Christians, to walk out of Homs. Some had been too weak or were still recovering from their injuries to walk a mile in the hot sun and were transported out by a cast-aside rickety old bus repurposed for the day. The more able-bodied men and women, relieved to be alive, walked alongside their children and grandchildren, some carrying suitcases, others pushing strollers filled with belongings too heavy to carry, and then there was Sonia, feeling like she was part of the great Exodus, freed from bondage and allowed to escape, and musing in her hunger and near physical collapse if God would part the waters of the Red Sea and allow them to pass.

Though no more words were exchanged between them, Andrew seemed satisfied to allow Sonia to walk alongside him while Mary went off on her own, taking photos and scribbling notes and interviewing people. At one point, she came looking for Sonia in tears.

"I just dropped my phone and broke its glass cover, and it won't turn on. What if I've lost…"

"There's nothing to worry about. Even if it has malfunctioned, a computer expert can extract all your data and, if necessary, transfer it to a new phone. We'll take care of it in Beirut. Here," Sonia said, giving Mary her phone, "Continue doing what you need to do, and if we lose track of one another, we'll meet up at the end."

There was also a brisk traffic of former residents on their way back into Bab Amr and the Old City, eager, Sonia assumed, to check on their homes and belongings. Some had perhaps come in search of loved ones they had not heard from but who had, in all likelihood, been kidnapped at gunpoint and taken in the bowels of the Old City, never to be heard from again.

Sonia saw Frans' neighbor, Madame Chidiac, and ran up to her.

"I'm glad I can thank you in person for the use of your apartment, but I've also bad news. A week ago, both your apartment and Frans' took a direct hit. I'm afraid there isn't much left of either."

"Given what's happened here, I didn't expect to find much, but I'm glad you're safe, and Father Frans?" And Sonia explained where he had taken refuge.

"I'll be sure to stop by and say hello before I leave again. We've only come to pack up what we can salvage. We've taken a flat near my sister in Damascus."

"I'm happy for you, Madame."

And as they walked on, the crowd of well-wishers grew. Television crews and live interviews began popping up along the route, people were cheering, and pretty soon, the twelve hundred evacuees began to sing the Syrian national anthem, and all the bystanders and well-wishers joined in.

Up ahead, Sonia caught a glimpse of Fouad waving his hands in the air. There was a sandy-haired American whom she assumed was the US Ambassador, and there were UN and Syrian Red Cross officials, too, all waiting to greet them.

Sonia was momentarily surprised when the ambassador warmly embraced Andrew, but then she remembered they had met in the rehab center in Broumana when Andrew was recovering from his injuries. If her memory served her right, they had even boxed together under Joe's supervision. There was the inevitable photo-op, too, and in this instance, a particularly poignant one—two Americans, one who had helped the other escape from al-Nusra. Every newspaper and TV channel across the US will eat up that human-interest story, thought Sonia. She was surprised, too, when she saw Jenkins and Mary together a bit later, talking as if they already knew one another, but then she was a journalist and often in Damascus and had perhaps interviewed him at one time.

When Fouad took Sonia in his arms and kissed and hugged her, despite of her need for a shower, and smelly clothes and filthy makeshift eye patch, she let go of her desperate appearance, her fatigue and aching legs, unaccustomed to doing so much walking, and let herself be smothered in love and attention.

When she saw the display of food and drink, she let go of Fouad and seated herself at the table. As she was about to put something in her mouth, Jenkins came and sat beside her. He introduced himself and his aide, John, and thanked her for helping coordinate Andrew's release.

"How did you know?" she asked.

"Andrew just told me," and when she turned to see where Andrew was, she saw him and Fouad hugging and talking. At least those two are reconciled. That's something to be grateful for, she thought.

Sonia turned her attention back to the food on the table, and as she was about to grab a container of *jallab,* Jenkins spoke up, "That's pure date syrup, Sonia. When the body reintroduces glucose back into its system after near-starvation, it can cause sudden shifts in the electrolyte imbalance and create a major stomachache. I suggest you try some *rumman* instead," he said as he reached across the table and grabbed a glassful. "Here," handing it to her. "Pomegranate juice, no sugar. A much better option, but drink it slowly, along with a dry biscuit or two. Grab a bunch and stick them in your bag and nibble on them on the way home."

And when it was time to take their leave, Jenkins said his goodbyes, and a UN representative escorted Sonia, Andrew, Moussa, Mary and Fouad to a waiting van. Sonia and Fouad climbed aboard first and grabbed the first row. And when it was Andrew's turn, he ignored them when he got on board and chose a seat at the back of the van. Mary and Moussa, already chatting, climbed aboard last and grabbed the seats closest to Andrew. For a journalist, it did not get any better, thought Sonia. Mary would have the next two-plus hours, the time it would take to reach Beirut, to do an in-depth interview with Andrew and Moussa about their time with al-Nusra. As the van pulled out of Homs, Sonia forgot her hunger, Andrew's anger, even Frans' unwillingness to say goodbye, and leaned into Fouad's chest and promptly fell asleep.

# CHAPTER EIGHTEEN

ON THE DRIVE BACK FROM HOMS to his official residence in Damascus, Robert pondered the afternoon's events and felt pleased with their every detail, even if he had had little to do with their overall execution except to show up and be photographed with Andrew. It was the UN and the Syrian Red Cross who had taken care to provide the necessary first aid and nourishment for the twelve hundred refugees who had walked out, many in desperate need of consoling and reassurance at a time when their lives were in upheaval. He had left it to John, his aide, to notify the media that an America recently held by al-Nusra would be among the evacuees. Keen to cover a heartwarming story for a change, they had shown up by the dozens talking into their television screens, their thick cables and sophisticated equipment scattered helter-skelter across the road, eager to hear first-hand from someone who had survived seven months as an al-Nusra prisoner. Jenkins had grown quite fond of John, a well-educated, thirty-something. In spite of the illegal activities he had dragged John into, whether the rally in Darra or the one in Homs, both in support of al-Nusra, John had remained steadfastly loyal and discreet. John had also witnessed him enduring a severe dressing down from Bashar, never questioning the whys or wherefores. Jenkins' father would have also been pleased by today's event. It was a highly emotional occasion, the kind of heart-wrenching scenes voters would remember—Robert Jenkins, an accomplished diplomat and patriot, a man of high moral character, freeing an American physician along with twelve hundred other refugees.

After his photo-op with Andrew, Fouad had introduced him to Sonia Rizk, the unsung hero, in his opinion, who had somehow managed to convince the head of al-Nusra to release Andrew from captivity. He was eager to know how she had accomplished such a feat, but given her state of fatigue and near starvation, he knew not to bombard her with too many questions. They could wait. He planned to spend some time in Beirut before leaving for the States, and he hoped, given time to recover, she would be amenable to a debriefing at that time.

When he had a more precise idea of his arrival time, Jenkins phoned Nadia, who anxiously awaited news of Andrew's release. Just how relieved, he was eager to gauge for himself. She had yet to convince him that she no longer loved Andrew. When his car pulled up in front of his residence, Jenkins barely had time to get out and thank John for his good work when Nadia came running out of the house.

"Oh Robert, you did it," she said as she flung her arms around him. "You got him released. I'm so grateful. I've already called my father to give him the good news. You can't imagine how worried he's been for Andrew."

"And you, were you worried?" Jenkins asked.

Ignoring his question, she turned her attention to John.

"Won't you come in for a drink? I'd love to hear your impressions of today's events."

"Thank you for the invitation. That's most kind of you. Unfortunately, I still need to stop by the embassy. I have some work to clear up before heading home."

"Well, I hope I'll see you again before Robert leaves his post."

"I'm bringing him with me to Beirut, so, yes, by all means, you'll see him again."

"Excellent, well then, John, good evening, and thank you for bringing Robert home safely."

Nadia hooked her arm under Robert's, and as soon as John closed the car door and started the engine, they walked into the house.

"Come, darling, let's sit in the garden," she said, steering him in that direction. "Nademe's prepare us some lovely hors d'oeuvres, and I've put some Champaign on ice."

"Is there some kind of celebration?"

"There certainly is, Robert. You not only succeeded brilliantly in Homs, you've officially resigned your post. Two good reasons to celebrate, don't you think?"

"If you say so, but I need to shower first. Homs was filthy and miserable," and as he turned to leave, he asked himself why he hadn't insisted Nadia join him in the shower, but alas, he knew the answer. Nadia's eyes had flashed with excitement, and he knew those sparks were not for him.

"Okay, but hurry, darling. I want to hear all about today."

Nadia caught his hand before he headed upstairs. "Robert, have I told you how proud I am of you?"

"No," he smiled, leaning in to kiss her. "Tell me now."

"You listened to advice not just from me but from you father, and you made some monumental decisions. Not many men in positions of power could have done that."

"I love you, Nadia."

By the time Robert joined Nadia in the garden, she had already served herself a glass of Champaign.

"I'm sorry, I was too excited to wait."

He sat in the chaise lounge next to Nadia's, stretched out his legs, adjusted the pillow and laid his head back. "Pour me some Champaign, darling."

Nadia handed him his glass, and he took a long sip. "I needed that… now, I can begin. Where would you like me to start?"

"With Andrew, of course. How did he look? Had he lost weight? Did he have a beard? Was he able to walk out, or did he need assistance?"

"He'd lost an awful lot of weight. In fact, I hardly recognized him, but then, I'd only known him that one time in Broumana, and yes, his beard was long and straggly, and he was filthy and in desperate need of a shower, as was everyone else. He was accompanied out by a woman named Sonia Rizk."

Nadia's demeanor changed immediately. Brows furrowed, she sat up in her chair, turned and faced Jenkins.

"What the hell was she doing in Homs?"

He shrugged his shoulders and stared defensively at her. "I think she'd been covering the war. According to Fouad, she'd been there the last seven months. He couldn't wait to get her home. Sounds like he's madly in love with her."

"Too bad Fouad doesn't have better taste in women. Sonia's a bitch. I wonder why he never mentioned their relationship to me."

"Sounds like it was a wise move on his part given your apparent dislike for the woman. Whatever you think of her, Sonia single-hand-edly managed to get Andrew freed. We owe her an enormous debt."

"Andrew is free because of Sonia? Are you sure?"

"Isn't that what I just said?"

"Yes. But I can't believe it. Did she tell you that?"

"As a matter of fact, no. It was Fouad who explained the details of her adventure."

"I hate that bitch, Robert. I'm sorry, but there are no two ways about it. I've wished her dead any number of times. There's no punish-ment harsh enough for all the wrong she's caused."

Jenkins was taken aback by Nadia's violent reaction. "What does Sonia walking Andrew out have to do with your dislike of her? Seems to me we're talking two different things."

"I don't know if I can explain it, Robert. It's as if her walking out with Andrew was a personal affront to my dignity that someone who committed such a grave act of betrayal to both Andrew and me would be the one who walked him out. She doesn't deserve that honor. Does that make sense?"

"It's best I don't try to make sense of what you just said. Suffice to say, I get that you really hate the woman."

"With every cell in my body."

"How do you even know her?"

"We'd been friends for years, at least I thought we had. Our parents were close. She and I attended American University of Beirut together. We had the same circle of friends, and all along, she was the ultimate snake in the grass. She had an affair with my husband Elie before we married, and it was only later that I found out it continued during our marriage. She arranged to have me kidnapped by Jaafar. She ruined my life with Andrew. There, you have all the sordid details. Now I hope you understand."

"What I get, Nadia, or more accurately what I hear, is that you're still in love with Andrew. You make that abundantly clear."

"I already told you we'd gone our separate ways."

"That's not the same as saying 'I don't love Andrew anymore.'"

"Let me give you some more details so you can better understand why I feel this way. I had not been with another man for thirteen years when I met Andrew. When my husband Elie was finally declared legally dead, I finally permitted myself to fall in love with Andrew. Sonia had had a brief affair with him some twenty-five years earlier, and even though she had been the one to end it, she still loved him, as much as Sonia is capable of loving any man. When she discovered Andrew and I were to be married, she planned her furious revenge. She initiated contact with Jaafar, who confirmed Elie was still alive in a Syrian prison, knowing I would try to free him once I found out. She arranged my meeting with Jaafar, whom I had not seen since I had broken off our courtship some sixteen years earlier. I told you about my brief time with Jaafar when you accompanied me back to Beirut. Do you remember?"

"Yes, I remember everything you said that day, but there was never any mention of Sonia."

"Our discussion had been about Jaafar. You'd wanted to know how I knew him."

Jenkins was relieved to see Nademe come out of the kitchen carrying a tray full of food. He needed a few minutes to compose himself after Nadia's rant.

"More food, Nademe? We've only just begun to eat your smoked salmon canapes, which are divine. What are you bringing us now?"

"Shish taouk fresh off the grill, a green salad and a bottle of that white wine from Lattakia that you like."

"Splendid. Why don't you head off to bed now? It's rather late. We'll bring the dishes into the kitchen when we've finished."

"Thank you, sir. That's very kind of you... well, good night," and she walked back inside.

And turning to Nadia, he said, "You were telling me about Jaafar."

"Yes, he claimed to still love me and insisted he'd own me if I attempted to free Elie from prison, which I eventually did. I told you about that, too."

"Yes, you did."

"And that's when Sonia and Jaafar planned my abduction. There was one attempt when we were in south Lebanon together during the Israeli-Hezbollah war and the final one at my parent's home. So yes, I despise Sonia for what she did. She purposely threw me into the clutches of Hassan Jaafar, knowing he would turn me into his whore and someone Andrew would no longer want."

"How did you know that?"

"Andrew and I met once after my release. His immediate reaction, when he saw me, was disappointment, confusion. I'd begun to dress like Jaafar wanted me to in tight dresses, higher hemlines, more make-up, and Andrew had loved me for my natural beauty, at least that's what he said. More importantly, I knew in my heart that I'd changed. I wasn't the same Nadia. I resisted Jaafar's advances for the first two years. He respected that and never forced himself on me. When I finally agreed to sleep with him, it was because I wanted information about Sonia and the car bomb that caused her to lose her eye. I knew that if I agreed to have sex with him, he would tell me everything. It was then that I changed from a woman with a certain innocence into Jaafar's whore. I hated myself for that and so made every attempt to send Andrew away when we met. When he said he was in love with another woman, I was actually relieved. I'd met the woman when we were in south Lebanon. She was pure and as noble and as solid as he was, and

I couldn't have been happier for them, and that's how we ended our relationship."

"It's selfish of me to say this, but I'm also relieved to hear that Andrew loves another woman. In my mind, it makes me think you'll eventually come to fully love me. What I just said may not make any sense, but I'll grab onto any molecule of hope. But back to us, Nadia. I didn't fall in love with Jaafar's whore. I fell in love with a beautiful woman who quite literally swept me off my feet the first time I laid eyes on her. The same woman who spoke to me of possible war crimes if I continued my mission and who was responsible, in large part, for helping me turn my life around."

"The business with Sonia has nothing to do with you and my feelings toward you, Robert."

"Oh, but it has, Nadia. Your hatred has turned you into someone I don't know. I get that Sonia ruined that period of your life when you loved Andrew, but that was five years ago. In the meantime, we've met. You've become a major influence in my life. Put the past to rest. Discard your old baggage. Anger is a destructive force, and in the end, it'll only destroy you. Until recently, I'd spent most of my life angry at an absentee-father only to discover he had every reason to stay away."

"Why was that, Robert?"

"My mother's frequent affairs. She was lonely, and she was a romantic, a woman who had always had men in her life fawning over her. My father was not like other men. He loved her in his own way, I know that now, but he was never able to show it or play her romantic lover, something she desperately wanted. When he couldn't give it to her, she went looking for it elsewhere."

"How sad."

"Yes, he truly loved her, and by the time he was ready to tell her that it was too late. We have something beautiful going on between us, darling. You've said so yourself. Don't let anger spoil it. You're not ready to call it love, but I am, and I trust, in time, that you'll come to feel the same way. You've hinted as much, or have you completely fooled me?"

"Of course not, my darling."

Robert still was not sure. She admired him. That was a far cry from loving him.

Nadia got up from her chair and sat alongside him in the chaise lounge.

"Before we met, I'd spent four years in captivity, four years that were stolen from my life, four years that turned me from an innocent woman into someone I never wanted to become. I'm ashamed for what I've done."

"But that's not who you are now, Nadia. I've proposed marriage because I love the Nadia I know. In your head, you imagine someone else. It's simply not true. You had bad four years. According to you, you did some pretty awful things, but bad things don't change who a person is. Look at me. I've gone from someone who's done despicable things, including assassination plots, to killing a man in cold blood, to killing Syria's Intelligence Czar. If it weren't for you, Nadia, I wouldn't have changed. I would have continued doing exactly what I was doing, my government's dirty work—training insurgents to take down regimes the US no longer favored. I was a monster. You've turned me into a respectable person and brought out my innate goodness, the quality my mother instilled in me but one I had forgotten. Bad behavior doesn't change what's in a person's heart and soul. You're still the original, authentic and pure Nadia Khoury I want as my partner. You've been liberated from that dreadful period in your life." Jenkins laughed. "The irony is that I killed Jaafar, and that act of murder released you from bondage. I want to bury those deeds, make the past the past and move on and help you rejoice in who you are now, Nadia, the brilliant international lawyer, the lady who convinced me to resign my post and do something meaningful with my life. Why can't you see that and accept my love?"

"I've not refused your love, Robert, I embrace it with all my heart," and as she said that, she laid her head in his chest and cried. "I'm sorry, darling. I let my anger get the best of me. I've ruined a beautiful celebration. The last time I saw Andrew, the day I said goodbye to him, he said that Sonia's loss of her eye was karma enough for all the awful things she'd done. He was right, and maybe I had to spew out my anger just now to get it off my chest so I could move on and embrace your love. I'm going to work very hard at doing that, Robert."

"I hope so, silly woman."

As much as he hoped Nadia meant everything she said, there was still a lingering doubt as to her sincerity. What was the saying? He could only remember the gist of it—when someone insists too much about something, the opposite of what they are saying is likely true.

"Maybe I need some serious love-making to get me started," she smiled, looking up at him.

"I can take care of that right away," and as they stood to go in, they heard the phone ring. Robert looked at his watch. It was already nine-thirty.

"Who could be…"

Nademe, in her nightshirt and slippers, shuffled out of the house as fast as she could. "It's President Assad," she whispered excitedly as she handed him the phone.

"Thanks, Nademe, why don't you go back to bed. I'll be sure to bring the phone back in."

"Greetings, Bashar, and congratulations. The ceasefire went off brilliantly, as did the evacuation. It was a magnanimous gesture on your part to have agreed to the ceasefire, but you should have been there with me. The entire world saw twelve hundred people walk out of Homs, thanks to you, Bashar, and…"

"The ceasefire didn't hold, Robert."

Jenkins put the call on speaker phone, so Nadia could hear.

"What are you talking about?"

"As you know, all parties had agreed to a pause in hostilities for three days. I thought I'd put all necessary mechanisms in place, but this evening the army saw snipers taking up their usual positions and al-Nusra moving arms into new neighborhoods, at least that's what I've been told, and well, someone from Army command gave the orders to open fire, and the battle for the control of the Old City ignited all over again. Thankfully, anyone who had wanted to leave had already left, but according to the army, there are a few hundred people still there, by their own choice, mind you, but even if I wanted to intervene to save them, I couldn't. Al-Nusra isn't going to listen to me now."

"I wonder if it isn't ISIS insurgents who broke the ceasefire. They'd been edging their way into Homs and the Old City."

"It doesn't matter who it was. The damage is done."

"Can't the UN help?" Jenkins asked.

"Kofi Annan was so disgusted he's packed up his bags and left town."

Jenkins was glad that Andrew had gotten out and that he had been there to greet him. That photo op had put him on every newspaper across America according to his father, who had phoned him from Boston when he was on his way back to Damascus. Not only that, influential people across Massachusetts had phoned to pledge their financial support for his senatorial race should he decide to run. To what extent would the failed ceasefire affect their donations, Jenkins wondered? Not one iota. It was not his fault the warring parties had renewed their hostilities. In their eyes, he had freed an American from the grips of al-Nusra. Nothing else mattered.

"My resignation is official, Bashar, but I'll be here a few more days. If I can help in any way, please don't hesitate to call."

"Thanks, Robert, and good luck with your plans. Keep me posted."

"I will, Bashar. You do the same. We talked a lot about our mutual aspirations when we were last together. You have a fair share of things to do for your people, and most of them will be a challenge, so good luck to you, too. Goodbye, my friend."

After their last encounter, when they had spoken frankly and said what they had had to say to clear the air between them, he felt they had, finally, formed a bond, one that would continue well into the future. Syria needed a leader like Bashar, but he would have to work very hard to be that leader for his people.

"That's tough," said Nadia. "A ceasefire is only as good as the two parties who agree to it."

"Yes, all it takes is one small mistake to spoil everything. It won't be easy for Bashar to calm things back down."

"Certainly not. If, on a microcosmic level, he can't maintain a ceasefire, imagine on the macrocosmic level how impossible it will be to establish peace, especially if both regional and Western powers have different agendas for how they want the conflict to end and who they want left standing."

"And sadly, if they have their way, it won't be Bashar Assad."

"Thankfully, that impossible task won't fall on your shoulders, darling. You'll be out of here soon, and you won't have to worry about what happens here."

"That's not true. I care deeply about what happens here, especially since much of it's down to me. I helped plan the uprising. I trained the insurgents. You know the sordid details. I don't need to repeat my crimes."

"No, you don't."

"I have a lot invested here, my entire career, in fact, and on some level, even if I now see things differently, I would have wanted to somehow turn things around, given Bashar the tools to end the war, and leave on a positive note, having accomplished something good."

"What are you talking about? You got an American out. That's all anyone in the US will remember. Do you think Americans care what happens here? How many people have died in a war their government manufactured? Sadly, most of them wouldn't even be able to find Syria on a map."

The phone rang again. Jenkins thought it might be Bashar and picked up on the second ring.

"Robert..."

"Father, is everything all right?"

"Sorry, Son, I realize it's late there, but I've great news."

Robert again put his iPhone on speaker mode so Nadia could listen in.

"Senator McEnany has just announced he's been diagnosed with pancreatic cancer and is stepping down. I'm sorry for the man, but now the field's wide open for you, Son. Are you in? Can I move forward with our plans?"

"I'm in a hundred percent, Father. I even have the man I'll need to help me as I embark on this new career. He's my aide, John Jones, here at the embassy. I'm going to steal him away from the foreign service. He's personable, a quick learner and handsome—all valuable traits for a member of my soon-to-be-formed senatorial campaign. I've also found the perfect woman to be by my side. In fact, I've just finished having dinner with her. I'm trying to convince her to marry me. She's not only beautiful, she's an international lawyer and sits on the UN Commission for Human Rights."

Jenkins glanced over at Nadia. He was pleased to see her smiling.

"With your consent, I'd like to invite her to join us for Easter."

"By all means, I very much want to meet this woman. Like your mother, I've waited a long time to see you married and settled down."

Nadia spoke into the phone. "Since I'll be in New York at the UN, I'll definitely join you two for Easter. I'm eager to meet you, too. Robert has spoken very highly of you."

"That's a surprise," he said, and they all laughed and said their goodbyes.

"Will you also come to Boston when I launch my senatorial race?"

"Of course, my darling. I wouldn't miss it for the world."

"Speaking of busy schedules and future plans, I'll be heading back to Beirut tomorrow morning," she said. "I have some affairs to put in order before I leave for New York."

"Is that imminent? Maybe we can travel to the States together."

"I don't see why not. When you come to Beirut, we'll sit down and coordinate our travel plans. Any idea when you'll be coming?"

"I need at least two or three more days here to tie up loose ends and clean out my office."

"Good, that'll give me time to plan a little retirement party for you."

"I'd like that... but didn't you say you needed a little love right now?"

"I did," and he took her hand and led her inside and up the stairs to their bedroom.

Robert kissed Nadia deep and hard before he began undressing her. By this time in their lovemaking, she would have already begun undressing him, and when they were close to full arousal, they would have soared to the stars together and after, and when she'd caught her breath, she'd have burst out laughing, feeling satisfied, but she felt none of that this time. Her head was somewhere else. And when she would have normally nestled into his arms and fallen asleep, she turned her back to him and pretended to fall asleep. And as he lay his head on his pillow, thinking Nadia might believe she had been a good actress and fooled him, she had not. He had felt her lack of engagement, and it hurt him. She needed time. Once she committed to him, he thought, she would be his forever. Hadn't that been what she had done with Jaafar. She so much as said so when she described her rapport with him. Her relationship with Andrew had been different. Theirs had been true love, and this was the obstacle Robert was up against, what he had to convince her to relinquish if he was to finally win her heart.

# CHAPTER NINETEEN

THE DOORBELL RANG, and before Ani had time to answer, Nadia ran down the stairs and opened it. "*Bonjour,* Fouad, come in for a minute. Father wants to say hello before we leave."

Nadia no more than said Victor's name than he walked out of his study. "*Ahlan,* Fouad, I thought I heard your voice," greeting him in Arabic along with the customary kiss on each cheek. "I didn't get a chance to present my condolences. I was very sorry to hear about Joe."

"We all were…such a senseless death," Nadia said.

Fouad sighed. "I still can't believe he's gone. He was my best friend… and there was no better counterterrorism expert. His passing is a great loss."

"Speaking of good friends, how's Andrew doing?" Nadia asked. "It can't be easy for him, either, going back to that apartment where Leila was killed and where he and Joe had lived."

"He's surprisingly resilient, as only Andrew can be. We took a long walk along the beach yesterday afternoon. We talked and healed old wounds for which I'm grateful, and he got a lot off his chest, too. He's actually going back to work tomorrow. He doesn't know it yet, but Aziza has planned a welcome home party. I wouldn't be surprised if the entire camp didn't show up. Everyone there loves Andrew. I think he'll be quite pleased."

"No doubt," Nadia said, glancing at her watch. "*Yallah.* We'd better go. I made the reservation for 1:30. As hostess, I really should be there first."

"Carol and I will join you later for dessert," Victor said.

"Why not come with us now?" said Fouad.

"Oh, we'll let you young people have lunch together. We really just wanted to see Andrew and welcome him home… and say goodbye to Robert. Nadia told us he's moving to Boston. That'll be quite a change of pace for him."

Fouad nodded dismissively. "How's Moussa doing?"

"He's relieved to be back. Homs was terrifying. By the way, he's the one who told Andrew about Leila's death. Andrew forced his hand, but he didn't reveal any of the ugly details."

"I hope no one will," and looking at her watch again, Nadia said, "Let's go, Fouad. *A toute à l'heure,* Papa."

No sooner were Nadia and Fouad enclosed within his Mercedes and the engine hummed and the radio blared Lebanese pop music, than Nadia began to cry. "I'm sorry, I'm in such a muddle about what to do. There's so much going on, and I'm confused, and I couldn't hold it in another minute. The music, Fouad, it's a bit loud. Can you turn it down, please?"

He lowered the music with a button on the steering and asked, "What's bothering you."

"I hardly know where to begin. An hour ago, I got a call from the UN General Secretary. He wants to name me Special Rapporteur for Human Rights in the Levant."

"That's incredible news, Nadia. Congratulations. But wait, now I'm the one confused. What's so terrible about his offer?"

"Nothing. Wait." She wiped tears away from her face. "There's Andrew, and then there's our plan to bring down Robert. I can't go through with it anymore."

He looked at her aghast. "Hey, nothing can be that bad. Tell me. Maybe I can help."

"I'm a nervous wreck," sniffling while pulling a Kleenex from her purse and blowing her nose.

"I can see that."

"Yes, well, about Andrew. I wanted so badly to see him, but now I'm petrified. I wasn't nice to him the last time we met. In fact, I was downright ugly. What if he shuns me, Fouad? What if he doesn't want to see me?"

"You've nothing to worry about. Andrew will be very happy to see you."

"How do you know that?"

"Trust me. And he knows you took care of arranging Leila's burial in her village. He was very touched."

"Poor man, he's been through so much."

"Yes, he has."

"My bigger problem is Robert. After he killed Jaafar, you and I set out to bring him down, destroy him, make him pay for his crimes, not just Jaafar's but all the others, but I can't do it anymore. My relationship with him has gotten way out of control. Besides, in the strictest sense of the word, he has already been brought down."

"How do you figure that, Nadia? Has he stood trial for his crimes?"

"No, but he recognizes he did wrong and wants to make amends for his past mistakes."

"Bullshit, no one changes that radically. He's playing with you, Nadia."

"No, Fouad, it's worse. He's in love with me. He wants to marry me."

"How did you let that happen?"

"I didn't purposely let anything happen. It just happened. Apparently, I have this habit of bonding with men I spend time with. It's not intentional and appears to happen only if I discover they have a decent side to them. I was devastated when my husband Elie got arrested only to find out he was a scoundrel, so I never bonded with him. In fact, I should never have married the bastard, but, as you know, I accepted his proposal because Jaafar kept insisting I marry him. And then, under entirely different circumstances, I spent four years as his prisoner where

I found him engaging and likable and finally ended up bonding with him. I even mourned his death, for heaven's sake. The only natural, spontaneous thing I ever did was fall in love with Andrew. And now I have this dilemma with Robert to deal with.

"I didn't set out to change him, Fouad. I was supposed to help you bring him down, have him arrested and tried in a court of law. Instead, our relationship became more complicated as I began to spend more time in Damascus, finally discovering I enjoyed being with him, even when I still believed I was playing the good cop to a villain. I never suspected he'd fall in love with me. I assumed he treated our relationship as a fling, as I did, me just another of his many women. We spent a lot of time discussing his work. I listened to his perceived justifications for regime change and warned him he'd be tried as a war criminal if he continued. He knew my area of expertise was international law, and the more we talked, the more he began to see things from my perspective. And then, when his mother died, he was reunited with his father, and that, too, changed him, especially when he discovered they had both been doing their government's dirty work. His father had just retired, and influenced by his decision, Robert decided to do the same. Apparently, men in high-level positions of government and intelligence services assume they don't have to pay for crimes committed. He honestly believes he can walk away from his past, announce he's turning over a new leaf as a way of repaying society for wrongs done, and go on with his life. His goal is to change his government's foreign policy in the Middle East. And now, he wants me to marry him and be part of this next phase of his life."

"Okay, maybe I'm going to ask a stupid question, but what's wrong with that? I know any number of men who could easily fall in love with you, including myself, if I wasn't already taken."

"I'm flattered, Fouad."

She had to hold back from saying, And what an awful choice you've made, my friend. She wondered if Fouad had any idea how reprehensible Sonia was.

"Do you love him enough to do that, Nadia?"

"No," she said, crying harder. "There's only one man I truly love, and you know who that is, but that's an affair I'll never be able to re-kindle. As for Robert, let's just say I've grown fond of him, and with time I may come to love him. I've essentially promised as much. It's the only fair thing to do. He's trying so hard to win my love I don't want to hurt him."

"I've never heard anything more absurd in my life, and coming from you, of all people. Fair? Fair is having him tried for his crimes. The bas-tard doesn't deserve you. Let him go back to Boston. Tell him you'll follow him, if you need to tell him anything, and then cut off the rela-tionship once he's gone. Simple. *Halas.* I said I'd help, and *voila,* I have.

"To me, fairness means being honest, Nadia, and you're not doing that. He loves you. That's his privilege, but he doesn't own you. You're afraid to tell him the truth because you don't want to hurt him? That's not a reason to sacrifice your life for someone you don't love. I can't believe I have to tell you these things. It's as if you've thrown logic out the window when it's clear as day what you have to do."

"Oh Fouad, were it that easy. I admire what he's done and what he plans to do. He wants to be the next senator from the State of Massa-chusetts."

"God almighty. That's all the world needs. Another dirty intelli-gence officer turned politician. The man's a criminal, Nadia. He's plot-ted assassinations. I've read the dossier you gave me. His attempt on the Lebanese cleric's life alone killed dozens of people. Have you for-gotten that? When we were still in the CIA together, I saw him beat the shit out of a would-be-robber in Georgetown, then leave him for dead. He trained throat-slitting insurgents and sent them to Syria. The guy's got no redeeming qualities, Nadia. None."

"But there's another side to Robert now, a man who wants to right his wrongs. How can you fault someone who admits to wrongdoing and then decides to reverse course? 'Virtue never tested is no virtue at all.'"

"In my book, virtue is defined by moral excellence and ethical principles. Robert possesses neither, never did, never will."

"Possibly… it just adds to the confusion," and as she spoke, she pulled down the visor and inspected herself in the mirror. "Oh my God, Fouad, pull the car over. I need to fix my face. I can't let anyone see me like this."

"I don't know why you paint your face, Nadia. You're naturally beautiful. You need none of it."

"Men always say that."

And as she began to apply her make-up, an old man riding a donkey passed by her window. He was holding a plastic carrier bag from Spinney's Supermarket. Their contrasting circumstances suddenly embarrassed her, and as soon as he passed, she pulled out a wet wipe from her Chanel purse and rubbed off her eye make-up and the rouge from her cheeks until she looked more like the woman Andrew had once loved. Luckily, the dress she had chosen for the luncheon was something Andrew would have liked—black, elegant and stylish, yet simple—the same style dress she had worn when Andrew first laid eyes on her. She had also decided to let her long auburn hair flow across her shoulders the way he liked. Was this a conscious choice she made, she asked herself? She sighed with confusion and asked Fouad to drive on.

Nadia had chosen the Manara Palace Café along the Corniche just across from the sprawling grounds of the American University of Beirut. It was a restaurant popular with the locals for its high culinary standards but also for the way it took care to treat its guests with fine table linens, silver flat wear and china and, important to Nadia's taste in fine dining, flowers on every table. She had reserved their oval table closest to the sea in the quietest corner in the restaurant where her guests could be seated comfortably and enjoy the view along the coast. Concerned about any awkwardness Robert might feel toward Andrew and the confusion of her guests trying to decide what to order, she had gone ahead and chosen not only the mezze ahead of time to include her seasonal favorite—octopus cooked in its black ink—but her favorite fish dish, Samak Harra—sea bass cooked in hot peppers, onions, cilantro, tomatoes, walnuts, pomegranate molasses and tahini sauce, followed by knafeh—a shredded pastry with cheese filling—and a chocolate mousse cake, Robert's favorite.

After Nadia was greeted and fussed over by the owner, a close friend of her parents, she and Fouad followed the *maître d'* as he threaded them past tables with women elegantly dressed in heels and brightly colored silk confections, the men, tie-less, in dress slacks, casual sport jackets and Gucci loafers, to their table and there, to her surprise, sat Andrew. She had been as nervous as an adolescent on her first date at the thought of seeing him again. Yet, when he took her in his arms and kissed her cheeks, she marveled at how natural it felt, two lovers once engaged to be married, hearts throbbing, finally united, and she knew he felt the same by how tightly he held her. She gently pulled away, and with eyes flooding, examined him more closely. He had aged, and why wouldn't he have, she thought, after all he had been through, but beard gone and clean-shaven, he was still as handsome as the day they had met, yet there was both deep sorrow and wisdom there now, too, and she could only imagine what the death of Leila had done to him.

"You're as beautiful as the first time I saw you," he said and, obviously aware of how closely she was examining him, added, "I know. I've lost quite a bit of weight, but I'll make every effort to regain it—starting today."

Nadia laughed, feeling shy and happy, and thought how sharp and perceptive he had become, but she only said, "I've no doubt."

Before the other guests arrived, she invited him to sit on the opposite side of the table, facing her, and as she took her place, she glanced at Fouad, who had already taken his to the left of Andrew. He was smiling at her knowingly, which made her face feel hot. She glared at him.

"Robert and his aide, John, will be joining us, and so will my parents later, for dessert."

"I'm glad," Andrew said, not able to take his eyes off her. "I've missed them and your siblings, where are they now?"

"Maya's taken a job with an advertising firm in London, and Paul has taken over my father's law firm. Needless to say, Papa is thrilled that the family name will live on."

"And you, Nadia, what are your plans?"

"Oh, she has big ones," Fouad said, "she's just been offered…"

"Good afternoon, everyone," Robert said, announcing his arrival as he approached the table with John, his security aide, close behind. When he saw Andrew seated opposite Nadia, he remarked, as he kissed Nadia on the cheek, "Looks like I should have come earlier to get the best seat," and extending his hand, leaned across the table and shook Andrew's, and then Fouad's.

"Robert, why don't you sit here," Nadia said, pointing to her right, "And John, next to Robert. My parents will be joining us later, and I thought I'd let them sit here," pointing to her left. "They like sitting near the water."

"Very well," said Robert. "How are you, Fouad? I barely had time to talk to you in Homs."

"Much better now that we have Andrew back home."

"Have you taken time to rest?" Robert asked Andrew.

"A few days, but I start back to work tomorrow."

"Why the hurry? You deserve a bit of time off after what's you've endured."

"I admit the last seven months have been crazy, but I need some normalcy back in my life."

"I get that, but to be honest, I don't understand why you aren't calling it quits here and heading back to the States. Life is much calmer and more predictable there."

"My life's here now. Besides, after living here for so long, I'd probably find it boring."

"I hope that won't be my case. I'm headed home soon, but you probably already know that from Nadia."

Nadia was glad Andrew simply nodded his head. She did not want any confrontation between the two men, especially since it was likely Robert would have been the one to initiate it. She could already sense his jealousy with every word he spoke.

While the waiters filled the table with mezze plates with everything from tabbouleh to hummus with spicy ground lamb to muhammara, batata harra and beetroot dip, octopus and grilled shrimp, the maître d' offered Nadia's guests the choice of either arak or wine.

"What's a mezze without arak," said Andrew. "A tall glass for me, please, and look at all this food. I can't remember the last time I had anything good to eat."

"Arak for me, too," said Fouad, and Robert and John followed suit. "And Andrew, I suggest you try the octopus before I eat it all. It's a delicacy you'll only find in the spring of the year."

When everyone had been served, Nadia lifted up her glass, and as she was about to propose a toast, Sonia and Mary walked up to the table.

"Hello, everyone. May we join you?" Sonia asked.

Robert stood and said, "Of course, my dear, so glad to see you again."

"No," said Nadia, her bellowing voice clashing with the sound of a wave breaking against the seawall alongside their table. The wave had drowned out the severity of her tone. Calmer and with more dignity, she looked Sonia in the eye and said, "You may not join us."

People at nearby tables looked on, embarrassed. Another wave crashed.

Nadia was aghast at Sonia's unhealthy pallor, and her black eye patch only contributed to her careless appearance and unkempt hair. She almost pitied her, almost enough to say she could join them. Her weight loss was exaggerated, too, by the clothes she wore, half falling off her shoulders and her face, aged beyond her years, the wrinkles around her eyes and mouth particularly noticeable.

Nadia caught Andrew looking at her. He gave a gentle nod of his head as if to say, "it's all right. We can do this, you and I," before he said simply, "Nadia, why don't we just let bygones be bygones."

"And all those wrongs?"

He closed his eyes and shook his head. He politely overrode her objections and raised his hand to call the waiter. "Please set two more places."

"And I'm sorry I didn't get a chance to talk to you ladies in Homs," Robert said. "Perhaps we could find time this afternoon."

Whether an act of retaliation or plain jealous spite for her attention to Andrew, Nadia could not tell, but she was furious that Robert would so blatantly offer the woman he knew she hated such a conciliatory gesture.

"Of course," Sonia said, looking at Fouad for moral support after being so publicly humiliated. Fouad glanced at Nadia as if to say, "shame on you," and knowing how much courage it had taken for Sonia to walk up to their table and ask to be seated, he took her hand and kissed it. "And Mary, how about you?" he asked. "Would you be free to meet with Sonia and Robert after lunch?"

"It would be my honor to speak with the ambassador. We met briefly a few months ago in Damascus, but since then, I've compiled a lot more questions. I'm delighted to be given this opportunity."

"Well then, that's settled," Robert said. "Would you ladies care for some arak?"

"Gladly," Sonia said. Robert stood, and from the carafe the maître d' had left on the table, served Sonia and Mary.

When he sat back down, Nadia gave him a piercing stare. "You've got quite a nerve humiliating me like that," she whispered. "You know how I feel about that woman."

"As Andrew so justly said, it's time you put the past to rest."

"I'll be the judge of that, Robert, not you, nor anyone else."

"Not even Andrew?"

"Don't."

Poor Robert, even she did not think she would be so emotionally overcome by Andrew's presence. He felt the same way, too. She saw it in his eyes. What should she do with this rush of emotions? Was she to sacrifice her feelings to satisfy Robert or grab hold of the only man she had ever loved and run with him? The choice was easy, she concluded, but how to do it without hurting Robert? He had just given her an opening, hadn't he, when he had contradicted and humiliated her in front of her friends? Indeed, he had, and now, if she so chose, she had an excuse to break off her entanglement.

Robert stood, glass in hand and proposed a toast.

"As most of you know, I've recently resigned my post as ambassador. Syria has been both good and bad for me. On the negative side, I didn't do a very good job. Regime change was rigged from the outset, and that left little room for me to maneuver, and because of orders I was given by my government, I managed to create havoc and make myself an unwelcome guest of the Syrian government. In the end, the only positive I take away from Syria is the relationship I developed, against all odds, with Bashar Assad. My parting hope is that he survives. Syria needs a man like him. I say that as a person with full knowledge of what my government still has in store for Syria and with full knowledge that what I'm saying and will continue to say endangers me."

This is like a confession to exactly the right people, Nadia thought, and she admired him for having the courage to say it when it put his life in jeopardy. But where did his speech put her in her thinking? Clearly more conflicted, her mind flailing about in turmoil. Maybe she should forget the UN position, she thought, and the manner in which he had just humiliated her and agree to become a senator's wife. Didn't she owe that to a man of such bravery and conviction? Maybe, but could she love him?

Nadia watched Fouad as Robert spoke and, at a certain moment, caught his eye. With a nod and raised eyebrows, she managed to say, "See, I told you he was serious."

"In fact," Robert continued, "I muddied the waters quite a bit as my government's foot soldier, but I hope to be given a platform back home to turn those mistakes around. My immediate plan is to take a short break, a bit of R&R with my family in Boston, before launching what I hope will be the next phase of my life, a run for the Senate from the State of Massachusetts."

Nadia's guests politely applauded. There was Andrew, probably relieved Robert was leaving the area. Fouad, who would have preferred to see him go to prison. Sonia and Mary, both journalists, eager for a scoop on his motives and regrets as he moved on to another career. And Nadia, scared of the choices she would be forced to make.

"My father, who recently retired from government service, will be directing my campaign, and if I get the nomination in the spring primary, John Jones, my superb aide this past year, will leave the foreign service and join my staff."

Nadia turned her chair a bit and glanced around the restaurant as Robert spoke, relieved that the other tables had lost interest in her guests. They were chatting, laughing, offering good cheer, arms flung over chairs, women whispering one to the other while their husbands lit up cigarettes and cigars and ordered brandies and pulled up chairs and formed a circle and chatted among themselves. Despite Lebanon's violent history, this melting pot of civilization has managed to rebuild itself into something spectacular, and it was on days like this that Nadia was proud to be part of this extraordinary country, if only they could stop killing one another.

"I've also asked the woman I love to be part of my future. Nadia has agreed to consider my proposal. We'll be traveling together in a few days. I hope she'll decide to stay on in Boston until I can convince her to marry me."

Embarrassed to have to sit there and listen to Robert announce this to those present, she watched to see how Andrew would react. When their eyes met, she was unable to tell if he understood that none of these plans were set in stone, that she had agreed to nothing, that these tentative plans were all discussed before she had seen him again and knew she still loved him, and he, her.

Her parents arrived at the best and worst moment. Best because they offered a distraction from Robert's discourse, the worst because her emotions were not under control. Fouad, bless his heart, must have read her thoughts or seen the anguish on her face. He stood, welcomed her parents and took care to call the waiter and ask for two additional chairs to be put alongside Nadia and Andrew at the end of the table, and finally, suggesting the dishes be cleared and desert served along with coffee.

After Fouad, Andrew stood and embraced Victor and Carol.

"I can't tell you how relieved we are to see you back safely, Andrew. Promise you won't be a stranger in our house. Come often. You know how much we love you."

And then it was Robert's turn to greet Nadia's parents. "I'm so glad you could join us. This is my chance to say goodbye. I'll be leaving in a few days."

"We owe you a debt of gratitude, Robert. We'll never forget it was you who rescued Nadia from Jaafar's compound and escorted her back to Beirut. Thank you, and good luck with your future dreams. Nadia told us what you hope to accomplish."

And then it was Nadia, now more firmly in control of her emotions, who stood and welcomed everyone. She raised her arak and offered a toast. "To Andrew, welcome home. We're glad you've been safely delivered back to us. And to you, Sonia, I understand it was you who accomplished this incredible feat." Looking directly at her, she continued, "We will never forget your bravery. You stood up to al-Nusra at great risk to yourself and made it happen. Thank you."

"I appreciate those kind words, Nadia. Thank you."

Andrew smiled at her when she finished her tribute to Sonia. I knew you could do it, he seemed to say.

"And to Robert, the man who has taught me a great many things. Not many people are able to see the error of their ways, admit those wrongs and turn their life around. I'm very proud of you and what you've done."

Fouad then stood and, to Nadia's surprise, offered a toast to her. "To our dear Nadia, she's too modest to share her news, so I'm doing it for her. This morning the Secretary-General of the UN called her and offered her the position of Rapporteur for Human Rights for the Levant."

Everyone applauded, and her father sitting to her left, leaned in and kissed her on the cheek. "Well done, Nadia. I'm very proud of you."

"Thank you, Papa. With all the commotion this morning, I didn't have time to tell you and Mama, but I'm glad you're here to share in the good news."

And then she turned to Robert, "I realize this is as much a surprise to you as it was to me when I got the news. You can appreciate how much this position means to me, and so for the moment, we'll have to put any future plans on hold. I'll be expected to spend some time in New York, not sure how long, but eventually, my work will bring me back here for the foreseeable future. I'm very excited about this new and unexpected chapter in my life."

She was pleased when Robert kissed her on the cheek and congratulated her and relieved that he sounded as though he not only meant it but was genuinely happy for her.

Andrew winked, and his smile warmed her heart.

***

Later, when questioned, none of Nadia's guests could definitively say how it had happened, or precisely when, or if anyone suspicious had approached their table. And no one understood why a glass door behind Andrew and Fouad would suddenly shatter and fall to the ground. No one remembered hearing a shot fired, either. It had all happened so quickly. Nadia remembered having turned in her chair at one point to glance at the other guests. Had she observed any menacing activity? No, but then she was still in shock and unable to answer any questions the authorities asked. Could it have been someone seated directly behind him, or a waiter who had hidden a gun under a napkin and approached him from behind? If so, he had to have been a professional to have known to point the weapon directly at his brain to ensure a kill. No one could say for sure, but they agreed the assassin must have used a sound suppressor, maybe on a gun as compact as a Beretta, and that was why they were taken by surprise when Robert's head fell forward and hit the table. And even then, no one could quite understand where all the blood was coming from until Andrew turned Robert's head slightly to get a clearer idea of what had happened, and only then, realizing the full extent of his injury, understood a wound of that magnitude could only have come from a gun, fired at close range, for it had blown off the front of Robert's face, leaving a pulpy slab of what looked like ground beef, his mouth oozing the remnants of chocolate mousse and coffee, blood and sinew and brain fragments spilling into a scrambled mix and flowing in rivulets between the dishes on the white table cloth.

Nadia remembered everything in total clarity, even though she remained in shock for days. Andrew, staring at her big-eyed, when he discovered what had happened, John and Fouad, guns in hand, in pursuit of the assassin. Women screaming, their husbands escorting them out of the restaurant, her father, shielding her mother's eyes with his jacket as he ushered her away, the lone bullet found among the glass fragments, irrefutable evidence it had penetrated Robert's brain dura before exiting and shattering the door, miraculously missing Andrew and Fouad. The last searing image of Robert and the gory white tablecloth. And Andrew, hands on her shoulders as she sat frozen in her chair, his touch, even at such a horrific moment, bringing her solace and comfort.

CATHY SULTAN is an award-winning author of three nonfiction books: *A Beirut Heart: One Woman's War; Israeli and Palestinian Voices: A Dialogue with Both Sides;* and *Tragedy in South Lebanon. A Beirut Heart* was translated into Chinese in 2013. *The Syrian*, a political thriller, was her first work of fiction, followed by *Damascus Street. An Ambassador to Syria* is the third of a quartet on the Syrian conflict. Sultan is also a peace activist who served on the Board of Directors of Interfaith Peace Builders (now Eyewitness Palestine), an NGO based in Washington, D.C. She took her first trip to Israel/Palestine in March 2002 and subsequently co-led five delegations there on behalf of IFPB, including one to Gaza in 2012.

Sultan won USA's Best Book of the Year Award in 2006 for her autobiography *A Beirut Heart*; USA's Best Book of the Year Award in 2006 the category of History/Politics for *Israeli and Palestinian Voices;* 2006 Midwest Book Awards-Honorable Mention in the Category of Political Science for *Israeli and Palestinian Voices. Tragedy in South Lebanon* was nominated for Best Book of the Year in the Category of Political Science in 2008 and *Damascus Street* was a finalist for both the Eric Hoffer Award and the Montaigne Medal Award for its salient writing.

Made in the USA
Middletown, DE
28 October 2021